The bedsprings creaked beneath the specter's weight...

"...*Jule-yah*..." the figure said, its lip-less mouth moving mechanically up and down as those empty eye sockets looked up at her, spinning pools of black where even the ghostly blue light couldn't reach.

"...He did this to me, Jule-yah..." the skeleton mouth whispered, its voice thick and muffled, as though the tongue had swollen and now blocked the throat.

"...See what he *did* to me?..."

"No," Julia said, her voice only a hint of sound. She still felt herself falling away in a slow, backward spin.

"...*See what he* did *to me, Jule-yah*?..."

The thing on the bed reached out to her...

WINTER WAKE

D1300541

WINTER WAKE

RICK HAUTALA

WARNER BOOKS

A Warner Communications Company

Another one—as they *all* are—
for Bonnie...with love!

WARNER BOOKS EDITION

Copyright © 1989 by Rick Hautala
All rights reserved.

Cover art by Richard Newton
Cover design by Jackie Merri Meyer

Warner Books, Inc.
666 Fifth Avenue
New York, N.Y. 10103

Ⓦ A Warner Communications Company

Printed in the United States of America

First Printing: June, 1989

10 9 8 7 6 5 4 3 2 1

ACKNOWLEDGMENTS

I don't feel a book is really done until I've written the acknowledgments. It's something I feel I have to do to say thanks to the people who help me push, pull, nudge, and shove my books to completion. So, here's a little wave, a tip of the hat, and a great big THANK YOU to:

Mel Parker and Brian Thomsen, for showing interest in my work and for keeping the fires burning.

Dominick Abel, for doing everything a good agent can do.

Kathy Judkins, Chris Fahy, and Mike Feeney, for being my faithful manuscript readers and *still* remaining friends.

Mike Kimball, for all those phone calls that nursed me through that "next novel panic."

John Stewart, for continuing to make the *best* damned music I've ever heard..."strange rivers," indeed!

Bonnie and the boys...for everything else that matters.

Do you not see from what
acts of yours you suffer as you do?
To destruction self-inflicted
you fall so shamefully.

—Sophocles

CONTENTS

PART ONE

Clotho—
the Spinning
Fate

In the shadow of the hill,
Shall my soul be upon thine,
With power and with a sign.

Though thy slumber may be deep,
Yet thy Spirit shall not sleep;
There are shades which will not vanish,
There are thoughts thou canst not banish.
—*Lord Byron*

So shalt thou feed on Death, that feeds on men,
And Death once dead, there's no more dying then.
—*Shakespeare*

ONE
Coming Home

I

As John Carlson drove, his mind sifted through thoughts and speculations about what lay ahead—for both him and his family. After leaving home almost twenty years ago, there wasn't much comfort in the prospect of coming back to Glooscap Island. Hell! Why not admit it? There wasn't *any* for him! Of course his wife, Julia—as usual—was making the best of the situation, but that only made it worse.

The bottom line was that his father, Frank, needed them. Last spring, he had suffered a stroke which had left him partially paralyzed on the left side and subject to blackouts and memory lapses. The stroke was "very minor," as the doctor had said, but still worrisome. So he and Julia had been given two rather obvious options—either put him into an elderly care unit, hospital, or nursing home, or else move back to Maine and live with him so they could be there to help. If he had wanted to spend the rest of his life sleeping on the couch—or out in a snowbank—he would have said no when Julia insisted they move back to the island.

As it turned out, the land-surveying company John worked for in Vermont had connections with the Atkins Construction Company in Portland. His boss quickly arranged for an interview, and he got the job. So with a job and a house—on an island in Casco Bay with an ocean view, no less—things should have been . . . well, maybe not rosy, considering his father's situation, but certainly not as depressing as the cold, rainy drive was making him feel.

He noticed he was holding the steering wheel too tightly—even for such bad driving conditions. *His* bottom line, ignoring Julia's, had been that he didn't want to move back home—not to Maine, not to Glooscap Island, and *certainly* not to his father's house! It was like being sucked down a funnel, right back to the

one place he didn't want to be! He knew damned right well that
"you can never go home again," and his response had always
been—*Who the Christ would want to?*

"I think it looks kinda spooky," Bri said as she stepped out of
the car and looked down the stretch of the suspension bridge
leading over to Glooscap Island. Even with the hood of her raincoat pulled tightly around her face, strands of her light brown hair
stuck out and fluttered in the wind until the pelting rain matted
them down. Usually, Bri's eyes sparkled with the youthful excitement of a thirteen-year-old, but now, her mother saw, they were
dark with apprehension.

"Well, I hope it's not a bad omen," Julia said. She was standing
with John beside the U-Haul truck no more than fifty feet from
the bridge. Rain was coming down like hard pellets, rattling the
truck top and their raincoats. The road over the bridge seemed to
be dancing, vibrating with energy. Pencil-thin streams were dripping from the brims of their slickers, and Julia's sneakers made
squishy sounds whenever she shifted from one foot to the other.

Across the narrow bay, Glooscap Island was shrouded in an
October fog. Mostly, the land looked an amorphous gray, darker
than the sky that seemed to breathe and swell. The island actually
seemed to change its shape in the shifting mists. Close to the end
of the bridge, Julia could barely make out a few houses—or
maybe fishing shacks; she wasn't sure. The water in the bay was
black and gray, capped by white scud. The air was tangy with
salty spray.

The bridge, so John had told her, had been built back when he
was a boy growing up on the island. He had told her how the
island people had divided into two quite hostile camps—those for
and those against connecting Glooscap to the mainland. Before
the bridge, people had gotten to the mainland in one of two ways,
either on the Casco Bay Lines ferry or in their own boat. Those
folks opposed to the bridge saw easy access to the island as a
threat to their independence and quiet way of life. Those in favor
of the bridge saw it as a way to increase the population—and real
estate value—of the land. Easy access meant more people, more
houses, more summer folk, more jobs (if you ignored the impact
on the fishermen and lobstermen)—in sum, more money. Regard-
less, the bridge's existence was evidence enough of which side
had the greater pull in the state house. It all depended on your
point of view whether you thought it gave the Glooscap residents
the best of both worlds . . . or the worst.

II

Julia waited in the street with the car running while John slowly backed the U-Haul up the driveway to the garage door—actually, it was an old barn converted into a garage connected to the house by a breezeway. All but one of the windows along the top of the garage door were cracked or broken.

Surrounded by maple trees, the house sat on the corner lot between Shore Drive and Oak Street. It was a typical New England cape, quite a bit larger than Julia remembered it from the few times in the past when she and John had visited the island . . . larger and much more rundown. The formerly white paint on the clapboards was weathered to a dull yellow. The sheltered sides were chipped and peeling; the front had practically been stripped down to bare wood by the weather. Rain slanting in off the ocean gave the house a mottled, sickly look.

Time for a coat or two of Sears' Best, Julia thought as she surveyed the house.

The dull gray shingles on the roof were curling with age—"fish-lips," as they were called. It looked as though the next strong gust of wind—certainly the first northeaster this coming winter—would tear them away along with the antique storm windows with their green felt-lined frames. No newfangled doors and aluminum combination windows, much less triple-pane thermo-seals, for *this* house! The door in the breezeway sagged to one side, obviously loose on its hinges.

The maple trees in the side yard were spindly and gray, permanently bent landward from the prevailing sea winds. Their branches reached skyward like tired skeleton's hands, grasping but never holding the tattered clouds. Braced between two old maples was a stack of unused firewood which, by the rotted looks of it, would remain unused. All in all, the scene pretty much reflected how Julia felt inside—dull and dreary. She needed something to cheer her up, soon!

Julia drummed her fingers on the steering wheel as she watched John get out of the truck, go into the house by the breezeway door, and then, from the inside, run up the door. She wondered if he could even fit the U-Haul inside, the garage was such a cluttered mess, but John dashed out to the truck, started it up, and leaning out into the rain, backed it on in. The front end of the truck just barely made it inside so he could close the door—not that the rain couldn't pour in through the broken windows.

But only a portion of Julia's attention was on what John was doing. Most of her mind was occupied with thoughts about the house—their *new* home. She hoped it wasn't as bad as it looked on first impressions. Of course, she couldn't have expected Frank to keep the place up—not after his stroke, anyway. The rain didn't help, either. It beat down on a summer's worth of tangled weeds and uncut grass, and muddy runoff streaked the driveway.

She had wanted to take Bri into the house as soon as they got there, but she wanted John to be the first one to greet his father. In spite of their agreed-upon arrangements, they had set up the whole business of moving in with him over the phone, and she was nervous about their first face-to-face meeting.

Looking up at the large house—*God! In this weather, it looks like Noah's ark,* she thought—she began to wonder if they were doing the right thing. She wasn't blind to the heavy responsibilities they were taking on, even with the help of the nurse, who was going to be stopping by almost daily, but the reality of it all hit her hard.

John, meanwhile, had run the garage door down and was standing in the shelter of the breezeway, waving for her to bring the car up the driveway. Shaking her head, Julia put the car into gear and drove right up to the barn door and cut the engine. John began to unload the car as Julia and Bri got out of the car and approached the kitchen door of their new home.

Sitting in his wheelchair, Frank Carlson—Bri's new granddad —waited for them in the kitchen. If the house had appeared more run-down than Julia remembered, then Frank seemed much worse. Her strongest memory of him had been of a hearty, robust man who, in spite of being six feet tall and weighing over two hundred pounds, had carried himself with grace and an easy strength. The frail man sitting in a chrome-plated wheelchair, his thin legs covered by a frayed patchwork afghan, looked almost like an entirely different person. Only his face, which was much thinner and more wrinkled, remained the same.

"Frank," Julia said, approaching him slowly, as though he were an animal she didn't want to spook. "It's nice to see you again. How have you been?"

Frank made an odd clicking sound with his lips as he ran his fingers through his baby-thin gray hair. His eyes suddenly clouded over as he looked from Julia to Bri and back again to Julia. He shifted up in the wheelchair, and the motion almost knocked off the tattered slipper from his left foot.

"You ain't Abby, are yah?" he said, his brow furrowing.

"No, no," Julia replied. "I'm Julia . . . John's wife?"

"Course you are," Frank said, his eyes suddenly brightening. "Well, hell—I've been better," he said, his voice dropping to a low rumble.

"You've never met Brianna before," Julia said. "Bri, this is your Grandfather Carlson."

"It's—umm, very nice to meet you," Bri said, sounding to Julia like a schoolgirl reciting a memorized line.

She held out her hand to Frank, and after regarding her a moment, he held up his own hand and they shook. Bri found herself surprised by the warm strength she felt in the man's grip. His hand was callused and hard from a lifetime of work, but there was a gentleness when he touched her. When they broke off, she found herself staring at the blue veins and tendons that stood out beneath the thin, nearly translucent skin on the back of his wrinkled hand.

"Why don't I heat up some water for tea," Julia said, cutting into the awkward silence. She rubbed her shoulders and shivered. "By the time John gets inside, he'll be chilled to the bone."

"I got some Salada," Frank said as he started to roll his wheelchair over toward the kitchen counter. "None of that fancy-pants herbal stuff." He pronounced the *h* in herbal. Only Bri caught the little twinkle dancing in his eyes as he said this; she smiled back at him.

"I'll get it," Julia said, halting him. She went over to the stove and picked up the teakettle and inspected it before giving it a quick rinse and filling it with cold water from the tap. Its bottom was blackened.

Frank grunted. "It works well enough. . . . I just can't always get to it fast enough." He slapped his hand down on the armrest of the wheelchair. Pulling back hard on the wheels, he swung over to the table. The tendons in the backs of his hands stood out as thick as pencils as he moved, and both Julia and Bri saw his neck tighten with the effort.

Once she had the water heating up, Julia rummaged around in the cupboards, looking for cups and sugar. Frank seemed unwilling to tell her where to look, so she took the opportunity to go through the cupboards. She noticed that all of the food and only a few dishes, bowls, cups, and glasses were on lower shelves— within easy reach of someone who no longer could stand up. What surprised her, though, was the cleanliness of the kitchen. Everything was in order, stacked neatly away. From the condition of the outside of the house, she had been expecting to walk into a pigsty; this was a pleasant surprise.

Julia found the sugar bowl at last. It was on one of the higher shelves, so she figured Frank never used it. When she took the lid off, she was even more convinced—the sugar had dried to a single, solid lump. She put four cups on the table, and then leaned back against the counter while she waited for the teakettle to start whistling.

Bri was standing by the kitchen window, looking out into the back yard. She jumped with surprise when her grandfather spoke close behind her.

"There's a much fina' view out the living room window," he said. "Storm like this can really send the waves up over the rocks."

"Oh. I'll have to go see," she said.

Once Bri had left to check out the view, the silence in the kitchen got thicker; Julia felt it wrap around her like a heavy coat. She was trying—desperately—to imagine John growing up in this house, but she couldn't picture him here. Of course, back then things would have been much different—Frank would have been young and strong, like John was now; Dianna, Frank's mother, would have had her drinking, which would eventually kill her, under control; and John and his brother, David—who, unlike John, *hadn't* been fortunate enough to return from Vietnam—would have been racing through the house, whirlwinds of noise and activity. But no matter how hard she pushed her imagination, she just couldn't conjure up those ghosts from the past. This had been the home of a solitary, crotchety old man for too long.

"I have to say, you do seem to have gotten along quite well before now," Julia said. She winced as soon as the words were out of her mouth, realizing how they might easily be taken the wrong way.

Frank—who apparently was used to taking things the wrong way—snorted. His left hand, lying stiffly in his lap, twitched slightly.

"I mean," Julia continued, "the house is—isn't a . . ." She rubbed her hands together and was grateful when the teakettle started whistling shrilly and she could turn her attention to it and let her sentence die.

"I been having Hilda Marshall do a bit of housework a coupl'a times a week," Frank said.

"Well, I guess from now on you won't have to," Julia said. She finished filling the four cups, then went over to the window to see if she could catch any sign of John. She rinsed the kettle again, shook it empty, and put it back onto the stove.

Frank made a soft little chuckling sound and shook his head. "I been sayin' all along it weren't necessary for you and John to do this, yah know."

Julia turned and looked at him. Her mouth opened, but nothing came out. She was thinking, *If John didn't want us to come here, and he doesn't want us here . . . did I really force the issue this far?* And in spite of all her altruistic motives based on family ties and needs, for the first time Julia really wondered what she had gotten herself and her family into.

"Bri . . . honey," she called out, forcing a steadiness into her voice that she didn't feel. "Why don't you go out and get your father. Tell him I have some hot tea for him."

Bri came running from the living room, but she only got halfway to the kitchen door before John swung the door open and, in a gust of wind-blown rain, stepped inside. He shivered as he sloughed off his raincoat. Julia thought his face looked pale and tight, almost frightened as he glanced over at his father and nodded a silent greeting.

"So," his father said, his voice rumbling like distant thunder in his chest. "After all these years you finally come home to stay!"

TWO
Church Wood

I

"We probably ought to take a look around, don't you think?" Julia asked. She had gotten up from the table and was putting the empty teacups on the board beside the sink. She figured she would wash them later, after they had supper. The surprise would have been if Frank had an automatic dishwasher.

The storm was still rattling against the windows, but with the furnace rumbling like a friendly beast in the basement and the ceiling light spreading a warm, yellow glow all around, the kitchen felt extremely cozy. The only chill had been the not-so-disguised tension between John and his father. A blast furnace at full tilt, Julia thought, might thaw that.

"You'll have to 'scuse me from helpin' yah," Frank said. "I think Johnny remembers where everything goes."

He pushed his wheelchair away from the table and started moving toward the living room, where Bri, her tea getting cold on the coffee table in front of her, was sitting on the couch, looking out at the storm-tossed ocean.

Once Frank was out of hearing, Julia sighed deeply and shot John a withering look.

John took a deep breath and shook his head, covering his face with his hands as he rubbed his eyes. "I'm beat from the drive," he said by way of excuse, but when Julia didn't respond, he nailed her with a look and said, "This just isn't going to work out, you know." His voice was muffled by his hands. "I knew it all along, and I tried to tell you."

Julia, who was standing at the sink, felt her fists tightening. Granted, their first hour in the house had been tense, but she honestly felt that it was just a matter of time before everyone adjusted.

"He's used to being alone," she said, nodding toward the living room. She could hear the soft buzzing of voices as Frank and Bri talked. "After an active life like he's had, don't you think you'd be a bit resentful, being confined to a wheelchair?"

John shook his head and, sighing deeply, leaned back and looked up at the ceiling light. The cheap cut glass made the glow spin in watery circles in his vision.

"I think he's done pretty well, considering what he's had to adjust to," Julia continued. "I mean, feeling so confined and so dependent on other people . . . no wonder he's a little cranky."

John laughed at that and suddenly shifted forward, his voice lowering as if he were threatening her. "He hasn't changed—not one damned bit! It's just a matter of degree, not kind."

Julia wet a dishrag and came over to the table and wiped up the crumbs, scooping them into her hand, then rinsed them down the drain. She was determined not to let her husband's hostility and negativity get to her.

"I just wish you would give this a fair chance," she said. "After I—"

John laughed again and rubbed under his nose with the back of his hand. "Yeah, sure. Go ahead. Regale me with your story of your grandmother and what happened to her when she was put into a nursing home."

"That's not fair, John, and you *know* it," Julia said. She was wringing out the dishrag and now gave it an extra hard twist.

"Come on. Tell me all about how the staff treated her . . . or *failed* to treat her. About the time you came to visit her and she had crapped herself and had been lying in her own shit for—what? An hour or two? Certainly long enough so it had—"

"Stop it!" Julia shouted. She slapped the dishrag down on the edge of the sink. "That's not fair!"

"Oh, yes, it is," John said, pushing his chair back and getting up. "I think it's more than fair because, as far as I'm concerned, this is *your* gig."

With a ragged intake of breath, Julia turned away and looked out the kitchen window. She could hear her pulse making a soft, fluttery sound in her ears like a trapped bird; her throat felt as though she had swallowed something hard and dry. She started to speak, but all that came out was a sharp clicking sound.

"Little Miss Goody-two-shoes," John said.

Julia could see his reflection in the window, and she didn't like the smirk on his face . . . not one little bit. Taking a deep breath, she turned and looked at him, forcing her emotions to loosen up, to unwind.

"John—" she said, raising her arms pleadingly, signaling him that it was time to stop this crap and hug her. He hesitated for only an instant, then got up from the table and came to her, pulling her close. She lost herself in his heavy scent, grateful that she could let him hold her like this, if only for a moment. She twined her arms around the small of his back and, looking up, waited for him to kiss her. When he did, she couldn't help but notice his lips were cold and tight.

"You know," she said, pulling back and looking him squarely in the eyes, "this isn't going to work out unless you're with me on it."

John bit down onto his lower lip and nodded.

"And I realize," Julia continued, "that coming back here—to stay hasn't been easy on you. I know it isn't quite what you wanted to do—"

"Huh!" John said with a snort. "That could be called the understatement of the day."

"But—your dad *needs* us. He may be too proud to ask or even *hint* at it, but I can tell, and I'll bet you can, too. It means a lot to him that you would come back and help him like this."

"It means a lot to you, too—doesn't it?" John said.

Julia considered for a moment, then nodded agreement.

"And I know, in some ways, you've been so—so *pushy* about this because you want to make up, somehow, for what you saw happen to your grandmother. Uh-uh." He wagged his forefinger in front of her face. "Just this once, don't deny it, all right?"

Julia was silent for a long while; then she nodded.

"I promise you right now that I'll really try to make it work, okay? I really will—for you and Bri and me."

"And your father."

John nodded, but a flicker of resentment passed across his face. "Yes—for him, too. Come on, let's give Bri the grand tour so she can start getting settled in her bedroom. She *is* getting the best bedroom in the house, you realize."

Julia forced a laugh and gave him a playful punch on the shoulder. "You're just saying that because it was your bedroom when you were a kid."

"That's right, and look what a fine, upstanding adult *I* turned out to be."

II

"Is it true what"—Bri paused before saying the next word, as if her tongue wasn't quite used to forming it yet—"Granddad said?"

"What?" John asked. "What did he tell you?" He was leading the way up the stairs with Bri and then Julia following behind. Julia more or less remembered the house from the few times she and John had visited before, and she hung behind, wanting Bri— more than anyone else—to be excited about this move.

"About the 'church wood,'" Bri said.

When they reached the upstairs landing, John turned and looked at her. For just an instant, in the dim glow of light from the ceiling fixture, he thought her face looked . . . different. It was fuller, more mature. Her eyes were cast into shadow that—for just a heartbeat—made her look almost like a different person entirely.

"The church wood?" John said, his voice catching in his throat.

Bri was nodding. "He said this house was made from wood gathered from a whole bunch of buildings that had been torn down and stuff, and that some of it was made from what was left of one of the churches after it burned."

Julia shook her head, confused. "So what?" she asked, looking from Bri to John. "I'm sure back in the old days, when this house was made, they did stuff like that—recycled wood from other buildings. What's that got to do with anything?"

"Well . . ." Bri said, casting a nervous glance down the length of the hallway. Trimwork that had needed new paint at least ten years ago and faded wallpaper gave everything an unnerving gloom. Thick dust had gathered in every corner. "Granddad said that—even back when *he* was a boy, his mother used to say she could hear organ music—church music playing late at night . . . that the wood somehow echoed with it."

Julia snorted a laugh and shook her head. "Come on," she said. "He's just making that up to tease you. Let's take a look at what we've got here. We won't unload the truck till the rain stops, hopefully by tomorrow, so we have all night to figure out where we'll put what."

"Is it true, though?" Bri asked, her brow wrinkling with concern. "Or was he just, like, trying to get me worked up? He told me his wife, dad's mother, heard it sometimes, too—especially in the winter."

John and Julia looked at each other, each of them knowing they were both thinking that John's mother very well might have heard organ music resonating in the house. By the time John had left the island to go to the University of Maine, his mother was so far gone with her drinking that she might have seen pink elephants in the hallway, too.

"Look here, Bri," Julia said, placing her hands firmly on her daughter's shoulders and looking her squarely in the eyes. "I don't know your grandfather a whole lot better than you do—" She caught John watching her. "But I'd say he's just ribbing you."

Bri couldn't repress a shiver when she looked down the length of the dimly lit hall again. "Yeah, but—"

"No yeah-buts," Julia said. "Sure, there are going to be certain sounds you hear—creaking floors and squeaky doors and stuff like that—but that's normal in a house this old."

"Or even a new house," John added. "These days, with construction and materials so shoddy, you can hear all sorts of weird noises just walking from one room to another."

"But something like that sounds so . . . strange," Bri said, her voice hushed with awe.

"Don't go getting yourself all worked up," Julia said, pushing to the front. "Come on and take a look at your bedroom." She led the way down the hallway toward the farthest door.

Bri hesitated before following her and John. She turned and looked down the stairs, and her heart gave an extra-hard thump when she saw her grandfather sitting in his wheelchair at the foot of the stairs, looking up at her. He was smiling, but the thinness of his face and the hollowness of his gaze made it look more like a grimace of pain. Very slowly he raised his hand and, placing his forefinger to his lips, made a soft hissing sound.

It took great effort for Bri not to cry out. All she could think was, *Is this some kind of warning?* She knew already in the back of her mind that, for the first night at least, she was probably going to be lying there, staring at the ceiling all night, just *waiting* to hear the soft, wavering notes of organ music.

III

"You're not having second thoughts, are you?" John asked. A trace of a smile danced across his lips, but he tried not to let it show.

Julia's face, he thought, was a perfect copy of what Bri's had been while she was looking at what would be her bedroom. Frank had called out for someone—*anyone*—to come downstairs, and Bri had gone, reluctantly, to see what he wanted. Julia was pacing back and forth across the hardwood floor of the master bedroom, her eyes scrunched up as she tried to assess its possibilities.

Her first—and practically only—thought was that she was angry at herself for one slight miscalculation. If they were planning on staying here with Frank for however long, then she was damned well going to have to do a bit of "paint-'n'-paper" work, as they said about the handyman specials in the house ads. She couldn't figure out why John hadn't mentioned to her what a sorry state the house was in. For some reason, she had expected simply to move into the house, that the house would easily absorb them and their possessions—at least the ones they wouldn't put into storage. It had never even crossed her mind that, especially in the years since his wife died, Frank wouldn't have kept things up.

"Oh, no . . . no. Not at all," she said, shaking her head as she paced. "Although it does feel kind of funny, thinking we'll be sleeping in the same bedroom your parents used all those years."

"Well, you do look a bit . . . discouraged," John said.

Julia looked at him, took a deep breath, and let her shoulders drop. She could feel her lower lip beginning to tremble, but she didn't know whether to turn away from him or crumple into his arms and let all her frustrations out in a single, big cry.

"Yeah, I . . . I guess I am—a little," she said, forcing her voice to stay steady. "I don't think you realize just how . . . hard this all is for me, too, you know. Do you realize that, in all the time since we decided to do this—the whole time we were discussing it—"

"Arguing about it, really," John said.

"Well, whatever . . . I don't think you ever once thought about how all of this was going to affect *me*. I mean, in a lot of ways, you've got it easy. You're coming back to a place you know really well—the house you grew up in and all. There are still people around here who know you. Everything's familiar to you!"

John smiled as he came over to her and put his arm around her shoulder. He tried to pull her close, but she resisted.

"Do you have any idea what I'm talking about?" she asked, looking up at him, her expression firmly set.

John nodded. "Course I do."

"I mean, you've got a job lined up and everything," she said. "And what do *I* have to look forward to? I have your father to take care of and an antique house that looks like it hasn't been cleaned in years!"

"You're forgetting one thing," John said, his voice even and low. He glanced at the doorway, to make sure Bri wasn't out there listening. "*I* never said I wanted to come back here in the first place! Not *once*!" He shook his forefinger at her when he said the last word, and he waited, watching for her reaction.

Julia squirmed out from under his hold and walked over to the window. They had almost the same ocean view as Bri, except the large maple tree in the front yard blocked some of it. Her breath came into her lungs in a long, shuddering gasp.

"You really can't admit that by forcing this issue you just may have made a mistake, can you?" John said. He leaned one arm on the wall and, cocking his hip, regarded her with an icy stare. Julia could feel it penetrating the back of her head as she looked out at the rain.

"In all the years I've known you," he went on, "I'd have to say that's about the only real fault you have."

"What's that?" she asked, turning to meet his stare.

"You're so *damned* hardheaded. Once you commit to something, no matter what happens, you won't admit it when you're wrong."

"And you think coming back here to help your father is *wrong*?" she said, her voice quivering.

John nodded. "Yes—in a way, I do. I said all along that I thought the best thing would be to have him go into a nursing home where they could take care of his needs twenty-four hours a day."

Julia started shaking her head gently, but he went on.

"I know—I know what you'll say, but what happened to your grandmother was the exception, not the rule. The one thing you haven't accepted is that things *change*! The days of families— parents, children, grandparents—everybody living together in the old family homestead like this is . . . is just a half-assed romantic notion you've got." He raised his arms, indicating the dingy bedroom with a wide sweep. "Well, babe, this is it—this is the *reality* that's going to throw cold water right into the face of your romanticism."

He turned and strode out of the room, his footsteps sounding heavy on the stairs as he went back down to the living room. Julia turned and, pressing her face against the cold windowpane, with rain splashing the glass in front of her eyes, she finally let go, and hot tears started rolling down her cheeks.

IV

A short while later—after she had composed herself—Julia came downstairs. She put her best face on in front of Frank and Bri, but there was an iciness between her and John that remained even after the hour or so they spent dashing back and forth in the rain between the house and the car to get the few things they needed for the night.

Frank hadn't gotten any extra food for his newly arrived guests. He had a half-used package of hot dogs, a can of B&M baked beans, and two cans of Pabst lined up for his usual Saturday night supper, but there wasn't much else to eat in the refrigerator. "Hilda, the woman who does my cleanin' for me, usually gets me groceries on Monday," he said. That was the closest he ever came to apologizing.

Julia caught herself wondering if Hilda's shopping was as skimpy as the alleged cleaning she did.

"I reckon you could drive on down to Pottle's for a few things," Frank said. "'Less you feel like hauling on into Falmouth to the Shop 'n' Save."

Neither prospect appealed to either John or Julia, but finally— because John wanted to avoid bumping into anyone who might recognize him at Pottle's—Julia drove down to the corner store. She came back about a half hour later, grumbling about the outrageously high prices.

"Fella's got to make a livin'," Frank said sourly. "Y'could have gone to Falmouth if you wanted bargains."

"His prices are almost *double* what they are in Vermont!" Julia said, practically slamming the lettuce, tomatoes, hot dogs, and rolls onto the counter. She tried her best to keep her anger down while she and Bri made a salad and heated up the hot dogs and beans.

Supper was a tense affair, and Julia found herself thinking, if this was how it was going to be, there was no *way* things would work out. Every time she tried to make small talk, either John would not pick up on it or Frank would cut her short with a . . . well, it might not have been meant as a nasty remark, but she was feeling so sensitive, it sure felt that way.

The only real problem Bri had during supper was whenever she thought about Bungle, her cat back home, who had died a week before the move. The image of him lying dead on the wet grass with his fur matted down by the rain kept rising in her mind, and every time she had to choke back the tears. The few times someone—usually her mother—directed a comment at her, she would shake her head and say, "Huh?" forcing the person to repeat the question.

Frank seemed about the only person enjoying the "traditional" Maine Saturday night supper of beans and hot dogs. After the tension of driving across nearly three states, and the *worse* tension of their argument in the bedroom, Julia was eating so little she knew she was going to be munching something before bedtime.

"That was a good meal," Frank said, pushing himself back from the table and tossing his wrinkled napkin onto his empty plate. He started to pick up the plate to bring it over to the sink, but Julia quickly stood up and took it from him.

"I can get that for you," she said.

He looked at her, his expression dancing between irritation and gratitude. "I ain't no invalid, you know," he said softly. "A little something like this ain't about to keep me down for long." He slapped himself on the leg.

Julia went over to the sink and rinsed the plate under the faucet, then put it on the counter with the pans. She wanted to say something right away, to establish as firmly as possible that she saw her role here as one of *helper*, not nurse, but she was still feeling so tense from the events of the day that she said nothing and went back to the table to get her own plate.

"Mind if I smoke?" Frank said, reaching into the pocket of his cardigan and fishing out a battered corncob pipe and pouch of tobacco. When nobody protested, he rolled open the pouch and filled the bowl. Within a few seconds, he had the bowl stoked and, grunting his thanks, rolled his wheelchair into the living room.

They spent the evening sitting around, watching television. The conversation went about the same as it had at supper—not much was said, and there was very little content in it. When bedtime rolled around, there was a brief discussion about who would sleep where. After a bit of convincing, Bri agreed to roll out a sleeping bag on the rickety bed in her bedroom—"Just this one night," she insisted, and John told her he would unload the truck in the morning and put her bed together first thing.

Frank, of course, retired to his bed in the guest room, and even if he *had* offered to let Julia and John sleep there, which he didn't, they would have refused. Once Frank bid them good night and Julia had settled Bri in her room, she and John folded out the hide-away bed in the couch and made it up with sheets from the linen closet.

"These smell nice and fresh," Julia said as she tossed open the contour sheet so John could catch the other end.

John hesitated for a moment, looking at her with his eyebrows raised. "Umm," he said, holding the sheet to his face and inhaling deeply.

They worked silently together, spreading the top sheet and a heavy quilt over the bed. While Julia worked the pillows into the cases, John stripped off his clothes and went to brush his teeth in the bathroom. Julia hurriedly put on her nightgown and then collected both her and John's clothes and put them in the laundry room.

"Do you want the curtains open or closed?" John asked when he came back into the living room.

When Julia shrugged, he took the pull string and ran the curtains open. The sound of the metal runners was as harsh as a metal hasp being dragged over wood.

"It'll be nicer this way," John said as he stood by the window, looking out. In the distance, a blinking light flashed rhythmically —the lighthouse on Great Diamond Island, John told her. Off to the right, Julia could see the small yellow rectangles of a few neighbors' windows. Rain pattered against the glass, turning the view into a bubbly blur.

"It's awfully peaceful, isn't it?" she said after taking a deep breath. That wasn't what she was feeling inside, but she was tired and didn't want to start an argument with John, or say anything that would get him upset. Turning off the light, she came over and stood beside her husband, looking out at the night. Without hesitation, he put his arm around her shoulder and pulled her close. John made a soft sound in the back of his throat and glanced down at her.

"I—" she started to say, but he waved her to silence with his hand.

"I know what you're going to say," he whispered, his breath hot on her ear, "but you've got it all wrong. *I* was the asshole on this one. Ever since we got here, I've been acting like a—"

"You already said it," Julia said with a laugh. "An *asshole*."

"Oh, gee—thanks," John said, giving her a good-humored shake. "I can always count on you to say the right thing, can't I?"

"John, I—"

"You were supposed to say, no, honey, you *weren't* acting like an asshole. I understand. . . ."

"Come on, John, you know I was just joking. I realize you're pretty stressed out from the drive and all," she said. "Maybe I should have been a little more understanding myself. But what you said earlier—do you really think it's true?"

"About what?" John said. For just an instant he thought she was talking about the "church-wood" story his father had told Bri.

"About me being bullheaded?" Julia said. "That once I'm committed to something, I can never admit I'm wrong?" She looked up at him, her eyebrows arched, making her face look sad.

John nodded slightly. "I hope so," he said, snickering. "At least when it comes to me."

Julia's smile widened, and touching him gently on the cheek, she drew his face close to hers. They kissed long and passionately, and Julia shifted to press her body tightly against his. One of John's hands moved in a slow, sensuous circle from her shoulder up her neck to the back of her head. The other hand slid down the small of her back, pulling her hips against him.

When the kiss was finished, Julia, smiling, moved her hand from his chest down over his stomach and lower, into his underpants. She gripped his hardening manhood and gave it a gentle upward stroke.

"Maybe we should turn on the light behind us," John said with a chuckle. "Give the neighbors a show."

Julia grinned but then backed away, suddenly embarrassed that, in fact, someone outside might see them. She went quickly to the couch and slid in under the covers. Propping herself up on one elbow, she undid the top two buttons of her nightgown and said huskily, "Once you're through with the view, I've got something else to show you."

V

The blast of sound slammed into her sleep like a sledgehammer hitting the side of the house. Before she could even register where she was, Julia was sitting bolt upright in bed, letting out a loud scream.

"Wha—what is it?" John said as he scrambled off the couch, feeling blindly for the wall light switch. He slammed his knee into the coffee table and went down with a howl.

Julia was sitting up in bed, clutching the sheet to her chest. Her heart was pulsating in her throat, and her eyes were wide open, trying to take everything in. All she knew was that *something* . . . a horrendously loud noise, had driven through her brain while she was sleeping. She waited in the dark, listening to John scramble to his feet and hoping—if she heard the sound again before he got the light on—she would be able to identify it.

At the same instant John found the wall switch and snapped it on, the sound did come again. From outside in the dark came a low, throaty honk that gradually rose up the scale. Julia's fear-filled eyes latched on to John.

"Do you mean *that*?" he said, nodding toward the window. A smile slowly spread across his face.

The sound continued for another second or two and then abruptly dropped off into silence. As soon as it was gone, Julia had the sensation that it hadn't been there, that she was hallucinating it.

"What the hell *is* that?" she asked, her eyes darting frantically from John to the living room window. Outside, all she could see was the steadily blinking light from Great Diamond. The neighborhood was dark, and Julia glanced at her wristwatch to see what time it was.

Quarter past three! Who—or what—the hell would be making a sound like that at this hour? she wondered.

"It's only the foghorn out on Great Diamond," John said, still smiling. He walked slowly back to the couch and sat on the edge, letting his hand rest gently on Julia's knee beneath the covers.

"Does it—" she started to say but then cut herself off when the sound boomed out again, filling the night.

"Mom?" came Bri's voice from upstairs, tentative with fear.

Both Julia and John turned to see Bri as she came slowly down the stairs. She stopped halfway and, leaning over the railing, glanced around the living room.

"Hi, hon," Julia said.

"Is everything all right down there?" Bri asked warily. "I heard someone shout." She covered her throat protectively with one hand.

Julia flushed with embarrassment and shook her head. "Yeah—we're okay. The, uh—" As if a demonstration were needed, the foghorn sounded again. Julia cocked her thumb toward the window. "The foghorn on the lighthouse kind of caught me by surprise—that's all," she finished lamely.

"Oh," Bri said simply. She came the rest of the way down the stairs and sat in the rocking chair near the fireplace. She hadn't even heard the foghorn until just then. She was, in fact, rather surprised she hadn't. She had gone to bed earlier than usual and lain there, looking up at the ceiling, fully expecting to hear the low, throbbing notes of organ music reverberating in the woodwork. She had no idea what time she finally drifted off the sleep, but she had been expecting to wake up at the slightest sound.

"Well," John said, rubbing his hands vigorously together, "now that we're all up— Wait a minute, you want me to go get my father, too?"

"Don't be silly," Julia said, shaking her head.

"Hey—I just thought we could have a little party, that's all," John said. "No sense wasting the time now that we're all awake."

Julia rubbed her face with her hands and sighed. "Look, I'm sorry, all right? It's just that I didn't know what it was, and when I woke up and couldn't tell right away where I was, I guess I kind of panicked."

"Oh, real good, Mom," Bri said, glancing at John with a teasing twinkle in her eye.

"Well, we're up," John said. "We might as well make a party of it. Look, you two just sit there and enjoy the view. This'll help." He snapped off the living room light, plunging the room into darkness. "I'll go warm up some milk to soothe the nerves of anyone who might be feeling jittery."

"Sounds like a good idea," Julia said, "seeing as how your father doesn't have any *herbal* tea." She chuckled as her gaze drifted back to the window to the steadily pulsing light. When the sound of the foghorn came again, she was ready for it, and actually found it rather soothing—now that she knew what it was.

"Be right back," John said.

As her eyes adjusted to the darkness, Julia's nerves gradually untangled. She sat with her back against the couch and, patting the space beside her, asked Bri to come and sit with her. They didn't say anything to each other as they sat watching the weak flood of light come and go, come and go from the distant lighthouse. Each pulse of light showed them, faintly, an image of themselves reflected in the living room window.

"A lot or a little?" John called from the kitchen.

"A lot," Julia shouted.

"Umm—me, too," Bri said.

Julia lost track of how long it was taking John to heat up the milk. There was something so calm, so peaceful about the gentle patter of rain on the window, the drops glowing in bright beads with every flash from the lighthouse. It could have been a half an hour or more, for all she knew. At last, though, she heard footsteps approaching from the kitchen, and she and Bri straightened up.

John was carrying three cups filled with warm milk on a tray, using both hands and feeling his way carefully in the dark. At least he knew where the coffee table was; his shins still ached from the impact. He rounded the corner into the living room and was just about to say something when the light from the lighthouse came on for a moment and then winked off. In that moment, he saw—*thought* he saw—something that made his breath catch in his chest. His tongue felt too large for his mouth and made it impossible to speak.

"John?" Julia said softly, her voice drifting like a disembodied spirit out of the darkness.

John stood stock-still in the living room entryway, his whole body bathed in a cold sweat. He was waiting for the light to come again. In spite of the sudden ground swell of panic he felt, he couldn't move. He *had* to wait for the flash of light again, to see if his eyes had been playing a trick on him or if . . .

The dark square of the window suddenly blossomed with warm yellow again. John could vaguely distinguish objects in the room —the couch, the easy chair. . . . He held his breath until it began to burn in his lungs as he watched the brightening reflection in the rain-skimmed window.

"Holy shit," he muttered. At least he thought he said it aloud. It might have only been a thought.

The light grew steadily brighter, quickly reached its peak, then faded, but this time there was no doubt about what he had seen. The light illuminated Julia and Bri, casting their reflections in the window, but he saw something else that sent a ripple of chills racing up his spine.

Something gray . . . slouched and gray. It almost looked like a person! A person with his back to him, dangling from the end of a rope behind the couch, slowly twisting around. . . .

As the light from the lighthouse faded, the reflected image slowly dimmed, too. John wasn't sure if it was his eyes or his brain that registered it.

"You there, John?" Julia asked, glancing over her shoulder. "Come on. This is no time to be playing games."

John wanted to say something, but he still was unable to get anything more than a shallow breath into his lungs. It felt as though he were in the embrace of some giant who was intent on crushing the air out of him.

"John?" Julia called.

He could hear her shifting on the couch, but he just stood there, his eyes riveted ahead in the darkness, focusing on the spot on the picture window where he knew the reflection had been, where he knew, when the light came again, he would see . . .

It couldn't have been there, he told himself, but in the dark, he could almost feel the cold, dark body dangling in the space between him and the couch.

The darkness suddenly brightened, and the room filled with light once again. John was so wound up that he wanted to scream as he waited for the light to reveal the hanging, gray shape. The light came flooding into the living room, its brightness peaking, and then fading. John's numbed brain flooded with relief. All he had seen was Julia and Bri reflected in the window!

No one else! his mind shouted with glee. *There was nothing else there!*

He took a step forward, hoping his hesitation would be read simply as his caution in the dark.

"I—umm, I'm having a little trouble finding my way," he said. To his own ears, his voice sounded strangled and weak. "The lighthouse light kinda threw me off."

"Bri, get the light, will you?" Julia asked.

John stopped where he was, not willing to chance a spill while Bri went over to the wall and threw the switch. The living room was immediately bathed in warm—*steady*, reassuring—yellow light, John thought as he went over to the coffee table and carefully set down the tray.

"Well, well, well," he said, straightening up and brushing his hands together. "Lookee here. I didn't spill a drop."

He smiled with satisfaction at Julia, but all he could think about was what he had seen. *No!* he told himself. *What he had thought he had seen!* It had been a trick reflection of the lighthouse light, or something caused by the rain on the picture window.

Bri came over and sat back down on the couch next to her mother, bouncing up and down like a little kid. "Hey, this is fun," she said, reaching for the nearest mug. She held it in both hands and blew over the top before taking a sip.

Julia frowned and scratched her head. "All of us should be asleep, and we *would* be if that damned lighthouse foghorn hadn't scared me."

As he moved over to sit on the couch, John noticed that Bri and Julia were sitting in the same spots he had seen them in when the lighthouse light had been the only illumination in the room. With his back toward the kitchen, the hairs on the back of his neck prickled when he thought about the gray shape he had seen hanging from the ceiling behind the couch.

"Here you go, honey," Julia said as she handed him a cup of milk.

He took the cup, angry at his fingers for trembling as he raised it to his mouth. The momentary image of that gray figure was still burning vividly in his mind, as though it were etched in acid. He took a sip of the warm milk, but it tasted sour and clotted as it slipped down his throat.

"You okay?" Julia asked.

Damn her for noticing, John thought even as he smiled, nodded, and said, "Oh, yeah . . . sure."

Bri had stopped bouncing on the couch and was sitting now, staring at the blank rectangle of the window as the light pulsed on and off. She hadn't taken any more sips after the first tentative one.

The foghorn was still hooting in the darkness, but Julia realized she wasn't noticing it as much now that she was expecting it. She wondered about people who lived close to railroad tracks and had freight trains passing by late at night. Did they get so they never heard it when the midnight train went by?

"You know," Bri said suddenly, turning to look at her parents. "I was just thinking . . ."

When Julia and John saw tears welling up in her eyes, they had a pretty good idea that she had been thinking about Bungle.

"If—" she choked on the word but then forced herself to say it. "If Bungle was here right now, he'd be trying his best to take a lick out of my cup."

Julia said nothing as she placed her arm around Bri's shoulder and gave her a reassuring hug.

"If you'd like," John said, "maybe we can ask around on the island and get a new cat for you." His gaze followed hers to the black slab of the window, but his mind was filled with what he had seen—*No, goddammit! Thought I saw!*—reflected there. His mind played with the idea that somehow there had been someone outside looking in, and the trick of the reflection had just made it *look* as if he was in the living room.

But how the hell could that be? John wondered. *And who could it have been . . . a curious neighbor at three o'clock in the morning?*

He took a shaky breath, wanting to look away from the window but unable to. No matter how many times he told himself it had just been a trick of the glass, maybe something to do with the double-pane storm window, he just couldn't blot out that image of someone suspended in midair between him and the couch!

"No," Bri said, her voice sounding tight. "I don't want to get another cat." She slurped noisily as she took another sip of milk. "I think—I don't know. I kinda feel like Bungle would be really mad at me if he knew I *replaced* him so fast. You know what I mean?" The image of rain-matted fur and Bungle's sightless stare up at the gray sky rose unbidden in her mind.

Julia looked at her daughter and smiled knowingly. "Yeah . . . I think I do," she said, her voice low and warm. "When you lose someone you love, waiting is the right thing to do—to honor their memory." She appreciated being able to be the strong, knowing, and caring mother after getting scared like a little kid and waking up—well, *almost* the whole household.

"Well, hey, I don't know about anyone else," John said suddenly—a bit *too* suddenly, judging by the look Julia gave him. "But I'm sure feeling sleepy." In spite of the heat of the liquid, he gulped down what was left in his cup. "What say we all hit the sack?"

Julia was still looking at him as though he were an odd specimen; then she finished her cup of milk and, placing it on the coffee table, nodded agreement. "Yeah. Bri—get yourself back to bed. We've got a lot of unpacking to do in the morning—if this rain lets up."

"Well, you know what they say. 'If this rain keeps up, it won't come down.'" She kissed them each good night, and even though she didn't relish the thought of going upstairs in this strange new house by herself, she said a cheerful good night and boldly walked up the stairs to her new bedroom.

VI

"So, what's bothering *you*?" Julia asked once the light was out again and they were snuggled under the covers.

John rolled over and looked at her. His back was to the window, and the light from the lighthouse steadily blossomed and faded, casting faint yellow light onto the walls of the living room. He could feel a steely tension winding up inside him as he imagined, *That's all it was—imagination!*—that hanging gray shape reflected in the window.

Who the hell could it have been? he wondered, as his mind clicked off a few possibilities—none of which made sense. The lighthouse had shown the reflection only once . . . well, twice, but the first time had been so sudden, so shocking, he hadn't even registered it until the room had plunged back into darkness. The second time, when he had been *ready*, the image had looked somehow blurred, as though it was the pale reflection of a reflection, an image trying to condense into reality.

"Well?" Julia said, prodding him in the ribs with her fingertips.

"I—" His voice caught in his throat, and in spite of himself he suddenly rolled over and stared at the living room window. He was ready to see something—some*one* standing outside the house, a harsh black outline against the rainy night—but the window was empty—except for the circle of light from the lighthouse.

"God, John, you're acting like you're freaked out or something," Julia said. She rolled onto her belly, propping herself up on her elbows, and looked at him.

"You know, tonight when I was getting us the warm milk," he said, his voice rattling in his throat, "I thought I saw—I don't know." He shook his head and forced out a nervous chuckle. "I thought I saw—it sort of looked like my mother or someone reflected in the living room window."

"What the hell are you talking about?" Julia said. She paused, then laughed softly in the dark. "Is this another one of those stories, like that crap about the church wood that your father tried to scare Bri with?"

John shook his head vigorously. "Not at all," he snapped. "I just thought I saw something—that's all."

Julia felt blindly in the dark until she found his face and gave him a quick kiss. "G'night."

She was exhausted, and John's little spooky story, and even the steady *toot-toot* of the foghorn, didn't ruin the rest of her first night's sleep in their new house. She slept solidly until the morning sun came up over the ocean and lanced her eyes.

John, on the other hand, lay in the dark with his hands clasped behind his head as he stared blankly up at the ceiling. For the first time in his life, the haunting sound of the foghorn filled him with cold and lonely thoughts, and he pictured himself out on the night-stained ocean, tossed around and pulled helplessly by the rushing waves and tides.

Over and over, the ceiling would lighten with a wash of light and then fade, and every now and then he would snap his head to the side and look at the window, positive that in the corner of his eye he had caught a fleeting motion outside. Whenever he sensed something—some*one*—hanging from the ceiling behind the couch, he shivered and, staring up at the darkness, waited for the flash of light from the lighthouse to show him there was nothing there.

He finally fell asleep sometime just before dawn, but his sleep was as disturbed and restless as the dark, storm-tossed ocean.

VII

Like her father, Bri was also having trouble getting back to sleep. Up until she had mentioned missing Bungle, she had been doing fine trying to settle in her new bedroom, but once she remembered how much she missed her cat, how much she wanted him here, she found she couldn't get him and his rain-matted body out of her mind.

She made a mistake that helped keep sleep at bay. Of course her mother had no way of knowing it, and John apparently had forgotten that her bedroom was directly over the living room and there was a heating vent in the floor. She could hear everything her mother and father said as they tried to settle down to sleep. As soon as she heard John mention that he thought he had seen the ghost of his mother, she got out of bed and, ear close to the open vent, listened.

In spite of her occasional reading of a horror novel, she didn't *really* believe in ghosts or the supernatural. Like her mother, she wanted to dismiss what John had seen as nothing more than a trick of the glass, a doubling of one of their images.

The church wood was something else. Maybe it struck her fancy simply because she had never heard of a house actually echoing with sounds it had "heard" years before. The whole idea of wood still reverberating with centuries-old church music gave her the willies, and after her parents stopped talking and she was back in bed, trying to settle down, she lay in the dark just waiting to hear something.

Sleep tiptoed up on her despite her gnawing worry, and she drifted off after a while. Only once during the night did she hear something that dragged her awake. From inside the wall at the head of her bed, she heard a low thump and then a faint scratching noise. After a while another soft thump that sounded like a small pillow being dropped to the floor brought her out of sleep, and she sat up in bed, her sleeping bag pulled up to her chin.

Bri shook her head and rubbed her eyes, trying to decide if she had *really* heard it or if it had simply been part of the dream she had been having. It had sounded like there was something—something plump and heavy—moving around inside the walls, but she was still exhausted from the drive today, and she slowly settled back and let herself drift off to sleep. She decided she would mention it to her father or grandfather in the morning. Maybe—like the church wood—her new granddad would have a story about it.

THREE
Unloading

I

"Rats," Frank said. He spooned some Rice Krispies into his mouth and began chewing noisily. Several pieces of cereal fell back into the bowl when he continued to talk with his mouth full. "There's *rats* in the walls. Gotta 'spect that in an old house."

Julia looked wide-eyed at John, who silently shrugged his shoulders noncommittally.

"So I . . . I wasn't imagining it, then?" Bri said. She had been hungry when she first came downstairs, lured by the smell of eggs and bacon frying, but now her breakfast sat ignored on her plate as she listened to her grandfather. With the sun streaming like honey through the window, she felt great in spite of her poor sleep. One time during the night, she had awoken from a disturbing dream that had something to do with Bungle, her dead cat, and a girl she didn't recognize. In the clear light of morning, she was grateful that the vivid details had dissolved from her memory.

"You bet yer—ahh, bottom dollar there are," Frank said. He wiped his mouth with the back of his hand and took a sip of coffee. "Good coffee," he said, nodding thanks to Julia.

"Frank, honestly—" Julia said. "I don't think you should be filling Bri's mind with these stories." Given the freedom to do so, she would have gone on a bit more about the adjustments Bri was going to have to make, leaving her friends behind in Vermont to live on Glooscap, but she hoped that Frank would have figured that out by now.

"They ain't *stories*," Frank said, shaking his head quickly. "They ain't stories at all."

"Well, that nonsense about the 'church wood,' as you call it— what else would you say it is if it isn't nonsense?"

"Now maybe that's one thing," Frank replied, his eyes suddenly twitching and rolling ceilingward. Julia panicked for a sec-

ond, thinking he was about to black out, but he shook his head
and continued, "Them rats in the walls are another thing, though.
Living here so close to the mainland, 'tweren't hard for rats to get
over here. 'Specially on boats and all, but I'd bet plenty of 'em
swum over here, too. You go down to the wharf sometime, 'n'
you'll see. Tell her, Johnny."

For an instant, John glared at his father's use of what he considered his "little kid's" name; no one since high school had called
him Johnny.

"Tell her what?" he asked, tossing his hands up. "That there are
rats around the wharf? Of course there are."

"And in the walls! In the walls too, goddammit!" Frank
snapped. He brought his fist down hard onto the table, making the
silverware jump and clatter. Turning back to Bri, he said, "In the
fall they come in, yah know. Rats've gotta have a warm place to
live in the winter, same's anyone else. An old house like this has
enough space between the walls even a person could practically
fit in behind there. Round 'bout autumn, the rats start comin' in
'n' they stay inside the walls till spring."

"And you can live with that?" Julia said, wrinkling her nose at
the thought.

"Do they ever come into the house?" Bri asked, her voice
winding up a bit tighter. "Do you ever, like, *see* them?"

Frank shrugged casually. "Ahh, they ain't nothing. I figure
these rats—least their kin—have been coming into this house
since 'fore I was born. It's as much their house as it is mine."

Julia turned to John and said softly, "I want you to get some
D-Con or whatever—set some traps. I don't want to come down
here some morning and find a rat sitting on the countertop, nibbling on a loaf of bread."

"Hell," Frank said, his voice blending into a cackling laugh.
"They don't *nibble*. You ain't never seen these fellas. They're
big. Some of 'em get to be the size of a small poodle, and they're
at least twice as mean as an Airedale."

"Oh, just great," Julia said, her face darkening even more. She
nailed John with an even harsher look. "I mean it," she said. "I
don't want to see any rats in the house. They're . . . unsanitary."

"I sure as shi—" Frank glanced at Bri and corrected himself.
"Sure as heck ain't gonna do anything about it." He took another
spoonful of Rice Krispies and chewed noisily. "The last thing I
want is to have them rats *mad* at me." Turning to Bri, he added,
"They're like cats, you know—they can sense things people ain't
aware of."

Julia looked at Frank, wondering exactly how much of this was
truth and how much was bullshit. She was beginning to realize

that Frank liked to spin these little tales, make up stories just to get a rise out of someone.

"As exciting and as stimulating as this discussion is, I've got a truck to unload and get back to U-Haul. I don't want to have to mess around with it tomorrow," John said as he drained his coffee cup. "I'll be looking for volunteers."

Bri nodded and dug into her breakfast, taking huge bites of toast and eggs and washing them down with orange juice. Julia busied herself at the kitchen sink, anxious to start getting their own things unpacked so she could really start feeling as though they belonged in this house.

Rats in the wall as big as poodles . . . indeed!

II

The morning sun had pushed away the rain clouds, and a clear, blue sky vaulted in the sky, practically vibrating with intensity. Seagulls wheeled in the sky, tiny white specks moving in wide, lazy circles. Thin wisps of steam rose from the street as the morning sun warmed the asphalt. There was a brisk breeze coming in off the water, so in spite of the sweat John worked up unloading the truck, he had to wear a jacket against the chill.

John, his face dripping with sweat, looked out when a car stopped and a man stepped out, squinting in the sun. He waved to John, but it wasn't until the man was halfway across the lawn that John recognized who it was—Randy Chadwick, his old friend from high school.

"Well, I'll be a son of a bitch," Randy said as he stood by the end of the truck and held his hand up for John to shake.

"Son of a bitch, *yourself*," John said. He shook Randy's hand, then jumped down to the ground beside him. "So, I see you're still dragging your sorry ass around this island."

Randy smiled and nodded. "And I see *you're* dragging your sorry ass back to it. How the hell have you been, Johnny?"

"Fine . . . just fine," John said as he stepped back and looked at his friend.

It had been—well, not *that* long ago since he had last seen Randy Chadwick, six years ago, actually, when Randy had showed up at his mother's funeral, as he recalled. But even in the six intervening years, time hadn't spared Randy. He had once been the leanest, toughest-looking guy in the school—no doubt from the hard work he did back then, lobstering to help his family make ends meet. Now around his middle there was the bulge of a well-cultivated beer belly, and Randy's hairline had definitely receded a few inches. His face was tanned and deeply lined—either from worry or hard outdoor work. All in all, John's first impression was that Randy, who was only six months older than he was, looked at least five years older.

"I heard talk around town you might be heading back this way," Randy said. He snapped his head around when Julia came out the front door; then his eyebrows shot up as he quickly took her in. Turning to John, he winked lasciviously and nodded his immediate approval.

"Uh, Julia," John said, bristling at his friend's reaction. "This is my old friend from high school—Randy Chadwick. I've told you about some of the crap we used to pull. Randy, this is my wife, Julia."

"Nice to meet you," Randy said, offering his hand for Julia to shake. Looking back at John, he said, "I never heard you got married. When'd that happen?"

"'Bout five years ago," John said, shuffling his feet. "I would have thought my dad would have mentioned it to someone."

"Well, if he had, you know damn right well it would have been all over the island within a week," Randy said with a laugh.

Just then, Bri came dashing out of the front door and drew to a startled stop when she saw Randy standing there. John introduced her as his daughter, figuring Randy could do the necessary addition to figure out she was actually his stepdaughter.

"Well, Randy, we were just about to take a break for lunch," Julia said. "Would you care to join us?"

Randy glanced back down at his car as though it had just called to him, reminding him of something he had to do, but he shrugged and said, "I'm not particularly hungry, but I'll sit and have a soda or something with you while you eat." Turning to John, he added, "It'll give us a chance to catch up with each other. Christ—you're married! I can't believe it. Of all the people, you're the last one I thought would *ever* get married!"

Julia frowned at that, wondering what he meant, but she left her question unasked as she turned to go to the kitchen and slap together a few sandwiches. Embarrassed by her own awkward entrance, Bri followed her mother into the house.

John and Randy sat down opposite each other at the weather-beaten picnic table on the porch. For the briefest of instances, an awkward silence fell between them, but before long Randy got his jaw working and filled John in on plenty of local gossip. In the time it took for Julia to make the sandwiches, he told John more than he wanted to know about just about everyone they had gone to school with back in the late sixties.

While Randy was in the middle of a story about seeing a guy they had nicknamed "Booger," Julia came out with paper plates, napkins, and a platter loaded with tuna fish sandwiches. Bri was right behind her with a bowl of potato chips and several cans of soda and beer.

"Take what you want," Julia said as she plopped down onto the picnic-table seat. She let out a huff of air that flapped the strand of hair hanging down over her eyes. John thought she looked beat, and as he took half a sandwich, he smiled at her and said, "Thanks, hon."

Randy took a can of beer and popped the top. After a long swallow, he put it on the table and continued. "Course, I suppose you never heard from Abby, now, did you?" he asked.

John had just taken his first bite of sandwich and was chewing. Suddenly he leaned forward and coughed. Casting a quick glance at Julia, he muttered something none of them understood as he shook his head.

"Who's Abby?" Bri asked, looking back and forth between her parents.

Julia smiled thinly and echoed Bri. "Yeah—who's Abby?" She almost said something about Frank calling her Abby yesterday when they first arrived, but she let it drop.

Randy immediately picked up on what was happening and, frowning as he cocked his thumb at John, leaned forward and whispered, "I take it you never told her about Abby?"

Obviously caught in the embarrassment, John tried to turn it all into a joke. "Never saw any need to, actually," he said. Then to Julia he added, "She was just my girlfriend in high school." He swallowed the mouthful of sandwich and quickly took another bite.

"Uh-huh," Julia said. She sipped her Diet Pepsi thoughtfully, actually enjoying watching John squirm.

"It was . . . never anything serious," John added. He took a sip of his beer, grateful when he didn't choke on it.

"Nothing serious? Yeah, right," Randy said with a wide smile. "And the pope doesn't wear a funny hat! They were only the"—he glanced at Bri, then finished—"the *hottest* couple in the school. You'd see them everywhere together, during school, after school, hanging around Pottle's, intown Portland—everywhere, always holding hands and hugging." He leaned back and laughed with the memory. "They were *the* school couple—senior prom king and queen, the whole works."

"We were young and foolish," John said, shaking his head and wishing to hell Randy would just let it drop. As a matter of fact, he was beginning to wish Randy had never even stopped by—

unless he was going to offer to help unload. Right now, John wasn't quite geared up for all this memory-lane crap.

"So?" Julia said casually. "What's she doing now?"

"Probably married to a lobsterman with three or four little brats running around, right?" John said. "She's probably fifty pounds overweight and looks at least ten years older than she really is." He finished off his first sandwich half, and, after another sip of beer, reached for another.

"Actually, no," Randy said. "See, old Romeo here must've really broken her heart 'cause—what was it, two weeks before graduation? Something like that, she just split, left school, left the island. Gone. *Poof!* I'm telling yah, buddy," Randy said, leaning forward and slapping John on the back, "you must have really broken her heart!"

"You're not remembering things right," John said, his voice tight and strained. "*She* broke up with *me*."

"Oh, yeah . . . sure, sure," Randy said, chuckling. "You expect me to believe that?"

John shrugged. "It's the truth. She broke up with me and then the next morning she was gone. She told me she was going to leave. She had some crazy notion she could make it as a model in New York City."

His eyes flicked over to Julia, trying to gauge how she was taking all of this. She was probably as bored with it as he was. He knew something like this had to happen sooner or later, so maybe, he thought, it was just as well to get it over with. But if living on Glooscap was going to be a steady stream of high school and childhood reminiscences, he didn't want any part of it, and he was sure Julia would tire of it soon enough, too.

"But no one knows where she went, huh?" Bri asked. She, at least, seemed interested in Randy's story; she was finding it fascinating to try to imagine John as a boy growing up in this area. John was beginning to think, what with his father's and now Randy's stories, she was really getting an earful.

Randy shook his head. "All I know is, no one on Glooscap ever saw her again. Her parents and her sister . . . you remember Sally, Abby's sister, don't you?"

John shifted uneasily and nodded his head. "Uh, yeah, sort of. She was a couple of years ahead of us, as I recall."

Randy threw his hands up in a helpless gesture. "Well, *anyway*, none of them ever heard from her again. Abby just plain disappeared."

"Boy, that's weird," Bri said.

"How about you and Ellie?" John asked, hoping to change the

subject. "You guys are still together, aren't you?" He scooped a handful of chips onto his plate and started munching them.

"Oh, yeah, sure," Randy said. He drained his beer can and put the empty on the table. "Ellie's like what you said about Abby— married to a lobsterman with—well, she's got only two snot-nosed little brats clinging to her knees, 'n' she ain't exactly fifty pounds overweight."

"Christ! You're still lobstering?" John exclaimed. "I thought you were going to get out of that."

Randy said, "Why? It may be hard work, but it's damned good money!" He was smiling, but then his face suddenly clouded over as he looked at John. "I'm kind of surprised you never heard from Abby again, though," he said. "I always figured you and she would end up together again. That's why I was—begging your pardon, Julia—surprised to find out you'd gotten married."

"Well, hey, you know—time moves on," John said. He finished off his second half of sandwich with a huge bite, stuffed a few more chips into his mouth, and finished his beer. Glancing at his watch, he said, "And speaking of time, if we don't get a move on, we'll be unloading this truck after dark." He waited to see if Randy would pick up on the hint that he might need help with something, but when he didn't, he was just as glad. He was positive a whole afternoon of Randy's stories would drive him crazy.

"Well, I thank you for the beer," Randy said, sighing as he stood up. "It's nice meeting you, Julia—and Bri. I'd like to help you unload, but I've got to take Ellie over to visit her mom. I could swing by and help you later this evening."

Julia, who had been dreading the thought of carrying their large bureaus upstairs, was all set to accept his offer, but John shook his head. "Oh, no, no. We've got the rest of it, no sweat."

"Once you're all settled in, though, Ellie and me will have you guys over for supper," Randy said. "How's that sound? We can talk over old times."

He started down the porch steps and on the walkway turned and looked back up at the old house. "Boy, oh boy—when I think about all the things we used to do back then." He smiled and, shaking his head, held his hand out to John. As they shook, he continued, "I've got to say, though, I never thought I'd see the day you'd come back here to live, not after how many times you told me how you just couldn't wait to get the hell off this island."

John shrugged. "Like I said, time moves on."

"Yeah, I suppose it does," Randy said, nodding. "For some of us, anyway."

III

"High school honey, huh?" Julia said, smiling wickedly. She and John had just finished wrestling the first of their two bureaus up the stairs and into the master bedroom. They were both panting with exhaustion but grateful that they hadn't taken any gouges out of the wall.

"Come on," John said, shaking his head angrily. "Just forget about it, will you? It was never as serious as Randy makes it out."

Julia grunted and shrugged. "It would have been nice if he could have helped us unload."

John sniffed and, wiping his forehead with the back of his hand, said, "He unloaded enough *on* us, I think."

Julia looked at him with one side of her mouth curling up into a half smile. "I'm just surprised you never mentioned Abby to me, that's all." She made it sound as if she was hurt, but really—she didn't know why—she was enjoying seeing John get so bugged. "Actually, you know, yesterday, when I first went into the house, your father asked me if I was Abby."

"He *did*?" John said, suddenly tensing and looking at her wide-eyed.

Julia nodded her head, picking up on his reaction—no matter what John said, there was some obvious tension here. "That's what he called me. I figured his confusing me with someone else had something to do with those blackouts he's been having."

"Umm—probably," John replied simply.

"What, was this Abby someone he wanted you to marry?" Julia asked.

John's mouth tightened into a hard line before he answered her. "Just the opposite," he said, his voice sounding small and wire-tight. "He did everything he could to break us up." He sighed and shook his head. "He was always telling me I shouldn't tie myself down to someone from the island. That I should wait until I went to college and found someone who wouldn't nail my butt to this friggin' place."

"Uh-huh, I see," Julia said, nodding. "So, by the sound of it, it *was* more serious than you said."

John turned on her, his eyes flashing with anger. "Look, it's ancient history as far as I'm concerned, so why don't you just let it drop, okay? Christ! I've got enough to deal with, getting the rest of our shit upstairs. Are we gonna work or shoot the breeze all afternoon?"

So, even though she knew she didn't have the whole story, Julia did let it drop, mostly because neither of them could do much more than grunt as they wrestled the second bureau up the narrow stairway. But once that last big piece was upstairs, it was almost a pleasure to carry in the broken-down pieces for their beds and the much lighter boxes of clothes, dishes, and kitchen utensils, books, and other assorted possessions. Both of them fully appreciated that they had sold off their living room furniture, figuring if Frank's turned out to be too old and grungy, they would simply buy something new.

By three o'clock, they brought the last box inside. John rolled down the truck door and pulled around to the side driveway, figuring it was too late to take the truck back to Portland today. He'd drive in first thing in the morning.

"I think I might go for a little walk," Bri said.

Both of her parents were practically sprawled on the couch in the living room. About the only thought on John's mind was that he wanted a very hot shower before he set to work putting their beds together so they could sleep in their bedroom tonight. He shivered whenever he remembered the hanging gray shape he had seen reflected in the living room window, and no matter how much he ached from unloading, he was determined not to spend another night on the fold-out couch.

Bri glanced at him, worldlessly asking if it was all right to go out for a walk alone; he, after all, knew more about the island than she did.

"I don't see why not," he said after taking a deep breath.

"Where were you thinking of going?" Julia asked. She glanced at the darkening sky outside the living room window. "I don't want you down by the ocean after dark."

"I was just thinking of going over to the beach across the street," Bri said. "Who knows? Maybe I'll meet some of the kids downtown."

"Don't you remember what I told you?" John said, smiling. "There *is* no downtown."

"Just make sure you're back before dark, okay?" Julia said.

"Okay, okay," Bri replied, and she turned to go.

IV

She looks almost as lonely as I feel was Bri's first thought.

She was standing on the side of the road, looking out toward the ocean through a break in the trees. A narrow path, winding down to the sandy beach, was lined on both sides by a tangle of pine and wild rosebushes. Rose hips the size of small apples speckled the dark brush with bright red dots. The breeze coming in off the water was tangy with salt. Waves lapped up on the shiny sands, leaving behind white lines of scud.

The girl Bri was watching moved slowly along the edge of the water, darting up higher onto the beach every time a wave slid landward. She was wearing an old heavy-knit gray sweater—maybe her father's, Bri thought, or her boyfriend's high school letter sweater—and blue jeans rolled up at the cuffs. Her sneakers had something that looked like pom-poms hanging from the laces. She left no footprints in the hard-packed beach sand.

The sky was darkening, and the ocean was stained a deep purple as Bri walked down the path and onto the wide stretch of sand. The waves made the soft, hissing sound of tearing paper as they slid smoothly over the sand. The beach was littered with tangled masses of kelp that tripped Bri up several times as she walked briskly toward where the girl had gone.

But the strange thing was, Bri couldn't see her anymore. Confused, she looked back the way she had come and then down the length of beach, trying to figure out if the girl could have gone that far in the short time it had taken her to come down the path. It looked to Bri as though the girl had gone—what?—maybe a quarter of a mile in the time it had taken her to walk the hundred yards or so down to the shore.

"That's weird," Bri whispered under her breath. The breeze off the ocean took her words and whisked them away.

Looking at the sand, she tried to find any trace of the girl's footprints in the sand, but the beach was as smooth and untouched as if it hadn't been walked on in days.

Maybe the tide's coming in and washed her footprints away, she thought, still walking along the beach, her eyes straining to find some trace of the girl.

Up ahead, she saw where a stream of fresh water running to the ocean had carved a deep gully into the beach.

Ah! she thought. *That's where she went—up there and into the woods.*

Bri scanned the sand for any footprints to tell her she was right, but she could find nothing. Looking behind her, she clearly saw her own footprints, a wavering dark line winding all the way back to the trail, and that was all.

Of course, Bri thought, *if she walked in the water she wouldn't leave any tracks. Maybe she saw me and doesn't want anything to do with me.*

And even though she clearly remembered seeing the girl carefully avoiding each wave as it came toward her, Bri told herself that *had* to have been what happened. She had seen Bri following her and had dashed away, up the gully and into the woods to avoid her.

"Some friendly place *this* is turning out to be!" Bri said softly to herself.

She bent over and picked up a worn piece of oddly shaped driftwood. After brushing the loose sand from it, she hefted it in her hand, cocked her arm back, and spun it end over end into the brush. It ripped through the branches and hit the ground with a dull thud.

"Welcome to our friendly little town!" she yelled, throwing her head back and shouting at the darkening sky. "So nice to meet you! You'll just *love* it here!"

Spreading her arms out, she started spinning around in a wide circle, her feet kicking up fans of sand. She wanted to laugh out loud, or cry. She didn't know *how* she felt other than very, very lonely. The wind in off the water brought tears to her eyes as she spun crazily around until she was sure she was going to fall flat in the sand.

"*Goddammit!*" she shouted, clenching her fists and shaking them. "*God-damn-it, damn-it, damn-it!*"

Bri lurched to a stop and stood there, knees locked and legs braced while the whole world spun around her—beach, sky, ocean—beach, sky, ocean—all twisted around until they blurred like smudged chalk.

Thinking she must look like she was drunk, Bri staggered from side to side, trying to regain her balance. With the sun gone, the chill of the air bit right through her thin jacket, and she knew she had to get home. Her mother would be furious if she was out after dark.

As she started along the beach, back the way she had come, though, something caught her attention from the corner of her eye. Squinting, she tensed and peered as hard as she could at the line of rocks and brush ahead of her, past where she had first come down onto the beach. It looked like . . .

"What the—" Bri muttered, thinking it was just a trick of the gathering gloom. It was *impossible* for her—the girl she had been following—to be all the way back down the beach, but sure enough, there she was!

Did she run all the way back there while I was screwing around? Bri wondered. *What the heck is she doing?*

Still not entirely convinced the girl was even there, Bri smiled widely and waved her hand over her head. She was looking directly into the western sky, which was glowing brightly as if there were a forest fire below the horizon, and that only intensified the darkness in the rocks and trees by the edge of the beach.

"Hello . . ." Bri called out, still waving her hand as she started toward the girl.

Yes, there was no doubt about it—she was standing in the gloom just at the edge of the brush. It sure as heck *looked* like she was watching her, but the girl didn't respond in any way. She just stood there stock-still, staring toward Bri. Her gray sweater seemed oddly suspended in midair, and the darkness seemed about to swallow her up.

"Hey! Wait! Hold on a minute!" Bri shouted. She pumped her fists as she ran, taking in deep gulps of air that burned in her lungs.

In a matter of seconds, Bri closed the distance between them, but then at some point she looked down so she wouldn't trip in the sand or on the kelp, and when she looked up again, the girl was gone. Bri drew to a halt and stared, frustrated, at the thick black line of brush against the fiery sky. The girl was gone—vanished.

"Hey!" Bri shouted. Her voice bounced back from the wall of rocks with an odd reverberation. She slapped her fists against her thighs and grunted angrily.

"Come on!" she shouted as she walked very slowly toward where the girl had been. "For crying out loud! I just want to talk!"

Her legs were aching from her run, and the air rushing into her lungs felt like liquid fire. She didn't even try to hold back the tears that were forming in her eyes and streaking down her cheeks.

"I just want to talk. . . ." she said, her words echoing softly. "How the heck am I going to make friends if nobody will even *talk* to me?"

Dejected, she turned away and headed back toward the path she knew would lead up to Shore Drive. It was way past time to be getting home; her mother was probably already worried. She kicked at the sand as she crossed the beach and started up the path, but then, not five steps into the woods, she jolted to a stop. Looking down, she saw a peculiarly shaped piece of driftwood. It looked oddly like a boomerang, and when Bri stooped down and picked it up, it felt strangely familiar in her hand.

She stood up and studied the piece of wood as she turned it over and over in her hand, wondering, could this really be the piece she had thrown into the woods back by the gully.

"Friggin' island!" she hissed, surprised to hear herself echo her father's use of the word *friggin'*. She threw the wood down as hard as she could, satisfied by the snapping sound as it broke on the ground.

"Friggin' bunch of weird people on a friggin' island," she said as she stomped up the trail back to the road.

V

Her mother had everything pulled out of the cupboards and lined up on the counter while she reached up onto the top shelf and scrubbed with a sponge and hot water. She looked around and down when Bri came into the kitchen from the living room.

"Nice of you to show up *before* dark," Julia said, scowling. "I was just beginning to worry about where you were."

"Just out," Bri said, going to the refrigerator and taking out a gallon jug of milk. She got a glass from the counter and filled it, then put the milk back and stood leaning against the countertop while she drank. She wanted to tell her mother about the girl she had seen, but she decided not to. Why get her mom all worked up, too?

"So, did you meet anyone on your walk?" her mother asked, as though reading her mind. Apparently satisfied with her job, she dropped the sponge into the pan full of sudsy water and eased herself back down to the floor.

"Naw," she replied.

"Hmmm," Julia said. Shrugging, she started putting some of the boxes and cans back into the cupboard. She inspected each item and, more often than not, dropped them into the trash can beside her. "God, some of this stuff must've been up here for years." The only thing that made her feel good was that she hadn't found any evidence of mice—much less poodle-sized rats —up there, so maybe Frank had been pulling Bri's leg after all.

"I don't think you have to worry, though," Julia said. "You'll be starting school tomorrow, and I'm sure you'll meet plenty of nice kids there."

Bri nodded and then drained off the rest of her milk. "Yeah, sure. I'll be the new kid, and no one will want to talk to me." She also wanted to say something about the girl she had seen on the beach, but her ignoring her had hurt Bri, and she *definitely* wasn't going to mention this to her mom.

"Do I really have to start school tomorrow?" she asked, her voice whining. This had been a point of discussion ever since they'd started packing. All along both of her parents had insisted she jump right into school so she could start adjusting to her new life, but now, with the reality of all the unpacking and cleaning they had to do, she was trying one last time to get a few days' reprieve—a week, if she got lucky.

Julia chuckled. "The 'new kid'—makes me imagine you as shiny and fresh as these shelves I just scrubbed."

"Yeah, but Mom—"

"No yeah-buts," Julia snapped.

"But you don't understand," Bri said.

"I understand plenty," Julia said, turning toward her with a frown. "I moved a few times myself when I was young, and I know how it feels to be the new kid."

"Things are different, though," Bri said weakly. She knew she had lost—and this had been the final round.

"Is Granddad home yet?" Bri asked. "I'm getting kind of hungry." She looked longingly at the kitchen table to see any evidence that supper was close.

"He should be back soon," Julia said, wiping her hair from her eyes. "If you're hungry, there's nothing stopping you from making a sandwich to tide yourself over."

Bri looked at her mother with wide, sad eyes. "Do you want me to starve?"

Julia shook her head angrily. "Look, Bri—your father and I are exhausted! Between unloading the truck and getting all sorts of furniture shifted around and cleaned up in here, I really don't have the energy to do a turkey dinner for you tonight, all right? If you want something to eat, get it yourself! And when you're done, you can get up to your room and start unpacking. I think your father has already put your bed together, so you might want to put some sheets and blankets on it while you're at it."

"God! You make it sound like I committed a capital crime or something," Bri said.

For a second longer, her mother's face remained hard; then, it softened and she said, more mildly, "Sorry, honey. I'm hot, tired, and cranky."

Bri nodded, further resolved not to mention the girl she had seen on the beach. Her mother left the kitchen and went upstairs, and Bri stood by the counter, silent for several seconds while she listened to her mother and father upstairs, moving something heavy, by the sounds up in their bedroom. Finally she went to the refrigerator and fished around a bit. The best she could come up with was the tuna fish left over from lunch, so she slapped together a sandwich, refilled her glass with milk, and walked into the living room to sit on the couch and eat.

Outside, the sky was dark. The distant flash of the lighthouse winked on and off, and the solitary streetlight on the corner spread a faint yellow glow over the road. A few falling leaves drifted by on the breeze, spinning in the rectangle of light from the house. Even with the sounds of her parents unpacking upstairs, knowing they were nearby, Bri couldn't have felt more lonely.

She ate and drank in silence, tossing over in her mind what had happened on the beach. She had wanted to tell her mother about the girl she had seen, but something—she didn't know what— told her not to. If anything, she thought, her mother would caution her about talking to strangers, no matter what! But how, she wondered, was she *ever* going to make friends if everybody on the island avoided her?

A car came down the road, and its headlights swept over the yard as it turned into the driveway and stopped. Bri got up from the couch and, looking out the side window, saw a man get out, take a wheelchair from the backseat, fold it open, and then help Frank out of the front seat and into the wheelchair. She could hear the buzz of their voices through the window but couldn't make out what they were saying.

After a bit of discussion, the man got back into his car and drove away as Frank started rolling his wheelchair up the walkway to the kitchen door. It was just as the car was backing around and its headlights swung around that Bri saw something—some-one—standing on the side of the road, under the maple tree across the street from the house.

She tingled with instant recognition. It was the girl she had tried to follow on the beach! She was standing there, not cringing or hiding by the side of the road, but looking up, bold as could be, at the house. She was wearing that same old gray sweater, and she had her arms folded across her chest. Her face—in that instant wash of light—had looked pale and her expression blank as she looked up at the house.

Can she see me? Bri wondered.

She cast a fearful glance up the stairway, wondering if one of her parents might be there and also be able to see the girl outside. The stairs were empty, though, and she could tell by the scuffling sounds that they were still unloading boxes and putting things away upstairs.

The car pulled away, and Bri wondered why it didn't even pause when the headlights shined directly on the girl for an instant. She heard the kitchen door bang open as Frank made his entrance, but Bri didn't say a word or move a muscle as she stood by the window, watching the dark roadside where the girl had been.

Once the car was gone, the light from the corner streetlight wasn't quite bright enough to illuminate the girl, and Bri started to think she had disappeared again—had pulled a quick vanishing trick like the one on the beach. The light cast thin shadows of tree branches onto the street, but underneath the tree the shadows were thick and black, impenetrable.

Bri knew at least one thing now—the girl *must* have seen her and, in all likelihood, had followed her home. There was no other way to explain her being outside the house. Bri wondered, though, why she seemed to be avoiding her...as if she just wanted to watch.

Maybe she's just shy...just checking me out before she tries to meet me. She's trying to figure out who I am, Bri thought, peering out into the darkness. She couldn't be sure if the girl was still standing out there under the tree or had gone home. *And just where is home?*

"Well, I see you folks got some work done while I was away," Frank said gruffly to Bri as he rolled from the kitchen into the living room.

Bri, feeling as if she had been caught doing something wrong, quickly turned away from the living room window and smiled thinly at her grandfather.

"Umm—Mom and Dad did most of the moving," she said, casting a quick glance over her shoulder at the window. She couldn't shake the feeling that the girl was still outside the house, looking in at her.

As if to prove the truth of her statement, Julia yelled from upstairs, "Bri! You know those boxes in your room aren't going to unpack themselves!"

With an exaggerated slouch, Bri smiled at Frank and then trudged up the stairs to her room. Going down the hallway, she called out to her mother that Frank was home, then went into her room to face the disaster. The old, squeaky bed was gone, and Bri was happy to see her own bed. With a loud whoop, she jumped onto the bare mattress and bounced a few times.

The bedroom door opened, and her mother poked her head inside. Her face was streaked with grime and sweat, and her eyes looked tired.

"I'm not interrupting anything, am I?" she asked as she eased into the room, her face registering disapproval at the amount of work she saw still needed to be done.

"Just—uh, just getting used to it," Bri said, slightly embarrassed. "Before I get to work unpacking."

Julia frowned as she moved over to the window and looked out. The yard was dark, and a fitful gust of wind rattled the panes. She hugged herself and shivered.

"I suggest you get a move on," Julia said, turning from the window to face her. "You've got school tomorrow first thing, and I don't want you complaining that you can't find anything to wear in the morning."

Bri nodded, got up from the bed, and bent down to open the first box within reach. It happened to be clothes, and she started loading up her bureau drawers while her mother leaned back against the windowsill and took a break.

Bri was torn, wondering if she should tell her mother about the girl she had . . . well, *met* wasn't exactly the right word—had *seen* on the beach, and now outside the house. It bothered her, kind of gave her the creeps that she had followed her back home and had waited outside, and maybe was still there watching her but not letting her talk to her. She jammed her clothes into the bureau, wishing, if nothing else, to lose her concerns in activity, but the thought of that girl out there in the dark and cold gnawed at her mind. She wished her mother would leave the room so she could take a peek out the window and see if she was still there.

"So tell me, are you getting excited about starting school tomorrow?" Julia asked.

Thank you, God, Bri thought when her mother pushed herself away from the window and started pacing the room. *Now if I can only think of some reason to go over by the window. . . .*

Trying to look casual, Bri shrugged as she took out several sweaters and refolded them before putting them on the top shelf of the closet. "I dunno," she said. "I mean, I'd rather—"

"We've already had that discussion," Julia said coolly.

"I know," Bri said, whining. She took one of her sweaters and unfolded it, holding it up for her mother to see. "But all I've got is *this* stuff. I don't have anything *new.*"

"I think that sweater's just fine," Julia said, "and besides, no one at the school is going to know it isn't new."

"But *I* will," Bri said, her eyes flicking angrily from her mother to the sweater. Then, with a sigh, she folded it again and put it on top of the pile in her closet. "Well, at least I won't be as out of style as that girl I saw. *She* was dressed like someone out of the sixties or something."

"What girl was that?" Julia asked.

"Oh, just someone I saw downtown," Bri answered as she sat on the floor and opened another box, this one filled with her stuffed animals. She picked up a blue elephant she had named Oscar and, stroking her chin, said, "Hmm, I think I'll keep him on the windowsill for now."

Her heart seemed to skip a beat as she crossed the floor to the window. One floorboard creaked underfoot, and she made a startled little squeak, but her mother seemed not even to notice. She stroked Oscar's blue fuzzed head, remembering Bungle before placing him on the windowsill. As casually as possible, she let her gaze drift outside.

Her heart almost stopped when she saw her! The girl was still outside, standing in the shadows on the opposite side of the street, looking up at the house. Her gaze seemed to be directed right up at Bri's window. The faint wash of the far-off streetlight gave her upturned face a gauzy glow, and Bri could see that she was *smiling*!

Behind her, her mother was saying something more about school, but Bri's mind shut her out as she looked down at the girl. Their eyes met—there was no doubt in Bri's mind. A cold jolt hit her in the stomach, and her hand was trembling as she let go of Oscar.

What is she doing? Bri thought, wondering if this girl was teasing her for some reason.

Steeling herself, Bri forced a smile onto her face as she slowly raised her hand and waved to the girl outside. She could see her own reflection in the glass, and the thinness, the hollowness of her own smile unnerved her. But then her smile widened into a genuine grin when she saw the girl raise her hand and wave back at her.

"Mom . . . come here," Bri said, quickly turning away from the window for an instant. "There's someone outside."

Julia came over to the window, but when they both looked outside, the girl was gone. Bri had almost expected it.

"She *was* there," she said, looking at her mother's face close to hers.

"Who was?" Julia asked.

Bri was silent for a moment as she weighed her words. There was still something in the back of her mind that told her not to say anything more about this to her mother, to just let things go. But one thing Bri had always prided herself on was her honesty with her mother—especially after the divorce eight years ago. Holding back on her mother would be like *lying*!

"This afternoon, when I went for a walk," she said softly, letting her gaze drift toward the window. "Down on the beach I saw this girl. . . ."

It didn't take long to give her mother the details, because not much had happened. She realized, as she spoke, that she felt the situation was more complex than it actually was. It all boiled down to the fact that she had seen someone who, basically, had ignored her. *So what was the problem?*

The problem was, she had followed her home and was hanging

around outside the house, and Bri had no idea who she was or what kind of person she was.

Maybe she was a nut case . . . a girl who had no friends and, because of that, had gotten—well, *weird*. Maybe she was into, like, kinky sex or something. Her mother had told her about *those* kinds of girls.

Or maybe she had a rotten home life, had a drunk for a mother and had been sexually abused by her father. Her mother had told her about *those* kinds of situations, too! Maybe this girl hung around other people's houses because they had the "normal" home life she didn't have.

Or maybe she didn't even *have* a home! Maybe her parents had both died, and she lived alone, say down by the wharf in one of the fishing shacks. Maybe, with winter coming, she was looking for a warm house to be invited into.

Or maybe, as Bri had thought before, this girl was just shy and *did* want to meet her but didn't know how to go about it.

There were far too many possibilities to consider, Bri realized, but she knew one thing—her thoughts would *stay* just speculations as long as she never got to meet the girl and talk with her.

"You're sure you saw someone out there just now?" Julia said, unable to disguise the tremor in her voice. She didn't exactly relish the idea of anyone from the island playing Peeping Tom with them.

Realizing she had to calm her mother, Bri shook her head as though confused. "I don't know for sure," she said. "Maybe it was just the shadows from the streetlight." She knew it hadn't been, but she didn't want her mother getting all worked up about it, what her father jokingly called, "getting your undies in a bundle."

"You know, I'm probably just imagining things," Bri said.

"Well, you either saw her or you didn't," Julia said harshly. She was exhausted from the day of steady work, and her nerves were frayed.

"I *know* she was out at the beach," Bri said, not wanting her mother to question her sanity. "But I probably just saw the shadow of a tree branch or something. There's no one out there now."

"I think I'm going to have your father take a look around, anyway," Julia said as she started toward the door. Before she left the room, she turned toward Bri and, pointing her forefinger at her, said, "And *you* get to work. No more gazing out the window. I want all this stuff put away"—she glanced at her wristwatch—"within two hours!"

VI

Frank went to bed earlier than usual, saying that his day out visiting had worn him out, but Julia, John, and Bri worked long into the night, trying to blend their things in with what was already in the house. They realized early on that much of their stuff would probably end up in storage in the garage, but there were several personal things—certain paintings and books and pieces of furniture—that they couldn't quite abandon. They wanted to wait to talk to Frank about certain things of his that might end up in storage.

"I just can't wait to hit some *real* sheets on our *real* bed," Julia said, glancing at her wristwatch and seeing that it was almost midnight. "We can't get it all done in one night anyway, so why don't we all get to bed. Bri, you've got to be in the principal's office at seven-thirty in the morning."

Bri grunted and opened her mouth, thinking one last time to register her protest, but she fell silent. After kissing her mother and father good night, she went up the stairs, put on her flannel nightie, brushed her teeth, and slid into bed. *Ahh,* she thought *my own bed!*

But in the darkened room, listening to her parents as they washed up from the day's work, she felt about as tired as she would have after ten cups of coffee. She clasped her hands behind her head and lay there, staring up at the ceiling, her eyes so wide open they felt as if they were glued that way.

First she told herself she was just waiting for her parents to stop clunking around in the bathroom, running the shower, using the blow-dryer, flushing the toilet. But soon enough they were quietly settled in bed, and the house fell silent. Still sleep didn't come, so she told herself she was tense and excited about starting school in the morning, but she knew the truth—she was just waiting to hear the low, throbbing strains of organ music echoing in the walls . . . or the soft thump of a rat scurrying around inside the wall.

At last, though, she admitted what she had known all along: she was wondering how long that girl had waited outside in the dark, looking up at her darkened window . . . or if she was *still* out there!

She glanced at the illuminated dial of her alarm clock. *Twelve forty-five! God, I'll never get up on time tomorrow if I don't get to sleep!*

Her fresh-washed sheets and pillowcase crinkled under her weight as she shifted onto her side. Her staring eyes fixed on the window and the dark silhouette of Oscar, the elephant. Beyond the glass, the night sky practically vibrated with stars, bone-white pinpricks in the black. The thin shadow of a tree branch swaying in the breeze caught just the edge of her windowsill, and even though she knew it didn't look anything like a hand or claw, the shadow unnerved her because she couldn't help but imagine there was *something* out there on the window ledge, trying to pry her window open, claw its way to her!

She wanted to say the heck with it and just roll over onto her other side.

Don't even look *at the window!*

Don't even think *about that girl, whoever she is!*

Forget about everything *and get some sleep!* She knew she wouldn't make much of an impression her first day at school if, on top of everything else, she fell asleep in her first class. But *trying* to fall asleep, she had found, was like trying not to think about something—the harder you tried, the more you failed!

With a deep sigh, she threw her covers off and swung her feet to the floor. A chill went up the back of her legs, but she barely noticed it as she moved slowly toward the window.

Will the girl still be out there? she wondered. *But no—that's impossible! How could she be?*

Bri held her breath until her lungs felt as if they would burst as she looked out into the thick darkness. Beyond the harsh, dark line of the horizon, the starry sky looked like powdered velvet. The street was bathed in the soft glow of the streetlight, but everything was quiet, everything was calm. The girl *definitely* wasn't out there on the side of the road.

"At least I can't *see* you," Bri whispered. Her face was close to the window, and her breath fogged the glass. Her view of the road blurred, and she could almost imagine the girl *was* still there, hidden in the tree's shadow.

Crouching by the window, Bri waited, taking shallow breaths and trying not to blink her eyes. She didn't want to miss it if the girl was there and tried to move away. And what began as a suspicion soon became a conviction. She *was* still out there . . . she *was* hiding in the dark, looking up at her window! Bri could *feel* her sad, lonely eyes reaching up out of the darkness, touching her.

With a sudden sharp intake of breath, Bri stood up and spun away from the window. Fishing around in the dark, she found her slippers and quickly slid them onto her feet. Then she raced down the stairs taking them two at a time, her hand sliding on the railing, guiding her in the dark. She dashed to the living room door and flung it wide open, the chilly night air slamming into her like a shock wave.

Once outside, Bri didn't hesitate a second. She ran around to the side of the house on Oak Street, her eyes trying to slice like lasers into the darkness. Both the streetlight's glow and the shadows it cast seemed more intense, more harshly lined as Bri ran to the edge of the lawn and then drew to a stop, panting as she stared at the opposite side of the road.

"Hello," she called, her voice a raw whisper. "Are you still out there?"

A chilling breeze circled around her ankles like tiny hands. Bri felt suddenly very alone and exposed. It seemed that not only was the one girl watching her, but a whole multitude of eyes had surrounded her and were staring at her, unseen from the darkness . . . eyes that were cold and hungry.

A shiver ran through Bri's body, and her voice sounded fainter as she called again, "Hey! Are you there?"

Her only answer was the fitful breeze hissing like a snake in the dried grass and weeds of the lawn. Her vision blurred as tears welled up in her eyes, and her throat felt suddenly parched.

"I *know* you're out there," she said, her voice weaker as she scanned the solid wall of the night. "I just want to talk." Her voice faded even more. "I just want to be friends."

The night remained as silent and unyielding as it was dark. No soft chirring of insects in the grass, no gentle call of night birds . . . only the wind sighing.

Her tears carved hot tracks down her cheeks. Bri felt nearly overwhelmed with loneliness, and she wasn't even sure who she felt it for—herself or for the girl.

Maybe, she thought, *for both of us because I know, I can feel that you've lost something like I have. I've lost my friends and my home in Vermont, and my best friend, Bungle, but what have you lost? Why are you so lonely?*

She turned and headed back toward the house, feeling with every step that, out there in the darkness, cold eyes were fixed on her like magnets. She mounted the steps and went back inside the house, grateful, at least, to be out of the cold wind. She leaned her back against the door to shut and lock it with a soft click.

"See anyone?"

The voice came to her out of the darkness, and she let out a loud squeal. It took her eyes a moment to adjust to the dark inside the house, but after a second, she saw the silhouette of her grand-dad in his wheelchair in the doorway of his bedroom at the end of the hallway.

"I—ah," she started to say, but surprise held its fingers around her throat, and words still couldn't quite form.

"Sometimes, you know," he said, his voice sounding distant, "I get the feeling, too, that there's someone out there." He started rolling down the hallway toward her, and as he got closer, she caught a glimpse of his face—his eyes were half open, looking blankly up at the ceiling.

"It's like . . . I don't know, for sure," he said. "Sometimes I can almost *grab* it . . . and then it's gone."

He shook his head as though to clear it, but when he looked at her again, his face registered surprise, as though he had just noticed her standing there.

"What're you doing up at this hour?" he asked sharply.

Unable to speak, Bri simply shrugged.

"Yeah—I wasn't able to sleep, either," Frank said. He snapped on the overhead light. The sudden flood of light was so bright it hurt Bri's eyes. Shielding her eyes, she squinted as she looked at him watching her. She felt suddenly very self-conscious, standing there in her nightie and slippers. Looking down, she saw dried leaves and twigs stuck to the hem of her nightie.

"I . . . it was the weirdest thing," Bri said, stammering the words. "I was . . . positive I saw someone outside the house."

Frank sniffed and scratched his head. "Could've been," he said. "Lots o' nights some of the fellas end up drinkin' late down on the wharf. Could've been one or two of them stumblin' home in the dark."

Bri wanted to tell him about the girl she had seen on the beach, but instead she bent over and started picking the crud off her nightie.

"Yeah . . . well, maybe," she said. It bothered her that she was unable to maintain eye contact with her grandfather, but it was spooky, the way he just sat there hunched up in his wheelchair, staring at her, examining her. And even *weirder* how he had spoken with her and then acted surprised at seeing her. She wasn't positive, but it was almost as if he was toying with her—as if he knew something and was just waiting for her to say the right words so he would know that she knew, too.

"It's late. Hadn't you ought to get yourself back up to bed?" he asked.

Bri feigned a yawn as she tossed the dried leaves she'd collected into the wastebasket by the coat closet. "Yeah," she said, nodding, "I guess so. See you in the morning."

"G'night," Frank said, not moving, but shifting just his eyes to follow her as she went up the stairs. "Pleasant dreams."

FOUR
First Day Jitters

I

Once John and Bri had left for the day, Julia felt more at loose ends than ever. It wasn't that there wasn't any work to be done. Far from it. They had unpacked only about a quarter of their things last night, and most of what had been unpacked still hadn't found a place yet in Frank's house.

Our house now, Julia thought as she sat at the kitchen table, her hands wrapped around a cup of coffee. For several minutes she sat there looking around, comparing this kitchen to the one she had left behind in Shelburne Falls. Granted, this one was much bigger, but her kitchen back in Vermont had been sunny and yellow and warm. How many times had she sat at her own table in that kitchen, drinking coffee and talking with Sue or Ann or any number of friends who seemed always to be dropping by. There had been someone visiting every day, but who was there to visit with here on Glooscap? She had to resist the almost overwhelming desire to take the phone and give Sue or someone a call. Maybe just talking with her for a few minutes would get her out of her blue funk. But the longer she looked from dingy cupboard to dusty corner, the more she wondered why she had so willingly gone into self-exile from friends and everything she cherished in Vermont.

As if in answer she heard a soft thump and, looking around, saw Frank maneuvering his wheelchair around the corner into the kitchen.

"Mornin'," he said, pausing to scratch his beard-stubbled jowls.

"I hope we didn't disturb you too early this morning," Julia said, standing up and making room so he could get past her. "John and Bri had to get a pretty early start."

"Ahh, I'm a light sleeper anyway," Frank grumbled. A little

twinkle lit his eyes when he added, "I was up late, listenin' to the organ music."

He reached for the coffeepot and cup Julia had thoughtfully left out on the corner for him, filled his cup, and twisted around in his wheelchair to place it on the table before going to the refrigerator for the milk.

Julia's first impulse was to get it for him, but she knew he was used to doing things on his own and that he would resent anything she did to patronize him. She slowly eased herself back into her chair, not sure what to say next. All she could think was, if Frank didn't turn into a much better conversationalist, she would have plenty of motivation to get to work unpacking soon.

Frank came back to the table, stirred a generous amount of milk into his cup, then, taking a sip, leaned back and smacked his lips.

"Well, this is going to be unusual," he said, placing his cup on the table.

"How do you mean?" Julia asked, afraid he was going to start in on how they would have to be much quieter in the morning.

"Havin' the coffee made when I get up," Frank said, taking another sip. "It's kinda nice. Do you serve breakfast, too—or do I have to fetch my own?"

Julia smiled and stood up. "Scrambled or over easy?" she asked, reaching for the frying pan.

"Actually, toast and cereal will do just fine," Frank said. "But I reckon you got enough to do without waitin' on me hand-and-foot. I can get it myself."

Is this some kind of test? Julia wondered, looking for an instant at Frank and trying to gauge what he really meant. He was smiling at her pleasantly enough, but beneath the surface was he silently measuring her? And if he was, by what standards?

"It's no problem," Julia said, opening the cupboard and taking down a box of Rice Krispies. She popped two pieces of whole wheat bread in the toaster, got the grape jelly from the refrigerator, a bowl and silverware from the cupboard, and placed everything on the table in front of Frank. While she drank her second cup of coffee, he set to work eating his skimpy breakfast. She wondered how he could eat cereal without any sugar, but decided it was probably on doctor's orders.

The bowl of Rice Krispies was soon gone, and he was halfway through his second piece of toast when he nailed her with an unexpected question.

"So, what in the hell's John's problem?"

His bluntness surprised her. With difficulty, she swallowed her mouthful of coffee before looking at him and saying, "Beg your pardon?"

"I said, what in the hell is John's problem?" Frank repeated. "It don't take a goddamned Sherlock Holmes to figure out that *somethin's* bothering him. 'N' since he ain't about to open up to me, I thought maybe you could give me a bit of insight."

Instantly, Julia ticked off the possibilities to herself. Of course she, too, had noticed that John was acting . . . well, a little bit *differently* for him since coming back to Maine. His starting smoking again had been the only overt signal she had picked up. *But*, she thought, *Frank knows him better than I do in some ways. What's he driving at?*

"I don't think it's anything serious," she said, wringing her hands helplessly. "I mean, I don't think it's anything more than the stress of relocating. You know, a new job and all, and—"

"And coming back home," Frank said harshly, "to live with me! To take *care* of me!" He curled one hand into a fist and brought it down hard enough on the arm of the wheelchair to make it rattle. "Kinda funny, actually, when you think how much I was always the one pushin' him to get an education so he could better himself." He snorted and shook his head. "Can't very well better yourself on an island like this!"

The resentment Julia felt bottled up inside of Frank genuinely scared her. Of course, in the years she had known John, he had told her plenty of things about what kind of father Frank had been and what kind of childhood he had had. When she compared John's childhood to her own, though, she concluded he had gotten off fairly easily; it certainly hadn't been like *her* life, being passed from foster home to foster home after her parents had died.

"I don't think it's fair of you to say that," Julia said softly. "He doesn't resent you."

She wanted to say more but cut herself off and, looking out the window past Frank, groped for the right words. She was about to continue when, from the corner of her eye, she saw something—a thin, almost indistinct shadow slide silently across the windowsill. For just an instant, the sunlight streaming in through the window had been blocked. She tensed, looking at Frank to see if he had noticed it, too, but his back was to the window.

Forcing herself to stay calm and look casual, Julia got up and brought her half-empty cup over to the sink. She leaned forward, looking back and forth out the window, squinting into the sun as she dumped the coffee out and rinsed the cup. As far as she could see, there was nothing—no tree branches or birds or anything that could account for the shadow she had seen. It had been so thin and fleeting, she was almost convinced she had imagined it, but she couldn't rid herself of the unnerved feeling that something had been outside there. It was probably just a bird flying by, she concluded, but that didn't dispel the odd sensation she had that the source of the shadow had been close to the house.

"To be quite honest with yah," Frank went on, apparently not noticing her distraction, "I think it's 'cause he doesn't like me— never has! 'Specially since his mother died. I think he still blames me for what happened to her."

"Don't be ridiculous," Julia said automatically. She reached out blindly and put her cup in the dish drainer but kept scanning the yard.

"Come on, Julia," Frank said. His voice had such intensity that she turned around and faced him. "We're both adults here, and if we don't speak honestly with one another, your living here just ain't gonna work. You know that, and I know that. Right?"

"Of course," Julia said.

Her back was toward the window, and she just about screamed from the sensation that there was still someone out there watching her! Her breath caught in her throat, and she found it difficult to look directly at Frank. She wanted to maintain solid eye contact with him because she didn't want him to read her mounting fear and take it to mean she was hiding something about John from him.

"Then you can tell me up front what the hell it is that's bothering' him," Frank said. "Since you folks got here, he's said maybe three words to me. 'N' if he hates me so much—"

"He doesn't *hate* you," Julia said, forcing her voice to stay calm and mild. But then she had to clamp her jaw shut when, glancing down at her hand resting on the counter, she definitely saw a shadow move over the countertop. Her back was being warmed by the sun, and she felt it suddenly go cold, *as though something had come between her and the shaft of sunlight!*

With a low grunt, she spun around and stared wide-eyed out the window, fully expecting to see someone standing outside looking at her. The cold spot on her back sent goose bumps rippling down her arms, and she had all she could do not to scream when she saw *nothing*.

There was no one out there; the sun poured, unblocked, in through the window.

"Are you all right?" Frank asked, for the first time noticing her agitation.

Julia nodded, rubbing the bridge of her nose. "Yeah, I just thought for a second that I heard something outside," she said tightly, shaking her head.

Frank kept looking at her, making her feel as though he could peel aside her exterior and look right into her deepest thoughts. Of course, she knew that John honestly hadn't wanted to come back to Glooscap, that he would just as soon have continued their life in Vermont and let Frank fend for himself, either at home or in a nursing home. But she couldn't tell Frank she had been the one who insisted that they come to help him out. She couldn't—she *wouldn't*—tell him that. If he and John had unresolved conflicts between them, no matter how thick the tension between them grew, they were going to have to be the ones to work it out, not her!

"Look, Frank," she said, "if you think there's a problem between you two, it's up to you to talk to John about it. He's your son, after all." She waved her hands for emphasis. She was barely able to repress a shiver as she wondered who or what had blocked the sunlight in the window behind her back.

Frank snorted and shook his head as though she had just delivered a joke. "Yeah . . . right."

"I'm not going to get between the two of you," she went on. "If you can't talk to him directly, then, yes, you're right—our being here *isn't* going to work out."

She heard the words she was saying, and she honestly meant them, but her mind was consumed by the desire to move from where she was standing with her back to the window. She was so tense, though, that she was afraid if she moved right now, she would let out a scream and run from the room. The sensation that somewhere, outside the house someone was watching her scared the bejesus out of her. And coupled with what Bri had said last night about the girl she had tried to meet down on the beach, Julia was beginning to have grave doubts—not about living here to help Frank—but simply about living on Glooscap Island. There *was* something strange going on here, no doubt, but she was convinced of only one thing: it had absolutely nothing to do with the tension between Frank and John.

"I really do have a lot of work to do," she said. She held her breath as she shifted away from the window, still feeling unseen eyes boring into her back.

She came over to the table and started clearing Frank's place, but he quickly grabbed his empty cereal bowl and said, "I can get it."

Knowing it was time to back off, Julia said simply, "Fine," and smiling a smile she didn't feel, she went out into the living room and got to work opening boxes of books and placing them on the shelves by the fireplace. She tried as hard as she could to lose herself in the work, but she couldn't shake the feeling all day that there had been someone out there watching her. And she knew she would never forget the chilled sensation on her back when she felt whoever it was come between her and the sun.

II

"My first impression, if you want the truth, is that you're walking right into the middle of a shit storm," Barry Cummings, John's new boss at Atkins Construction, said. He was a tall, heavy-built black man with a warm smile John had liked immediately.

After leaving Bri off at school, John had had trouble finding a parking place and had gotten into the office a few minutes late— making for a great first impression. The first thing Barry did was take him out of the office building and down the street to show him where he could be guaranteed a parking space—if he arrived before eight every morning. Then he gave John a quick tour of the office, introducing him to everyone they bumped into. After loitering around the coffeepot, making light conversation with the employees, Barry showed John his new office. The company had recently moved into a brand-new building on Commercial Street, and from his office window, John could see, off in the distance across Casco Bay, the hazy purple lump of Glooscap Island.

Ah! Home, sweet home! he had thought bitterly while looking out over the water.

Now, working on their second cup of coffee, he and Barry were leaning over a huge blueprint unrolled across John's new work desk. The room was pleasant enough, clean and well lit, but perhaps a bit too small. John figured he, being "low man," had been given the smallest space.

The blueprint they were looking at was of the lot divisions and proposed road plan for Surfside Ledges, a condo development being built by the Freedom Corporation, one of the biggest land developers in the Portland area. It just so happened that the project was being built on the northeast side of Glooscap Island, on the ocean side of two small hills known locally as The Brothers that overlooked Whale Cove.

"Everything looks fine to me," John said after scanning the plan a few minutes.

Glooscap was a relatively small island, and even though he hadn't been home in years, he knew just about every square foot of the place. As a boy, he and his friends had ranged far and wide over the island, playing guns or whatever. Just past Larson's

Pond, where they had gone skating every winter, the area around The Brothers was—at least back then—one of the few woodsy places on the island. Huge oaks mingled with second-growth pines right down to the shore's edge. On the extreme tip of Whale Cove was Haskins' farm, about fifteen acres of cleared land, an old farmhouse, and a falling-down barn. The condo development, he could see, was situated so it had a beautiful view of the outer islands of Casco Bay.

"Oh, the plans are fine. Nothing wrong there," Barry said, straightening up and rubbing the small of his back. "It's the— let's call it the 'local opposition.' The people who *don't* want to see condos going up on their island."

John shrugged and stood back from the drafting table. Keeping his eyes focused on the blueprint, he drained his coffeecup and lobbed it into the trash can, waiting for Barry to continue.

"You must realize how tough it's getting, I suppose," Barry said at last, a faint smile on his lips. "The local environmentalists start screaming about—I don't know . . . whatever. Saving the breeding grounds for Arctic terns is the latest one I've heard. The environmental impact, as they're so fond of saying."

"But Freedom's gotten all the necessary clearances and permits, right?"

"Oh, yeah—sure, sure," Barry said.

"So any protest is pretty much a waste of time, then."

"That doesn't seem to stop them, though. There was quite a stink awhile ago about banning any more noncommercial fishing uses of—Well, that was in Portland harbor, but there's also been a lot of ruckus raised about some developing down in the Old Orchard Beach area, so it's been putting some heat on what Freedom Corp's doing out on Glooscap, as well. Lot of people on the island are bitchin' and moanin' about how they want to keep out-of-state money from ruining their island."

"I suppose that's only natural," John said, letting his gaze drift out across the water to the distant hump of the island. "Of course, you don't really hear them bitching when those out-of-staters buy their lobsters, do you?"

"Never," Barry said.

Seeing the planned construction had started John remembering the times he and his friends had spent racing around the woods, the times he and one of his girlfriends had met in the woods and in the hayloft of Haskins' barn and fooled around. Back in those days, just copping a quick feel on the *outside* of your girlfriend's shirt was a major accomplishment. Anything more and, as the guys used to say, you were an "all-time skin master"!

"So what do you think?"

"Huh? What?" John said. He was torn out of his reverie, suddenly aware that Barry had asked him a question he hadn't heard.

"I'm not keeping you awake with all of this, am I?" Barry said, smiling.

John started to apologize, but Barry waved him to silence. "Hey, I know. You're not even in the office for an hour, and here I am bombarding you with all sorts of bullshit. What I asked was if you felt like you were caught in the middle, seeing as how you do have to live with your neighbors on the island. They might not take too kindly to the fact that you're involved with this project."

"Oh, no—no," John said, shaking his head. His eyes kept wanting to wander back out the window to the island, but he looked down at the blueprint instead, focusing as hard as he could on the thin, dark blue lines that represented the reality that hovered in the pale haze on the horizon. "It's just . . . well, everything's still kind of spinning for me. It's going to take me awhile to absorb it all."

"Hey, man, I understand," Barry said. "What say around lunchtime we go up to Carbur's for a sandwich. We can go over this in more detail. That is, of course, unless you want to start out with another project first."

John took a moment to consider. It might make sense to back down from this if it really was such a volatile issue. And the bottom line was, he wasn't so sure himself how he really stood on this issue. He knew he couldn't very well work as a land surveyor and develop a sentimental attachment to the way things used to be. Progress was progress, and with more people moving to the Portland area, more housing space was needed. Condos— whether you liked them or not—were places where lots of people could live on a relatively small area of land, and land development was going to happen. The best hope was that the developers would show responsibility with what they did.

But then again, this wasn't just *any* condo project. This was on his home turf! Places he used to go to play baseball and skate and slide in the winter, places where he drank with his friends, where he tried to get laid were going to be ripped down and dug up to make room for a row of buildings that, judging by the sketches Barry had showed him, looked more like a stretched-out beehive than a place for people to really live.

"Is this road going to be anywhere near a . . ." He let his voice trail off as he stared down at the map. In the silence that followed, he felt Barry's eyes boring into him. He looked at his boss, his pencil poised in the air. "There's a grove of oak trees out around here," John said, swallowing with difficulty. "I used

to—it's a sort of special place to me from when I was a kid."
Again he swallowed, and the sound his throat made seemed unnaturally loud in the small office. "It's not noted on the blueprint,
but I was just wondering if the road here goes anywhere near it."

Barry craned his neck forward and looked at the blueprint, considering for a moment. "Actually, I think most of those oaks are
going to have to be cut down to make way for the road," he said.
"We tried to work the road around them so we could spare them,
but there's just too damned much ledge farther to the north, and
you can see the buildings have to go where they're placed."

"Cut down, huh?" John said. His throat had gone suddenly dry,
and he wiped his mouth with the back of his hand. "Well, that's
progress, I suppose. Say, where was that water cooler again? It
must be the heat in this building—it's really drying me out."

"Yeah, sure—out by the coffeepot," Barry said, picking up his
empty Styrofoam cup. "Come on, I'll show you. I'm due for a
refill, anyway."

FIVE
Meeting Audrey

I

Julia didn't know what Frank did to fill up his days, but he did
make every effort to keep out of her way, and eventually, as she
threw herself into the job of getting their things unpacked, she
stopped wondering and worrying about him. Judy Bartlett, the
local nurse, still came by every morning to help him—mostly
with his physical therapy. The bottom line for Julia, though, was
that Frank had, after all, made it on his own—even after the
stroke—before they moved in. In fact, she began to question just
how much he really needed them there.

She spent the better part of the first day cleaning the
bathrooms, upstairs and down, and then sorting through their toi-
letries and towels. Most of the towels Frank had were frayed,
faded, and full of holes, so she threw them away without a second
thought and replaced them with their own.

Once that was done, she started in on the bigger project of making her own kitchen utensils and the foods her family preferred fit in with what Frank already had in his kitchen. At one point early on the first afternoon, she sought Frank out in his room to ask him if he minded her plugging in the microwave.

"Microwave be damned!" had been his response. "Anything that cooks stuff in plastic and won't let you cook in metal is *unnatural!*"

After a while, she started to catch on that he was joking much of the time. Regarding the microwave, she discovered that the wall plug wouldn't handle the grounded three-prong plug, anyway. She left that particular problem for John to figure out.

She was concerned, needless to say, about how Frank would feel about her throwing away—or at least putting into storage—his old toaster—an antique Sunbeam that shot out sparks every time it popped—his battered aluminum pots and pans, tarnished silverware, and an assortment of things Julia couldn't even figure out how to use. He told her to chuck anything she didn't want. " 'S your kitchen now 's much as it's mine," he told her. So, using the empty boxes from her own unpacking, she packed up anything she thought might someday be usable and threw away the rest.

Although at first it had looked like a formidable task, the actual job of cleaning turned out to be not so bad once she got started. Of course there were some corners—especially inside the stove —where the grunge had built up over the years and would *never* be clean again, but Lysol and elbow grease took care of just about everything in the kitchen. Later in the week, she even spent an afternoon and evening repainting the trimwork in the kitchen, and she got John's promise that some weekend soon he would repaper the living room. All in all, she thought, in spite of first impressions she, John, and Bri were settling into the house quite well.

That wasn't to say there weren't some conflicts. Although he warmed up some, John still wasn't very talkative—especially to his father. But even when it was just John and Julia, she noticed a tightness about him that she hadn't seen there before. Frank, for his part, tried to break the ice several times, but as soon as he met any resistance from John, his own horns went up and they were silent with each other.

Julia didn't like living with this tension, but she told herself— and would have told Frank if he had spoken to her about it a second time—that John was adjusting to a lot of things all at once, particularly his new job, and she was sure he would mellow eventually.

By Thursday night, though, Julia was beginning to wonder.

When John came home from work complaining of a splitting headache, she casually told him to get some aspirin from the bathroom medicine cabinet. The next thing she heard was a roar and then a torrent of swearing.

"What is your problem?" she asked in amazement. She was standing at the kitchen sink, up to her elbows in cold water, rinsing fresh spinach for supper.

"This god damned . . . *cover!*" John shouted. He shuffled into the kitchen, his knuckles white as he tried to twist off the cap. "What's the name of this? *Panadol?* Damn it! They should call it *Damn-itol* or *Jam-itol!*"

"Here, let me try," Julia said, shaking her hands dry and taking the bottle from him. She put her thumb under the edge of the cap and with a quick flip, sent the cover flying halfway across the room. "Sometimes you just need a woman's touch," she said with a laugh as she shook two pills out into his hand.

John scowled as he popped them both into his mouth and washed them down with a cup of water. Without a word, he turned and strode into the living room, leaving Julia standing there. "You're welcome," she said, softly enough so—she thought—he didn't hear.

It hadn't been that big of an event, but to Julia, now that she was watching for it, it was very significant. Coupled with several other incidents, each relatively harmless on its own, it all added up to trouble. *Trouble because something was bothering John, and he wasn't saying what it was!*

Julia had her own problems to deal with, as well. Throughout her day, she did the typical things—grocery shopping, cleaning, unpacking, and rearranging furniture. But almost all the time, she felt there was something strange about the house—well, not so much *about* the house as *around* it.

Maybe, she told herself, it was just John's agitated state seeping into her own perceptions.

Or maybe it was Bri's loneliness working on her nerves.

Then again, maybe it had something to do with Frank's noncommunication with his son.

Or possibly Frank's bitter hostility at being confined to a wheelchair after an active, full life.

It could have been some or *all* of these, but Julia felt certain there was something more. . . .

A *presence* in or around the house was the best way she could describe it to herself, a feeling or vibe. More times a day than she really cared to think about, as she was working she would get the eerie sensation that she was being watched. The skin on the back of her neck would suddenly go cold, and her armpits would feel damp and clammy. Sometimes she would quickly turn around, expecting to see Frank sitting silently in the doorway, watching her, but the feeling also came at times when she knew Frank was out visiting with friends and she was positive she was alone in the house.

"I think this house might be haunted," she said to John one night. It was Friday night, and tomorrow would mark the end of their first full week on Glooscap.

The light was out and they were tucked into bed. She had an arm and a leg draped over him, pulling his body close. She could feel her warm breath bouncing back at her from the pillow, but the reassurance of John's being there didn't eliminate the chill she felt on her back.

"Yeah . . . sure it is," he mumbled, smacking his lips and rolling onto his side away from her. As soon as she said the word *haunted*, John's mind had filled with the image he had seen that night in the living room.

A slouched, gray shape suspended in the air by the couch!

It had been a person, he was sure of that, but it had been hanging with its back to him. In his imagination, though, the body was slowly swinging around, and his heart pulsed coldly when he expected to see—and *recognize*—the face!

Sighing, Julia flopped over onto her back and stared up at the ceiling. It was an indistinct gray blur that, strangely, seemed to come closer and recede with each breath. In the silence that followed John's reply, she lay there listening to his low, steady breathing. She wasn't sure if he really was asleep or simply faking it to avoid talking to her.

The darkness pressed in close, rubbing against her like a soft animal, and when she began to sense that even now, in the dark somewhere, eyes were fixed on her with a cold, steady stare, a low whimper started to build in the back of her throat.

"John?" she said softly, pulling him even closer.

"Huh?" He heaved a deep sign but stayed where he was, his back to her.

"Honey . . ." She slid her hand under his arm and gripped his chest, then slowly moved down his belly, willing the warm solidness of his body to remove the fear she felt mounting inside herself. She knew how she spent most of her time—*admit it, Julia old girl, all of the time!*—worrying about *other* people. Frank, and John and Bri; they were *always* on her mind. . . .

But what about me? she thought, tension coiling inside her like a hot wire.

Her hand slid lower down John's belly and, gripping him hard, she started stroking him. Raising her head from the pillow, she brought her mouth close to his ear and flicked her tongue out like a kitten lapping milk.

John's breathing caught; then with a moan he rolled onto his back. Even though she couldn't see his face clearly, she could tell he was looking at her in the dark.

"Not now, honey," he said, his voice crusted with sleep. "I had a bitch of a week, and my head is still killing me."

"That's *my* line," she said with a chuckle. "Come on." She slid the covers down, exposing his bare chest. "We haven't fooled around all week. We don't want to start acting like a couple of old farts, now, do we?"

She leaned down and gently nibbled his nipples, and felt him getting hard.

"Really, Jule—" John said, sounding a bit more awake.

"You know what I'm thinking?" Julia said, bringing her face up to plant a wet kiss firmly on his mouth. Her tongue darted between his lips and lingered there for a while. When the kiss was through, she continued talking so he wouldn't be able to voice the protest she knew would come. "I was thinking, now that we're really getting kind of settled in here, maybe we ought to start thinking again about having a baby."

"Come on, Julia!" John said. "Get practical!"

He hiked himself up in the bed, trying to keep her at bay, but he was rock-solid in her hand, and he couldn't resist when she lowered her head and started sucking on him. With a deep sigh— a perfect mix of pleasure and irritation—he leaned back while she sucked until he was ready to burst.

"I can tell you like it," Julia said, pausing for a moment and looking up at him in the dark.

She, too, was lost in the pleasure of the moment, but as soon as she stopped for an instant, a deep, dark fear began to twine within her. She was positive she was being watched.

"You *know* I like it," John said. He reached down, slid his hands under her arms, and pulled her up until their faces almost touched in the dark. "But I don't want to start in again on this bit about having a baby, all right?"

"I . . . just—" Julia began to say, but she cut herself off, afraid the trembling she heard in her voice would give her away.

"We've been over it time and time and *time* again," John said, holding her firmly in his embrace, "and I just don't think we should do it. I don't know why you keep at it like this!"

"But you—you know how much it would mean to me," Julia said. She still couldn't get rid of the feeling that there was someone else—not just the two of them—in the room. The urge to scream and make a lunge for the light became almost overpowering. She could feel cold, hard eyes staring at her from the surrounding darkness. Her body started to shake.

John found her lips in the dark and kissed her, holding her suffocatingly close. But as they were kissing, Julia's mind was still dwelling on that unseen presence she felt in the room. It was almost as if someone was trying to communicate with her, reach through to her but, like a weak radio signal, didn't quite have the strength. With a whimper, she broke off the kiss and pushed John away.

"For Christ's sake, Jule, is that all sex is for you now? A *function?*" John snapped. "You ruin it for me every time!" He kept his voice low so he wouldn't disturb Bri or Frank, but she could tell he wanted to shout.

"No, honey. It's not that."

"Bullshit! I think it is! For the past—what? At least a year, now, that's all I hear from you. I want to have a baby! *I want to have a baby!*"

Julia could feel her tears building, but her voice was too constricted to say anything. Oh, it was true enough; she *did* want a baby, and she didn't see why now wouldn't be a good time for it, but it was the eyes that were affecting her now . . . *the eyes* she felt drifting around her bed in the darkness, lurking—even during the day—just at the edge of her perception *like the pale reflection of a cloud's shadow. . . .*

"I mean, at this point in our lives, I don't think we need the added burden of a new baby, all right?" John said. "Think of it! Diapers, two A.M. feedings, baby-sitters, the whole thing! Christ, it would *ruin* the life we've gotten used to!"

"We could use Bri for a baby-sitter," Julia said. "She's old enough." Her voice sounded flat and emotionless to her, but apparently John didn't notice.

"I don't think that's exactly fair to Bri, either," John said. "Look, when we gave it a try last year and it didn't work out, I thought you were satisfied. You have a fantastic daughter, and—"

"But I always thought you wanted a child of your own," Julia said, her voice a throaty whisper. "I mean, I know you love Bri. I think you're a fantastic father for her, and I don't think having a baby will take away anything between you two; but *I* always wanted and I thought *you* wanted us to have a baby together."

"Come on, Jule," he said, pulling her even tighter. "You know we gave it a fair try, and it just didn't work out."

Julia struggled within herself to find security in his hug, but she couldn't shake the feeling of being watched. The idea that there was a little soul hovering in the darkness by their bed, a baby just waiting to be born inside her both touched and terrified her.

"Yeah, sure—we tried," she said, "but we didn't do everything we could. . . ." She let her words drift away because she knew she was close to saying something she would regret.

"Fine! Go ahead and blame me," John said. He snorted in the darkness, and she felt him pull away from her. "You know, just because I won't get tested to see if I can even *have* a baby, it doesn't mean I'm—I'm worried about my masculinity or anything."

"Don't be silly! I know that," Julia said. She tried to hug him tighter, not caring now if the tears fell or if he knew they fell. All she wanted was to hold him. "It's just that—well, I have needs, too; and sometimes I get the feeling you just don't care about what *I* might need. I know what I'd be getting into having another baby. And if it's something I want, I just—" Her voice hitched in her chest, and she pulled back to wipe at her eyes with the heels of her hands. "I don't see why you won't go along with it."

"There are a million reasons I could give you," John said.

But you don't feel the eyes watching you . . . the baby who's waiting to be born, she thought, unable to repress a shiver.

"And there are a million reasons *I* could give you why we *should,*" she said. "But I would think . . . I'd *like* to think you'd do it just because it's what I want."

She pulled away from him, sighing deeply as she settled her head in the well of her pillow. Her first impulse was to get up and go downstairs to sleep on the couch. *Let him stew a little!* she thought bitterly.

Tears were running down either side of her face and soaking into the cotton pillowcase. John made a futile attempt to touch her, to comfort her, but she resisted, rolling away from him onto her side. The darkness closed in even closer . . . so close it felt like a second layer of skin, but Julia didn't feel quite as much fear anymore. All she could wonder was,

Who's out there, waiting to be born?

II

Saturday morning dawned bright and clear. Across the street from the Carlson house, there was a rockbound point of land jutting out into the ocean almost half a mile. The island people called it Indian Point. The ground sloped downward from the street, ending abruptly at the rocks, simply dropping off into the ocean as if a piece of it had broken off, or a giant had taken off a huge bite. Right up to the rocky edge, the ground was covered by a dense growth of scrub pine, frail saplings, wild roses, and other tangled bushes which Bri didn't even recognize. Tiny birds—either sparrows or finches—darted through the trees, their warblings whisked away by the steady wind off the water.

All through the week, Bri had spent as much time as she could —right until darkness fell—wandering the sandy beach and the ledges farther along the shoreline, where glittering tide pools swarmed with nearly microscopic life. Waves swept in, sometimes gently, sometimes crashing over the seaweed- and kelp-bearded rocks. But now that there was plenty of daylight available to her, she was determined to hack her way, if necessary, through the thick brush and explore as much as she could of Indian Point.

The wind off the ocean wasn't just chilly; it was downright cold. It sent bubbly white sea foam flying, and it whistled shrilly through the trees and bushes, filling the air with the sweet smell of pine. Bri shivered, and she pulled her collar tightly around her neck at first, but after walking for a while, she warmed up from the exercise.

To her great surprise and relief she found a whole network of paths winding through the undergrowth. Apparently she wasn't the only person who liked to get away for some solitary thinking. This was such a gorgeous piece of land, she wondered why no one had ever built out here. She figured it was probably protected, either by the state or private ownership. The paths at least indicated that, whoever owned the land, they didn't mind people using it.

Bri was hoping against hope that the girl she had seen last Sunday would be out here again this weekend. All week she had built up so many fantasies, so many wild and implausible stories about her, she was actually beginning to dread meeting her. The mundane reality of who she was, where she lived, and why she looked so lonely walking the shore might possibly be better left undiscovered.

But in spite of all that, Bri still couldn't shake the idea that she and this girl could be friends. Speaking only for herself, of course, Bri felt so lonely, so adrift on Glooscap, all she wanted was one person, one good friend to give her some kind of access to life here on the island . . . someone she could go with to the mall and to the movies and out to eat.

She paused to watch as a sea gull wheeled overhead, stalling and drifting in the strong breeze, its wings flashing a too-brilliant white against the blue sky. Its mournful cry came to her on the wind, and with a sudden fluttering, it swooped down and landed in the water, where it rode the shifting swells, looking too tiny to survive in such a cold and lonely place.

Like me, Bri thought, feeling her eyes water as she turned her face into the wind and licked her upper lip to taste the salt. She was amazed that the gull wasn't picked up by one of the waves and sent crashing against the jagged rocks.

She lost all sense of time as she kept her eyes focused on the solitary gull, losing him and then finding him again in the white foam of the waves. The horizon was dotted with the sharp outlines of islands farther out, but Bri kept her concentration close to shore, trying to *feel* what the gull felt as he was tossed about. Her thoughts were drifting, bobbing on the water with the gull, but then suddenly the back of her neck began to prickle and she was snapped back to full awareness by the sensation that someone was watching her.

Her mouth was half open, as if she were about to speak as she turned and looked back along the path she had come. A tight constriction gripped her chest when she saw that there was someone standing in the shadows of the low-hanging branches. The figure was almost totally camouflaged by the tangle of tree limbs and dead leaves still clinging to the trees.

She's there! Bri thought, her breath catching in her throat with an audible click.

The girl from the beach was standing there, looking at her!

Bri licked her lips and sucked in a quick breath before trying to speak.

"Ah—hello," she said.

Bri was looking at the girl over her shoulder, and now she slowly turned her whole body around. Something in her mind made her think that this girl was like a frightened animal, and Bri didn't want to do anything to spook her.

"I—uh, I thought I might bump into you here today," Bri said tentatively. She shruggged her shoulders awkwardly. Both of her hands lifted up and indicated the expanse of ocean behind her. "It's so beautiful down here. I can understand why you like to come walking down here."

Standing in the tangle of bushes, the girl didn't move or say a word. She stood there so silently, Bri actually began to wonder if she really was there at all.

Maybe I'm imagining things, Bri thought. *She's just an illusion . . . a play of light and shadows.* She was suddenly aware of how dry her throat felt.

"Hey, come on," Bri said, taking one small step in the girl's direction. "You don't have to be afraid of me." She gave a quick little laugh that sounded unnaturally loud to her own ears.

The girl simply stood there looking like a frightened animal as she peered through the branches. Her eyes were the only things about her that moved, darting back and forth, from Bri to the ground and back to Bri. Her face had a pinched quality to it, and it looked unnaturally pale, especially for someone who apparently spent as much time outside as she did. Her hair, Bri noticed, was thick and long, a dull black—the exact color of the shadowed tree branches she was hiding behind.

"I know you saw me last week over on Sandy Beach," Bri said. She took a few more steps toward the girl, but for some reason it looked to her as though they got no closer. "I've been thinking all week that we probably ought to meet. I think we're—what would Anne of Green Gables call it? Kindred spirits? That's it."

"Maybe," the girl said, her voice a low, throaty whisper that was whisked away quickly by the sea breeze. But with that single word, Bri just *knew* they were going to be friends; her tone of voice carried with it a lost loneliness that mirrored her own feelings of being without friends on the island.

"Come on," Bri said, waving her forward with her hand. She glanced over her shoulder at the tossing swells heaving up on the rocks, sending white spray flashing into the sky. "I mean, walking alone out here can be fun, but sometimes it's nice to have someone to talk to, don't you think?"

The girl didn't answer right away; she closed her eyes and, tilting her head back, took a long, slow inhalation of the salty air. When she opened her eyes again, she was looking directly at Bri with a look that was both distant and piercing.

"Sure," she said, her voice still just a low thrum.

"Well, then—come on," Bri said, waving at her more vigorously. "I don't bite, for crying out loud."

The girl seemed to deliberate for a few seconds, apparently weighing the solitary freedom she was giving up against the companionship she might be gaining. Then, ducking beneath an overhanging branch, she stepped out onto the path in clear view.

The first thing Bri noticed was that, in full sunlight, the girl's hair took on a richer, deeper hue that made her face look all the paler. Her eyes were dark brown and had a distanced warmth that Bri had never seen before in anyone's eyes. As the girl moved toward her, Bri couldn't help but be surprised at how small she really was. Having only seen her fleetingly and at a distance, she had for some reason expected her to be much taller than she actually was. But her smile, faint and fleeting like the rest of her, was also genuinely inviting.

"My name's Brianna Mullen," Bri said, holding her hand out for the girl to shake. The girl's hand was freezing cold in her grip, and she wasn't surprised when the other girl quickly broke off the contact. As soon as they let go, she slid her hands into her sweater pockets. "Everyone calls me Bri, though. I live up on—"

"I know where you live," the girl said, looking Bri squarely in the eyes without blinking. "Your last name's Mullen?"

"Well, my mom's married to John Carlson," Bri said. "You must know Frank Carlson. He lives in the house up on the corner. Anyway, my real father's name is Mullen, so that's why her name's different from mine." When she was finished, thinking she already had blurted out too much, she shrugged awkwardly and waited for the girl to introduce herself.

"Oh," the girl said finally, nodding her head slightly. "So you're not *his* daughter."

"Oh, no. My real father lives in Cooper Falls, New Hampshire. He's a schoolteacher. But, umm, what's your name?" Bri asked before another awkward silence could descend.

The girl's gaze had drifted out over the water, and she—just as Bri had been—seemed captured by the seething power of the ocean.

Kindred spirits, indeed, Bri thought.

"My name's . . . Audrey," the girl said, a faint smile twisting one corner of her mouth. "Audrey Church." She turned and started walking slowly down along the rocky edge. Bri hurried to catch up with her as she leaped from rock to rock.

"And—uh—how exactly do you know where I live?" Bri asked, a teasing smile on her face. They were keeping well back from the water's edge, but because of the unevenness of the ground, they couldn't stay next to each other.

"This is a pretty small island," Audrey said. "It doesn't have too many secrets. Word gets around pretty fast."

As they walked, Bri was astounded at how effortlessly Audrey clambered over the rocks. It seemed as though she moved easily up and over large rocks that Bri, rather than scrambling up, would just as soon walk around. Bri struggled to keep up with her, but before long she found herself almost too winded to talk.

"Was that you outside my house last weekend?" she asked when they had reached the tip of the headland and stopped to look out across the bay to Portland. The purple-hazed outline of the city looked like a mirage.

For just a flickering instant, Audrey remained hypnotized by the ocean, her eyes fixed on the distant city skyline. Then, shaking her head, she turned to look at Bri.

"Outside your house?" she said, a look of genuine confusion on her face. "I—I don't think so."

"You don't remember? Last Sunday?" Bri said. "I saw you

down there on the beach and tried to catch up with you, and—well—you kind of avoided me. But I thought I saw you outside my house later that night."

Audrey shook her head and, again looking her squarely in the eyes, said, "No. I mean, I remember taking a walk on the beach—at least I think I did. . . . I like to take walks on the beach. I suppose I might have walked past your house on my way home."

"Come on," Bri said with a nervous laugh. "You're teasing me."

She tried to swat Audrey playfully on the back, but she twisted quickly to one side, and Bri missed her. The move was so quick, Bri almost lost her balance and fell. Looking down at the more than ten-foot drop to the water, churning with foam and seaweed, Bri felt a cold dash of panic in her stomach. Audrey's face remained impassive, as if she either hadn't realized how close Bri had come to falling over the edge or else she didn't care!

"It was pretty late at night," Bri said, her voice winding up with tension. She took a few steps away from the drop. "You—or someone—was out under the streetlight by the side of the house."

Audrey shook her head. "I wasn't really . . . unless it was, like I said, when I was on my way home."

"So, tell me where you live? What are you into?" Bri asked.

Audrey didn't answer for a few seconds as she squinted, looking out over the ocean. Bri was beginning to accept that this was typical of her—to act as if she was either considering her response or hadn't heard you at all and had her mind on something else entirely.

"I'm over on the other side of the island," she said at last, indicating the general direction with a vague wave of her hand.

Bri thought of an odd image; each of Audrey's words was a milkweed puff, and as soon as a word was out of her mouth, it was zipped away by the breeze. She had the curious feeling that when she listened to Audrey speak, she wasn't *really* sure she had said anything. Her words were like water that instantly evaporated as soon as they were spoken.

"I was wondering, too, why I didn't see you all week at school," Bri said. "I kept hoping I'd bump into you so we could meet, but—I mean I thought I saw you once or twice, but you must be in high school, huh?" She shrugged and slapped her hands against her legs, as though she could provide no answer herself.

"It's my . . . parents," Audrey said, her face suddenly darkening. "They don't put a whole lot of trust in the school system. They don't really want me to go because they don't think I'll get the right kind of education."

"What, are they fundamentalists or something?"

A confused smile flitted across Audrey's face. It was the most expression Bri had seen so far, but it had such sadness to it.

"No. My parents . . . they're—" Audrey started to say, but then she cut herself off and turned from Bri to look over the ocean again.

Bri couldn't help but finish the sentence for her; in her mind, she clearly heard the words *no, they're dead*. She didn't know she knew; it didn't make any sense, but *dead* was the word she was positive Audrey was going to use to finish her sentence.

No, she thought, *I'll bet it's because she's poor. Just look at that ratty old sweater. She won't tell me where she lives because she's so embarrassed about her home.*

Bri shivered, hugging her arms to herself. They started walking again, angling around the curve of the shore, along the landward side of Glooscap. Here, sheltered from the wind, Bri realized how much of a sweat she had worked up trying to keep up with Audrey, who continued to climb seemingly effortlessly over the rocks. Up ahead, around the bend, they saw the gray-weathered pilings, ringed with seaweed, that marked the entrance to the harbor. The sea was calmer here, everywhere dotted with the brilliant markings of lobster buoys and anchorage floats.

When Bri started off toward where the rocks dropped off and the beach flattened out, Audrey drew to a sudden halt. Her eyes —which had looked so warm and brown before—now took on a steely coldness, looking almost blue as she stared across the narrow harbor toward the assortment of wharfs and fishing shacks.

"I—I don't want to go over there," she said, shaking her head. She turned to Bri with that scared-animal look in her eyes. It struck Bri as really strange how she could change so suddenly, and with apparently so little reason. The only sound besides the gentle rush of waves along the shore was the far-off putt-putt of a lobster boat rounding into the harbor from the opposite side of the island.

"What—? Is there someone over there you don't want to see?" Bri asked.

At least by the way Audrey was acting, Bri had the impression there was someone she was embarrassed or shy about seeing. Maybe her father was one of those drunken lobstermen her father was always complaining about, or maybe she had had an argument with her boyfriend who worked down on the docks and she didn't want to bump into him just yet. But other than the lobsterman rounding into the harbor—and he was far enough away so he wouldn't have been able to tell who they were—the only other people in sight were the small, dark specks of the men hanging around the fishing shacks.

"I just don't want—people to see me when I'm out for a walk. That's all," Audrey said, looking back the way they had come.

Bri glanced at her watch, then back out to the point of rocks they had just left. She wanted to spend the rest of the day with Audrey, get to know her and maybe figure out where she was coming from, but it was getting close to lunchtime, and she had promised her mother she'd get her room done this afternoon.

"D'you want to come up to my house for lunch?" Bri asked.

Audrey seemed to let the question settle in her mind for a few seconds before answering. Her eyes flitted back and forth, not focusing on anything. Finally she patted a bulge in her sweater pocket and said, "Thanks, but no. I'm not hungry."

"Come on," Bri said. "After lunch, I told my mom I'd finish unpacking my things. You won't have to do any of the work, but it'd be nice to have someone to talk to while I work. I can show you—"

"I don't think so," Audrey said distantly, cutting Bri off cleanly.

"Then why don't I go home and fix us some sandwiches? I can get us each a bottle of soda, and we can make a picnic of it."

Audrey shook her head vigorously. "No!" she said. "I like to spend my time out here alone!"

Does that mean me, too? Bri wondered. She had been thinking they would be fast friends—*kindred spirits*—and was stung by the sharpness of Audrey's reply. The wind off the water whistled in her ears, and looking out over the empty ocean, she felt how deep and cold Audrey's loneliness was. Her eyes started to burn with tears, and not just from the stiff breeze.

"Well, then," Bri said, feeling again as if she were approaching an animal she didn't want to spook, "after I have lunch, maybe I'll bump into you again."

"Maybe," Audrey said. Without even a backward glance, she started walking back out toward the point of land. Her slouched, frail figure, dressed in that bulky gray sweater, quickly blended in with the tumbled rocks, and she was soon lost to sight.

" 'Bye," Bri called out. Her voice sounded flat and dead to her ears. The wind blowing straight into her face stuffed her words back into her mouth. She had the curious sensation that she was talking to herself—had been all along—and, embarrassed that someone might see her, she turned and started back along the path up to the road.

III

All morning while she worked at painting the window trim in the living room and John did the wallpapering, Julia found it best to keep away from John. It wasn't so much that he was still angry at her from their argument the night before. They had had that discussion often enough before. No, she sensed a different kind of tension circling around him like a hungry shark in the water, like a whirling storm wind. His eyes, when he looked at her, seemed to smolder with a hidden fire, almost as though he had seen something he didn't want—or didn't dare talk about. Whatever it was, it was something deeper than anything she had felt in him before. Another silly round of talking about having another child certainly wasn't the cause.

Julia's first thought was that it mostly had to do with unspoken and unresolved feelings between father and son. Once she and John could talk to each other—maybe tonight—she was going to push him about making a more honest effort, as he had promised her, to stop acting like he was still a child under his father's roof. He would have to work to connect with his father as one adult to another.

Meanwhile, though, she found it best to work away at what she was doing and let him work at what he was doing, limiting their conversation to questions about the color of the paint or requests to help hold a piece of paper in place while measurements and cuts were made before gluing.

It was a little after noontime when Bri burst into the kitchen, her cheeks glowing red, her eyes wide with excitement. Julia was at the kitchen sink, washing the latex paint from her brush.

"Well, don't you look like the healthy one," Julia said. "I hope you're invigorated enough to get that room of yours straightened up." She tore off several paper towels and wiped the paintbrush across them.

"I finally met her," Bri said excitedly as she shrugged off her jacket and hung it on the wooden peg beside the door.

"Met her? Met who?"

"Audrey. Her name's Audrey Church," Bri said, practically bouncing with excitement. "Remember that girl I said I saw on the beach last Sunday? Well, I finally bumped into her, and we spent almost all morning just talking and stuff."

"You don't mean that girl who was hanging around outside the house, do you?" Julia asked.

"No—no. That wasn't her," Bri replied. "I guess I was mistaken about that." She knew that wasn't what she really thought; Audrey's denial that morning had seemed thin at best, but she didn't want her mother ruining this friendship just as it was starting. "Audrey's a really neat person."

"Well, that's nice," Julia said. She finished wiping the brush and tossed the used paper towels into the wastebasket. After carefully placing her paintbrush on the edge of the counter, she asked Bri, "What would you like for lunch? Will soup and a grilled cheese sandwich be okay?"

"Sure," Bri replied automatically. "I asked her to come up to the house for lunch, but she said she didn't want to."

"Who? What are talking about?"

"Audrey—the girl I was telling you about," Bri said, her voice taking on a frustrated edge.

"Oh, yeah—right," Julia said, nodding. She went to the refrigerator and took out the sliced cheese. "The soup's in the cupboard over there. Do you want to start heating it up while I get the sandwiches ready?"

"Don't want to, but I will," Bri muttered, unable to stop the ripple of anger she felt at her mother for throwing a wet blanket over her excitement. She got the soup—her favorite, Campbell's minestrone—and snapped it under the electric can opener. But all the while, as she poured the soup into a pan and put the pan on the stove, she was thinking about Audrey and wondering why she would spend so much time out in the cold on the beach.

When lunch was ready, Julia called John and Frank to the table, but this lunch—like all the other lunches and dinners so far—was frosty; there was little conversation with any content. Bri had had such a damper put on her excitement, she didn't even bother to mention Audrey to either her father or grandfather. Frank groused about the poor reception on the TV in his room, and wondered aloud when Glooscap would get cable. John just complained about the poor quality of the wallpaper glue he was using. Julia simply ate her soup and sandwich in silence, wishing to heaven everyone would keep his complaints to himself.

After lunch, when Bri and Julia were clearing the table, Bri casually mentioned that she was planning on taking another walk down to Indian Point.

"Oh no, you're not," Julia said firmly, pointing at her with the sponge she was using to wipe the table. "You told me this morning you would get the rest of those boxes in your room unpacked, and you're not taking one step outside of this house until you do."

"But, Mom . . ."

"But *nothing!* That's the last word on it until it's done!"

So Bri spent the bulk of the afternoon in her room, scowling and throwing things into bureau drawers and onto closet shelves. She had the radio tuned in to a loud rock station—WBLM—just to irritate her mother.

Her bedroom windows looked out over the street toward Indian Point, and several times Bri stopped her mad dash to empty the boxes in order to kneel on the floor, elbows resting on the windowsill, and look out at the granite-bound point. A few times she thought she saw motion that could have been Audrey scrambling around on the rocks, but it was too far away, and it might just as easily have been water sweeping in over the rocks.

She had finished by three o'clock, and after flattening all of the boxes—John had said he wanted to save them in the rafters of the garage in case they ended up moving again soon—Bri raced downstairs.

"All done," she announced proudly as she ran into the living room.

Even with the living room furniture pushed aside, she couldn't believe how different the room looked now that her parents had finished with it. The walls looked alive, not drab like some dusty room out of the last century, and even without the curtains up, the trimwork around the windows looked brand-new.

"Could always use another hand," John said, looking down at her from his perch on the stepladder as he wrestled a glued piece of wallpaper into place.

Bri smiled and shrugged. "Actually, I was kind of thinking I'd head back out to the point. You've been telling me all along that fresh air was one of the bennies of living here."

"Not when there's work to be done," Julia said, shaking her head as though disgusted.

"Come on, Mom. I just want to take a walk and see if I can find Audrey."

"Who's Audrey?" John asked sharply. He had turned back to his work, but now he lost his grip on the edge of paper. As it started to slide away from him, he made a grab for it and almost ended up doing a half-gainer off the ladder. He did manage to snag the paper, though, and regain his balance.

"She's the girl I met down by the beach today," Bri said casually. "Her name's Audrey Church."

John cast a quick look over at Julia, but she had already heard it all and was concentrating instead on the trimwork.

"I—uh, I don't know of any family named Church living on the island," John said, frowning. "Are they new here?"

Bri shrugged. "She didn't say one way or another. Can I go now, Mom?"

Julia gave a loud huff, the breath stirring the hair hanging over her forehead. "I don't care. Get out of here," she said, and that was all Bri needed. She pulled her jacket on in the kitchen and was out the door before Julia could catch her breath and tell her to be home before—not *after*—dark.

But Bri's excitement soon faded. She followed the twisting trails through the scrub growth, clambered over the rocks, and walked the length of Sandy Beach three or four times, but there was no sign of Audrey anywhere. Feeling sad for herself, and thinking that Audrey had absolutely no interest in being her friend after all, Bri wanted to cry. But in spite of the cold, she didn't give up all afternoon. Finally, as the sun started lowering in the west, she turned and headed back to the house, wondering if this morning had been not just her first, but maybe her *last* chance to talk with Audrey Church.

<u>SIX</u>
A Certain Slant of Light

I

"Bri can take you down to Sandy Beach and show you the ocean anytime," John said. "And besides, that's what the tourists come to Maine to see. I can show you parts of this island the tourists *never* get to see. Come on."

Sunday morning had dawned, like the day before, bright and clear. Frank, as he usually did on Sundays, had gone off to church at nine, so Julia didn't feel as if she was shirking her duty when she, John, and Bri took off for a prelunch walk.

"Don't you think we should be finishing up the living room today?" Julia asked.

"Hey, come on! You've been complaining all week about my seeming uptight. So, consider this my chance to unwind. Right up here's where we used to play cowboys and Indians all the time."

"If this is going to be a nonstop nostalgia trip, I'd just as soon you hooked up with Randy so the two of you could go at it together. I can just head on back to the house and do some paint-ing," Julia said. She halted for a moment but let him tug her arm so she'd follow along.

They had crossed the road behind the house and were trudging across a field, heading toward a fairly steep incline, which John had informed them was called Bald Hill. The crest of the hill was thickly forested with pine and hemlock, so Bri wondered aloud how it had come to be called "bald."

"Maybe back in the old days there weren't as many trees," Julia offered.

"Actually, back when my father was a kid, most of the woods in the middle of the island were burned flat. Luckily no homes burned, but the lobstermen say this hill looks like a bald man's head from out in the bay."

"Local color galore," Julia whispered.

She was keeping her steps high so the knee-high grass wouldn't trip her up. Summer's grass was mostly dead and yellow; dying weeds were browned and bent over everywhere. Milkweed pods had burst open, and their white fluffs were drifting by on the breeze. A few crickets, not yet killed off by the frosty nights, chirred in the deep grass, but they were the last remnant of sum-mer. There was no doubt the hand of autumn had touched the woods and fields here.

Bri was dragging several paces behind them both. She kept stopping and looking back down the hill toward the ocean. From this high up, she had a clear view of Indian Point and a part of the beach. Off in the distance, the skyline of Portland was clear-cut against the western sky. In all, the view was gorgeous, but all Bri could wonder was, *Is Audrey walking around down there now?*

"That's called the Hook Road over there," John said, pausing and pointing off to the left. "Bri!" He waved for her to catch up with them. "Come this winter, I'll take you out to Larson's Pond for some skating. Even if there's a heavy snow, the wind off the ocean usually blows it clean as a whistle. You can go for a mile or more."

"Sounds great," Julia said. She slitted her eyes and, leaning her head back, took a deep, noisy inhalation. She could feel the sun and the wind easing her nerves, untangling them. For the first time, she began to wonder how much of John's uptightness was really her own being reflected onto him. He was right, she had to admit—this was what they all needed!

Bri was still dawdling behind, kicking at the dead weeds, so after waiting a bit longer, John and Julia decided to ignore her and go ahead at their own pace. They entered the deep, cool green shade of the woods and started up the gradually steepening path.

Glancing over her shoulder, Julia caught a glimpse of Bri's yellow headband. She called out, "Come on, Bri! You'll get lost if you don't keep up with us!"

John shook his head as he went on without slackening his pace. "There's just one path. She'll be fine as long as she sticks to it."

"You know this place," Julia said a bit sharply. "She doesn't."

When it was apparent Bri wasn't going to come running after them, they went on ahead anyway. The forest floor was littered with curled brown leaves—mostly beech and maple. Thick groves of pine held the deep green they would have all winter. Sea gulls flew by high overhead, their raucous cries drifting to them on the wind.

"You know what I notice most?" Julia asked after a while. "There aren't any—oops, there's one, but it's the first one I've seen." She bent down to pick up the rusty beer can by the side of the trail and, after inspecting it for a moment, tossed it deep into the brush. "Well, there isn't *much* litter around here."

John shrugged. "Thank God for returnable bottles and cans, I guess," he said. "There's a grove somewhere along here. I can't remember exactly where, but when we were in high school, I used to come out here drinking with the guys."

"What—no girls?" Julia asked with a snicker.

John shook his head. "Naw, this was like a private spot for the guys. When we wanted to fool around, we'd go out to—" His voice caught in his throat, and he had a fit of coughing before he could finish.

"That much fun, huh?" Julia said, laughing.

"We'd . . . go to . . ." John said, sputtering. He had his hand over his mouth and was trying to catch his breath. "To Haskins' barn . . . on the other side of the island." He wanted to say more, but a sudden, vivid image rose in his memory.

He saw a face, pale and slack. From between nearly bloodless lips, an unnaturally thick tongue protruded. The face held an expression of agony, of intense pain. Even in death.

"Are you all right?" Julia asked, her face creasing with worry as she swatted John on the back.

Bending down, bracing his hands on his knees, John coughed and sputtered, then sucked in a deep breath. He pounded on his own chest, gasping. His eyes were watering, blurring his vision, but even now the traces of what he had imagined lingered like visual echoes in his mind.

"That isn't how you usually react when you think about sex," Julia said, laughing now that it was obvious John was going to be okay. She widened her eyes and smiled wickedly at him. Casting a quick glance over her shoulder to make sure Bri wasn't within hearing range, she said, "Maybe Haskins' barn is where I'll have to get you if I want to make a baby."

The coughing fit finally subsided, and John's breathing returned to normal. The momentarily clear image began to fade in his mind. Wiping his eyes with the back of his hand, he tried to say something but then simply signaled for Julia to be quiet about it. At last, with Bri still trailing behind, they continued their walk side by side up to the top of the hill.

If the view was gorgeous from halfway up, it was fantastic from the top. Shimmering blue ocean stretched away in three directions. The horizon was broken by dozens of islands, and everywhere small specks of boats, some with full-bellied white sails, glided over the water: weekend sailors taking advantage of what could be the last good weekend before pulling their boats out; lobstermen making a late morning haul; one of the Casco Bay Lines boats, heading out to Peaks Island.

"Not a bad little view, is it?" John said, coming close to Julia and encircling her waist with his arm. His coughing fit was all but forgotten as they looked over the scenic beauty.

Julia snuggled into the hug, letting herself fill with contentment. "It *is* nice," she said, but even as she said it, she felt something cold take hold of her heart.

It wasn't just that she still couldn't see Bri somewhere down the slope, hidden by the trees. . . .

It wasn't just that a whole week of unspoken hostility between John and his father had stripped her nerves down. . . .

And it wasn't just the uprootedness she felt, leaving behind her home and friends in Vermont.

No, it was all of these and something more. . . . There was a vague, dark . . . *something* more!

"Over there is Blanchard's Orchard," John said. "They've got —at least they *used* to have—the best damned apples in the state. Macs and Cortlands and a couple of other kinds. Next summer, we'll have to go apple picking, okay?"

As he spoke, Julia was so filled with a dark, churning dread, she barely registered his words.

What? she wondered, feeling her stomach twist with uneasiness. *What the hell's wrong with me? I can't even let myself have a good time and enjoy a nice walk like this.*

"Sure . . . sure," she replied softly. She couldn't help but wonder if John was picking up on her agitation. She looked up at the sky—perfectly cloudless except for way out on the horizon to the south. She looked down at the dried brown and yellow hill gently rolling down to Shore Drive and the band of houses that ringed the island. Everywhere it was peaceful and quiet, but she still felt it—a cold, black, nameless *dread* coiling like a dark snake around her heart.

"Where's Bri?" she said, suddenly snapping to attention. She glanced quickly at John, then stared down the path they had followed to the crest of the hill.

"Don't worry—she'll be along in a minute," John said mildly.

Now the nameless fear suddenly had a focus, and Julia became convinced that Bri was in danger. She didn't know how she knew, but she knew! Pulling roughly away from John, she started down the path a few steps. Cupping her hands to her mouth, she yelled as loud as she could.

"Bri! . . . *Bri!*"

Her voice rolled down the hill and echoed back up at her with an odd reverberation. The pine trees surrounding her suddenly felt ominous, as if they were closing in on her, and she expected any minute to see . . .

What? she wondered, so frantic she was nearly speechless.

"Come on, Bri!" she yelled. "Answer me! *Answer me!*"

II

"Hey, Bri."

Bri stopped walking and stood stock-still in her tracks when she heard the voice call to her. It drifted to her softly on the breeze . . . so softly it *could* have been the wind whispering in the pines. Her eyes darted to both sides of the path leading through the pine woods. She couldn't even tell which direction it had come from.

The yellowed carpet of fallen pine needles covered the ground on both sides of the trail, and there was no indication of anyone having walked in there. She was just about to start walking again when something, a faint stirring of motion off to her left, caught her eye. Far back, under the deep emerald-green shadows of the pines . . . was that a shadow, or was there someone standing there, looking at her?

There is someone there! Bri thought, her eyes widening with frantic fear. She glanced quickly up the trail where her parents had disappeared, wishing to God they were somewhere in sight. She didn't dare call out to them.

What if that's some crazy person lurking in the woods? A killer, she wondered, feeling a sudden pressure in her bladder.

She strained to see into the thick shadows under the pines, but it was as if night were still clinging to the dark hollows of the land. The shadows were so intense they seemed to vibrate with an ultraviolet purple.

"Bri . . . over here. . . ."

The voice came to her again, striking her eardrums like feathery velvet. It was coming at her from all around, wafting through the pine branches more like the scent of pine resin than a real sound. She looked frantically up at the green of the trees reaching to the blue sky, but she found no reassurance there. The dark shadows under the trees seemed to be shifting and twisting into a shape that looked almost like . . .

"*Audrey?*" Bri said. Her voice sounded more like a bark. "What the heck are you—?"

The deep shadow under the tree coalesced, and it *did* look like her new friend. Audrey was standing in the deep pine grove, looking straight at her, beckoning her to come to her. Although Bri couldn't actually see her eyes, she could *feel* them watching her. . . .

"Come on—cut it out, Audrey," Bri said, forcing a lightness into her voice which she didn't feel. "You really had me scared for a minute."

She took a step forward, convinced she could see Audrey standing in the shade, beckoning to her, but as she got closer, the shape seemed to shift away, and then Audrey was gone like a pattern drawn in the sand, erased by the wind.

Confused, Bri halted halfway between the path and the spot under the pine trees. A fitful gust of wind waved the branches, sighing with a low, snakelike hiss, and she saw the interplay of shadows and light that could have made it look as if someone was standing there. But no one was there now!

"Audrey?" Bri called out, her voice frail, almost a whisper. Scowling, she turned and started back toward the path, but just then the voice called her name again.

"Bri . . ."

Am I imagining it? she wondered, as she tried to hold back a rising flood of panic. *Am I going nuts or something?*

"Bri . . . over here. . . ."

With a sudden shout, Bri raced forward to the place where she thought she had seen Audrey. Her heart was hammering in her chest; the sides of her neck were pulsating as she swung her hands at the trees to clear her path. Pine branches swished and snapped back into her face, and then she broke into the clearing. She spun around in a wild circle, scanning the woods for the source of the voice.

"Is this another one of your tricks?" she shouted, clenching her fists in frustration. "Like disappearing on the beach?"

The thought struck her that it might not even have been Audrey. It seemed more like something some kid might cook up to tease her, make her think she was crazy.

"Well, you don't scare me!" Bri yelled. She picked up a rotting branch and swung viciously at the branches around her. On the third or fourth swing, the branch snapped in her hand and hit the needle-covered ground with a dull thud.

"Over here. . . ." the voice whispered again. It was so faint this time, Bri almost didn't notice it. She was so worked up, she knew she wasn't acting rationally as she kicked and scuffed the forest floor.

"Screw you, Audrey!" she screamed, spinning around so her voice projected in all directions. "Screw you *all!*"

As her voice faded in the woods, she spun on her heel, thinking to head back to the path and catch up with her parents, but again a shadowy figure deeper in the woods caught her attention. Stunned, Bri froze in midstride and looked. There was no doubt now that it was Audrey. She was standing in the shifting shade of the trees, one hand raised and slowly motioning for Bri to follow.

"Over here . . . Bri. . . ."

"No, goddammit!" Bri shouted. "I'm not going to play any of your stupid little games!"

She waved her hands in frustration as she started backing away. "I'm sick and tired of your . . . *teasing* me!" Tears flooded her eyes, making the dim figure look even more indistinct. "If you want to be friends, Audrey, we can be friends, but I'm *not* going to play stupid games!"

Saying that, she quickly turned and started running back toward the path. Her footsteps were muffled by the thick carpet of pine needles, and moving soundlessly, she had the momentary impression that she was drifting—flying, as if in a dream. Low-hanging branches swished and smacked her face, and one caught her headband, almost pulling it off, but she kept running, wanting to put as much distance as she could between her and Audrey.

Her mind was spinning like a tornado as she ran. She was thinking how much she liked Audrey, how much she wanted to have her for a friend, but she was also thinking that she really didn't know a thing abouth her. She acted so . . . *strange.* She started to picture her as the Ally Sheedy character in *The Breakfast Club*—a spooked-out weirdo who dressed funny and acted like she wasn't all there. "She's got the phone, but no dial tone," as her friends in Vermont would have said.

As she ran, though, a jolting fear gripped her. She suddenly realized that she should have crossed the path by now. It was a well-trodden path; it would have been impossible to miss it. *But why hadn't she come to it already?*

The air rushing into her lungs felt like fire, and she was grateful for the heavy panting sound filling her ears. Otherwise, she might still hear Audrey calling to her.

"Bri . . . over here. . . ."

She nimbly leaped over deadfalls and dodged trees and boulders as she ran, but the farther she went, the more she knew she was in trouble!

Oh, God! I'm lost! her mind screamed. She didn't slacken her pace, but she started looking frantically around for any sign of a clearing, a break in the thickening woods where she could get her bearings. It seemed as though the woods were getting deeper, thicker! Up ahead, she could see a big boulder sticking up out of the earth like a solitary giant's tooth. She *knew* she would have remembered seeing something like that!

A whimper, so low it sounded strangely disembodied, escaped from her throat as she ran, and then she saw, straight ahead, a dense grove of pines almost dripping with deep shadows. And in those shadows, she saw someone standing . . . someone *beckoning* to her!

She tried to stop quickly, but the pine needle–covered ground was slippery, and she fell down, skidding like a baseball player sliding into home plate. Her right foot plowed up the pine needles, exposing thick, black soil, and it was only luck that got her hands into position to save her from smashing her face into the ground. Her nose was filled with the dank, earthy smell of fresh soil.

"Bri . . ."

The sound filled her mind, but she wasn't sure, she *couldn't* be sure if it had really been there or if it was just an echo in her mind. Her chest felt as if it was going to burst from the pressure pushing out from inside her. She knew if she screamed she would probably strip her throat of flesh.

Pine needles and forest mulch flew into the air as she scrambled to get back up. Her panic was blind now, and she ran back the way she had come, figuring that, in her confusion, she had gotten turned around and missed the path.

Head uphill, her mind shouted. *They're up at the top of the hill!*

She clenched her fists and pumped her arms, pushing away the pain in her desperate run. Her knee was numb from the fall she had taken, and she wouldn't have been surprised, when this was over, to see that she had a nice, deep gash from a buried rock.

If this ever is *over!* her mind whispered.

The effort of running up the steep slope of the hill took its toll on her soon enough, and before long she was lurching and stum-

bling forward more than running. The muscles in her legs felt
unstrung. It felt as if there was a presence behind her, something
dark and nameless closing the distance between them, but she
didn't dare look back as she ran.

Just run . . . run! she commanded herself, but she was close to
her limit now; exhaustion was twisting inside her body, peeling
away at her muscles, shredding her lungs. And then, with a startled shout, she tripped and fell forward.

At first she thought she had stumbled over a fallen tree. She
barely registered that her foot had hit something soft and yielding.
But as she was scrambling to get back to her feet, she looked
down and saw something that sent a mind-numbing wave crashing through her brain. The sunlit woods all around her suddenly
telescoped into a laser-narrow beam focused down at her feet.
Lying on the ground was the *thing* that had tripped her—a horribly decomposed body . . . a *human* body!

Bri stared at it, gaping. She took a gasping breath, but that only
crammed her scream back down into her chest. Only the top half
of the body was exposed; from the waist down, it was covered by
thick, black mulch. Wind and weather—and possibly wild animals and carrion birds—had stripped away all but a few tatters of
flesh. A few remnants of clothes, heavy with mold, clung to the
bleached skeleton. The eye sockets, like two dark inkwells, stared
sightlessly at the swaying pines overhead.

Bri's heart felt as though it had contracted into a fist-sized
stone. Her teeth clamped down hard together as she stared unbelievingly at what lay at her feet. A scream wanted to burst out of
her lungs and throat, but there was no air, no pressure to let it rip.
Bright spinning spots of light exploded in front of her eyes, but
the darkness of those two vacant eyes grew stronger, pulsating,
swelling, swallowing her. Her head was spinning wildly, and she
felt as if she were drowning, being pulled into those two black
sockets.

Barely aware of anything except that sightless skull staring at
her, she struggled to get up, to get away. Her arms flailed in the
air as if searching for a handhold. Her feet suddenly slipped on
the slick carpet of pine needles, and she went down again. Her
head hit a glancing blow on a tree trunk, and then the darkness of
those vacant eyes completely filled her mind.

III

"You're *sure* you're feeling all right?" Julia asked. She was
sitting on the edge of Bri's bed, holding a cold washcloth on her

left temple where she had skinned it against the tree trunk when she had fallen. Bri had complained of a headache, but the Tylenol she had taken fifteen minutes ago already seemed to be kicking in.

"Yeah . . . I mean, it still hurts, but I don't think there's any brain damage or anything," she said, forcing a tiny laugh.

"Well, you sure had me and your father worried," Julia said. She took the washcloth away, refolded it, and then held it to Bri's head again. "You've got to remember, when you're out for a walk like that, never to leave the trail. You found out today how easily you can get lost."

Bri nodded, even though the motion sent a sliver of pain shooting through her head. She opened her mouth, about to tell her mother that she wouldn't have left the path but she had seen Audrey, her friend, in the woods and had wanted to follow her. Telling her mother that, though, she decided, might be a mistake after all, so she remained silent.

When she had come to in the woods, with her father gently slapping her face to bring her around, she had immediatley started babbling about the decomposed body half buried in the forest floor. No matter how much she insisted that's what she had seen, her parents had shown her—pointed directly at—the rotting deadfall she had tripped over. When she had gotten more insistent, they had clearly pointed out where her foot had kicked the log, removing a big piece of the rotting wood. They showed her that the ground was scuffed where she had fallen and then tried to scramble to her feet. "There couldn't possibly be someone buried there!" her father had kept repeating.

"But I know what I *saw*," she had protested. But the protestation had gotten gradually weaker until she finally accepted their suggestion that, in her panic—maybe after she had bumped her head—she had imagined seeing the dead person there.

Even though serious doubts remained, she finally told them she accepted their explanation—if only they would drop it for now and let her rest. The pounding in her head, though fading, still sent jabs of pain through her skull. In her heart, she *knew* what she had seen, and she was smart enough to know that, if she kept insisting she had seen a dead person instead of a rotten tree trunk, they might have a strong argument for brain damage. There wasn't the slightest trace of humor in *that* thought.

"Well, you sure had us worried when you didn't answer me," Julia said, shaking her head.

The whole incident, Julia thought, had been . . . well, *unusual* wasn't the most accurate word to describe it, but so far it was the closest she could come. No matter how much she thought about it, she just couldn't account for the weird sensation she had gotten, while she and John were standing at the top of Bald Hill, looking out at the beautiful view, that Bri was in trouble. John's rambling reminiscences about playing out here as a boy should have been soothing, nostalgic; they should have given her a sense of the rustic childhood *she* had never experienced. Instead, she had been filled with a dark foreboding and—as it turned out—a very accurate fear for Bri's safety. All she could think was

What if I hadn't thought something was wrong? What if Bri had been out alone when she got hurt? What if I hadn't insisted to John that we go back and look for her?

She laughed, trying to dismiss all of these thoughts as typical fears of a mother, but the truth was, Bri *had* been in trouble. She *had* gotten lost. She *had* fallen and hurt herself, maybe more seriously than it seemed. If they hadn't combed the woods for her—they had been looking for more than a half hour before they found her!—she might still be out there, unconscious in the woods.

That body in the woods, Julia thought, feeling a tingling echo of the dread she had experienced, *could have been Bri if we hadn't found her!*

She repressed a shiver as she smiled fondly at her daughter and stroked her hair back.

"Who knows?" she said, letting her smile widen even though she was still trembling inside with dread. "Maybe this will be good for at least a day off from school."

"Maybe," Bri answered sleepily. "Actually, I'm feeling kind of wiped. Would you mind pulling the shades so I can sleep?"

"Not at all," Julia said. "You just make sure you tell me if that headache doesn't go away. You got hit in the tenderest part, you know."

Bri grunted as she snuggled down into her pillow, careful to keep the hurt side of her head up.

Julia went over to the window and pulled down the shade. She wanted to feel relief, but she couldn't The sense that *something* was wrong . . . something had been wrong and was *still* wrong . . . that there was trouble brewing, just wouldn't go away, no matter how many times she told herself to stop worrying—Bri was safely home now.

The darkened room was filled with the sound of Bri's deep, even breathing. Julia stood by the window, watching her daughter and feeling those feelings all parents have—that she would do absolutely anything to keep her from harm! Quietly she tiptoed to the door and eased out into the hall, letting the door click softly shut behind her.

"Please," she whispered, staring at the solid wood door. "Please let my baby be all right!"

IV

"Oh, yeah—sure!" John said, his eyes narrowing as if he were in pain as he paced back and forth in front of the picture window. He continually slapped his fist into his open palm, making a flat, wet sound. A stub of a cigarette was hanging from his lower lip. "It was a *great* way to start the project. I should have that much fun every goddamned workday!"

Julia was sitting on the couch, sipping a glass of rosé as she watched her husband pace. He had come home from work late, and the first thing he did was grab a glass and fill it half full of whiskey. When that was gone, he filled it again, but now the glass was forgotten on the coffee table as he strode back and forth across the living room floor.

"And do you want to know the worst thing about it all?" he said, smirking with disbelief. "It wasn't just that this truck driver—whoever the hell he is—decked this guy because he's opposed to these condos going in and tried to stop his truck, or that this guy who got hit is probably going to try to sue his ass off. Hell! Not just the driver! He'll probably go after the whole damned company as well. *Christ!* Maybe he'll nail *my* ass because I stepped in between the two of them and tried to stop the fight! No, the worst thing is—"

Imagining I was looking down at a waxy-pale, dead face! That I was covering that dead face with handfuls of dirt! his mind screamed.

He didn't say that out loud. For just a second, he paused and took a drag of the cigarette in his hand. He clenched it so tightly between his fingers he just about crushed it.

"I—uhh, I'm there, helping this guy get up off the ground, you know, and fucking Randy Chadwick is standing there, smiling at me like I'm some kind of Benedict Arnold because I'm working out there!"

He exhaled noisily, went over to the coffee table, and ground out the cigarette in the ashtray. He immediately lit another, sending a plume of smoke up to the ceiling.

Julia ducked her head to one side, trying to avoid the billow of smoke, and smiled weakly. "Come on," she said mildly. "It probably wasn't as bad as you thought. You told me Randy said he wasn't really actively protesting—that he had just showed up to see what was going on."

"Yeah—sure," John snorted. His eyes fastened on his whiskey glass, and he picked it up and took a swallow, wincing from the burn as it roared down to his stomach. "And then I said to him . . . I actually said to him, 'Small world, isn't it?' I can't fucking *believe* that was the best I could come up with!"

"You were probably a little more concerned about the guy who'd gotten punched," Julia said. "For crying out loud, John, give Randy a break, and watch your language—Bri's upstairs, doing her homework."

"Sorry . . . sorry," John said softly, but he didn't stop his pacing and angry puffing.

"You didn't hear any more about it this afternoon, then, did you?" Julia asked, keeping her voice as mild as she could, no matter how much she didn't like the anger bubbling out of John.

John shrugged. "Nothing when I got back to the office, but Barry and I were on the site the rest of the day. We didn't leave the island until well after five o'clock."

"But you said the cops never came, so maybe this guy doesn't really have a case—not if he didn't report it to the cops."

"Jesus!" John shouted, then cringing, he glanced toward the stairs and lowered his voice. "He had a good twenty or twenty-five witnesses there. I don't think he'll have any trouble getting a few of them to back him up. Jesus! I mean, this could really turn into a—what was it Barry said? He said I was stepping into a *shit storm*. I'm telling you, it's enough to make me want to quit the damned job and do something else!"

Julia chuckled softly under her breath. "Yeah . . . sure."

"I mean it," John said, his face suddenly serious. "We don't need the money from my job the way we used to—not living here. There's no mortgage."

"You've got to remember, Bri's going to be heading for college before long."

John waved his hands in front of his face. "We've got money in savings, and we can always take a school loan. I don't see why I have to bust my ass day in and day out anymore. I could—I've got it!" He snapped his fingers in the air. "I could be a lobsterman like my old buddy Randy. Get a boat and a few traps—nothing much to get started, and spend my time out on the water."

"Be serious," Julia said, shaking her head.

"I am! I think most of the way I feel about this friggin' island is because of the way my father was always pushing it at me, telling me I *had* to go to college, I *had* to leave this island if I was going to do something better with my life. Hell, he even broke—"

John caught himself, but in the sudden silence that followed, he locked eyes with Julia.

"He broke . . . *what?*" she asked pointedly.

John looked down at the floor, considering for a moment. He shook his head sadly from side to side. "I was going to say that he was responsible for breaking up me and Abby back in high school."

"Oh . . . really?"

John shifted nervously from one foot to the other, then went over to the picture window, drew the curtain back, and stared out at the ocean. "I remember thinking, if I had a dollar for every goddamned time he told me not to end up getting married right out of high school . . . Christ, he practically forced us apart so I'd go off to the university! But I don't want to talk about that! I was talking about my goddamned job!"

"And how you wanted to become a lobsterman," Julia said with a smirk.

"Well, think about it! I mean, I could deduct the purchase of a fancy-ass boat with a forty-band shortwave radio. We could take every winter off and go to Florida if we wanted. I'd be out to work before dawn and back home by noon if I didn't get *too* serious about it."

"And you'd be working in storms and rain and cold," Julia said. "Listen to yourself. You're making it sound like it's your conception of paradise, for crying out loud. All I ever heard from you before was how much you always wanted to leave home because you wanted to be something more than a lobsterman."

"Maybe that was my father talking more than me," John said, shrugging as he took a drag on the cigarette and stared thoughtfully out the window. Evening was coming on fast, and the water had turned a deep purple against the indigo sky. Small black specks—either sea gulls or lobster buoys—rose and fell with the swells.

"I'm just saying I don't need this kind of pressure," he said softly, his face close enough to the window to fog the glass. "I don't need the hassles and the bullshit."

Julia shifted uncomfortably on the couch. "Well, I can agree to that." She paused and took a sip of wine before continuing. "But I don't think it's just your job that's getting to you."

John wheeled around and stared at her, his face a network of shadowed, harsh lines. *Did I let something slip?* he wondered, panicked.

"I think, for one thing, you've got to stop acting like a—" Julia glanced in the direction of Frank's closed bedroom door. Faintly, she could hear the muffled sounds of the TV. Lowering her voice, she finished, "Stop acting like a child around your father. Ever since we moved back here, you've been acting *different*, some-how."

John finally noticed that the cigarette in his hand had burned down to the filter. He sneered and dropped it into the whiskey remaining in his glass. Then, heaving a deep sigh, he turned to look out the window again.

"It's just that you've been acting so uptight all the time," Julia said. She got up and walked over to him. Standing behind him, she encircled his waist with her arms and pulled herself tightly against his back.

"If I've been uptight lately, it's with a goddamned good reason," John muttered.

"And just what do you mean by that?" Julia demanded. She spun him around so he was facing her and looking her squarely in the eyes.

"I mean . . ." he started to say, but then his voice trailed away, and his gaze went blank for a moment. Then, shaking his head, he looked back at her. "I mean *everything*. My job, my father, living here—all of it is just eating away at me!"

"Including me?" Julia said, her voice husky as she pulled him closer.

John was silent for the space of several heartbeats, but before he could reply, Julia pushed herself away from him.

"It's me, too, isn't it?" she said, feeling a dull hollowness beginning to grow in the pit of her stomach. "I'm getting on your nerves, too, aren't I? Because of wanting a baby . . . right?"

Slowly, barely perceptibly, John lowered his head in a nod. "Well—you've got to admit, you *have* been more than a little bit pushy about it," he said.

His words sliced her like a razor, and Julia's first impulse was to lash out at him for hurting her. She wanted to shove him away and run upstairs, leave him to wallow in his own depression and self-pity. *Christ!* she thought angrily. *Let him smolder if he wants to! What's he got to be so damned upset about?*

But because she didn't act out of reflex, her second—and better—response was to ignore her own hurt and try to see what he meant by what he'd said, try to understand what he was going through. Even she had to admit that she might have been pushing a little too hard on the baby issue. But it was more than slightly painful to hear it put so bluntly.

"The way you've been going at it," John said, "makes it more like a job than romance. God! I mean, we can't even screw for fun anymore. It has to be 'trying for a baby'!" He clenched his fists in frustration and stared at her, not seeing how much his words were hurting. "No wonder you hadn't gotten pregnant in the year we were trying! You're putting so goddamned much pressure on me, my fucking sperm is probably fried by the time I shoot it out!"

Julia's eyes were stinging as she looked at her husband, wondering if this really was the man she had married five years ago. A small corner of her mind was whispering that, just like with her first husband, Sam—Bri's father—she was doing it again—grabbing and holding on so tightly, she was actually driving him away from her. But she knew in the core of her soul that it wasn't just her; it wasn't about the job or the house or the baby she wanted. It was something about *him*, too, something *deeper* . . . something that was stripping his nerves raw!

"I know—" she said, her breath hitching in her throat. "I probably have been a little too . . . pushy about it."

"Pushy! Christ! You've been positively demanding! 'Come on! Let's fuck! I want to have another baby!' Jesus!" John's face flushed red as he glared at her.

"Okay, okay!" Julia said weakly, unable to control the shaking in her voice. She turned and walked away from him and stood with her hands on the couch back, staring at him and wondering, *Who the hell is to blame here? What the hell is going on?* She could feel her anger growing in swells like the ocean when a storm is brewing.

"It's just that Bri—"

"Hey, come on now," John said. "You know I love Bri as much as—hell, *more* than if she was my own daughter."

"I know you do," Julia said sullenly, "but I want to have a baby with *you*. So yeah, okay—I seem a bit demanding, but I don't mean to be."

"You may not mean to, but that sure as hell is the way you come across," John said. "God, I'm lucky I can get it up at all with that kind of pressure!"

"We don't have to have a baby," Julia said as tears began to roll down her cheeks. "I mean, I want one, I really do, but if you're so dead set against it, we don't have to. Maybe we should adopt instead. God knows there are enough kids in the world who need a chance."

"It isn't that!" John shouted, followed by a deep sigh. "It isn't that at all. I just don't want to have a baby, plain and simple! And even if I did, the way you're pushing so hard at it takes all the fun out of it."

"Fun?" Julia said, her face twisting with a lopsided smile. "I don't think you can call having a baby *fun*. I mean, you never had one of your own before. You don't know how much work they are."

"That's not the point, either," John said.

"And what exactly *is* the point?" Julia snapped.

Something in her tone finally got through to John; it broke down the wall they had so quickly thrown up between them. It hurt him to see the way she cringed away from him as he started toward her, but he held his hands out to her, and after a moment's hesitation, she came around the couch and collapsed into his arms, letting herself be nearly smothered by his crushing hug. Seconds expanded into minutes as they stood there holding on to each other as if they were desperately clinging to a life raft in the middle of a storm-tossed ocean. Finally John reached down and gently prodded her under the chin, raising her face to his for a long, slow kiss. At first her mouth was nothing more than a cold, hard line, but gradually the ice melted, and she playfully darted her tongue between his teeth.

The kiss was long and slow, and when they broke off, John put his mouth close to her ear and whispered, "I'm sorry." His breath washed warmly over her ear, and she tried to ignore the tinge of whiskey on it.

"Me, too," she rasped, unable to control the sobs that shook her body.

"And . . ." He paused, clearing his throat before continuing. "And if it really means that much to you, okay, I'll go along with it. We can really give it a shot."

"Give *what* a shot?" she asked, not wanting to hope he meant what she thought he meant.

"Having a baby," John said, stroking her back with the heels of his hands. "We'll try to have a baby—if it means that much to you."

She smiled up at him, her eyes glistening with tears. She was incapable of letting him know now just how much it meant to her, but she was sure, over the next few months, she could make him understand.

SEVEN
Frank and Julia

I

The small band of sunlight that wedged between the curtains cut across the foot of the bed with laser intensity. The room was muted, with warm yellows and browns, dusty with age. John saw spinning motes of dust, caught for an instant in the sunlight and then gone, winking out like old stars. The only thing in the room that didn't look old and used up was the shiny chrome wheelchair.

John watched the sleeping figure of his father, not even sure if he really was seeing the bed sheets rise and fall with the low, steady breathing, or if it was just an illusion. He felt a momentary panic when he remembered how his mother, dead and lying in her casket, had appeared to still be breathing.

"Uh, Dad?" he whispered. He was holding a breakfast tray in both hands, so he had to ease the door open with his hip. The air in the room was musty and stale; it also had a peculiar undercurrent of . . .

What? John wondered, searching his mind. When it came to him, he gasped softly, his hands involuntarily clenching on the edges of the tray. *It smelled almost like a barn. Rotting hay—dry, blackened tatters of cobwebs and dust—the moldering smell of an old dirt floor . . .*

When John looked again at his father's sleeping face, the sickly glow of dingy sunlight made it look as though Frank's face had been sprinkled with dirt. John staggered backward a step when he imagined seeing his own hands scooping dirt over his father's dead face, covering him with thick, black, wormy soil.

Frank was lying on his back, his face turned away from the door. His left hand, looking frail and nearly bloodless, was flung up onto his pillow. He didn't stir as John, his heart hammering in his throat, came a few steps farther into the room. John's eyes were riveted to his father's hoary, yellowed fingernails, and he couldn't help but wonder if that's how *his* hands would look when he was that old.

"Hey, uh—Dad," John whispered as he tiptoed closer to the bed. "I've got some breakfast for you."

He was about to reach out and shake his father's shoulder when he suddenly became convinced his father was dead! He wasn't breathing! There was no pulse in the neck, no flicker of the eyes beneath his eyelids!

John became convinced that, when he had imagined seeing his own hands dumping dirt onto his father's face—*had it even been his father's face?*—it had been a premonition, or maybe his subconscious mind registering the truth first, before he was consciously aware of it. . . .

He's dead! John's mind screamed.

He almost dropped the tray when he took three quick steps backward. The backs of his legs felt as if they were made of rubber that was rotting, fraying; icy waves centered in his stomach and rippled out through his body.

That's the smell! his brain screamed. *Not a barn smell! The smell of death!*

He looked frantically at the door as though help were going to come charging into the room, and his mouth tried to form words. The only sound that came out was a strangled *Arggh*. He backpedaled, and his foot caught on something. When he pulled out his hand to catch himself, he let go of the tray. With a loud clatter, it hit the floor. The impact sent the glass of juice, a cup with two soft-boiled eggs, silverware, and napkin flying. John hit the floor hard on his tailbone, sending an electric jolt of pain up his spine.

"What the hell?"

A surprised shout caught in John's throat when he saw his father suddenly sit bolt-upright in his bed and turn to look at him, sprawled on the floor.

"Jumped-up bald-headed *Christ*! What the hell are you *doing*?" Frank shouted. His eyes were wide with fright, and his lower lip was trembling.

John looked down at his crotch, where the wet stain of orange juice made it look as if he'd lost control of his bladder. Remains of the eggs were splattered everywhere. Shards of broken glass and porcelain littered the floor. John was grateful he hadn't cut himself.

"I—uhh, I was bringing you breakfast in bed," John stammered. He picked up the paper napkin and, getting up slowly, wiped the wet stain on his crotch.

"Hell of a way to wake a guy up!" Frank said, shifting around on his bed. He sat up and, looking at John, gave a half smile. "What the hell you tryin' t'do, give me a heartie?"

John wondered if he looked more frightened or comical, but either way, he burned with embarrassment. "I just thought . . . before I went to work, I'd bring you a bit of breakfast," he said as he knelt down and gingerly began picking up the largest of the broken pieces.

"What happened?" Julia said, poking her head into the room. "I was just getting up, and I heard a crash." She quickly assessed the situation and sadly shook her head. "Did you get hurt?"

John grimaced and, shaking his head, said, "No, just lost a glass and a couple of eggs. Nothing serious, but I am going to have to change for work, though."

"Let me help you with that," Julia said, coming over and kneeling down beside him.

"Well, what the hell is this, anyway?" Frank said, "D'yah think I'm too damned feeble to come to the breakfast table myself?"

He hiked himself up in the bed and awkwardly shifted his feet to the floor. He had to grab the cloth of his pajama leg and pull on it to get his useless left leg to move. The motion made the pants leg roll up, and John caught a glimpse of his father's thin white leg, laced with blue veins that stood out like thin cords under his skin. The muscles looked flaccid, almost useless.

"No, I thought we could have a bit of a talk while you ate," John said, looking down at the shattered remains of the breakfast, now piled up on the tray.

"Talk?" Frank said, frowning. "What in hell've we got to talk about?"

Julia gave John a soft, sympathetic look, when she realized what he had been trying to do; probably because of their discussion last night, John had taken what she had said to heart and decided to try to break down some of the barriers that stood between him and his father. The attempt—even though it failed— touched her, bringing tears to her eyes.

"Go on," she said, not looking up as she waved a hand over her shoulder at him. "I'll get the rest of this. You've got to get cleaned up for work."

John stood up and went toward the door, but he hesitated for a moment, looking back at his father sitting on the edge of his bed. The old man's face was perfectly neutral, as if he either couldn't guess at what John had been trying to do or he just didn't care.

"Do you even *like* soft-boiled eggs?" he asked.

One side of Frank's mouth was still twisted up into a crooked smile. Shaking his head, he said gruffly, "No . . . not really."

II

After cleaning up the rest of the mess, Julia left Frank at the breakfast table, happily plowing through his habitual bowl of Rice Krispies, while she went upstairs to talk with John. Before he left for work, she wanted him to know that she, at least, appreciated what he had tried to do, even if his father didn't.

But when she came into the bedroom, it was almost as if there was a different John knotting his tie in front of the mirror over his bureau. His mouth had a distinctive downturn, and his eyebrows looked like two dark shelves over his eyes as he looked at her in the reflection. There were deep creases in the corners of his eyes, but she couldn't decide whether they were from hurt and embarrassment, or from a bottled-up rage he was trying desperately not to let out.

"Well," Julia said, easing into the room and gently shutting the door behind her, "no one's going to fault you on your intentions."

John snorted, finished with the knot, and jerked it up tightly under his neck—too tightly, actually; he gagged and wiggled his finger in under the knot to loosen it a bit.

"Son of a bitch!" he said, sneering as he grabbed his sports coat and shrugged his shoulders into it. "He doesn't know how to appreciate anything. Never did, so I guess I was a fool to think he'd be any different now."

Julia had her mouth set in a firm line, and she shook her head in vigorous denial. "You can't say that. You don't know how he feels."

Again, John snorted. "How he feels? Who gives a sweet shit how he *feels*? If he never lets it show..." His eyes flashed brightly in the mirror, glaring at her as he adjusted his lapels. "He could feel like the frigging savior of the world inside, but if he doesn't *do* something about it, what goddamned good is it? Fuck it!"

He took a comb from his bureau top, ran it quickly, savagely through his hair several times, then slammed it back down onto the bureau.

"There—I guess I'm all set," he said, turning to look directly at her for the first time.

"You look great," Julia said, coming over to him and giving him a tight hug. "Maybe before you go, you can try to say something nice to him."

John pushed her away and angrily shook his head. "Honest to

God, it's like he's...*shit!*" He laughed and shook his head. "Christ! You say you want to have a baby so much! You don't need one! You've already got one right there, downstairs! Hell, probably in a year or two, he'll get so bad he'll even start shitting himself. Then we can buy some industrial-size Pampers and *really* have a blast with our seventy-three-year-old baby!"

"Come on, John. That's not very nice."

"Nice? Who cares about *nice?*" John shouted. "I try to do something nice for him, and what do I get? He acts like I dropped the tray on purpose to wake him up! Maybe he thought I was trying to scare him to death so I could get my goddamned inheritance, such as it is. And what'll that be? This house and a mountain of overdue bills? No way! If I try to do something nice for him, does he even say thanks for trying? Oh, no, no way. Not Frank Carlson! He doesn't even know the frigging word *thanks!*"

"Keep it down—he'll hear you," Julia said, waving her hands at John.

"I don't care if he hears me," John shouted. "I mean, what kind of thanks are *you* getting? You're stuck home all day doing what? You're taking care of an old man who should have been put in a nursing home and—"

"And *forgotten?*" Julia snapped. "Is that what you want?"

John scrunched his eyes shut tightly and banged both hands on the bureau in front of him. The comb bounced once, then fell to the floor. "No, that's not what I want, but *Christ*, Julia, is this what you want? To be hanging around the house all the time, just watching him slide down the tube?"

"I'm not...unhappy," Julia said softly, feeling in her soul she was telling at least most of the truth.

"Well, I don't see that you're all that happy, either," John said, scowling. "And five years ago when I married you, that was the one thing I wanted to make you—happy."

"And I told you what I thought would do that," Julia said, softer still.

"Oh, yeah, sure—having a baby," John said. He stretched out his arm and glanced at his watch. "Shit! I'm going to be late if I don't get a move on," he said. "I can grab lunch in town."

He started toward the stairs, but Julia touched his arm, halting him. He wheeled around, facing her with anger. No, she thought. *Maybe not anger. Hurt* seethed in his eyes.

"Well, even if he doesn't say it, I want to say thank you just for trying."

The glare in his eyes almost melted. John leaned forward to kiss her firmly on the mouth. He didn't know why, but for some reason he felt a sudden, powerful stirring of sexual energy. If he hadn't been running late, he would have been tempted to grab her and carry her to the bed. He'd give her the baby she wanted, all right!

"I really have gotta go," he said after breaking off the kiss. He went quickly down the stairs and out the front door. *So he won't have to go through the kitchen and see his father,* Julia thought, feeling sadness well up inside her like a dark tide.

"Call me when you get to the office, okay?" she called.

"Yeah—sure." And then he was gone with a slam of the front door. Julia stood at the top of the stairs, waiting until she heard the car start up and pull away before going back downstairs. By that time, Frank had finished his cereal and gone back to his bedroom. Through the closed door, she could hear the indistinct buzzing of his television. She couldn't help but wonder how much Frank had heard of what had been said upstairs, but she tried to dismiss it as she set about getting busy for the day. Judy Bartlett would be over soon to take care of Frank. Julia just wanted to get—and *stay*—busy.

III

"I think the whole idea is downright . . . *sinful*! That's what it is!" Frank said with a grumble. It was a chilly but sunny Saturday afternoon, and he was sitting in the kitchen, talking to Julia while she washed the lunchtime dishes.

John had driven over to the condo construction site to recheck a few angles and elevations so work wouldn't be delayed on Monday morning. Bri, as usual, was off on one of her long walks along the shore. Julia found herself wondering from time to time if Bri's walks might not be as solitary as she said they were, if maybe she really was meeting a boy down there. She was considering giving her a serious mother-daughter talk that evening. Julia—as she had been all week—was alone in the house with Frank.

"It's just a bit of harmless fun," she replied as she opened the plastic bags and poured the tiny M&M bags into a bowl. "It's a fun little holiday for the kids." She smiled pleasantly at Frank, but what she really wanted to do was laugh at him outright.

"It's a holiday for Satan, that's what it is!" Frank said. "It's bad enough they celebrate it at all, but on *Sunday*! The Lord's day!" He banged his fist down on his wheelchair armrest, making it vibrate.

"That's why the trick-or-treating is tonight instead of tomorrow night," Julia said.

"People don't seem to realize that once they start opening themselves up to this . . . *devil* stuff, it gets to a point where they can't stop it, 'n' it can just overwhelm 'em!"

Unable to stop herself, Julia snickered, and it immediately blended into a full laugh. She turned to face Frank, fully convinced he was smiling behind her back at the put-on he was creating. But Frank was about the farthest from smiling she had ever seen him; he was frowning, and his jaw was set in a grimace that doubled the lines in his cheeks.

"I'll bet when *you* were a boy, you did your share of trick-or-treating," Julia said mildly.

She had found over the past few weeks that—as the old expression went—Frank's bark was worse than his bite. Frank scowled and grumbled a lot—and some of that was justified, considering that up until four months ago, he had been a hale and hearty man. But now he was confined to a wheelchair, and no matter how much his doctor said there was a chance that, with exercise and luck, he would be able to walk again, he knew he was going to be wheelchair-bound until he died. *This was it . . . the end of the line!*

That couldn't help but sour anyone's attitude, Julia thought, and what with his frequent memory lapses—he had called her by at least four different names since they moved in: Abby, Dianna, Ruth, and Marcia—she tried to deal with him patiently. When he got into these tirades, though, it was difficult not to snap. What bothered her most was that, even in the short time they'd been living with him, his outbursts seemed to be increasing in frequency and intensity. And now he was starting in on something as harmless as Halloween!

"When you're a kid," Frank said, "young 'n' foolish, you do plenty of stupid things—things you'll live to regret . . . if you're lucky 'n' smart." He blinked his eyes, holding them closed for several seconds before continuing. "Sure, I done things I wished I'd never done! We all have. I just think makin' a national holiday out of devil worship is going a bit too far!"

"It's not a national holiday," Julia said. "It's just a custom. A little fun and a few harmless pranks. Tell me you never soaped up a window."

Frank's scowl deepened as he looked down at his useless leg. His lower lip began to tremble, and Julia felt a jolt of rising panic when, for just an instant, she saw his eyes flutter and roll upward.

"I was reading an article in *Reader's Digest* or somethin' about these kids—teenagers—who got involved with those dungeon games, and they did a spell or something that actually raised a demon that possessed 'em. They killed two girls. Should've killed themselves!"

"Come on," Julia said, laughing softly. "You don't actually believe playing a game caused them to do that, do you?"

"I *read* it," Frank said, as if that was the final authority. "These kids got possessed and ended up killing—what was it? Maybe three or four people in their town before they turned themselves in. Said they wanted to be exercised."

"You mean exorcised?"

"Whatever! The point I'm trying to make is, even something like Halloween can unleash these demonic forces."

"A couple of dozen kids roaming the neighborhood asking for candy hardly seems like a threat from hell," Julia said.

"Go ahead!" Frank shouted, pointing at her with a trembling hand. "Go on! Laugh at it! You'll see! Once you open the door to these things, sometimes you can't shut it. They'll get you in their power 'fore you know it, and 'fore you can get away from 'em! You know, it ain't slipped my attention that since you got here, you and John ain't been to church. What's the matter with you people anyway, ain't you religious?"

Oh, boy! Here we go! Julia thought.

She took a deep breath and sighed, shaking her head. They had spent a lot of days with just the two of them in the house, and from discussions they had had and little comments Frank had let drop—especially on Sunday, when Josh and Allen Stubbins came to take him to church—she had suspected that this topic would come up eventually. Now Frank had taken the opportunity of bitching about Halloween to get around to what he was really after.

"It's not that we're not religious," Julia said, leaning back and bracing herself with her hands on the counter.

Before she got any farther, though, Frank interrupted her. "Me and Dianna tried to bring John up right as a boy, yah know? But even back then, he was so damned headstrong."

I wonder which side of the family he gets that from, Julia thought.

"We took him to church, did what the baptism service says—put the scriptures in his hand—but it didn't seem to do no good. I was kind of hoping you'd be the one to bring him back."

"I don't want you to get me wrong, Frank," she said, hoping what she was feeling didn't show. He could talk away about his religion, but that didn't stop him from letting fly a curse whenever his blood pressure went up. "But John and I just don't buy organized religion. We feel that religion is—"

"Buy! You said you don't *buy* religion? It isn't something you buy!"

Julia cocked her head to one side, resisting the temptation to mention some of the more recent incidents involving television evangelists and their pitches about buying salvation, and other things, such as seedy motel rooms and private parties.

"I really don't want to discuss it," Julia said. "I don't want you to misunderstand me. I think—and John thinks—religion is a personal thing, an individual choice."

"There's only *one* way," Frank said, his voice taking on an almost preacherly resonance. "I would think—even if not for your own sake—you'd want to do something for Bri."

Julia rubbed her hand over her face, wishing she was anywhere but here right now. It was taking greater and greater effort not to snap out at him.

What the hell's it to you, anyway? It's our business, not yours how we raise Bri! Don't talk to me about being a hypocrite! Look at your relationship with your own son!

Julia took a deep breath and measured her words. "I feel that, when it comes time, Bri can decide for herself. I don't want to push her one way or the other."

"It ain't a matter of *pushing,* for Christ's sake," Frank said. "It's a matter of guiding—directing. A child can't choose for itself. If you don't show it the way, Satan will be there to grab 'em down, 'n there won't be time to 'decide for yourself,' as you say."

"Bri's not a child," Julia said as mildly as possible. She literally had to bite down on her tongue to keep from pointing out that she felt her daughter could decide for *her*self, not *it*self. "And if you want to get right down to it, *you're* not setting the best example, what with your swearing like you do all the time."

Frank shook his head angrily. "You may not have noticed it, but I've been makin' an effort not to cuss, 'specially when Bri's around. But I talk the way I talk from spending most of my life on the docks. I ain't saying I'm perfect myself, but—"

"No, I don't think you are," Julia snapped, "but you *are* saying you're better than I am and John is, and I don't think that's one bit fair."

It was an effort to make her motions appear unhurried, but she grabbed the sponge, wet it under the faucet, and quickly wiped the crumbs off the table. While Frank sat there speechless, she tossed the sponge into the sink, rinsed her hands, then dried them on the dish towel hanging from one of the cupboard door handles.

"John and I know how we want to raise Bri," she said, her voice low, almost trembling. "Now, I can appreciate your concern, but when it comes to Bri—whether it's something as silly as whether or not she'll go trick-or-treating, or something as serious as the condition of her soul—I think I, as her mother, can handle it, if it's all right with you."

She knew she was glaring at Frank, and she knew she was taking some advantage of him, standing so close to him he had to tilt his head back to look up at her. But she was angry enough not to care. If he wanted to, he could treat John like he was still a boy, but he surely wasn't going to tell *her* how to raise her daughter, church or no church!

"Look, uh, if you don't mind me using your car, I think I'll go out for a drive," Julia said backing off.

Frank's face remained expressionless as he pointed toward where his car keys hung on a nail by the door. "I ain't ever gonna use that car again," he said gruffly.

"If Bri comes back while I'm gone, tell her I'll be back in an hour or so. I think I'll zip over to the condo site and see what's going on."

Frank said nothing, and he didn't move as Julia grabbed her jacket and the set of car keys and walked out to the car in the barn. As she opened the barn door, got into the car, started it up, and backed down to the street, all Julia could think was, *Screw it! If he's going to give it to me, he's going to have to learn that I'll shovel it right back!*

IV

John's car was parked on the side of the road with its trunk wide open. The transit box was on the roadside, open and empty, and some of the equipment was gone. As Julia pulled up behind the car and parked, she wondered how he dared leave all of his equipment out like that. Wouldn't somebody driving by be tempted to steal it?

She got out of the car and scanned the area, looking for him, but there was no sign of him anywhere. He had said he would be working with Barry today, but he hadn't mentioned whether he was going to pick him up in town first or meet him out here at the site. If Barry had driven to the island this morning, they might be off in his car, maybe getting lunch. She glanced at her watch and saw that it was a little after one o'clock.

On her left, the open, flat field sloped gently down toward the ocean. Its thick mat of yellowed grass and weeds had been flattened and torn up by the heavy equipment, but other than a few mounds of thick soil, there wasn't much that would hide him from view, so she turned to the other side of the road, toward the trees and dilapidated barn. Cupping her hands to her mouth, she shouted John's name several times as loud as she could.

Her voice didn't seem to carry very far, however. It bounced back at her with an odd flatness. With only the devastation of the ground breaking and one deserted, weather-grayed house and barn in sight, she was filled with a sense of loneliness. It surprised her how desolate, how unsettled this end of the island seemed. It made the southwest tip of the island, where they lived, seem downright thriving.

She called out John's name several more times before she concluded he and Barry—if they weren't getting lunch—were probably off in the woods across the road. Hadn't John mentioned something about the old barn and some trees that were going to be cleared out?

Pocketing her car keys and making sure her car doors were locked, Julia started out across the field toward the barn. She paused now and again, turning back to look at the view from the field. The wind off the water had a clean taste to it, chilly and invigorating. She couldn't deny that it was a beautiful spot, and whoever ended up living in the condos out here was going to have a gorgeous view into outer Casco Bay.

She also felt a strong sense of the place's past and what it would be losing. The gray house with its partially caved-in barn, looking out over the cold gray sea, spoke of a distant, less complicated, and less hurried way of life—the kind of life, actually, John must have experienced growing up out here, an older, more timeless way of life. Even though she had no personal attachment to the land, she felt a sadness when she saw these fields being chewed up by thick-treaded bulldozers, and knowing that the house and barn would be bulldozed to make room for luxury living—the kind of living probably no one presently living on the island could possibly afford.

The dead, silvered grass swished at her legs, and the sound, combined with the salty breeze, reminded Julia of the day last week, when they had gone for a hike on Bald Hill. Looking to her left, she could see the treeless ridge rising above the thick screen of woods. Along the edge of the field, most of the trees, predominantly oaks, had been stripped bare by the cold weather.

A bluejay singing its harsh song suddenly darted out of the woods. Caught by surprise, Julia jumped and tensed until she saw the harmless blue flash dipping over the field.

Why so jumpy? she asked herself, looking around to see if anyone was nearby and had seen her jump. She considered why, but she thought she knew the answer—being out in the open like this made her feel exposed, vulnerable. She had never really felt comfortable in wide open spaces, so she hurried her pace to bring her closer to the trees.

Once at the edge of the woods, beneath an old, spreading oak, she stopped and called again for John. The echoes of her voice died away, and she strained to listen, but no reply came.

"Damn it," she muttered, looking back at the path she had trampled through the dead grass. She could see the tops of several wooden stakes that had been driven into the ground and flagged with orange plastic tape to mark boundaries. She knew John had been here, but when? Those markers could have been driven in any time last week.

From here, she could see the back of the barn with its shingle-less roof and fallen-down outbuildings. The side door was hanging open, and although at this distance she couldn't hear it, she could see that fitful gusts of wind were slamming the door open and closed against the side of the barn. The two windows on the side of the barn had long since lost any trace of glass, either from boys' stones or the winter storms that slammed straight into this northeast side of the island.

While she was looking back at the barn, Julia felt a tingling between her shoulder blades, a sensation that someone was watching her. A little rush of fear went up her backbone when she remembered how, just last week, Bri had gotten lost in these same woods on the other side of the hill. After they had found her, she had insisted that she had seen a human body half buried in the ground. That idea sent a wave of goose bumps rippling over Julia's arms.

As she looked around, trying to see if there really was someone watching her or if it was just her overactive imagination, Julia's eye was drawn by a shifting motion inside the darkened doorway of the barn. She sensed almost immediately that this hadn't been where the feeling of being watched had originated, but it sure looked as though there was someone inside the barn. Thinking it might be John, and wanting unaccountably to get some distance between herself and the trees, she started across the field at a brisk pace.

"Is that you, John?" she called once she was halfway to the barn. She kept her eyes focused on the opened door as it swung back and forth. The closer she got, the louder the banging became; before long she could hear the shrieking of rusted hinges.

The ground around the barn was littered with the refuse of a collapsed chicken coop, old tools and machinery, two rusted plows and a harrow, the burned-out shell of an ancient car—Julia couldn't determine the model or year—and several stretches of barbed wire and slat wood fences, now knocked flat. The air was filled with the smells of age and rot. Everything combined to give the side yard the illusion of a devastated battlefield, and nostalgia or not, it would probably be a good thing to get this mess cleaned up, Julia thought as she walked gingerly through the rubble.

She went to the side barn door and braced it open by leaning against it with one hand. The wood was weathered to an almost marble smoothness, but when the wind almost tore it out of her hand, a sliver of wood lanced into the heel of her palm.

"Ahh! Shit!" Julia shouted, quickly pulling her hand away from the door and looking down at the dot of blood that welled up like a ruby bead. A tiny splinter was sticking out of her palm, enough so that it was easy enough to grab with her fingernails and pull it out. Squeezing with thumb and forefinger, she forced the blood to flow, then put the cut to her mouth and sucked on it. The coppery taste of blood filled her mouth, and she spat it onto the ground.

The split second she did that, she thought she heard a soft chuckle come from the darkness inside the barn. Julia's breath caught in her throat, and she looked wide-eyed at the opening, wondering if she had really heard laughter or if it had been the sighing of the wind in the grass.

Leaning forward, but careful not to commit herself to entering the barn, she looked inside, trying to pierce the dark gloom. A heavy, musty smell filled her nostrils as she looked in at the broken-down stalls, the collapsed workbench, the rickety ladder and trapdoor leading up to the hayloft, and the arching beams of the roof—*no doubt populated with spiders and bats,* she thought, shivering. Harsh, bright lights in the roof—the spaces between planks where the shingles had been torn off—let in slanted shafts of sunlight, but as soon as the pure light of day entered the barn, it seemed somehow to be swallowed up by the dusty gloom. If it was possible, the place seemed more decayed on the inside than it did on the outside.

If from a distance she *had* seen motion inside the doorway, there didn't seem to be any evidence of it now. The only sound was the harsh whistle of wind as it zipped in through cracks and holes in the barn. The only motion was the gentle swirl of dust spun up into the rafters by the breeze and then allowed to descend slowly through beams of sunlight.

"Don't go in there!" a voice shouted behind her, echoing across the field.

Julia had just shifted her weight forward and was about to step into the barn when the unexpected shout came, making her spin around with a frightened squeal. She looked up and saw John running toward her from the woods. With a cautious backward glance inside the barn, she started toward him, smiling and waving. She couldn't believe how happy she was to see him, and she found herself hoping he hadn't seen how much he had surprised her.

"What the Christ are you doing out here?" he asked once they met in the middle of the field.

Taken aback by the almost hostile tone in his voice, Julia refrained from hugging him as they looked each other squarely in the eyes. After the gloom of the barn, the brilliant sunlight made Julia's eyes water.

"I just wanted to see what you were doing out here," she stammered. "I hadn't really seen the construction that was going on out here."

"Well, you shouldn't be snooping around here," John said. There was a tenseness in his body that more than bothered her; it scared her. It was almost as if she had surprised him at something, and he hadn't liked it at all!

"I was just taking a peek inside the barn," Julia said defensively. "This is Haskins', right? An old place like this is kind of interesting."

"Well, you've got to be careful," John said, his voice low and firm but still sounding unnaturally tight. "An old barn like this could collapse anytime without warning."

"I don't think I was in any danger," Julia said, looking back over her shoulder at the barn. "It's lasted this long. I'd say it'll hold up a few more winters."

John shrugged. "Well, it'll all be torn down and gone by next spring, anyway, once we start on this side of the road."

"Kind of a pity, though, don't you think?" Julia said. Her mind was focusing on the sense of loneliness, the wistful feelings for the past she had experienced out in the field.

"Why'd you come out here, anyway?" John asked sharply.

"I saw your car on the road and figured you were still here. You didn't hear me callling?"

John shook his head. "Must not have. I was checking the farthest boundary line over there." He waved his hand in the general direction of the woods.

Julia squinted and, looking out across the field, was struck by something curious. If he had been off in the woods not too far from the big oak tree where she had been, why hadn't he heard? Why hadn't he answered? He certainly would have been close enough.

"Everything's all right back at the house, isn't it?" John asked.

Julia nodded, but she noticed that he still seemed agitated—as though she had interrupted him at something.

"Sure," Julia said vacantly as she looked around the field. "Everything's fine. I just wanted to see what all the fuss was about out here. Hey, I thought you said Barry was going to be helping you today."

John hesitated a moment, then said, "He left awhile ago—must have pulled out just before you got here. I'll bet you passed him on the road."

Julia shook her head, fairly positive she hadn't passed anyone on the road. But what bothered her more was the feeling that when John spoke, she couldn't dismiss the feeling that he was lying to her, that he was hiding something.

What the hell is going on here? she wondered. If she'd had a more suspicious nature—and if she hadn't known John as well as she did—she might have suspected he was meeting a woman. But the idea that John was having an affair was totally ridiculous. Even if, by some remote chance, he was meeting with someone he didn't want her to know about, why would they meet out here, on a cold, windy field, or in Haskins' barn?

No! Julia told herself. She knew him well enough to know he wasn't screwing around, but then, what was he doing out here, apparently alone?

"So, did you leave your surveying equipment in the woods?" she asked, looking past him toward the lines of trees.

John glanced nervously over his shoulder, his eyes momentarily widening as though he half expected to see someone. Then he shook his head. "No—it's down by the road near the house. I was—uh, just walking the boundary line. It was all mapped out before I got the job."

"Oh," Julia said simply, noticing that he didn't have the surveyor's maps with him. She couldn't shake the feeling that earlier, when she had felt so strongly that she was being watched, it had been John hiding in the woods, and not letting her know he was there, until he yelled to her not to go into the barn.

But why? she wondered. Was she being ridiculous, suspecting something was going on that she wasn't supposed to know about? Was the truth simply that Barry had left early, and John had been walking the boundary line alone? That he really hadn't heard her calling him, and then saw her for the first time just as she was entering the barn? Or *was* there more?

"Say, I haven't had lunch yet, and I'm hungry as a bear," John said. "If Dad and Bri are all squared away, why don't you and I take a drive into town for something. I heard there's a lobster house just over the line in Yarmouth that's supposed to be terrific."

"Sure," Julia said. "I've already eaten, but I'll join you. Actually, I wanted to talk to you about your father. We had a bit of a religious discussion this morning."

"Oh, boy," John said, rolling his eyes upward and reminding Julia unnervingly of Frank when he had his momentary lapses.

"It wasn't anything serious," Julia said. "We can talk about it at lunch. I'll get your car and bring it around. Why don't I meet you in front of the house over there?"

They each started out across the field in different directions. Julia was enjoying the prospect of a relaxing lunch, just the two of them as they hadn't been for too long. The thought of what John might have been hiding from her receded as she walked, leaning her head back and inhaling deeply of the ocean air.

As she passed the open barn door, once again freely swinging open and shut with the gusting wind, she couldn't forget the sensation she had had of seeing motion in the darkness inside. She couldn't push aside the feeling that someone was hiding somewhere nearby, watching her, reaching out to her with a cold, icy hatred.

Julia shivered and didn't start to feel better until she was past the barn. She cast a fearful backward glance at it when the door slammed open with a resounding bang against the barn wall. She had to force herself not to look inside, into the musty gloom, and most of all, she tried not to speculate who might be waiting there in the darkness.

V

"I always thought he was bad, and by the sound of things, he's gotten worse," John said. He tipped his head back and sucked noisily on one of the small lobster legs. When he had gotten out the tiny nugget of meat and swallowed it, he wiped his chin with his napkin and took a sip of beer.

Julia sat with her hands folded in her lap. She hadn't been hungry, and she had never really cared for lobster, but John had insisted that she try a "real Maine" lobster. Watching him work away at his, though, had taken away what little appetite she had had.

"Maybe we can get this one in a doggie bag," she said, frowning as she pushed her plate away.

"They're best when they're hot out of the pot," John said. He took his lobster and ripped off one of the large claws. Using a nutcracker, he broke the thick shell and extracted the wad of speckled meat.

"Yeah, well, I'm going to have to pass for now," Julia said, feeling her stomach churn as she watched him dip the meat into the melted butter and then stuff it into his mouth.

"So, anyway," John said, still chewing as he spoke, "you and the old man squared off. And you think you came out on top, huh?" He chuckled. "That'd be a first."

"How was he as a father?" Julia asked. "I mean, you've told me quite a bit before, but you never really got into the religion part of it."

John shrugged and wiped his hands on his napkin. He stared out the window at the bay for a moment, then said, "I don't think he was into it as much back when I was a kid. At least, not as bad as you make it sound. I mean, we'd go to church and all, but it was never the hellfire and brimstone you said he laid on you."

"Not exactly hellfire and brimstone, but he was pretty pushy about it, saying there was only one way to get to God and going on about how Halloween is a holiday for Satan."

"Well, *that* I've heard before," John said, snorting with laughter before taking another drink of beer. Julia was glad to see him actually relaxing and enjoying himself. *Maybe,* she was thinking, *this is all we needed—to get out together now and again.*

"I think I always figured he'd end up a Bible-thumper," John said, still snickering. "Especially after my mom died. I think it's some kind of guilt thing because he feels like maybe he was responsible for her dying." John suddenly stopped short and started coughing—so hard, in fact, his face turned bright red and his eyes began to water. It took awhile for the fit of coughing to subside, but when it was over, he wiped his face with a fresh napkin and smiled weakly at his wife.

"You okay?" she asked, settling back into her seat.

John nodded his head quickly.

"Yeah . . . yeah," he said, his voice still a bit strangled and sounding like someone else's. "I'm . . . God! I must've swallowed down the wrong pipe."

"I'm not surprised, the way you're going at that lobster," Julia said. "Take it easy. We're not in any hurry."

"Yeah," John said. "But let's talk about something else besides my father, all right?"

"Sure thing," Julia said, and they turned their conversation to things other than Frank or John's condo site or Bri's problems making friends at school. Their time in the restaurant and their pleasant drive home went by too fast, and looking back on it later,

Julia realized it was one of the last times they had a genuinely good time together.

EIGHT
Trick or Treat

I

All week, off and on, Julia had wondered if Bri was planning on going trick-or-treating. Granted, she was a bit old for it, but last year she and a few of her friends had dressed up and gone out, and they had had a great time. Julia was hoping Bri had made friends with at least one or two kids from school so she wouldn't sit home moping all evening.

At four-thirty, as the sky was starting to darken, Bri got the bowl of candy from its hiding place on the top cupboard shelf and placed it on the small table by the front door. She opened the front door and stared up at the thin branches of the trees, which looked like black lace against the fading sky.

"So, you're not going after all, huh?" Julia said when she came into the living room and saw Bri leaning out the door. Bri shrugged, shut the door, and went over to sit in the armchair, her feet splayed awkwardly in front of her. She grunted some kind of reply, but Julia didn't need to catch the words to get the meaning.

"How about that girl you told me about? Audrey's her name, right?"

Again Bri grunted. Leaning forward, she reached around the doorjamb and grabbed a bag of M&Ms. She peeled it open and popped several into her mouth, chewing noisily as she stared blankly at the floor.

"I haven't really seen her since that time out on the point," she said. A thin glob of chocolate formed at the side of her mouth, and she wiped it away with her fingers, then licked her fingers.

"Give her a call, why don't you?" Julia said. "It's not too late to throw some kind of costume together."

Bri shook her head and dumped some more M&Ms into her

mouth. After chewing and swallowing, she looked at her mother and said, "Her name's not in the phone book. I already checked."

"What, is it unlisted or something?"

Shrugging, Bri made a move to grab another bag of candy, but her mother stepped forward quickly and gave her a light rap on the back of the hand. "Uh-uh. Leave some for the kids."

Frowning, Bri turned back around in the chair and sighed.

"She didn't want to be friends, I guess," Bri said, and Julia could see her lower lip beginning to tremble. "We just talked that day—that's all."

"But you said you thought she seemed nice," Julia said.

"Not nice enough to want to be friends," Bri said. Now that her mother had moved over to the couch, she snatched one more bag of candy—uncontested, except for the frown Julia gave her.

"I had kinda hoped we'd have a class or something together, so we could get to know each other, but all week I didn't see her. I think she must be in high school. Otherwise I'd have seen her around."

"She must be if in two weeks of school you haven't bumped into her even once."

"Oh, I've seen her a few times—at least I *think* it was her, but—I don't know." She shook her head quickly, confused, as she tried to put the pieces of the mystery together.

"Did you ask any of the other kids about her?" Julia asked.

Julia was thinking back to her own high school days, and to one of her classmates in particular. Her name had been Ann—Ann Clifford—and she had been the "new kid" the beginning of sophomore year. She had been so quiet and withdrawn, the kids gave her the nickname Phantom. Slowly, though, as the school year went on, Phantom loosened up, and she and Julia became close friends—at least until they went their separate ways after graduation. But several of the students never did accept her into their tight little circles.

Julia felt torn about what advice she could give Bri. If this Audrey was the class scapegoat, one of the school's loners, then it would be nice of Bri to befriend her. The expression "misery loves company" kept drifting into her mind, but she dismissed that. The cliché she thought of to counter it was, still waters run deep. On the other hand, if Audrey was some kind of social misfit—and no one was better than junior high school students at tagging and tormenting social misfits—it wasn't going to help Bri's acceptance into the school social structure to be associated with her.

"I asked a couple of the girls, but what they told me was there wasn't anybody named Audrey Church in the school. I think they were just putting me on."

"Well, they must have been, unless Audrey doesn't go to school. You said she acted sort of funny talking about her home life. Maybe she's dropped out or something."

"I don't know," Bri said. "Maybe her parents work and she has to stay home to do housework or take care of a younger kid or something."

"Well, then, maybe that's it. Both her parents work, and she stays home to baby-sit. Dad drove Granddad over to his lodge meeting tonight, but when they get home, I'll have to remember to ask Frank about the family. He should know them if they live on the island."

Bri shrugged as though it really didn't matter anymore, but before she could say anything, there was the sound of running feet on the front walkway, and a chorus of voices bellowing "Trick-or-treat!"

Both Bri and her mother went to the door to see the troop of costumed children on the doorstep. As Bri put a handful of candy into each bag as it opened up in front of her, she addressed each child as the character he or she was. The tally was one witch, two ghosts, and—what practically sent Julia into hysterics—an IRS auditor, complete with blood-splattered rubber ax in hand. Seeing a knot of parents standing down by the road edge, Julia waved, but only one of them waved back. She consoled herself with the thought that the holiday was for the kids, anyway.

After the first round of kids, though, only two other groups came up to the door all evening. It wasn't for lack of trick-or-treaters out and about. From the living room window, Julia could see dozens of children, white sheets or vampire capes flapping behind them as they raced up and down the street. The streetlight cast long, lean shadows on the street. But not many of the trick-or-treaters made their way up the walk to the Carlsons' door.

"I guess there'll be plenty of M&Ms left over, huh?" Bri said, once it was obvious that their house was being avoided.

"Just don't let your father know about it, all right?" Julia said, winking.

"No problem," Bri said, smiling thinly. "But why do you think they're not coming up here?"

Julia shrugged as she went to the window and looked out on the now fully dark street. Eerie silhouetted figures flashed by under the corner streetlight, but she could tell there wouldn't be any more visitors tonight—not unless they got a late night window soaping.

"It's probably because your grandfather hasn't given out Halloween candy for years," Julia said.

"How do you know that?" Bri asked, opening another bag of M&Ms and filling her mouth.

Not wanting to go into the "religious" discussion she and Frank had had that afternoon, she simply shushed Bri and went to turn off the light over the front steps. She took what was left of the candy and went into the kitchen.

"I thought you said I could have that," Bri said, following behind her.

"You've had more than enough for tonight, I think," Julia said. "God, you'll be in a sugar coma before long." She put the bowl back up onto the top shelf and swung the door shut firmly. "You'll know where to find it tomorrow."

Bri's disappointment registered on her face, but she could tell it wouldn't pay to argue. Taking a deep breath and letting her shoulders droop, she said, "I've gotta admit, this has been one of the *funnest* Halloweens I've ever had."

Julia smiled and shook her head. *"Funnest?* Did you honest-to-God say *funnest*? I'm really going to have to talk to your English teacher."

"Okay, the *most fun* I've ever had," Bri said, waving her mother away as she reached out in an attempt to tickle her. "This has been the *absitively, posolutely, bestest* night of my life. There —are you satisfied?"

"Much better," Julia said, bursting out with laugher. "Your command of the English language is surpassed only by your natural grace and charm." She jabbed her forefinger into Bri's armpit and wiggled it until she squirmed away.

Chuckling even while she knew it was to hide her own disappointment, Bri forced a yawn. "I think I'll wash up and go to bed early tonight. Maybe read a little before I crash."

"It's only"—Julia glanced at the clock over the refrigerator—"a little past eight. Come on. Keep me company until the men get home. We can play a game or something."

"I don't think so," Bri said, as she started moving slowly out of the kitchen toward the hallway stairs.

"Then maybe there's a good movie on TV," Julia said. "One of the local stations has *got* to be showing *Night of the Living Dead*."

"No—really," Bri said. "I haven't been sleeping that well lately. I just want to unwind. I'll see you in the morning. G'night."

Julia suspected that Bri was heading to bed so early because of her disappointment about missing trick-or-treating, and she wished she could make it up to her somehow, but she also knew that she couldn't—it was going to be up to Bri to make her own friends here in Maine.

"Good night, then," Julia said, giving her a little wave. She stood in the kitchen, listening to Bri's footsteps as she slowly trudged up the stairs.

II

Lying in bed, her attention just barely on the words dragging by her eyes, Bri could hear the sounds of the kids whooping it up in the street. Laughter and screaming and hollering echoed in the still night, repeatedly drawing her eyes to the cold blank of the window. Several times she turned off her reading light and got out of bed, crouched by the window, and looked out. A pale quarter-moon rode low in the sky, and Bri found herself disappointed that it hadn't been a fat-belly full moon casting long blue shadows beneath the parade of figures in the street.

But the moon wasn't the only thing that she felt disappointed about; she honestly wished she could have gone out tonight and whooped it up with a bunch of friends. She wondered if right now in Shelburne Falls, Lisa and Veronica and Debbie and the others were out cruising the streets. Remembering the friends she had left behind in Vermont only made the cold hollowness in her stomach feel worse.

"Damned silly holiday, anyway," she whispered as she went back to bed and slipped under the sheets. The book she was reading—*Anne of Avonlea*—lay facedown on her pillow, open to the page she hadn't been able to concentrate on. Sometime after eleven o'clock—an hour or so after she heard her father and grandfather come home—she turned off the light and snuggled down under the covers. Sleep, though—like reading—didn't grab her, and she lay there, staring up at the indistinct gray ceiling.

What brought her to full attention was a low, steady throbbing sound that seemed as much a part of the night as the darkness. Now that she had noticed it, she couldn't even say for sure when it had started. Propping herself up on her elbows, she looked over at her window, where the shadows of branches, thrown by the streetlight, danced like stiff-jointed skeletons on her windowsill. Her room was hushed, perfectly quiet.

Leave it to me to freak myself out on Halloween night, she thought as, confused, she closed her eyes and concentrated, trying to pull back the memory of the sound that had disturbed her.

She wasn't sure if it had been real or in her imagination, but she held her breath and didn't move for several seconds as she waited for the sound to come again.

Tension coiled inside her like a cold snake, and when the sound was repeated, it caught her so much by surprise, the only sound she could make was a strangled click in her throat. She was awake! She *knew* she was! And drifting out of the darkness, winding and twining with a soft, subtle whisper, were the soft strains of organ music! *Church* music!

Bri wanted to leap from her bed, but like a child whose imagination has convinced her that there are alligators in the dark under her bed, she didn't dare bring her feet out from under the covers. Her heart was hammering a tinny drumbeat she felt mostly in her neck as her eyes darted around the room, trying to find which direction the music was coming from.

It seemed to be coming from everywhere!

The notes blended together, swelling and throbbing with a pulsating power that, Bri sensed, was being held in check. The tune —*yes! There was a definite tune!*—seemed familiar, but Bri couldn't quite place it, other than that it was definitely a hymn— church music!

"The church wood!" she whispered, her throat so raw and dry she wasn't sure whether or not she had actually spoken.

As soon as she realized she really was hearing the church wood, she felt the walls and floor of her bedroom vibrating, resonating with the sound of the organ. The vibration worked its way into her bones, making her tingle. She imagined that, if she dared get out of bed and look at herself in the mirror, she would see that she was glowing with an eerie blue light!

This has got to be a dream! her mind screamed. *But it can't be! I'm awake! I know I am!*

Remembering a trick someone had once told her about how to tell if you're dreaming or not, she held her hand up in front of her face and stared at it.

Yes! That's my hand!

Slowly she flexed her fingers, never letting her concentration waver from her hand, but still the soft organ music throbbed in the darkness like a hulking animal presence in the room, a part of the living darkness. The more she concentrated on it, the more it seemed to fade, until it was just on the border of her hearing.

The rawness in her throat got worse, and Bri realized that she was breathing too fast. She was sucking in quick gulps of air through her mouth. It took all the mental effort she could muster to try to calm herself down and inhale slowly through her nose, but no matter how hard she tried to calm herself down, her nerve endings felt stripped raw as she listened to the organ music rise and fall like the heavy sough of ocean waves.

"No . . . *no!*" she said, moaning softly as her eyes darted around the darkened room, trying to find the source of the receding sound. Like a will-o'-the-wisp, it was elusive, shifting around the room every time she tried to hone in on it. First it would seem to come from the corner by the window, and then, as soon as she looked in that direction, it would shift over by the bureau. When she looked there, it would seem to be coming from inside the closet.

She wanted to cry out, yell for her mother to come into her room, but no matter how hard she tried to steady her nerves, whenever she thought she might have enough air in her lungs to shout, she would try to swallow and the dry lining of her throat would feel as if it was burning.

Suddenly a sound hit her ears like the snap of a rifle. It wasn't much . . . just a quick little pop that drew her attention away from the organ music now softly filtering into her room from behind the headboard. The new sound was so sharp and sudden, Bri thought for an instant that it had been inside her head.

Maybe I'm so scared I popped a blood vessel! she thought, her fear mounting even higher.

But the sound came again, and this time she had no trouble identifying at least where it had come from, if not the sound itself. Something had hit against the window glass.

With a sudden flurry of motion, Bri threw her bed covers aside and jumped to the floor, making it over to the window in three long strides. It seemed as though the organ music stopped the instant her feet hit the hardwood floor.

She felt as if she were breathing dry dust as she crouched on the floor and looked out into the night. The moon was out of sight, so only the weak glow of the streetlight lit up the side yard. A low-hanging mist swirled and eddied between the trees and crept up onto the edge of the road. Everything was hushed and calm; the night sky looked like fuzzy velvet.

And then another *snap* hit the window right in front of her face. Bri jumped back with a startled squeak tightening her throat. Instantly she realized what was going on. *Some of the island kids are out there,* she told herself. *They're tossing pebbles against the window to scare me.*

Slowly she eased herself up to the window again and, hands gripping the sill, looked out, trying to determine where the kids were hiding. They could be across the street, behind the maple trees, but she thought more than likely they were pressed up against the side of the house, out of sight until they darted out and tossed another pebble up at her bedroom window.

Bri felt an element of calm return as she sat on the floor, thinking this all through.

The organ music . . . Well, that *had* to have been part of a dream. Even though she didn't feel as if she had been asleep, she must have drifted off, and—this being Halloween—she had let what her granddad had told her about the "church wood" in the house work on her nerves and invade her sleep. That was clear enough.

But what about the—?

She jumped again when something went *pop* against the glass. She leaned forward quickly, hoping to catch the pebble thrower before he darted back to cover.

She reached up to the window lock and snapped it open, ready the next time the culprit threw something.

Try as she might, though, she couldn't get the window to budge. She stood up and felt to make sure she had it unlocked, rather than locked, but the catch was open. Last weekend she had had the window open to air the room out, so she knew it *did* work. *Why not now?* she wondered as she pushed upward as hard as she could. It was while she was struggling to raise the window that she chanced to glance down and see the figure standing by the side of the house. She—Bri knew right away it was a girl— had her head tilted back and was staring up at her bedroom window, looking at her, her pale face floating in the darkness below as though she were looking up from the bottom of a well.

"Audrey?" she whispered, recognizing her. "What in the heck?"

She knew Audrey couldn't hear her, not with the window shut, so she redoubled her efforts to get it open. Standing in a crouch, her knees locked, she pushed as hard as she could against the sash, and finally it slid up. A cold wash of night air swept in over her, raising goose bumps on her arms as she stuck her head out the window and looked down. A fitful gust of wind lifted her hair.

"For crying out loud, Audrey! What are you *doing* out here this late?"

She had no idea what time it was, but the moon was down and the street was filled with an eerie, silent darkness. No hint of the coming dawn brightened the vault of sky.

Audrey didn't say a word, but she continued to stare up at Bri. It looked as though she had, after all, been out trick-or-treating. Her face had a pale, white cast to it, as if she hadn't yet washed off her white face makeup. In the feeble glow from the streetlight,

Bri could see dark, heavy lines underneath Audrey's eyes. Her mouth was opened, but she said nothing.

"What the heck do you want?" Bri whispered, hoping she wouldn't wake up her parents.

Slowly Audrey shook her head and raised her hand in a beckoning gesture. Bri knew she was signaling for her to come down, but the gesture—*the same one she had seen her make to her that day in the woods!*—sent a shiver up her spine. She shook her head.

"No—I can't come down! God, it's late! Shouldn't you be home?"

Audrey remained silent as she waved her hand slowly up and down. Her eyes seemed never to blink, and Bri could feel the coldness of her stare working its way into her heart.

Suddenly, though, she understood what was going on, and she didn't like it one bit. Audrey wasn't any different from any of the other kids on the island. She had no interest in being her friend, and she was pulling this spooky stunt just to freak her out.

"Look, Audrey, I—" Bri started to say, but to her ears, her voice sounded oddly distorted, as if she were speaking directly at a wall and her words were bouncing back at her.

"Come with me," Audrey said, her voice faint, feathery. She was still slowly beckoning Bri with a hand that looked as pale and polished as white marble.

And as cold, Bri thought, shivering.

"You should be home," Bri said. "I'll meet you on the point tomorrow, okay?"

Audrey didn't reply for a moment, but then she said softly, "Come with me . . . now."

"Don't be ridiculous!" Bri hissed. "It's almost—" She turned her head to glance at the clock by her bed, but it was turned away from her and she couldn't see the dial. Dashing quickly to her bedstand, she grabbed the clock, saw that it was a few minutes before one in the morning, and then went back to the window. Somehow she wasn't surprised when she saw that Audrey wasn't there. Actually, she had the peculiar sensation that Audrey never *had* been there, that she was dreaming all of this just as she had the church-wood organ music.

After rubbing her shoulders to warm up, she slid the window back down and, working hard to convince herself she had imagined everything, was just getting back into bed when she heard a heavy thump from downstairs. It sounded like something had hit the front door.

"Jesus," Bri whispered under her breath as she got up and went out of her bedroom and down the stairs, tiptoeing as lightly as she could so she wouldn't wake her parents or grandfather. Through the sidelight window beside the front door, she saw the shadow of someone—*Audrey*—standing on the front steps.

Bri's hand was shaking as she fumbled with the lock and turned the doorknob. As the door swung open, a cold gust of wind swirled into the foyer, easily tearing through the thin fabric of Bri's nightgown. The words she was going to say—telling Audrey to go home, she'd see her tomorrow—were forming in her throat, but they were suddenly jammed back down with a sharp intake of breath. The doorstep was empty. Just the wash of light from the streetlight carpeted the granite slab of the step.

"What the—?" Bri managed to say, taking an involuntary step backward. She was positive she had seen Audrey's shadow. Then, with a start, when she focused farther down the walkway, she did see Audrey standing down by the road.

How could she get away from the door so fast? Bri wondered. With that thought, her suspicion became a conviction—Audrey, and probably several other kids, were using Halloween night to tease her; they were trying to scare her.

"I know what you're up to," Bri called out to the solitary figure standing down by the road. She had to admit that the effect was good—the soft yellow glow of the streetlight, the silently swirling ground mist, the fitful gusts of chilling wind. And Audrey's face . . . so pale, so blank looking.

"I know you're just teasing me," Bri whispered harshly. "So why don't you just leave me alone?" She could feel herself wanting to cry, her lower lip trembling, but she wouldn't let herself break down—not in front of Audrey and the kids who were probably hiding in the darkness beside the house, snickering at her.

But Audrey, obviously, wasn't going to stop—not yet, anyway. Again she slowly motioned with her hand for Bri to come outside. Her voice carried softly, like a velvety murmur from the dark. "Come here with me. I want to show you something."

"No way!" Bri shouted, unmindful now of waking up her parents. She took several quick steps forward out into the night, bracing her fists at her sides as though ready to fight. "You guys have got to stop it! Stop *teasing* me, for crying out loud!"

Her eyes darted to each side of the front stairs, but she didn't spot anyone else hiding there, watching her. Her anger, sparkling red in her mind, became a hot flush of blood coursing over her cheeks.

"If you don't go away and leave me alone, I'm going to tell my parents!" Bri yelled. Her voice echoed in the night with a muffled dullness. When she looked back down by the roadside, though, she was stunned into silence; Audrey was gone. Suddenly and silently, she simply wasn't there!

Bri shivered with the cold and, figuring Audrey, knowing the joke was played out, had simply ducked behind a tree, was just turning to go back into the house when she sensed more than saw or heard someone moving beside the house to her left. Just as she turned to look, a face popped out of the darkness, stopping mere inches from her own face. The cold dash of panic that hit her nearly blinded her, and in that first frightening instant, she didn't recognize Audrey's pale face, eyes and mouth wide open, so close to her she could feel the chill of her skin.

"Tell him . . ." Audrey said, her lips moving with an odd disunity with her words. "I want you to tell your father something."

Bri wanted to ask what, but it felt as though thin fingers were pressing in the sides of her neck.

"I want you to tell your father that you saw me tonight," Audrey whispered, her breath cold and dank on Bri's ear.

"I—" Bri started to say, but that was all that came out.

"Tell him you were talking to . . . *Abby!*" The last word was long and drawn out, and seemed to reverberate in her ears . . . *like the church-wood music*, Bri's fear-numbed brain registered.

And with that last word, Audrey suddenly ducked back, dissolving into the darkness like a passing cloud. Bri's lungs hissed as she took in a deep gulp of air and then forced it out as a long, wailing screech. She didn't feel her legs give out underneath her, and was just barely conscious of slowly falling down. She didn't feel her knees slam into the hard stone step, didn't feel the cold stone as she fell face first onto the walkway. The next thing she was aware of was her mother and father talking softly to her as they leaned over her and rubbed her face with a cold washcloth.

III

"I'm really worried about her," Julia said later in their own room. It had taken her and John more than an hour, until well after two o'clock, to calm Bri down and get her settled back in bed. Knowing dawn was only a few hours away, Julia was half-tempted to stay awake and enjoy the peace and quiet before everyone got up for the day.

"I—" John said, then paused and, lacing his hands behind his head, stared for a moment at the ceiling. "I just think it was a harmless prank that—"

"*Harmless?*" Julia said, wanting to shout but holding back so she wouldn't wake up Bri. "Do you call scaring her so badly she faints *harmless*? She's lucky she landed the way she did. She could have banged her head really hard on the steps!"

"You didn't let me finish," John said. "I think it was a harmless prank that just got a little out of hand. I mean, from the way Bri described it, they really had it worked out—what with her seeing that girl Audrey down by the road, and then having someone jump out from behind her." He chuckled in spite of himself. "You've got to admit, it's a pretty elaborate prank."

Julia was sitting cross-legged on the bed, looking at John and not believing what she was hearing. She also didn't like what she was thinking, that he wasn't taking Bri's experience seriously because she wasn't *really* his daughter by blood. Maybe that allowed him to see the slight bit of humor in all of this. All *she* felt was defensiveness and protectiveness for her daughter.

"I just don't think it's fair of those kids—whoever they are— to tease her like that," Julia said, grimacing and shaking her fists with frustration.

"But if you look at it from the other side," John said mildly, "you could take it as—well, almost a hopeful sign."

"What the hell do you mean by that?" Julia snapped.

"Well . . . I mean they at least consider her important enough to tease. I honestly don't think it's that serious."

"It *is* serious if someone gets hurt!" Julia said angrily.

John shrugged and said, "Yeah, but she didn't get hurt bad. Mark my words—at school on Monday, I'll bet the kids treat her a little better, and before long, she'll be in with them."

Julia snorted and shook her head. "Yeah—or by Monday they'll have thought of some other way to tease her . . . some other little practical joke, and if it's anything like this last one—well, who's to say they won't stop until they put her in the hospital?"

"I think you're definitely overreacting to this," John said mildly. He reached over and turned off the light, plunging the room into darkness. John fluffed his pillow and, with a deep sigh, sank his head down into it.

For several minutes, Julia didn't move. Still sitting cross-legged on the bed, she listened to her husband's steady breathing, her eyes focused on the distant darkness out toward the horizon. She was mulling over everything that had happened, everything they had said, but she couldn't quite bring herself around to John's point of view. What those kids had done to Bri was downright mean-spirited. A prank's a prank, but at least in this instance—*because it's my daughter,* Julia thought—they went too damned far. If there was a way to find out who had been outside the house, she most assuredly would be making a few phone calls

in the morning. First off, there was Audrey Church. That might
be the place to start.

"What do you think she meant by that?" Julia said suddenly.

John, who had already drifted back to sleep, rolled over and
groggily muttered, "Huh?... What?"

"What that girl said to Bri... to tell you Bri had seen Abby.
Why would she say something like that?"

Even though it was dark, she could feel John come fully
awake, his body tensing. He heaved a deep sigh, shifting in the
bed. When he spoke, his voice just barely masked the tremor in
it.

"I have no idea," he said. "I mean, obviously it's someone's
idea of a sick joke. For all I know, Randy Chadwick might have
put this Audrey up to it. Maybe he's trying to spook me a little—
give me a little Halloween scare."

"Do you think she meant *your* Abby... your high school
sweetheart?" Julia said.

"How the Christ should I know?" John snapped. His fist hit the
mattress with a soft thump. "I mean, for Christ's sake, this was a
bunch of kids pulling a stupid Halloween prank. That's all it
was!"

"Yeah, but then why mention Abby?" Julia said. She shifted
around and lay down on the bed, not even bothering to get under
the covers. Watching the black rectangle of the window, she knew
she wasn't going to be able to get back to sleep now.

For a long time, John lay there silent in the dark room. Julia
could tell by his breathing that he wasn't asleep. His breath
rasped gently in and out, in and out. Julia wanted to say more, to
question him further, but their night's sleep had been ruined
enough already, so she lay there, staring at the window, not saying anything.

IV

After getting back into bed, Bri listened to the low-level buzz
of her parents' voices as they talked in their bedroom. She
couldn't hear what they were saying, but she had a pretty good
idea. She was just grateful that the sound of their talking masked
the other sound—the low, echoing organ music that she thought
she might otherwise hear if the house were perfectly silent.

Finally, sometime close to dawn, she drifted off to sleep, but
like a swimmer who is constantly doing surface dives, she kept
coming up to the surface to take a gulp of air before going back

down. The dreams that shifted through her overworked brain were gross, distorted replays of the night's events.

The face that had loomed out of the darkness at her, in her dreams now became distorted and rotted, with loose flaps of skin hanging down in shredded chunks. Sharp, dirt-caked teeth grinned at her as the mouth opened in wild, soundless laughter.

The figure that had been standing down by the road became a thin, wafting, transparent shape that drifted, lifting unnaturally off the ground with each cold blast of the wind. Pale, white arms swaying like strands of kelp, tossing gently in the push and pull of the tide.

Audrey's upturned face now floated up the side of the house and stopped level with Bri's second-story bedroom window. Her cold, vacant stare, eyes like inkwells, drilled into Bri's heart, into her soul, like icy spikes.

Several times Bri woke with a start and found herself sitting up in bed, her eyes fastened on the gradually brightening rectangle of her window. She knew she would have screamed if she had seen even the hint of a shadow out there, and even when she saw that there was nothing in the window—no face leering in at her—her conviction that there *was* someone outside, hanging just below the window ledge just out of sight, became so strong she wanted to scream. The only sound she could make, though, was a soft whimper as she snuggled back under the covers so she would be safe. With dawn brightening the sky, she finally slipped into a deeper sleep and stayed there until well after ten o'clock the next morning.

PART TWO

Lachesis— the Assigning Fate

I dreamed last night a deathly dream. Perhaps
The morning will dispel it if I speak it...

—Euripides

Terrors compelled me,
to terrors I was driven.
I know it. I know my own spirit.

—Sophocles

NINE
Wharf Rats

I

It was the first day of November, and the weather seemed to know it. Monday morning dawned cold, windy, and raw, with rafts of clouds spreading like steel gray hands over the island. The early morning sun, looking like a low-wattage light bulb, shifted in and out of the clouds like a teasing dancer.

At first John thought the nausea he felt in his stomach when he first got out of bed was just another case of the morning blahs, but even after breakfast—which he barely touched—he didn't feel any better. Worse, actually, and during the drive in to Portland, the twisting in his stomach got even more intense.

After he had parked the car and walked up to the Atkins office, the backs of his knees were feeling like sponges. He went straight to his office, nodding a greeting to the usual crowd gathered around the coffeepot in the conference room. A few minutes later, Barry poked his head into the room, a steaming Styrofoam cup in each hand.

"I brought you a cup," he said, his smile wide and pleasant.

John simply nodded as he slouched in his chair, barely able to focus on Barry's face.

"You getting real serious about your work so soon, or's there something bothering you?" Barry asked as he sidled into the room.

John shifted forward in his chair and supported his head with both hands, elbows propped on the desk. He looked at Barry, forced a smile, and grunted. Just thinking about taking a sip of coffee sent his stomach into a whirlpool.

"I'm—uh, not feeling so well," he said.

Barry chuckled, apparently not realizing how bad John felt. He put the coffee cup on the desk next to John and said, "Well, what with working even on Saturdays, making the rest of us look like slugs, it's no surprise you feel like shit on Monday morning." He glanced out the office window at the gun-barrel sky. "'Specially a crappy Monday morning."

"I don't mean to—" John started to say, but he couldn't finish because his stomach suddenly felt as though someone had connected with a solid jab in the gut. Spinning quickly around in his chair, he grabbed the wastebasket beside the desk and ducked his head into it. With three loud heaves, his entire breakfast splashed into the metal can, splattering like rain on a tin roof. Barry took an involuntary step back, his eyes wide with surprise.

"Jesus, man," he said, watching dumbfounded as John continued to retch into the bucket. "If you're feeling that bad, why didn't you just call in 'n' stay home?"

John looked up at him with glazed eyes. "I didn't know I was—" But that was all he had the chance to say as a series of dry heaves shook his body.

"Lemme get you a glass of water," Barry said as he hurried from the room, returning in a matter of seconds with another cup and a handful of paper towels. He handed them to John and then stepped back, wrinkling his nose from the ripe smell of vomit.

John nodded his thanks and took a quick sip of water, but that seemed only to give his stomach something more to throw back out. After wiping his mouth with a paper towel, he was back with his head in the wastebasket.

"I, uh, think you'd better head home," Barry said once the second wave was over.

John nodded his agreement, but when he stood up, he wasn't so sure his legs would be strong enough to carry him down the hall to the elevator, much less to the parking lot. If he had been feeling better, he might have found it funny, how the room seemed to be expanding and contracting with every breath he took. He felt oddly dissociated from his hand as he reached out for his coat. It took an incredible effort to put it on. *Screw buttoning it up!*

"Don't worry about the wastebasket. I'll get it," Barry said, stepping aside to let John walk past him and into the hallway.

Placing his hand on Barry's shoulder, John forced out the word "Thanks," and made his way slowly toward the elevator.

The drive home was so hallucinatory it reminded John of the couple of times during college when he had experimented with LSD. The worst aspect of it all was the time dilation. It seemed to take almost an hour just to get out of town and across Tukey's Bridge. The construction on I-295 didn't help any, but even after he was on Route 1, he had the curious sensation that the road was a greased incline, and he just was not getting anywhere. To keep himself from falling asleep, he rolled the side window halfway down and let the cold air wash over him. He shivered, feeling his nipples harden, but it was better than falling asleep at the wheel.

By the time he got to his turnoff at Foreside Road, the whole world looked and sounded as if it were submerged in deep water. By the time he was crossing the bridge onto Glooscap, his teeth were chattering with fever chills. He rolled up the window and clamped his coat collar tightly around his neck, but that didn't do any good. Finally, by the time he spun the steering wheel for the turn up into the driveway, there were bright yellow spots zigzagging like meteors across his vision.

He stopped the car halfway up the driveway, not caring that he left it at an angle that blocked the garage door. All he cared about was getting upstairs into bed and letting the fever and chills work their way through his system. The only positive aspect about the whole damned thing was that, since this flu had hit him so hard and fast, maybe it would leave as quickly.

"I'm home," he called out as he shouldered open the door and lurched into the kitchen. His voice barely carried above a whisper, but he could tell from the silence in the house that both Julia and Frank were out. Bri had left for school when he left for work, so that left the whole house to himself and his misery.

The churning in his stomach felt slightly better, but figuring a sip or two of ginger ale would settle things down, he opened the refrigerator, grabbed the nearly empty half-liter bottle, and twisting off the cap, drank several swallows. With a rumbling belch that almost brought everything up, he went over to the counter, fumbling for a pen to leave Julia a message to tell her he was upstairs in bed and not to disturb him.

He found a pencil and notepad, but when he went over to the kitchen table and sat down, a sheet of paper lying squarely in the center of the table caught his eye.

"What the—?" he muttered, picking up the paper and looking at it. A sheet of paper had been torn out of a notebook; the three ring holes were ripped. At the top of the first thin blue line, a single letter—or was it a number?—had been scrawled in heavy pencil.

I

Dizzy with fever, John scowled as he looked at the page, trying to figure out what the hell it was. It no doubt had come from Bri's notebook; she had probably started to write something and then changed her mind. Most likely, in the flurry of activity to get to the door in time to catch the school bus, she had forgotten to throw it away.

With a quick flexing of his fingers, John crumpled the paper into a tight ball and, twisting around in his chair, tossed it at the wastebasket. It hit the rim and bounced onto the floor beside the refrigerator. Rather than getting up and putting it into the wastebasket, though, John stood up and, shaking with chills, made his way painfully up the stairs. The joints of his arms and legs felt like hot wires as he took off his shirt and pants and slid under the covers. Within seconds, he was flirting with sleep, and throughout the rest of the morning, his awareness skimmed like a seabird just over the surface of sleep.

As his fever raged, vague dreams and images twisted through his mind. Several times, he became convinced there was someone in the room, standing at the head of the bed. . . .

How can that be, he wondered groggily, *when the bed is up against the wall?*

But that was the feeling he had as he wrestled with sleep. Maybe it was Julia, back from wherever she had gone. But if it had been her, she no doubt would have talked to him, asked him how he felt, maybe gotten him some more ginger ale.

He remembered leaving the bottle of ginger ale on the kitchen table, and like someone lost in the desert who sees a distant oasis, he wanted nothing more than to get that bottle of ginger ale and gulp it down. But he didn't have half the strength he needed to get downstairs, and even if he did, he knew he couldn't make it back upstairs to bed. At one point, he dreamed he *did* get down to the kitchen, but when he grabbed the bottle and tilted his head back to drink, his mouth was suddenly filled by a flood of soft-bodied, gray things—*maggots!* He woke up, sputtering and spitting, but —surprisingly—didn't throw up again.

Over the course of the morning, the clouds had shifted and sunlight now filtered into the room. In his brief moments of clear consciousness, John watched motes of dust, brightly illuminated, spinning like planets and then winking out as they drifted into shadow. The shadows themselves—cold and blue—seemed to shimmer and sway, at times creating the watery illusion that the bedroom furniture was moving, shifting soundlessly across the floor.

The worst part of it was the sense he had that someone was hovering around the bed as he lay there tossing and turning. The image he had seen—*When?* he wondered—rose in his mind with shocking clarity.

A slouching gray shape dangled from the ceiling, frayed rope digging deeply into the flesh of the neck. The head was snapped to one side because of the broken neck. The face, gray and bloated, was turned away from him, but in his mind he saw the face turning . . . slowly turning . . . to look at him. The eyes, cold and lifeless, were slowly opening!

The image rose in his mind and fell away like the surge of the tides. Every now and again, John would hear what might have been a soft, indistinct voice whispering close to his ear . . . so close, in fact, that he could almost imagine the cold, dead breath washing over the side of his face like ice water. He couldn't understand the words, and whenever he turned his head to see who was there, the voice would shift to the other side, still hissing and whispering weakly like a radio signal struggling to increase its gain.

Sometime in the early afternoon—he knew it was afternoon because, in a moment of clarity, he saw that there were no longer shadows cast across the sill of the east-facing bedroom window —he imagined a hand reaching out from behind the bed and gently brushing the sides of his neck. Icy darts shot up to the base of his skull when he felt the cold fingers gently stroke his throat just under his jaw. The touch—*like the whispering voice at his ear*—was feeble, as though, as much as those hands might want to grab him, they didn't have enough substance or strength . . . not yet, anyway.

Throughout the afternoon, the voice whispering to him from the head of the bed seemed to gain in strength, so he could actually make out a few of the words. Lying there with his eyes closed, John tried to focus his awareness, imagining it as a beam of laser light cutting through the darkness, but no amount of concentration would bring the voice in any clearer.

". . . didn't . . . fault . . . haven't . . . yours . . ." the voice hissed, wavering up and down the scale.

Moaning and tossing his head in the fever-hot well of his pillow, John tried to reply, thinking that whoever was trying to speak to him had an important message for him.

". . . you . . . realize . . . fault . . ."

John's muttered responses were no more coherent than the babble of words he was hearing. He blurted out fragments of thoughts, none of which, in his more lucid moments, made any sense even to him.

Sometime in the afternoon, Julia came upstairs—*yes! It was really her!*—and asked him if he needed anything. Grateful at last to actually see someone and not just *feel* there was a person in the room, hands reaching to him from the headboard of the bed, he shook his head and rasped a single word, "No."

"I'll check in on you in a bit, then," Julia said, edging over toward the door.

John stirred, opened his eyes, and as best he could, because of the swirl of images and memories in his brain, tried to tell her what he had been imagining. In broken phrases, he communicated fragments of the hallucination to her, and she listened patiently until he settled back down into bed.

"The fever's doing this to you," Julia said mildly. She came back over to the bed and, sitting on the edge, gently rubbed John's forehead. His skin felt like a live coal under her fingers. His hair was matted down in a ring of sweat. He seemed to pull away from her touch, though, so she stood back up and, easing the door shut behind her, left him there.

During his next waking moment, John figured she must have come back into the room after he had fallen asleep, because— after another particularly frightful dream, in which he began to feel pressure being applied to his throat, *like a noose slipping tighter*—he awoke with a start and, seeing the glass of ginger ale, grabbed it and gulped it down greedily. Within a minute, he was kneeling on the bedroom floor with his face over the wastebasket, coughing and sputtering as his stomach spewed it all back out.

Julia came rushing into the room and, after helping him back into bed, handed him a cold washcloth for his face. But the chilly cloth on his forehead only reminded him of those hands he had imagined reaching out, feebly trying to touch him, trying to choke him. Once she was gone, he let the washcloth drop to the floor and sank back into a thin, disturbed sleep that would last long into the evening.

II

Earlier that day, after Bri and John had left and after Mrs. Bartlett had visited with Frank and gone, Julia asked Frank if there was something special she could do for him. She was still feeling guilty about their argument about churchgoing, and she wanted, once and for all, to make it up to him.

Frank didn't answer right away, but she was beginning to understand that it was his way to silently consider things before answering. It may have seemed typically Yankee, but it also suited Frank's personality perfectly. After a few minutes, though, he nodded his head and said, "Yeah, I spose there's somethin' you could do for me."

"What's that?" Julia asked after a short pause, trying the un-hurried Yankee style on for size.

"I was thinkin' how it's been awhile since I went down to the wharf. See who might be around. 'S probably deserted, but we could give it a shot."

Unlike just about everyone else on the island, Frank had never lobstered for a living; he had worked for years at the CMP power plant on Cousins Island, and had retired seven years ago. But almost all of his friends around town were lobstermen, and on days off, he usually visited them down on the docks for a bit of drinking and cardplaying after their day's work was done.

Julia readily agreed, so around ten o'clock she rolled Frank out to his car, helped him into the front seat, then collapsed his wheelchair and put it into the backseat.

"You'll have to tell me where to go," she said as she started up the car and backed out onto Oak Street.

Frank nodded and made a slight motion to his right as she drove to the stop sign at the intersection of Shore Drive. After the right turn, just past Pottle's, he nodded to the left, and she turned down onto a road marked Wharf Road.

"Might wanna slow down for this," Frank said, but his words were a second too late. When the asphalt abruptly ended, the car bottomed out on the potholed dirt road. The incline down to the water was quite steep, and with the shimmering gray water straight ahead, Julia felt a momentary panic, thinking, *What if the brakes let go?* She could imagine the car gaining speed as it bounced over the short swath of grass and then shot out into the cove.

But the brakes didn't let go; the car squeaked to a stop at the bottom of the hill. The dirt road branched left and right, and Julia sat waiting for more directions. For a moment, Frank just sat there, too, wondering why she wasn't moving.

"Oh—take a left, I spose," he said. "Might's well see if Fren-chie's round." Julia obliged with a left turn.

Driving past the fishing shacks, Julia was struck by the thought that, as postcard pretty as they might look from the ocean, the close-up reality of these ramshackle buildings reminded her more of third world poverty in the Caribbean. On both sides of the dirt road were the tiniest and—if they had been painted and refin-ished—the cutest little buildings. But she could see that those that did have doors usually had slats of cardboard filling most of the windows. The single windows looking out onto the road were likewise mostly all broken, the holes filled either with newspaper, cardboard, or moldering cloth.

Everywhere the ground was littered with empty beer cans, whiskey bottles, crushed cigarette packs, assorted food wrappers, empty fuel drums, piles of gray-weathered lobster pots, tangled ropes, and stacks of brightly painted buoys. Weeds, now dead and brown, choked the narrow alleys between the shacks, which were backed by a long wall of thick granite blocks. Other than the buoys and the boats riding at anchor in the harbor, there wasn't a single thing in sight with a fresh coat of paint.

"It's—" Julia started to say, but then thought better of it. She had been about to say, *"It's depressing,"* but she instantly thought, who was *she* to judge? It wasn't as though the lobster-men couldn't afford to keep up appearances; they just weren't into them. *Let the outta-staters think what they want and be damned!* seemed to be the attitude.

"Don't see no one," Frank said, squinting as he scanned each side of the road, peering into the darkened doorways as best he could as Julia drove by. "Why don't you park over there by the boat yard?" He pointed to a wide open area off to the left. Up the rise of the hill, Julia could see what must have been the back side of Pottle's store.

"I won't get towed or anything, will I?" Julia asked as she slid the car into Park and clicked off the ignition.

Frank snorted with laughter and said, "I got a feelin' they'll recognize my car even though it's been in the barn ever since—" To finish, he slapped his useless leg with the flat of his hand.

"Oh, I've been using it some," Julia said as she got out and went around to the passenger's door. After taking the wheelchair from the backseat and unfolding it, she set the wheel lock and helped Frank swing up off the car seat and into the chair. He shifted his hips from side to side, getting comfortable.

In the shelter of the harbor, the air was much warmer than up at the house. She tipped her head back, and, closing her eyes for a moment, inhaled deeply. The mingled scents of ocean-fresh air and rotting bait, tinged with wet rope had a rawness that, while unpleasant at first, actually was rather invigorating. Julia was filled with a sense that this was where honest, hardworking men spent their days from before sunrise until after dark. In spite of how many times she had heard John bitch about the narrowness and the grubbiness of the world down by the harbor, Julia almost envied the salt-of-the-earth feeling the place had.

"Where to?" she asked, taking hold of the handle grips. She was just leaning forward to release the wheel lock when the sharp report of a gun shattered the air, followed an instant later by the whine of a bullet ricocheting off a rock. Three more shots cracked off in quick succession. Julia crouched low, her panic-stricken face level with Frank's.

Frank was smiling, watching her. Then, shaking his head, he said simply, "Yup . . . it sounds like Frenchie's around."

"What's going on?" Julia asked, her eyes darting from side to side, trying to locate the source of the shots.

Frank pointed to the left, down by the water, where a man wearing a nearly shapeless red felt hat and dingy tan coat was sitting on the edge of the wharf. He had a rifle cradled in his lap and was leaning forward, studying the tumbled granite blocks of the wharf that jutted out into the cove. Sunlight made the water sparkle farther out, but the man was peering into the shadows in close where the water rippled like ink.

Before Frank could respond to Julia's question, Frenchie brought the rifle up to his shoulder and the sharp report cut the air three more times. Each bullet whined like an angry bee as it bounced off the rocks.

"Yo! Frenchie!" Frank hollered, raising his hand up to cup his mouth. His voice didn't carry well, and it took several more shouts to get the man's attention.

Finally Frenchie turned, but he didn't rise from his perch. He signaled instead with a wave of his hand—which clenched the neck of a wine bottle—for Frank and Julia to join him.

"Down around to the right there's a bit of road," Frank said, so Julia released the brake and pushed in that direction. The rutted dirt road, though, wasn't much good; the wheelchair bounced and wobbled viciously. A few times, Julia was afraid she was going to tip Frank out onto the ground, but eventually she made it to the wharf edge, and once she struggled the chair up onto the relatively smooth rock surface, pushing Frank was a bit easier. She didn't wonder very long why Frenchie didn't come to help; as soon as they got close to him, it was obvious he was three, maybe four sheets to the wind.

"Fine mornin', ain't it?" Frenchie said.

His face was a dense network of deep lines crisscrossing skin that looked more like leather than flesh. His hat shaded his eyes, but from underneath the uneven brim, Julia could see his eyes sparkling like chips of amber. His jowls were covered by white stubble. His smile, when Frank introduced Julia to him, exposed a row of rotted and browned teeth.

"Pleasure to meetcha," Frenchie said.

"Nice to meet you, too, Frenchie," Julia said as she shook hands with him. His grip was dry and hard from a lifetime of pulling on lobster trap lines. It wasn't until she bent over to fasten the wheelchair brake that she saw the real reason Frenchie hadn't helped her get Frank's chair onto the wharf. His left leg had been amputated from just above the knee. The loose flap of pant's leg was folded up and pinned shut.

"Frank told me 'bout you and John movin' in with him," Frenchie said. "He didn't tell me you were so pretty."

Slightly flustered, Julia looked down at the ground. Everywhere the rocks were splattered with sea gull shit and litter. She had been wanting to sit down but decided against it.

"So how's the huntin' been today?" Frank asked.

"Had betta," Frenchie said, shrugging his shoulders and tipping the wine bottle to his lips. Old Duke sloshed back and bubbled as he took several gulps. Then, with a satisfied smack of his lips, he handed the bottle to Frank, who took a slug without pause. After Frank had his first swallow, he offered the bottle to Julia, but she shook her head and mumbled a quick "No, thanks."

"I tell yah, as the years go along, them sums-a-whores are gettin' smarter. I swear they are," Frenchie said, squinting as he turned his attention back to the shadows under the stone blocks.

Julia strained her eyes, trying to see anything other than the sea-weed-collared rocks and inky water. Frenchie, though, obviously saw something because just then he snapped the rifle to his shoulder and popped off two shots.

"Damn!" he snarled, shaking a clenched fist in front of his face. "Missed 'um."

Frank looked around at Julia and, reading her confusion, said, "Yah see, ever since Frenchie lost his leg, back in—what was it? 'Seventy-nine?"

Frenchie nodded but didn't take his eyes off the wharf.

"Yeah—'seventy-nine. He's took it upon himself to rid the docks of wharf rats."

Julia raised one eyebrow, silently questioning if anyone other than Frenchie could see these rats.

"Used ta think I could do it, too," Frenchie said as he took the wine bottle from Frank and drank deeply. "Thought for a while there I was makin' progress, but them sums-a-whores breed like *rats*," he finished, ending with a chuckle at his own dumb joke. "They come up from the wharf, too, 'n get into people's houses."

"Yah see," Frank went on. "The accident that resulted in Frenchie losin' his leg all came about 'cause a rope he was dependin' on let go, and Frenchie claimed—"

"Didn't *claim*!" Frenchie snapped. *"Know!"* The knuckles of his hand holding the wine bottle turned white.

"Yeah, well—Frenchie knows the rope let go 'cause some rats been gnawing on it and weakened it. Ever since then he's been campaignin' against the rats. Says he's gonna be like the Pied Piper, and get rid of all the rats on Glooscap."

"Damn well gonna try, anyway," Frenchie said. He suddenly clamped the bottle between his thighs, aimed, and shot again. The bullet whistled in the air as it ricocheted and then went *plink* into the water.

"Course, that gets to be a real problem when you consider just about every boat that ties up here can be crawling with rats in the hold," Frank said. "Not to mention they can swim across the bay even if they don't bother to use the bridge."

Frenchie looked at Frank and shook his head sadly. "You're gettin' to be damn-right depressing on such a nice day, you know that?"

"Just fillin' Julia in a bit, is all," Frank said sullenly.

Julia could hear in his tone of voice the unspoken thought, *So, here we sit. Two useless old men. Might as well be drunk.*

"I honestly don't see anything out there," Julia said, craning her neck as she tried to pierce the shadows of the wharf.

"Surprised you can't," Frenchie said "Some of 'em get pretty damned big."

"As big as poodles?" Julia asked, remembering what Frank had told Bri after she had heard thumping sounds in her bedroom wall at night. She suspected she was being strung along with a variation on the old fish story.

"Sure," Frenchie said. "Reckon some of 'em—'specially the smart ones like that one I just missed—might live long enough to get that big. They can get pretty mean 'n' nasty, too. I seen one of them rats attack a German shepherd and do a pretty good job on him before the dog decided to call it quits."

Julia looked at Frank to see if his face would reveal that she was being put on, but as far as she could tell he didn't let on that she was. Her concern was whether the family might be in any danger from big, vicious rats living in their house.

"There!" Frenchie said, pointing to a spot just above the water-line. "See 'um?"

The water lapped gently at the base of the wharf, and the un-evenly cut rocks created a maze of shadowed cracks and spaces as jumbled as the lines of Frenchie's face. The darkness under the rocks was so black it seemed to vibrate in contrast with the water, but after staring as hard as she could where Frenchie was point-ing, she did see something—a vague shifting. Then her heart skipped a beat. Perched on the edge of a rock, shaded by an overhang, was the biggest rat Julia had ever seen in her life. His plump bulk really *did* look as big as . . . well, a small poodle.

Julia watched the motionless animal for several seconds, and

she was just beginning to think she might be imagining it when
the sharp report of Frenchie's rifle made her jump. Beneath the
loud gunshot, she thought she heard a little squeak. But there was
no doubt that she saw the dark bulk flip off the rock and land in
the water with a big splash.

"Damn straight! Got 'um!" Frenchie said before taking a victory swallow of wine. "One less o' them sums-a-whores!"

"Couldn't you get fined or in trouble for doing this?" Julia
asked. Her eyes were still focused on the spreading ripples where
the rat had sunk beneath the water. The only reply she got from
both Frank and Frenchie was snorting laughter.

Now that he had scored, Frenchie apparently felt a little more
sociable. He put down his rifle, turned on the rock to face Frank
and Julia, and withdrew a new bottle of Old Duke from his coat
pocket. Twisting the cap off, he offered the first sip to Julia.

Thinking, what the hell, Julia held the bottle up and toasted
Frenchie. "To one less son-of-a-whore rat," she said, smiling. She
took a gurgling swallow, then handed the bottle to Frank.

Frenchie motioned for her to have a seat on the rock beside
him, so she sat down, and for the rest of the morning and on into
the afternoon, the three of them sat there, talking about just about
anything and everything that came up as they watched the boats
entering and leaving the harbor. The lulling sounds of motorboats
and gulls crying as they wheeled overhead were only shattered
whenever Frenchie shouldered his rifle and cracked off more
shots at the "sums-a-whore" rats.

Around noon, Julia walked up to Pottle's and bought them each
a submarine sandwich—an "Eye-talian," as Frenchie called them
—some chips, soda for her, beer for Frank, and another bottle of
Old Duke for Frenchie. Julia ended up tossing half of her sandwich to the gulls that had swooped in almost as soon as they
started eating.

While they were eating, two more men—obviously brothers
and maybe twins—joined them. Frank introduced Julia to Herb
and Mark Winslow, who stood around, adding their opinions and
comments to everything that was said until, sometime around one
o'clock, they drifted off, saying there was a poker game in one of
the shacks. Frenchie declined, saying the hunting was "too
damned good to give up."

When Julia noticed that it was after two o'clock, she reminded
Frank that Bri would be home from school soon, so they should
probably get back to the house. Saying good-bye to Frenchie,
who looked as though he planned on sleeping right where he was,
she rolled Frank back up to the car, helped him in, then loaded his

wheelchair into the backseat and started the motor. The last thing she heard, as she backed around in the boat yard and then started up the steep dirt road, was the sharp report of Frenchie's rifle.

"I can honestly say I enjoyed myself," she said as the car labored up the incline to Shore Drive.

Frank sat with his hands folded in his lap, his face clouded by a deep scowl. His wrinkled eyebrows reminded Julia of the thick, shadowed rock ledges that made up the stone wharf. She put on her turn signal for the right turn onto Shore Drive.

"I can understand why you enjoy going down there," she went on. "That Frenchie is quite the character."

"Oh, yeah!" Frank snorted. "All of us are just up to our ears with local color," he said sourly.

"What he said about those rats bothers me, though," Julia said, gently probing the topic.

"What about 'em?" Frank said sharply.

"Well, it's just that—I mean, do they really come up from the docks and get into people's houses?"

"I told yah that's what it is if you hear any noises in the walls. It's the rats." His eyes suddenly rolled upward, staring blankly at the car ceiling. "Unless it's—who the hell is that?"

"Who?" Julia asked, shifting her eyes from the road to Frank, wondering who he had seen and where.

"Huh?" Frank said. He turned to her, and his eyes suddenly snapped back into focus.

"The rats," Julia said. "I was asking you about the rats. Can they be dangerous? I mean, they carry diseases and if one of them got into the house, what if one of us gets bitten or something?"

"T'ain't never been a problem before," Frank said, scowling. "Don't see why you should make it one now."

Julia wanted to say more, but by the time she turned onto Oak Street, a cloud had fully descended on Frank, and she knew anything else she might say would only prompt a snappy reply from him, either, even though she knew she couldn't talk to him about it directly, at least not yet.

It's being confined to a wheelchair that's getting to him, she thought. *Seeing Frenchie only reminds him all the more that he and his friends are getting old, dying off.* She was filled with a feeling of helplessness, and wished there was something she could say or do, but she knew there was nothing.

"Hm. I wonder why John's home so early," she said as soon as she saw his car parked at an odd angle in the driveway. She had to park down by the road because she couldn't get her car around John's without driving onto the grass.

Frank shrugged, looking as if he didn't know or care what John was doing.

And on top of everything else, Julia thought, *that—the way he and John interact—only makes matters worse.*

"Probably forgot something and had to dash home to get it," she said more to herself than to Frank. Her mind was still more occupied with the question of how she could learn to communicate with Frank.

While she was getting his chair out of the backseat, she remembered a prayer her grandmother had taught her long ago: "God, grant me the courage to change what can be changed, accept what cannot be changed, and the wisdom to know the difference."

Possibly, she thought, *that's why Frank has gotten so much more involved with church recently. He's working on accepting what's happened to him, what can't be changed.* But that thought only made her feel all the more guilty for the argument they had had over the weekend.

"I hope you didn't mind my tagging along today while you were visiting with Frenchie," she said when she opened the car door and gave him the support he needed to swing out into the wheelchair.

"No—not at all," he said, his mouth close to her ear as she did her best to lift him. It was a struggle, but she got him settled into the chair and started pushing him up the walkway.

Julia felt, though, that he didn't mean what he had said. She had the sense that he had tolerated her only because she had asked to come along in the first place. Now that she thought about it, she was convinced he would never have asked her on his own.

She wanted to say something to him, to reach out and communicate with him so badly it pained her, but she found him to be defensive most of the time. In those few moments—like this morning—when he let his guard down, she found him to be a genuinely enjoyable person, but those moments were rare. As she wheeled him up to the kitchen door, though, she silently vowed that, while she wouldn't be pushy about it, she was definitely going to keep trying.

A few minutes later—when she found John upstairs in bed, tossing and turning with a fever—everything she had been thinking was forgotten.

TEN
High School Memories

I

Although the rain let up on Thursday, by Friday afternoon another storm roared into the area, bringing chilly winds and a pelting, cold rain that changed to sleet in the evening. Over John's half-hearted protestations that after four days home sick he still didn't feel totally better, Julia had accepted Ellie Chadwick's invitation to their house for supper. Bri had also been invited, but by using the excuse that she didn't want to go out on such a damp, cold night, she convinced her parents to let her stay home with Frank. She stood in the kitchen doorway and waved to them as they dashed through the freezing rain out to their car.

After her parents had driven off, Bri joined Frank in the living room where they settled down for a few games of checkers. Bri won two of the first three games rather handily, and she began to suspect that her grandfather was letting her win. Halfway into the fourth game, she decided to make a stupid move, just to see what he would do.

"D'you really wanna do that?" he asked, scratching his beard-stubbled chin. The sound it made was like sandpaper scraping on wood.

Bri pretended to examine the board, then nodded, and he saw the opening and took the jump.

"Aww, I didn't *see* that," she wailed, leaning back in her chair and slapping her forehead with the flat of her hand. "That'll teach me."

Frank smiled as he removed her two captured pieces. "You just ain't got your mind on the game's all. What yah thinkin' about?"

"Oh, nothing much," Bri said. Now that she had blown a move, she looked at the game with renewed intensity.

"Well, I can imagine one thing on your mind is you're thinkin' there are probably better things to be doin' than sittin' around the kitchen, playin' checkers with some old fart."

Bri had her head down, but now she looked up at her grandfather and tried to figure out what he was getting at. He was smiling at her, but there was a trace of sadness or concern in his eyes.

"No," she said. "Not at all. I'm having fun."

"Oh, sure, sure," Frank said. He pushed himself away from the table and rolled over to the refrigerator. Opening the door, he reached in and grabbed two cans of beer. "You wanna have a sip of beer with me?" he asked, holding up the two cans.

Bri shook her head. "No, thanks. Maybe I'll get a Pepsi or something after this move." She had never liked the taste of beer whenever her father had let her try a sip. Besides, she was concentrating on the board, trying to find some way out of the hole she had so stupidly dug for herself.

"Oh, yeah—that's right. You kids like to smoke pot instead of drink, right?"

Bri wrinkled her nose as she looked up at him. "Come on. You know not every teenager has a drinking or drug problem."

Frank popped the flip top of his Pabst, then rolled back to the table. "That ain't what I read in *Reader's Digest*," he said. His face was completely deadpan, and Bri had no idea whether or not he was joking. Maybe, she thought, he was just trying to distract her.

Finally she thought she saw the best move she could make for now, so she slid her piece on the board and sat back, waiting for Frank to make his move.

"You know," Frank said after taking a sip, "I've been noticing you go for a lot for walks down by the beach."

Bri felt herself stiffen and instantly thought, *Yeah, sure. I'd rather be spending a rainy night like this with some friends . . . say, Audrey.*

"I like the beach," she said, her voice taking on a defensive whine. She felt a ripple of impatience when her grandfather didn't even look at the checkerboard, much less contemplate his next move.

"Oh, it's nice, all right," he said. "Where do you go?"

This was beginning to feel like the Grand Inquisition, but Bri didn't want to be mean and tell him to mind his own business. "I just walk around—mostly on Sandy Beach and out on Indian Point."

"You know, you've got to be careful out there," Frank said. "Them rocks—they can get pretty slippery when the tide's out."

"I know. I've taken a few little slips," Bri said.

"'Specially after a storm like this," Frank said, nodding toward the rain-beaten window. Bri followed his glance. "It'll probably be a nice day tomorrow, but you know that storm's still right off the coast. Them waves'll be pretty high—'specially on the headlands. Every now and then, a big one'll come up, and if you're too close to the edge—*whoosh!* You're in!"

Bri wondered if what he was saying was true, or if he was saying this to scare her for some reason, to keep her away from the point.

"I had a friend—name of Robbie Makkonen. Smart guy. Grew up here on the island. Knew all about the moods of the ocean. He went out fishing off the point one day after a hurricane, and a wave swept him right out to sea."

"Did he drown?"

"Darn tootin' he drowned. There's a pretty wicked undertow off them rocks, so if you go out there—'specially after a storm—you make sure you stay well back from the waves, okay?"

"Don't worry," Bri said, nodding her head. "I will. Are you going to take your turn or just rattle your dentures all evening?"

Frank sat back, surprised and secretly pleased at her use of his own pet expression for talking too much. He sipped on his beer, then glanced at the board. "I swear you ain't got your mind on this game," he said as he jumped two of her men and landed on her side of the board.

"King me," he said with a laugh.

"King yourself," she snapped. She tossed him one of his captured pieces and glared at him with mock anger. Then they both burst out laughing, long and hard, when—accidentally on purpose, as he said afterward—Frank's elbow knocked the board and jiggled all the pieces around.

"I win by default," Bri cried out, standing up and shaking her clenched fists over her head. "Let me get a Pepsi to celebrate, and then I'll see if I can make it four out of five!"

II

The supper Ellie served was surprisingly good—a dish she called "Greek-oregano chicken," along with fresh green beans, salad, and home-baked bread with real butter—something Julia didn't allow in their house because of the ever-increasing spare tire around John's middle. By the time Ellie brought out dessert —carrot cake with whipped cream—the conversation had fewer awkward silences than at the beginning of the meal. Ellie and Julia in particular found they had a lot in common, while Randy and Frank kept their discussions on a more superficial level.

After dessert, with coffee in hand, they went into the living room and settled down. Their conversation remained on a fairly shallow level as the two couples tried to feel each other out. For Randy and John, it was a slow discovery of who the friend from high school had become over twenty years.

John had taken the time to look at and analyze Ellie, thinking it was miraculous how much she had changed in twenty years. He remembered her as a petite, rather plain, but certainly not unattractive girl, but since high school—and two children—she appeared to have aged significantly. There were dark circles under eyes he remembered as being sparkling blue and lively. Her hair, which he had remembered as being full-bodied and a shimmering brunette, now looked limp and lifeless, with strands of gray. She was still a small person, and she still had a rather rounded, attractive figure, but she looked frail and drained of life. John thought she seemed much older than her years, and that merely confirmed his thought that living on Glooscap wore people out before their time.

Even Randy, John thought, looked a lot older than John felt he himself looked. His hairline was definitely retreating, and his stomach swelled out enough so it hung out over his belt buckle. He looked strong and healthy, especially his hands and forearms, but John couldn't reconcile this man with the thin, wire-framed boy who had been the baseball team's star pitcher and the school's top scholar. He didn't bother with college after high school, choosing instead to do what his father had done for a living— haul lobster traps.

Maybe working outside every day, winter and summer, had aged him, John thought, but John was a surveyor, and he was outdoors a lot. It had to be something more than that. It couldn't be as simple as that they were just getting older, could it?

No, John thought, feeling almost bitter as he thought of how he looked compared to Randy. *It's living on this island that'll drain the life out of you!*

When Randy hauled out *Summer Days and Summer Nights*, an old Beach Boys album, and put it on the turntable, the conversation inevitably headed down memory lane for a while, but John —feeling increasingly uncomfortable—quickly lit a cigarette and steered the topic around the past.

"So, uh, what do you folks think about Freedom Corporation's condo project on the other end of the island?" John asked. "I get the feeling it doesn't have the backing of a lot of folks around here."

Ellie smiled weakly. "Yeah—Randy and I both signed the petition against it. At this point I don't suppose there's much we can do to stop it."

John laughed aloud as he looked at Randy and said, "I doubt it, now that they've broken ground. But Jeeze, Randy, I never would have taken you for an environmentalist."

"Randy's no *environ-mentalist*," Ellie said before Randy had a chance to open his mouth. She pronounced the word with contempt, as if it were something dirty. "It's just that the condo isn't the most popular thing on the island right now, you know."

"I'm beginning to pick that up," John said. "On a couple of different occasions, now, there have been people out there protesting, carrying signs like it's Vietnam or something. And you must've seen on the news where that truck driver and some protestor slugged it out." He leaned forward and flicked the lengthening ash of his cigarette into the ash tray, catching Julia's frown in the corner of his eye.

"To tell you the truth, John, you're not exactly the most popular guy on the island now, either," Randy said. He was smiling, but John—having known him so well—caught the subtle intensity in his voice.

"What do you mean by that?" John asked. He couldn't help but catch the nervous glance that passed between Randy and Ellie, as if she was trying to tell him, *Would you please shut up?*

"The fact that you're working for these people—the Freedom Corporation—" Randy said. "I mean, I didn't want to get you all worked up about it, but—" Randy shrugged as he searched for the right words. "Well, you know how it is. Some of the guys down at the wharf were shooting off about how, if you were born and raised here, maybe you should have a little respect for the Glooscap way of life."

"The 'Glooscap way of life'?" John echoed, arcing an eyebrow. "I've never heard it put quite that way."

Not so subtly, Ellie made an attempt to get Randy's attention to get him to be quiet. He ignored her, though, and went on.

"Well, you haven't been around here for quite a while. Come on, John. You must realize how people feel about condos and big developments going in! It's ruining our way of life."

"But maybe that's just the point," John said, feeling his anger rise. "*That* way of living isn't possible anymore. The world goes on, you know. You can bury your head in the sand, but times change."

"Oh, I know that," Randy said. He sat back casually on the couch to signal that he personally did not share the opinion he had expressed. "I'm just telling you what I heard. That a few people around town are kinda surprised you'd work for someone like the Freedom Corporation."

"I work for Atkins—a *surveying* company," John said stiffly. "That's all."

In the back of his mind, a thought flickered to life. As he looked at Randy, sitting there, smiling good-naturedly at him, John couldn't help but wonder if Randy was more serious than he let on. And now that he thought about it, maybe that little prank outside their house on Halloween night had been intended for him and not Bri. Maybe Randy hated what John was doing!

The Beach Boys had been wailing about summer and surfing and girls all the while, and when the record clicked off it produced an awkward silence.

John laughed aloud nervously and tossed his hands into the air as though he had just been dealt a terrible poker hand. "Hey—look, Randy. I had no idea what projects were going on when I took the job with Atkins," he said. "I mean, I took their offer because we had to move back to help out with my dad. No one said anything about a condo site on Glooscap until after I had accepted the job.

"But don't you think it's wrong?" Ellie said, leaning forward and nailing him with a hard, earnest look.

"All I know is progress moves on," John said. He shrugged, looking to Julia for support, but she sat there, helplessly silent. "People are moving into the state, and they have to live somewhere. They want to live on the islands because of the beauty. No one moves to Maine to live in a city. You stay in New York or Boston for that."

Ellie frowned and shook her head. "But don't they realize," she said, "that they're destroying the Maine they're moving up here to experience? By the time they all get here, it won't be here anymore. It'll be gone to make room for more condos!"

"I don't know—I guess that's the price we have to pay for living in God's country," John said, trying to lighten things up. Nobody seemed to pick up on his sarcasm, so he let it drop.

"Actually," Julia said, "John was just telling me a couple of days ago that he thought he should quit his job and become a lobsterman."

Randy's burst of laughter was sudden and loud. Ellie looked angrily at her husband, but he was laughing so hard, he shook and almost dropped his half-empty coffee cup.

"Oh, that'll be the day," he sputtered. A fleck of spit shot out of his mouth, and he wiped his mouth with his napkin. "I'd want to have the television film crews there to report *that*! The day you go out in a lobster boat is the day I'll put on a three-piece suit and start selling life insurance."

"Come on," John said. "What is this, shit-on-your-old-buddy week?"

His cigarette had long since burned down to the filter in his hand, so he dropped it into the ashtray. He started to reach for another, but this time caught Julia's stare and let his head drop to his side.

"No, I just . . . it kills me trying to imagine you on a lobster boat. You wouldn't know the first thing about it." Randy tilted his head back, practically howling at the ceiling with laughter. "After everything you said about . . ." Smiling widely, he shook his head. "I just can't picture it."

"You ought to go out some morning with Randy and give it a try," Julia said, picking up on the teasing. Her eyes were twinkling with merriment as she glanced at Ellie and Randy.

"Yeah, you should," Ellie added. "Some Saturday morning, you ought to hop into the old *Bait Barrel* and go out with Randy. See what it's really like."

"Can't be any worse than building condos, huh?" John said.

Tears were rolling down Randy's face. "Do you remember what you wrote in my yearbook?" he said. He was laughing so hard now he could barely catch his breath.

John shook his head and, deciding to hell with Julia's discomfort—*if they're going to tease, I'm going to smoke*—took a cigarette and matches from his shirt pocket. His hands shook slightly as he struck the match and lit up.

"No," he said, blowing the smoke out through his nose. "I don't remember."

Ellie was already up from her chair and halfway up the stairs before Randy stopped laughing. His cheeks were bright red. A minute later, Ellie returned, handing her husband a dark blue, imitation leather–covered book. Without reading the title stamped in fake gold on the front, John recognized the 1966 edition of *Rocks and Pebbles*, his and Randy's high school yearbook.

"Check it out, my man," Randy said, still shaking with suppressed laughter as he came over beside the chair where John was sitting and flipped open the book. He hurriedly fluttered through the first few pages until he came to a page with a skinny, short-haired boy staring at the camera with wide-eyed surprise.

"Let's talk about a rabbit caught in the headlights of an oncoming car," Randy said as he held the book open with both hands and displayed it to both Julia and Ellie.

"I don't know," Julia said thoughtfully. "I think he looks kind of handsome. Let me see."

She held out her hands for the book, and when she took it, her first thought was that it was funny how she barely remembered seeing John's graduation picture. Just once, when she and John had first met, they had sat together and looked through his high school yearbook. She realized now that she had only seen the book that one time; she hadn't even come across it while they were packing for the move to Maine.

"Pretty cool dude," Julia said. "Radical hairstyle." She handed the book back to Randy after studying the picture for a moment, trying to see the man in the boy.

"Oh, he was cool, all right," Randy said. "Just look at how *long* that hair is!" Again, his laughter was so loud he snorted as he doubled up.

"Come on, give it a rest, will you?" John said. He glanced briefly at the picture, thinking how strange it was that this really had been him. The hair that had seemed so outrageously long back then was, in fact, barely touching the tips of his ears. And his eyes did look like the eyes of a scared animal caught by the headlights of an oncoming car.

And that's just what they were! his mind whispered.

He tried like hell to control his hand as he raised the cigarette to his mouth and inhaled deeply.

"Notice what he wrote for me," Randy said. Clearing his throat, he held the book at nearly arm's length and read with a stern, professorial tone. " 'To Randy C. Probably the only person who *really* knows how much this day means to me! I hope we stay friends in the years to come, but we can't if you end up smelling like a bait barrel.' Isn't that sweet?"

"Actually," Ellie said, "that's why Randy named his boat the *Bait Barrel* . . . in honor of you."

"I'm touched," John said, placing his hand over his heart. "I truly am."

"Could I take another look at that?" Julia asked. Randy handed her the yearbook, and she sat silently flipping through the pages while Randy continued to needle John.

"That might not be such a bad idea, though," Randy said. "We could head out early some Saturday morning, and you can see just what the job is. I don't remember a single time you've been out on the ocean for *any* reason."

John squirmed in his chair and repeatedly flicked the tip of his cigarette into the ashtray. "Oh, no. I don't need anything like that. I know all I need to know about lobstering. It's hard work and it's smelly." Turning to Julia, he said, "Just stand downwind of this guy after he docks, and you'll be convinced, too."

Randy leaned over close to his ear and, just as he did in the old days, whispered, "Come on . . . what are you, a *pussy*?"

Grimacing, John shook his head. "I just am not interested,

that's all," he said. He could feel, for the first time, that Randy's behavior was getting beyond teasing. He could feel himself becoming mad at Randy—and not just the old Randy he had known twenty years ago. For the first time since they'd gotten there, John earnestly wished Julia had declined the invitation, and if she could have read his mind right then, he would have flashed the message, *Let's get the fuck out of here!*

"Hey! What's this?" Julia asked, her voice suddenly cutting off Randy's next comment. John, at least, was grateful for the relief from the tension.

"Let me see," Randy said, moving over to Julia's chair and looking down at the book spread open on her lap. For an instant, John didn't like to see his old high school buddy sitting close to his wife like that. Randy studied the yearbook page for a moment, then muttered, "Well, I'll be a son of a bitch."

"Randy!" Ellie said, casting her eyes ceilingward.

"Look at this," Randy said, taking the yearbook from Julia and showing it to his wife.

Curious, John also got up from his seat and came over to look at the book. As soon as he saw the page, he recognized it, and when he saw what was wrong, cold chills hit him in the stomach like a fist.

"Well, look at that, why don't you," Ellie said, shaking her head with wonderment. "One of the pictures has faded."

"That's the weirdest thing I ever heard of," Randy said, holding the opened page up to the table light and turning it so he could see it at different angles. The page was of the graduating class portraits, but right across the middle there was a blank strip where there should have been a photo, name, and description. Even under a bright light, there simply was no trace of the missing photograph.

"I wonder what—Jesus Christ!" Randy said, his voice a sudden bark. "John, this is where *Abby's* picture was! What the hell could've happened to it?"

Pretending interest but fighting the waves of cold that practically made his teeth chatter, John craned his neck to look at the blank spot on the page as Randy angled it back and forth under the light. He had looked at that picture often enough to know exactly what should have been there: Abby's smiling face—her soft, rounded cheeks, her long, dark hair hanging to her shoulders, and that quotation he had always thought was so damned stupid: "Fresh of spirit and resolved to meet her perils constantly."

"It just ain't there," Randy said, with confusion written all over his face. Marking the place with his finger, he hurriedly flipped through the other pages of the yearbook, checking to see if there was any other damage. Then, apparently satisfied, he reopened it to the missing picture.

"Maybe they used . . . I don't know, some kind of cheap paper or printer's ink or something," Julia volunteered, but she knew that was a foolish idea, because if that was the case, other parts of the book would have suffered as well.

"Well, I'll be damned," Randy said with a shrug. "I just can't figure what might have happened. There's no sign of damage anywhere." He turned the yearbook over in his hand and inspected the sides and back. "You have a yearbook at home, don't you?"

John shrugged. "I suppose so. I haven't really taken the time to look for it lately."

Randy frowned and said, "If you think of it, why don't you check to see if your picture of Abby is still there? I'd kind of like to know."

"If I think of it," John said. It was an effort to keep his voice from trembling, but he managed to add, as brightly as possible, "I guess it's like some memories . . . they fade away after a while."

"I'm gonna take this to the photo store in Portland and see if they can explain it," Randy said, still bothered by the whole thing.

"Boy, it *is* sort of weird, don't you think?" Julia said. "I mean, you said no one's seen Abby in—how long? Since right before graduation? And then her picture fades from the school yearbook. It sounds like something right out of *The Twilight Zone.*" She rubbed her shoulders and shivered.

"There's got to be a more reasonable explanation," John said. His voice was low and even, and apparently only he heard the tremor in it.

After a few more minutes wondering aloud about what might have happened to Abby's picture, Randy finally put the yearbook away. That also, thankfully, seemed to stop any more nostalgia for the evening, and they spent the rest of their visit talking about raising kids, how Frank was doing following his stroke, and jobs —but *not* condos. Around nine-thirty, John gave Julia the signal that he was ready to leave, so they said their thank-yous and, bundled against the raw weather, started for the door.

At the door, Randy nailed John with his bright eyes and crooked smile and said, "So, are you gonna do it?"

"Do what?" John asked, dreading what he thought was coming.

"Go out lobstering with me someday. If nothing else, it'll give you a chance to realize how lucky you are to have the job you've got."

"I don't know," John said. "Maybe."

Randy swung the door open and held it for them as they dashed out into the rain toward their car. John went first and held the car door open for Julia, who practically threw herself onto the seat. Her face was dripping wet from the short time in the heavy rain.

"I had a good time," she said softly, wiping her face with one hand and waving to the Chadwicks, who were standing in the doorway. "How about you?"

"Okay, I guess," John said, but he punctuated his comment with a low snort. Leaning to one side, he fished the car keys from his pocket, turned on the ignition, and looked over his shoulder to back down out of the driveway. "I wasn't all that pleased with some of the things Randy said, though."

"Oh, he was just teasing you," Julia replied. "And—I don't know—maybe what he said explains why the people around town haven't been all that friendly."

John's mouth was set in a firm, hard line as he pulled into the street and started forward. The headlights did their best to push back the cold darkness "Yeah, well, one thing you've got to admit. I sure as hell don't look as old as Randy does. God, he's aged a lot!"

Julia regarded John in the soft glow of the dashboard light, then said, "Oh, I don't know. I don't think they looked all that bad. Maybe a little more weathered than you and me, but they didn't seem that old. You want to know what I'm still ticked off about, though?"

"Yeah—what?" John said, fully expecting Julia would say something about how Randy had given him a hard time about working for Atkins and the condo project.

"I'm ticked that I still don't know what she looks like," Julia said, her voice taking on a dreamy quality.

"Huh? Who? What are you talking about?" John said. He looked at her face glistening wet in the light reflected from the wet street as they drove slowly toward home.

"Abby—that's who," Julia said softly. "I wish that picture hadn't faded from the yearbook. I still don't know what your old girlfriend looks like."

"I don't want to talk about it," John said tensely. "All right?" He forced a sharp laugh and, keeping his eyes straight ahead on the road, added simply, "But one thing you can believe—she wasn't half as pretty as you are."

And in his mind, he involuntarily finished his sentence, *Not anymore, she isn't!*

ELEVEN
After the Storm

I

Bri had pretty much given up on the idea of trying to meet Audrey again and make friends with her. Well, at least that's what she told herself when she set out for her walk on Saturday morning. The whole week had been lousy at school, and she was trying her best to accept the fact that—at least for now—she wasn't going to make friends easily if at all, either at school or on the island. This depressed her somewhat because she had been part of such a close-knit group back in Vermont. On her walks, she thought a lot about the way things used to be.

The day had dawned clear and bright, just like her "new" granddad had said it would. The breeze off the ocean was raw and invigorating, tangy with salt; it tasted funny on the back of her throat when she breathed through her mouth. Waves were piling up high on the rocks—huge swells that crested just as they hit. White spray went flying high into the blue sky. Driven toward land because the sea was still so rough farther out, sea gulls spun and dove among the breakers, looking for crabs that had washed up onto the rocks.

The storm had stripped what little foliage remained on the trees on Indian Point. The winding paths were mired with mud and rain-battered leaves. In order to keep her boots relatively clean, Bri had to skirt some pretty deep puddles. Halfway out onto the point, she saw what could have been someone's footprints in the mud. Her instant thought was, *Audrey's out for a walk, too,* but she pushed aside her excitement, determined not to say a word to Audrey if she saw her.

It'll serve her right for what she's done to me, she thought as she mentally catalogued Audrey's offenses: trying to scare her on Halloween night, ignoring her, maybe even actually hiding from her at school, and that trick she had pulled on her out on Bald Hill, hiding in the deep woods and calling to her. . . .

"Yeah, screw you," she said sullenly as she kicked a divot in the wet turf.

More and more, Bri was coming to see the ocean as her only real friend on the island. Oh, sure, there was always her mother and father, and—truth to tell—she had honestly started to enjoy being around her grandfather. Still, she felt it was only when she came down near the ocean that she could think and feel her own honest thoughts, and then there was no need to say them aloud because there was nobody else around.

Off in the distance, Bri could see the Great Diamond lighthouse. The crystal-clear air made it look much closer than she knew it was. The steady breeze in off the water carried a lonely, distant hoot from some offshore light or buoy. Bri's eyes started to water as she eased down off the slope and started climbing around on the slick, black rocks.

Tangles of seaweed and frayed rope, driftwood, and even a few smashed lobster pots littered the rocks, making it look almost unfamiliar to Bri. She thought she was beginning to know this area like the face of an old friend, so it surprised her to see how much one storm could actually change the shoreline. Whenever she found some washed-up wood or rope, she would pick it up and toss it back into the ocean. The activity gave her something to do, a sense that she was restoring the point to what it had been before the storm.

In the lee of a huge rock, half-buried in the sand, she saw something glittering—a piece of shattered green glass worn and rounded by the working of the waves. As she bent to pick it up, someone spoke from behind her.

"Looking for buried treasure?"

Bri was so taken by surprise, she barely registered what had been said. She was even more surprised when she turned and saw Audrey smiling down at her from the bluff. The sun was directly behind her, and her long hair blew in the wind like tangled smoke. She cast a long shadow over the rocks all the way to Bri. The bright sunlight and the brilliant blue of the sky blurred her features.

"Lots of treasure," Bri said, instantly mad at herself for not sticking to her resolution not to speak with her if they met. She wanted just to walk away and ignore Audrey—let *her* feel what it was like to be ignored. But instead Bri simply stood there, tossing the beach glass from hand to hand as she looked up at Audrey.

"They say there's supposed to be pirate treasure buried somewhere around on this island," Audrey said.

"Well, whoop-te-do," Bri said, not really caring if Audrey got mad and left.

"Can I look for buried treasure with you?" Audrey asked. Her voice was pleasant and mild, so soft it seemed as though she was standing beside her, not at the top of the rise.

She still hadn't moved from her position looking down on Bri. When she moved to get out of Audrey's shadow, the sunlight stung her eyes so she had to shield them with her hand.

"I'm just walking," Bri said. "It's not up to me what you can and can't do."

Audrey let out a soft laugh, barely audible above the whoosh of the wind off the water. Breakers roared against the rocks, and the air was filled with the cry of sea gulls. When Bri turned to continue making her way along the shoreline, Audrey noiselessly climbed down the rocks and suddenly appeared at her side. They walked for quite a while in silence, their hands in their pockets and their faces turned away from the cold wind.

"How come you're acting so . . . strange?" Audrey said at last. "I thought we were friends." They had rounded the point and were heading toward the harbor. The ocean was much tamer on the landward side, but there was still plenty of evidence of the storm washed up on the rocks.

Bri shrugged as she recalled the first—and only other—time she had walked out here with Audrey. *Talk about acting funny,* she thought, remembering how Audrey had been afraid of being seen by anyone on the wharf. She wasn't surprised when Audrey suddenly turned on her heel and said, "Let's go back on the other side. I like to watch the waves come crashing in."

Not caring one way or another, Bri turned with her and started retracing their route around the point. She was burning to say something to Audrey, to ask her why she acted so . . . well, *funny* wasn't the word. *Mean* was more like it.

What have I ever done to you?

Don't you want to be friends?

Why do you think it's so much fun to tease me?

These and other questions rose in her mind, but she didn't ask any of them, figuring she'd just give it a rest and see how Audrey treated her today. If they spent the morning together and had some fun—then fine. If Audrey suddenly took off, leaving her behind —then fine. She just wasn't going to push it anymore!

"I just *love* it when the ocean's so wild," Audrey said, stopping in her tracks and turning her face into the wind. Her hair blew straight back, exposing her face, and as Bri looked at her, she felt a sudden chill. She realized that, until now, she had never really taken a good look at Audrey—that Audrey had always, unaccountably, kept her eyes averted. As she looked at her now, she was shocked to see how thin and pale she actually looked. Although she couldn't have been older than sixteen, the corners of her eyes were wrinkled like an old woman's, and her lips were thin and cracked. Her jawbone stuck out as though the skin covering it was no more than paper-thin. She looked, to Bri, like someone who hadn't eaten or slept well in years.

"Don't you just *love* it?" Audrey asked.

When she turned and looked directly into Bri's eyes, Bri had to struggle not to scream. Audrey's face—even while she was looking at it—seemed to be shifting, changing. It wasn't just the interplay of the shadows from her windblown hair. Audrey's face, her skin seem to be losing what little fleshy muscle tone it had; it was dissolving down to the skull beneath. Her eye sockets were shadowed, and Bri had the terrifying illusion that her eyes were actually *gone* . . . that Audrey was staring at her from bony, empty sockets!

In a roaring rush, she remembered the decomposing body she had seen that day on Bald Hill when she had fallen. No amount of insisting by her father or mother was ever going to convince her that she hadn't tripped over a human body in the woods. And now . . .

Am I losing my mind? she thought as waves of frantic fear tugged at her.

"Is something the matter?" Audrey asked. She leaned closer to Bri, and in Bri's terrified imagination, she saw—not thin, fleshy lips, but the clacking teeth of a skeleton. The voice didn't come from Audrey's thin throat . . . it was in the roaring air all around her. *It was inside her own head!*

"No . . . I . . ." Bri managed to stammer.

I'm going crazy! her mind screamed as she tried to convince herself this wasn't happening! *It's just a trick of light! The reflection of the sun on the water is making her face look ripply like that!*

Swept up in a blind panic, Bri finally found the willpower to tear her eyes away from Audrey and look down at the ground. She stared intensely at the rough, black texture of the rocks, trying to root herself in what was real and solid. But the details of the rock surface seemed to be dancing with energy. Sharp lines of light and shadow cut her vision like razors, and her panic only swelled higher, stronger.

"For crying out loud, Bri," Audrey said, her voice nothing more than a velvety ruffle. "Cut it out! You're scaring me! God, you look like you've seen a ghost."

Audrey's voice had the soft tone of caring, of concern, but beneath that, like the clammy draft of wind snaking along the floor of an old house, there was an undercurrent of . . . *enjoyment* at Bri's discomfort.

"I . . . No, I . . . uh—" But that was all she could say. The next thing she knew, there was a cold, embracing wetness crashing down on her, instantly blocking out the sunlight as it swept over her. She thought she was falling . . . fainting, but as the towering wave tore at her legs, she realized in a flash of panic that she had been swept off the rocks and plunged into the icy ocean water.

Somewhere in the back of her mind, she heard the exact words her grandfather had said to her the night before . . .

'Specially after a storm like this, her grandfather's voice rang in her memory. *That storm's still right off the coast. The waves' ll be pretty high—'specially on the headlands. Every now and then, a big one' ll come up, and if you're too close to the edge— whoosh! You're in!*

I'm in! Bri thought as a burning coal of fear struggled against the numbing chill of the water.

She didn't know if she said it or simply thought it, but the next time she opened her mouth to scream, all she got was a mouthful of briny water. She gagged and sputtered, trying to blow it out, but the water was all around her, stinging as it flooded into her nose, throat, and eyes.

I'm drowning! . . . Oh, God! Help me, I'm drowning! her mind shouted, but at the same time she knew she wasn't dead yet. She sensed that she wouldn't be able to struggle so hard if she were already dead.

She barely felt the pain as her body was tossed and scraped against the rocks. It seemed as though the water cushioned her from slamming too hard. Besides, the tide was pulling her back out to sea. Her arms and legs were flailing wildly as she tried to resist the backward pull, but she was like a tiny piece of driftwood being tossed and pulled wherever the ocean wanted to take her.

As she struggled against the downward drag of the water, Bri's mind seemed to register everything in slow motion. She was surrounded by bubbly green water—numbingly cold—right up over her head. There was something tangled around her legs, something slippery and tough. It felt like slimy hands trying to pull her down, and in her mind, she imagined the green, barnacle-crusted hands of drowned sailors grabbing at her. A small, rational corner of her mind knew that it was really kelp wrapped around her legs, but whatever it was, it was assisting the waves in keeping her under.

In her mind at least, she was screaming as she strained to bring herself up to the surface that shimmered like a fire above her head.

If I can just get a breath of air, she thought. *Just a breath of air . . .*

It struck her as increasingly peculiar how she seemed to have so much time to think about things. She felt herself slowly twisting and bending with the currents, drifting as though in free-fall. She remembered hearing someplace that drowning was supposed to be a relatively painless way to die. . . .

Painless, yes . . . but what about the panic?

She was kicking her legs as hard as she could, trying to get free of the tangling seaweed and get to the surface, which now looked like the end of a long, shimmering tunnel. It caught her by surprise when her efforts were rewarded and without any sensation of moving upward, her face burst up into the air.

With a throat-tearing roar, she swallowed air into her lungs in one huge, salty gulp, just enough to let out a shrill scream.

"Help! . . ."

She was shocked to see how far away from the land she was. There wasn't any way of knowing how long it had been since she had fallen in. It could have been a few seconds or several minutes.

Audrey must still be nearby, she thought as she paddled frantically against the tide. *Why doesn't she help me?*

"Help! . . ."

Another wave swept up over her, beating her under with its surging power, but Bri's legs were free of the kelp—*the fishy, dead hands*—and she was feeling confidence now as she kicked up to the surface. There was still such a ferocious downward pulling on her legs, she fully expected to be pulled under again, maybe for good this time.

Going down . . . down for the third time, her mind whispered.

But the waves weren't cresting this far out to sea, and the air rushing into her lungs made her feel she had an honest chance to survive. If only she could catch the landward drift of a wave and let it wash her up without smashing her against the rocks. She tried to get her bearings relative to the beach. She looked longingly at the distant strip of sand and wondered if she was going to be able to make it that far. The water was so cold, her arms and legs felt like lead. They could barely move, but she knew she had to make shore . . . and soon!

As she struggled to aim toward the beach, though, she realized something else . . . something that sent a dizzying spiral of fear through her. She just might make it, but then, she thought, *What about Audrey? Audrey wasn't on the rocks!*

"Oh, my . . . God!" she sputtered. As she kicked toward land, her head kept bobbing under water, and when she surfaced, sputtering and blowing, she stared frantically all along the shore for some sign of Audrey.

What if she got swept in, too, and drowned? Oh, God! No! Or maybe she's gone for help. . . .

Between her and the shore, the waves were cresting, spewing up plumes of white spray as they broke. The dismal beach looked as if it was miles away.

Can I make it? . . . Can I make it? she kept asking herself as she struggled against the undertow. The story her grandfather had told her just last night, of his friend who had been washed away and drowned after a storm kept playing in her mind.

Whoosh! You're in!

Swept far out to sea!

The absolutely only bright spot in the whole thing was, she realized, that it didn't look as though she was going to be washed up against the rocks. The current had taken her well away from Indian Point. She knew she would never survive a pounding against the rocks. If she drifted that way, sometime that afternoon, or maybe tomorrow, a lobsterman or someone taking a walk on the point would find her bruised and bloodless body smashed against the sharp granite shore!

No! she shouted in her mind. *No!*

The waves were tossing her about roughly, but she could see that she *was* getting closer to shore.

Every joint in her body felt like stretched rubber, cold and twisted, as she stroked toward the shore. Every muscle was chilled and stiff, almost dead feeling. Her lungs felt as though she had inhaled at least a gallon of briny water, and her nose and the back of her throat were on fire.

As she got closer to shore, she could literally feel the adrenaline kick into her system. She pounded the water with her hands and did powerful scissor kicks. She saw the stretch of smooth, sandy beach getting closer . . . closer.

"Whoo—" was all she got to say when a wave suddenly picked her up from behind as though it were a single, powerful hand, and, lifting her up, carried her toward the beach.

I'm flying, she thought, and in an instant of panic, believed that maybe she *had* drowned . . . maybe she was already dead, and the ocean was simply tossing her soul about on its surface as it were a leaf, floating on a pond.

The wave continued to build, carrying her forward with a rush that threatened to tumble her over, feet over her head. The icy water surged around her, both lifting and pulling, until she thought the moment was never going to end... she was going to spend eternity rolling head over heels forward until she blacked out... and never came out of the blackness.

Then a wash of churning white foam exploded into her face. She felt herself falling, and with a muscle-wrenching impact, she landed face first on the sand. The wave crashed over her and quickly sucked back off the sand, trying to snatch her back, but it retreated, leaving behind a crumpled form, facedown on the sand.

Bri struggled to her feet, coughing and sputtering. She viciously spit the sand from her mouth. A quick glance over her shoulder revealed another, even larger wave barreling in toward her. She lunged forward like a football player, diving for the last yard to the goal line just as the wave smashed into the beach. Cold hands grabbed her by the backs of the knees, but she had enough momentum to carry herself the rest of the way. With a long, warbling groan, she collapsed flat onto the dry sand and simply lay there, staring up at the sky.

I made it! I'm alive! she thought as relief and exhaustion battled inside her. She wanted to stand up and jump with a whoop and, at the same time, to sink as deeply as she could into the comforting and relative warmth of the sand. The thin November sun shone down on her face with a steady hammer beat.

What about Audrey? Bri thought, looking around with a surge of panic. *What if she's drowned? What if she didn't make it!*

Tears stinging her eyes, Bri staggered to her feet and scanned the beach, quickly turning her head from side to side for a sign of Audrey. She tried to push aside the mental image she had of Audrey sinking slowly into the cold, green depths of the ocean with seaweed tangled around her legs and arms and throat as she drifted down beneath the tossing waves.

"Audrey!" she shouted, cupping her hands to her mouth and spinning around in circles. Anyone watching from the road would have thought she was drunk as she lurched first this way and then that way, shouting Audrey's name.

The stiff breeze off the water soon counteracted the feeble warmth of the sun and Bri clutched her shoulders and rubbed them vigorously. She stared at the tossing waves, wondering if, maybe, she would see Audrey's gray sweater bob up, or her hand reaching futilely to the sky as she went down.

Going down for the third time....

"The rocks..." she said, her throat raw from yelling. She figured she might be able to see better if she got to the rocks, and maybe they would give her some shelter from the chilling wind.

She started across the sand, barely watching where she stepped because her eyes were fastened so intensely on the rocky point of land. But she had taken no more than ten steps before she saw—

"Oh, my *God!*"

Standing on the rise of land, silently, motionless with her arms at her sides, staring at her with a blank, passive expression, was Audrey. The wind whipped her hair like a tattered banner and ruffled her heavy sweater but she seemed somehow not really *there*. That was the only way Bri could explain it to herself. It was as if she were an illusion.

"Audrey . . . ?" Bri called, walking forward with a few lurching steps. The chill had invaded her muscles now and was cramping them up. She had heard the term *hypothermia,* the life-threatening loss of body heat, and she wondered if that's what was happening to her. Would she be able to get home and get warm before her body just gave up?

"Audrey. . ." she said, softer, almost pleading as she held up her hands. Her teeth were chattering so loudly they sent bright little pinpoints of pain up into her head.

As she got closer to Audrey, feeling immense relief that she hadn't been swept away by the ocean, another thought intruded on her, and she came to a dead stop.

Why didn't she go for help?
She's just standing there doing nothing!

Bri and Audrey stood staring at each other for a long time. No words passed between them, but then Audrey suddenly turned and walked away, disappearing as silently as a puff of smoke below the edge of the land. First she was there . . . then she was gone, just like *that!*

Bri just stood there, her mouth gaping open as she thought, *Had she really been there? Maybe I imagined her.*

She didn't take long to contemplate it, though. Chills were shaking her entire body, and she knew if she didn't start for home, her muscles were going to give out on her. She would collapse in the sand and die of exposure. Telling herself this was it—she would *never* trust or even try to see Audrey again—she started up the slope of the beach toward the road and headed up to the house.

II

Bri lucked out, as far as she was concerned. When she got up to the house, her parents had left a note saying they had gone out shopping. Her grandfather was in his room, probably asleep, with the TV blaring away. There was no one to question why she was dragging herself home, soaking wet and shivering. In the kitchen, she sloughed off her drenched and sandy clothes, threw them into the washing machine, and went upstairs to take a long, hot shower. The hot water helped a little to relieve the deep aches in her muscles and joints, but even after she had slipped into a clean flannel shirt and jeans, shivers racked her body all afternoon as she sat on the couch, idly watching TV and reading. Her mind kept turning back to Audrey, and she found herself wondering why she had just stood there doing nothing while Bri floundered in the water. Why hadn't she tried to help?

By late afternoon, after her parents had gotten home, the chills had gotten much worse, and after supper, she lay down on the couch and covered herself with a heavy blanket, complaining of a headache and chills. She thought her symptoms were from her dunking in the ocean, but eventually she realized that she must have the flu her father had just gotten over.

Her parents considered canceling their plans to go to the movies in Portland, but Bri insisted that she would be fine—all she needed was rest.

"I can take care of her as long as she stays down here on the couch," Frank said. Turning to Bri, he added, "'Sides, I've got to even up the score with a coupla games of checkers . . . if you're up to it."

"Maybe later," Bri said, snuggling the covers right up to her chin. The TV was on, but she barely noticed it as she drifted off to sleep.

"Anyway," Frank said to John and Julia, "you two git a'goin'. You need some time out. Things're under control round here."

So they went, driving away just as the sun was coloring the sky with a vibrant orange. Frank sat for a while, silently watching Bri as she slept, then he rolled into the kitchen and got himself a beer. He grabbed a copy of *Reader's Digest* and sat in the doorway to the living room, drinking beer and reading.

An hour or so passed, and the house was silent except for random creakings as floor joists registered the drop in temperature. Bri started to stir, and Frank came quickly over to her and waited for her to open her eyes. When she finally did, she looked up at him with a distant, glazed expression.

Frank smiled sympathetically as she tossed her head from side to side, groaning. Then, with a mighty effort—*not as much as I needed to swim for my life though*, she thought—she sat up on the couch and met her grandfather's look.

"I told you, didn't I?" he said after a long stretch of silence.

Bri felt her face flush, wondering exactly what he meant.

"Well," Frank said, leaning closer to her. "Didn't I?"

"Tell me what?" Bri asked. The fever was raging in her body, flushing her cheeks, but worse was that she did know exactly what he meant.

"I told you to stay away from the shore after a storm," Frank said gruffly. "I told you it was a dangerous place to be."

"I didn't—"

"Tut-tut," he said, waving a pointed finger in front of his face. "You might not want to tell the truth to your folks—for whatever reasons—but don't you go lying to me, 'kay? I know you had a bit of trouble down there on the point."

"How . . . how do you know that?" Bri asked.

Her first—and practically only—thought was, if her parents found out what had happened, they might make her stay away from the point. She didn't ever want to see Audrey again, not after what she had done, and *not* done, but she didn't want to give up her walks down there, either. Since moving to Maine, that was pretty much the only pleasure she had found.

"I suspected something happened," Frank said. His eyes seemed to get cloudy for a moment, then he shook his head. "Now I *know*. You want to fill me in?"

Knowing she was caught, and actually wanting to unburden herself to someone, she told him everything that had happened— even the part about how she knew, as soon as she saw Audrey standing on the bluff, that she hadn't even tried to get help. It felt good to unload, too. Just saying the words so another human being could hear them was an immense relief.

"But how did you know something had happened?" Bri asked once she was through. "I mean, did someone see what was happening and then call the house?"

Frank shook his head. "No. You might've been real careful 'bout gettin' your wet clothes into the washer, but you left your sneakers in the entryway, soakin' wet and covered with sand. I didn't realize it was as serious as it was till you just told me."

Embarrassed, Bri looked down at her hands folded in her lap. Besides the fever, she could feel something else—something cold and sad and lonely twisting in her gut. Her lower lip began to tremble, and she knew she was going to start crying—*damn it!* As much as she tried to hold it back, she couldn't.

Frank dropped his magazine to the floor and quickly came over to the couch, reaching out his arms to her. Leaning forward off the couch, she felt awkward trying to hug him in his wheelchair, but she was also grateful for his warm strength as he pulled her close to his chest and gently patted her back. She felt the rough texture of his sweater on her face and inhaled its musty old-man aroma as her tears flooded from her eyes and soaked into the old wool. In one corner of her mind, she knew she would forever link that particular wet-wool smell with her grandfather and how much love she felt for him right then.

She cried so hard her body started to tremble, but at last the waves of loneliness—*like that icy ocean and those cold, barnacle-crusted hands*—receded. Just having someone to hug was enough to dull the pain. Sniffing, she sat back on the couch, grabbed a Kleenex, and started wiping her eyes and nose.

The living room was silent for several seconds as they sat there looking at each other, each knowing they had started to develop a deep bond.

"You know, you ought to tell your folks 'bout what happened," her grandfather said.

Bri sniffed and nodded, but he seemed to sense that she didn't really mean it. It saddened him to see that same distance growing between Bri and her mother that he had felt between himself and John ever since John was a teenager.

Maybe, he thought, *it's just the way things are.*

"But it ain't just what happened today, is it?" Frank said softly.

Bri's face twisted through a whole gallery of expressions as she groped for the words, any words that might get at what she was feeling. They didn't have to be exactly the right words... anything close would do right now.

"It's just that they just don't understand what I'm going through," she finally managed to say, although her voice was scratchy. The fever was laying soft, hot pressure on the back of her head. Her self-image right now was that of a dingy, torn sheet tossed casually into the corner.

Frank smiled, a warm, sympathetic smile, and reached out to pat her gently on the knee. "I don't think parents ever *do* understand what kids go through. You may tell yourself when you're a kid that, once you have children of your own, you're gonna remember what it's like, but by the time you do, things have changed you enough—'n' times have changed enough—so even though you may honestly want to understand, you just can't anymore, no matter how hard you try."

Lord knows, I tried, he thought to himself, and he couldn't push aside the feeling that, for him and John, it was already too late.

His words only made Bri feel all the more helpless and alone, but the fact that he was saying them to her—and it wasn't just her thinking them to herself—made her feel ... well, about as good as she could.

"It's really up to you, you know," he said. "If you don't tell them what you're feelin', how're they supposed to know?"

"I've told them hundreds of times, but they won't listen to me! They never do!"

"Oh, I don't know about that," Frank said. "I think—hell, I *know*—your mom and dad happen to love you a lot, 'n' it bothers them that you aren't happy here. . . ." His voice trailed off as he thought, *Because they had to come here to help me!* And seeing what it was doing to Bri cut his heart like a razor slice.

"Yeah . . . well," she said, but before she could say more, a wave of shivers raced through her body. Her teeth chattered, and when she sniffed loudly, tiny spinning lights danced across her vision.

"I think right now all you need is rest," Frank said. "I was kinda hopin' for a coupla games of checkers, but I—"

"I can play," Bri said, trying to brighten up as she sat forward on the couch. But the sudden motion made the pressure in her head get worse, and she collapsed back on the couch and closed her eyes.

"Maybe you oughta head on up to your room," Frank said. "The checkers'll wait."

Bri opened her mouth to protest, but instead she shifted her feet to the floor and, dragging her blanket behind her like a loose robe, she mumbled a "g'night," and shuffled slowly up the stairs.

"Hope you're feelin' better in the morning," Frank said.

He waited at the foot of the stairs, listening as she walked slowly up to her room. Her bedroom door clicked shut behind her, and then he heard the squeaking of the bedsprings as she climbed into bed. He didn't move from his position until he was sure she was asleep, but even then, he didn't feel as though everything was done, as though everything was safe.

There was something else in the back of his mind that he knew he was supposed to have told her. It had come to him while they were talking, but before he could say it, it had faded again, like a tiny flame that had gotten blown out. All he knew, as he stared silently up the stairwell toward Bri's bedroom door, was that it had something to do with that girl Audrey she had talked about—

Something to do with her!

III

She's back!

The words came crashing like a tidal wave into John's mind as he stood in the kitchen doorway, staring in astonishment at the dim reflection in the picture window. And almost instantly, his second thought was, *Why did I think* she?

They had come home late from the movie because they had had to wait for the second show. Supper at Tortilla Flat had taken a bit longer than they had planned, and by the time they found a parking space—which, on a Saturday night at the Maine Mall Cinema, was pretty close to a miracle—the Mel Gibson movie had sold out. It was either another movie, certainly *not* the gory-looking horror movie *Night Siege,* or wait. So they killed time wandering around the Maine Mall and got back to the cinema in plenty of time.

Julia seemed to enjoy the movie almost as much as John did, but it turned out to be nearly as violent as Gibson's last one, so there were a few scenes where she snuggled her face into John's chest until he signaled it was okay to come up for air. As soon as they got home, Julia went upstairs to check on Bri. She poked her head into the room, saw that she was sleeping soundly, and then tiptoed downstairs. Frank's door was closed and the TV was silent, so they figured, without Bri's company, he had gone to sleep early as well.

While Julia waited in the living room, John fixed them each a cup of tea. As he was carrying the tray into the living room, he was overwhelmed with a sense of déjà vu—the feeling that this had happened before—when he glanced at the window and saw two people reflected in the window—Julia and . . . *someone else!*

He remembered the last time this had happened, on their first night in the house. The sudden blast of the foghorn had woken them up, and Julia and Bri had waited on the couch while he heated up some milk for them. The living room had been dark except for the steadily blinking lighthouse beacon. Rain had been beating against the window, and he had seen—*no!* he told himself, *thought he had seen*—a dark figure hanging from the ceiling.

This time, a single reading lamp was on in the living room. Bri was in bed. Through the picture window, just like that other night, John could see the lighthouse, but no rain beat against the glass. Centered in the middle of the window, though, was that same figure, the same indistinct blur. It certainly *looked* like a person, he thought, but this time he tried not to let himself panic. He stopped in the doorway and stared at the glass.

"Something the matter?" Julia asked, turning to look at him.

He wasn't sure, but it seemed as though the second reflection, which had its back to him, was slowly turning around to face him.

Is there some kind of double reflection or something? he wondered. He moved his head from side to side, studying the change in perspective. Everything in the room—even the weird double reflection—seemed to shift. It was too dim, too vague to pin down exactly, but whatever it was, it did look like another person.

"No, there's . . ." He shook his head and, with as few steps as possible, put the tray down on one of the end tables and went back to where he had been standing in the doorway. As soon as he looked at the window, he saw that the double reflection was still there, but damned if he could figure out if it was Julia's or . . .

No! It couldn't be anyone else!

"Raise your hand and wave it," John commanded.

Frowning, Julia did what she was told, and John watched, fascinated, as both reflections raised their hands. The clearest reflection of Julia's back was easily recognizable, but the second one—even as it waved its hand—looked somehow . . . different.

"Come here a minute," he said, motioning her over. "Stand right here." Julia came over and stood where he told her to. "Now watch when I sit down on the couch."

He walked over and sat exactly where Julia had been, turned to face her, and said, "Look at my reflection in the window. What do you see?"

"All I see is your back," Julia said, frowning with confusion. "Why?"

"No, no . . . look *carefully* at the reflection. Right where the light from the lighthouse is." He raised his hand and waved it from side to side. "Now what do you see?"

Julia squinted as she stared at the window, but all she could see was the rather clear outline of her husband, waving his hand over his head like a fool. She told him so.

"There isn't, like, a double reflection there?" he said, turning around for a look at the window himself. "Can't you see a dimmer secondary outline of my shape?"

Julia shook her head. "No . . . just you. Is this some kind of joke?"

John was looking back and forth from Julia to the window. He was frowning as he tried to see if she was standing exactly where he had been.

"Move back and forth a little and keep looking at the picture window, where I told you. Tell me if anything changes."

Again Julia did as she was told, but after a while stopped and, shaking her head, came over and sat beside him on the couch.

"I guess it's a good thing we didn't go see that horror movie instead of waiting," she said. "I think you're too suggestible. Can I have my tea before it gets cold?" She reached for the tray on the end table and almost dropped it when John suddenly shouted, "Wait! Stay right where you are!"

He got up quickly from the couch and went back to the kitchen doorway, staring at the picture window. Julia, meanwhile, was sprawled awkwardly across the couch, looking at him over her shoulder as if she feared he had gone crazy.

"This isn't the most comfortable position," she said.

"Just a second," John said. *She* might not have seen the shadowy reflection—and, by Jesus, it had looked like another woman reflected in the glass—but *he* had . . . and it was there again! He moved back and forth, up and down, trying to see it more clearly, but every time he thought just a slight shift would make it clearer, he would move a fraction of an inch and it would be gone like smoke.

"John, this is getting just a tad ridiculous," Julia said. She shifted around into a sitting position and took one of the teacups. Testing the liquid with her lips, she nodded and said, "It's still warm. Come on and sit down and relax."

"Just a second," he said. Keeping his eyes fixed squarely on the window, he made his way across the living room floor, feeling his way around the furniture. He barely noticed the jolt of pain when he bumped his shin on the coffee table.

When he got right up to the picture window, it looked almost as if there was a stain embedded in the glass itself, and that somehow it got lighter and darker, depending on the angle he viewed it from. He came right up close to the glass, trying to see beyond the superficial reflection of the living room, with his wife sitting on the couch, watching him in amazement. Bending over, he put his fingers to the glass and rubbed it with small, circular motions.

"I never noticed a blemish in this glass before," he said. "Did you?"

"Will you cut it out and get over here?" Julia said, slapping the couch cushion beside her. He could tell she was starting to get upset with him, but damn if it *still* didn't look as if it there was a second vague figure hovering just at the edge of vision, *like a photographic negative on one of those old-fashioned glass plates*, he thought.

"God," he said, straightening up. "That is so strange."

"You're the one who's strange," Julia said. "There's probably just some tiny imperfection in the window that's distorting the light."

Cupping his chin in his hand, John studied the picture window a second longer; then he went back to the couch and sat down with a heavy sigh. Julia handed him his cup of tea—now totally cold—but he seemed not to notice as he sipped it. They carried on a casual conversation for quite a while, brushing at times on a few more serious problems, particularly Bri's lack of adjustment at school, but John's eyes were constantly drifting back to the window, trying to get a fix on what he thought he had seen there. Every so often, especially just as he was turning to look away from the window, the dark splotch—which *might* have resembled a human shape—would seem to whisk away just before he turned and looked at it straight on.

"What the hell are you doing?" Julia finally asked out of frustration. "You're hardly hearing a word I'm saying."

"No—I, uh . . . just keep thinking I see something there," John said. "That's all."

"Well, what? What do you think you see?"

John shrugged nervously. "I told you before; I think it's some kind of double reflection, but sometimes it seems to move even when you and I aren't moving."

"Maybe the house is haunted," Julia said. A sly smile spread across her face, and she held her hands up like a witch and whistled *The Twilight Zone* theme music.

"Cut it out," John said, pushing her away.

"No, seriously," Julia said. "Maybe it's your mother's ghost come back."

"That's not very funny," John said, frowning deeply.

"I'm not joking. I mean, this is an old house and all. Who's to say it doesn't have a few spooks hanging around in the rafters? Don't you ever hear sounds at night, like bumping and banging around inside the walls?"

"That's the rats my father was telling you about," John said with a snicker. "Unless it's my father trying to get down the hallway to the bathroom without turning on the light." He laughed, but the laughter sounded thin and unconvincing, even to his own ears.

Wharf rats as big as poodles, banging around inside the walls! Julia thought, unable to repress a shiver. No, before she chalked up anything to a ghost in the house, she figured she'd better eliminate some of the more reasonable explanations first.

"It's just that—" He cut himself off quickly because he had again caught just a hint of motion in the corner of his eye. This time he was convinced it had been there, that someone had gone past the window outside the house. Instantly he remembered what had happened to Bri on Halloween night, and his first thought was that good old Randy Chadwick was out there, snooping around, for whatever reason.

Julia jumped when he turned quickly and looked at the picture window. "What?'" she asked. "Did you see something?"

"No, no . . . nothing," John replied. He drank the last bit of cold tea and glanced at his watch. He was surprised to see that it was already after midnight. "I think we ought to hit the sack. I'm not used to staying up this late."

Julia stifled a yawn and nodded agreement as she stood up. She put their empty cups onto the tray and carried them into the kitchen while John went over and turned off the living room light. As the room was plunged into darkness, he couldn't help but wonder what the darkness hid. What reflections would there be in the picture window *now* if his eyes could pierce the darkness? Or who might he see standing out in the dark, looking in at them?

He met Julia at the foot of the stairs, and arm in arm they went up to their bedroom. After a quick wash-up, they tucked themselves into bed, kissed good night, and rolled over to sleep. But, as late as it was, sleep was elusive for John, and as he drifted in and out of a thin slumber, his mind played with what he had seen . . . and *thought* he had seen . . . reflected in the living room window. In his dreams, thin, dark shadows kept trying to resolve into clearer shapes . . . shapes that were taking on sharper definition . . . shapes that were struggling to gain substance. . . .

TWELVE
"Dem Bones"

I

After all that had happened on Saturday—some of which Bri never told her parents—Sunday was a relatively relaxing day. Frank, as usual, went to church in the morning and spent the afternoon visiting with friends. Bri was feeling better, but still not well enough to get out of bed before noon. Then, after a light lunch of toast and juice, she went back up to bed. She was secretly hoping to have at least one day off from school. Julia and John had finished off the living room painting and papering last weekend, so they spent a leisurely afternoon browsing through the *Maine Sunday Telegram*. The one time John mentioned that he might snap on the football game, Julia threatened divorce, so the TV was quiet all day.

From her bed, Bri could see Indian Point, and several times throughout the day, she thought she saw someone walking around out there. The figure, though, was little more than a dark dot in the distance, and the rough terrain blocked her view most of the time. She suspected it was Audrey, but after what had happened yesterday—how Audrey had just *stood* there when she had been swept away by the wave and not gone for help—Bri never wanted to see Audrey again as long as she lived!

Julia was grateful for their free time this afternoon because she found John starting to unwind. Throughout the morning, he had still seemed wired, but after lunch, and her joking about divorcing him if he watched football, he started to seem like the old John she used to know, the fun, relaxed, easygoing John.

"You said awhile ago how you might want to find something else for a job," she said. "Were you serious?"

They were sitting side by side on the couch, the Sunday paper a fluttered mess around their feet on the floor. John was drinking a beer, which was unusual for him before evening, but Julia didn't feel at all as if he needed it to unwind.

Staring thoughtfully at the top of the can, his finger flicking the pull tab and making it hum, he shrugged. "I dunno," he said, shaking his head. "I guess I was pissed off. I wasn't serious about being a lobsterman, but . . . I don't know, it would be kind of nice not to have so much pressure."

"Is there really that much pressure in what you're doing now?"

John took a swallow of beer. "Enough. You know, Randy wasn't just making that up about me not being the most popular resident of this island. And even if I *wasn't* working for Freedom, being the new guy at Atkins and all, I sorta feel I have to prove myself more than the guys who have been there awhile. You know, sometimes I feel like—you know what my father used to say?"

Julia arched an eyebrow.

"Like I've been shot at and missed, shit on and hit!"

"Colorful," Julia said, smiling in spite of herself. "But do you have any alternatives?" She shifted forward and placed her hand gently on his arm. "I mean, realistically?"

"No—not really," John said, slouching down and—to Julia's surprise—actually snugging up closer to her. After the way he had been acting since they moved to Glooscap, this rather surprised her.

"Why don't you take up Randy's offer?" she asked. "Give lobstering a try with him. Who knows? Maybe you really would like something like that."

John's laughter came out with a snorting spray. "Oh, I can see it now. *The Old Man and the Sea.* Come on—give me a break!"

"Just a suggestion," Julia said, nestling her face into his chest. What she was thinking now had nothing to do with his work. She was weighing in her mind whether or not she should again try to bring up the subject of having a baby. She hadn't come up with any new angle, but maybe, since he was in such a good mood . . .

"I guess I'll toss this," John said, heaving a sigh and standing up after taking one last sip of beer.

Julia opened her mouth, about to say something, but then remained where she was, watching the moment slip away.

Maybe later . . . tonight, she thought.

"I'll go check on Bri," she said, also rising. "See if she needs anything."

From the kitchen, John could hear her as she went up the stairs. It seemed as though every step on the stairway had a rusty-nail creak in it. He went over to the entryway and tossed the empty into the bag where they collected the returnable bottles and cans. Pausing for a moment in front of the refrigerator, he considered having a second beer but then decided to have a Diet Pepsi instead.

As he was reaching up into the cupboard for a glass, he saw something from the corner of his eye and, turning, saw that there was a single sheet of notebook paper folded in half and stuck in between the sugar and flour canisters. A spark of recognition made him frown, and at the same time he remembered the weird sense of déjà vu he had had the night before when he had seen that strange double reflection in the picture window.

He slowly lowered his hand from the cupboard. He couldn't control the shaking as he reached out and took the sheet of paper. From upstairs, he could hear the soft *buzz-buzz* of Julia's and Bri's voices. He knew his father wasn't around, but he couldn't shake the sensation that someone was watching him as he flattened the paper open on the countertop and quickly scanned what was written there.

I WON'T...

A dash of chills raced through him when he recognized the same heavyhanded pencil marks. He chuckled softly to himself, but that did nothing to relieve the tingling tension that had started winding up in the pit of his stomach. He was aware that his breathing had gotten rapid and shallow.

Is this the same piece of paper I saw before? he wondered as he held it up to the light, inspecting it. He was pretty sure he had crumpled up that first note and tossed it into the wastebasket, so he was certain this couldn't be that one. But it looked—even down to the torn notebook ring holes—*exactly* the same . . . except for the additional word WON'T.

"Won't *what?*" he said aloud. There was a spot on the back of his head that felt as though someone was staring at him from behind with a hard, icy look; his scalp was tingling. He turned around quickly, but there was no one there.

The trembling in his hands got worse as he tore the sheet of paper several times, each tear making a sharp, hissing sound. When the note was nothing more than a little pile of rough squares, he sprinkled them like huge snowflakes into the wastebasket, then crammed them down beneath the day's trash so they couldn't be seen. Then he got a glass from the cupboard and the Diet Pepsi from the refrigerator, and while he was pouring himself a full glass—even though now he felt he could really use that beer, after all—he heard the sound of Julia's footsteps as she came back downstairs.

"How's she—" he started to say, but he was cut off by Julia's sudden shout.

"What the hell did you do in here?"

Confused, John put the Pepsi down and came into the living room to see Julia standing there, an expression of total confusion on her face. The newspaper which had been lying on the living room floor was now a shredded mess. Several sheets had been torn into long ribbons and strewn about like party streamers.

John was just as confused as Julia, and he held up his hands helplessly. "I didn't do a thing," he said, thinking if Bungle were still alive, they could blame him.

"Is this some kind of joke?" Julia asked, looking at him with a harsh expression on her face. "After that number you did last night about the reflection in the window, are you trying to play some kind of trick on me?"

"No . . . honest, I—" John said. He went over to the pile of torn newspaper and picked up several ribbons, letting them slide like ticker tape from his hand to the floor. Shaking his head, he looked back at Julia.

"Are you sure *you're* not trying to play some kind of trick on *me?*" he asked.

"Come on," she replied. "I was upstairs with Bri. And why the hell would I do something like that, anyway?" She paused and, staring at the paper, suddenly clutched her shoulders and shivered. "Do you think it could have been those rats your father was taking about?"

"What do you mean?"

"You know—maybe those wharf rats that live in the walls were trying to get some of this paper—I don't know—for nesting or whatever." She looked back and forth along the floorboards, trying to see any sign of where the rats might have come out of the wall.

In his memory, all John could hear was the harsh ripping sound as he had torn up the note he had found in the kitchen. He couldn't help but wonder if there was a connection somehow. "It doesn't *look* like rats could do something like this. I mean, it's all torn so evenly on the side. I would think rats would *gnaw* things, but—hey! I suppose anything's possible."

"I don't like it," Julia said, still nervously scanning the walls. "I don't like it one bit! If one of those can come out and start chewing on our newspaper in the middle of the day, what else might they do? Don't you think they might get into our food? Or what if they attack us when we're sleeping? Remember hearing about that baby in New York City, where the mother found a rat in the crib chewing on the baby's face?"

"They don't do stuff like that," John said. "That's right up there with those albino-alligators-in-the-sewer stories. You've got to remember, I grew up here. We never had a problem with them before."

"Yeah—*before*," Julia said. "But it sure looks like we do now! Rats can be really dangerous!"

As he started to scoop up the shredded pages—and now that he looked at it, it didn't seem quite so bad; only a few pages were torn, and it *did* look like a rat could have done it—John started to laugh. He was remembering one of Bri's favorite books when she was little, *Mrs. Frisby and the Rats of NIMH*. The image of a real rat wearing a pair of wiry bifocals and reading the *Maine Sunday Telegram* was just too much for him. Shaking with laughter, he crumpled the newspaper into a tight ball and, thinking, *This will hide that ripped-up note all the better,* went into the kitchen and stuffed it into the trash.

Julia followed him into the kitchen and, checking the time, said, "Your father should be home soon. I think I'll just heat up some soup for supper, if that's all right with you."

John nodded. "Sure . . . I'm not that hungry, anyway." In fact, his stomach was still twisting from the tension he had felt when he had found and read that note.

I WON'T...
Won't what?

After cramming it into the wastebasket, he barely gave the ripped newspaper a second thought.

Seeing his Pepsi still sitting on the counter, he poured it into a glass and headed back to the living room. "I guess I'll just pop on the TV and see what the score is," he said, trying his best to ignore the withering stare he knew Julia was giving him behind his back. But he had other things on his mind—things that, at least for now, he didn't want to think about.

Like, *What in the name of sweet Jesus did that message mean?*

II

All day Monday at work, John felt a sense of gathering dread, and by the time he left for home that evening, he knew why: tomorrow he was scheduled to go out to the Surfside condo project. Whenever he thought about the field where Haskins' barn stood, the barn tottering so badly it looked as if it would collapse with the next breeze, he couldn't help but think about the times he had spent out there while in high school. And some of those were memories he would just as soon not stir up.

The sun had just set as he was driving across the bridge onto Glooscap, and even though he knew Julia would be waiting on supper until he came home, and even though he honestly didn't want to, he turned left after the bridge instead of right, intending to drive past the construction site. He kept telling himself he just wanted to glance at the site so he could see what progress had been made and he would know what to expect in the morning.

The workers had left for the day, and in the gathering gloom of night, their silent, abandoned machinery looked like dinosaurs frozen in time. Everywhere the land showed marks of their passing, with huge chunks of earth carved and piled up like mountains on the moon. Everywhere there were deep-treaded wounds on the land. Like blank, unseeing eyes, frozen puddles in the rutted dirt road reflected back a pale image of the sky.

As John rounded the corner and glanced up at Haskins' barn, a shiver raced through him. He was tempted to stop and go up there, to see what work had been done around it. He knew one thing he was going to have to check was the levels for the road that would be carved into the trees past the barn.

But even though he slowed the car, he couldn't bring himself to stop. There was no way, he thought, that he was going up there— not alone, not with night falling so fast!

Stepping down hard on the gas, he rounded the corner a little too fast. His tires skidded in the dirt the trucks had spilled on the asphalt, and as the car swerved around the corner, he felt a momentary panic that he might veer off the road. If he lost control and went over an embankment, then he might be stuck out here *alone* at night!

The thought clenched his heart like a cold fist, and he gritted his teeth, holding tightly to the steering wheel until the tires grabbed the road and held. He felt some measure of relief, knowing the road was firmly under his wheels again, but in his rearview mirror, he could see the plume of dust his tires had kicked up, swirling like storm clouds behind him. And no matter how fast he raced down the road toward home, he couldn't quite dispel the gnawing feeling of dread that churned in his gut.

He wondered if he *ever* would. . . .

III

"You've got to have a talk with your father, or Mrs. Marshall, or *whoever!*" Julia said when she met John at the door.

He stepped into the kitchen, shook off his heavy coat, and hung it on a peg in the entryway. Dropping his briefcase to the floor, he grabbed Julia with both hands and pulled her close for a kiss.

"Why?" he asked.

"Well, someone's been screwing around with the furniture," Julia said. "I went out to the store this afternoon, and when I came back, the couch had been moved over toward the wall. I had a hell of a time pushing it back into place."

"Didn't Bri stay home from school today?" John asked. "Maybe she moved it so she could see out the window."

"Bri didn't move it," Julia snapped. "There's no way she could have."

"Then I don't suppose my father could have, either."

"So then it must have been Mrs. Marshall. She must do it when she comes in to clean. I told your father he didn't need to have her come in anymore, but he insists. He says he's paying her with his money and that she's come to depend on the income, so he doesn't want to fire her."

John shrugged. "Well, if she's screwing things up, maybe it's time we spoke to her," he said.

"Maybe you should talk to her," Julia said. "You could call her right after supper."

"Sure . . . I suppose," John said. He picked up his briefcase and carried it into the living room, where he deposited it beside the telephone desk. In a moment he had returned to the kitchen.

"And there's something else," Julia said, folding her hands in front of her as she stood by the kitchen table. John raised his eyebrows questioningly.

"I don't want to go pointing a finger, accusing anybody," Julia said softly, "but I'm missing some jewelry."

"You're sure you haven't just misplaced it?" John asked.

Julia shook her head. "Positive. It's nothing really valuable, but I haven't been able to find a necklace and two pairs of earrings. You know my gold-link necklace? And my two pairs of Laurel Burch earrings—the ones with the birds on them."

"And you think maybe Mrs. Marshall has helped herself to these?" John said.

"I don't want to point a finger at anyone," Julia said. "I was just wondering if you knew where they were."

One side of John's mouth eased up into a smile. "No, those earrings don't really go with anything I have," John said. "I haven't been dressing up in drag lately. You know I'm trying to give that up."

"Oh, aren't we the comedian tonight," Julia said. "Come on, John!"

"I know," John said, snapping his fingers. "We've got gremlins!"

"I'm serious," Julia said with a flash of anger. "That was some of my favorite jewelry."

"Well, don't look at me," John said. "Ask Bri. Maybe she borrowed them. Or do you think Mrs. Marshall might have lifted them?"

"I . . . I don't know," Julia said.

"Well, we can either ask her about it or simply tell her not to come by anymore, that we don't need the help."

"That might be the best way to handle it," Julia said. "I don't want to come right out and accuse her. But—hey, they'll probably turn up soon, anyway. Why don't you call Bri down for supper? I'll see if your dad's awake. Oh, and there's one more thing."

What now? John thought even as he forced himself to smile.

"I told you I had gone to the store," Julia said. She bent down and opened up one of the cupboard doors and took out a rather large brown bag with *Trustworthy Hardware* printed on both sides. She handed the bag to him and said simply, "I don't care *what* your father says about it, either. I want you to put these out."

John opened the top of the bag and, looking inside, saw three large metal rat traps with shiny, mean-looking teeth.

"After you give Mrs. Marshall a call, you can smear those with something—the guy at the hardware store suggested peanut butter—and put them up in the attic. I don't want any more rats getting into my house!"

"What happened to your live-and-let-live attitude?" John said.

"I still have it," Julia replied with a sly smile. "I'll let the bastards live, as long as they don't come into my house!"

"Fair enough, I guess," John said. He refolded the bag and put it on the counter beside the toaster. He didn't exactly relish the idea of setting the traps—or cleaning them, if he managed to catch anything—but he knew once Julia had her mind made up, there was no denying her. If there *had* been, they never would have moved to Maine in the first place. . . .

Supper went peacefully enough, even after Julia informed Frank that she absolutely didn't want Mrs. Marshall coming by to do cleaning anymore. She didn't mention the moved furniture Hilda hadn't put back into place, much less the missing jewelry. Instead, she said it was an insult to her own housekeeping abilities to have someone else do any of the work, and *that* was *that!*

After supper, Bri went straight up to bed, saying she still felt drained by the flu. Frank and Julia went into the living room to watch the evening news while John cleared the table and did the supper dishes. It was Bri's turn, actually, but he told her he would give her a break as long as she paid him back once she was feeling better.

From the living room, Julia shouted to him, reminding him that he had a certain phone call to make. John almost countered that, since he had work to do on the plan he would be using the next day, and since she was the "heavy" in this instance, she should call. Instead, he picked up the phone book and flipped through the pages to find Hilda Marshall's phone number.

He rifled through the pages, looking for the *M*'s when he saw something—a piece of paper—stuck inside the phone book. His stomach dropped as soon as he saw it because he instantly recognized what it was. . . .

A sheet of notebook paper folded in half . . . with its punched ring holes torn . . . and something written on it in heavy-handed pencil!

He could see the scrawled words through the paper. Whoever had written it had borne down so hard it had almost gone right through the paper. John almost dropped the phone book as he hurriedly unfolded the paper and read what was written.

I WON'T FORGET...

"Hey, Jule?" he called out, aware that his voice was shaking.

"Yeah?" she replied over the televised sounds of gunfire and a reporter's voice-over.

He felt his throat go suddenly dry, and he wasn't even sure his next words would come out, but instead of going into the living room, showing her the paper, and asking what this was all about, he tore the paper into the smallest fragments he could and rolled them into a tight ball.

"Uh . . . oh, nothing," he said in little more than a croak. "Nothing . . . I've got it."

He went into the bathroom down the hall and sprinkled the torn paper into the open toilet bowl. He had to hit the flush three times before they all disappeared with a sucking gurgle, but even as he watched the water swirl the fragments of the note away, he *knew* he was going to see that note again—next time, no doubt, with another word added. He wondered if Julia, or Bri, or maybe his father was playing some kind of trick on him, and he decided that, no matter what was going on, the best thing to do was simply ignore it.

IV

"Because I don't particularly like rats, that's why! Is that all right with you?"

Julia was standing with John in the upstairs hallway. She shushed him with a wave of her hands, indicating Bri's closed bedroom door with a quick nod. What bothered John the most was the smirking smile on her face as she watched him, flashlight, hammer, and nails in one hand, bag of traps, jar of Skippy peanut butter, and a knife in the other.

"Well, I don't particularly like them, either," Julia said, eyeing the attic door. "But I don't see why you can't just go up there and set a few traps."

"If it's so damned easy, why didn't *you* do it this afternoon?"

"I never knew you were so scared of rats," Julia said, her smirk widening into a smile.

John sucked in a deep breath, held it, then let it out with a slow whistle. His eyes practically danced in his head, flicking between the attic door and his wife.

"Everybody has his thing, all right? Some people can't stand snakes, others can't handle spiders. Mine just happens to be rats," he said. "Are you going to come with me?"

Julia thought for a moment, but even considering that he had already done one "dirty" job tonight, calling Hilda Marshall and telling her not to stop by the house to clean anymore, she just didn't want to go up there. She could barely stand being here in the opened doorway. Crawling around in a dusty, dimly lit, confined area, even if it *wasn't* infested with rats, wasn't exactly her idea of a fun time. She chastised herself for thinking it, but baiting the rat traps seemed like a man's job.

"You take care of it," she said as she took a few steps away from the door. "I'll wait here and listen for any screams, okay?"

"Thanks," John said, shaking his head with disgust. "Thanks a whole pant-load!" He opened the attic door and put his foot on the first step, but before he started up, he looked back at Julia .

"You're sure you won't reconsider? This is your last chance."

"Go on," she said, waving her hand at him. "Just get it over with."

He reached out for the light switch on the wall, snapped it up and down several times, but somehow wasn't at all surprised when the bulb upstairs didn't come on. None of them had been up into the attic since they move into the house, mostly, John told himself, because storing stuff up there instead of in the garage made it feel like more of a permanent commitment to staying. He still had in the back of his mind that, if he had his way, they would be moving off the island and out of Maine sometime soon.

With a flick of his thumb, he snapped on the flashlight and let the oval of light slowly wash up the stairs to the top. Only the floor of the attic was insulated, so cold air came rushing down at him as soon as the door was open. The breeze stirred up a thick layer of dust and cobwebs in the stairway. With one last inhalation of fresh air, John braced himself and started up the stairs. Shivering, he told himself his reaction was only because of the cold air.

I won't see any rats, he kept telling himself. *They'll run and hide as soon as they hear me coming.*

The floorboards creaked underfoot. When he reached the top of the stairs, he stood in a crouch, looking back and forth to each end of the attic, trying to decide the best places to set the traps.

Again he thought of *Mrs. Frisby and the Rats of NIMH*, and

he chuckled softly, wondering if perhaps he might see a rat wearing Julia's gold necklace and earrings.

"Look out! Behind you!" Julia suddenly yelled from down in the hallway. John swung his flashlight around and scrambled to one side, just barely registering Julia's cackle of laughter.

"A real comedian, you are," he snarled. "Why don't you just go downstairs and let me handle this, all right?"

He snickered softly to himself, but he was thinking there was nothing funny about the sweat-slick grip he had on the paper bag and the flashlight. The musty attic air, which probably hadn't circulated in a decade or more, filtered into his throat like fine-grained sand. The chill of the night air made his breath come out as a fine mist.

Looking around, he saw that sometime recently his father had brought some things up here. Everything was hazy with the thick layer of dust, but he recognized several pieces of furniture. There was the old easy chair his father used to read his newspaper in at night. The red covering was laced with holes from which yellow tufts of stuffing hung out like curdled cream. An old coffee table, with its chipped and splintered top, was buried under several bundles of tied-up magazines. Some of the twine had rotted and snapped, fanning the magazines—they looked like old copies of *Life* and *Look*—across the rough-cut pine flooring.

Farther in, he could see several boxes jammed so full of old clothes the cloth was hanging out the sides. Sleeve ends and hems looked frayed, as though they had been . . . *chewed,* he thought, even though he didn't want to admit it. He was hit by a wave of nostalgia as he scanned the accumulated family history. Fragments and pieces of his childhood—maybe even his collection of plastic soldiers and his old Lionel train set—were stored up here, collecting dust, their boxes good for nothing more than to provide material for rats' nests.

Was that actually his mother's fancy blue wool coat, the one she used to wear every Easter, hanging from a nail in a rafter?

And wasn't that the sleeve of his father's military uniform, the one John used to wear when he played soldiers with Randy, sticking out of that box?

John had been moving slowly down toward the end of the attic, cautiously watching for any sign of rats, but there were no droppings on the floor that he could see.

He froze when he heard a soft scuffing sound behind him. His neck and shoulders were tingling as he snapped around, his flashlight beam weaving and darting as it tried, like a bloodhound, to sniff out the source of the noise.

Had that been a rat sneaking in among the piles of junk? he wondered. *Or was Julia still at the foot of the stairs, making noise just to tease him?* He hadn't heard her go down.

"That you?" he called out. His voice, dry from the attic air, was nothing more than a harsh whisper.

Off to his left, he thought he saw just the faintest hint of motion, but by the time he brought his flashlight beam to bear on it, it was gone. Swearing softly under his breath, he scrunched down and opened the bag from the hardware store. Bracing the flashlight under his arm, its beam directed at the open mouth of the bag, he took out the first trap along with the jar of peanut butter and the knife.

He had three traps to set and, if he'd had his choice in the matter, he would just as soon have set all three up by the door. Let the damned rats come to him! But rats, he figured, were probably smart enough to avoid something so obvious as three traps lined up side by side.

John snorted as he spun off the jar lid and scooped up a glob of peanut butter. He nailed the anchor chain to the floor, bending over the nail to make sure, no matter how big a rat he caught, he wouldn't crawl away dragging the trap behind him. Then he smeared the bait pan, spread the teeth-lined jaws apart, and locked them open with the spring bar. Gently, he placed the trap on the floor, pushing it with his foot over by one of the piles of boxes.

He had just started to stand up to go to the other end of the attic when, again, he heard a rustling sound, this time much louder and closer. A thin dew of sweat broke out on his upper lip, and he felt a deep, urgent churning in his gut. He waited, tensed, in one position for so long his arms and legs began to ache, but he didn't want to move—not yet.

"Jule . . . if that's you fooling around . . ." he said, but as he was waiting to hear even just a hint of a giggle, something moved over by the old recliner. A thick, heavy body dropped with a thump to the floor and quickly scurried out of cover not five feet from him.

John let out a startled gasp when a rat—*God! It was one of the biggest rats he had ever seen in his life!*—stopped, turned, and looked at him, nailing him with a cold stare. Its beady little eyes looked like shiny black balls glistening with oil. The rat laid back his whiskers and, exposing its chisel teeth, chattered angrily at John, who still hadn't found the strength to move.

Christ! He's going to attack me! John thought in a flood of panic. He could see the open attic doorway—his only escape!—beyond the rat. *It might as well be a hundred miles away!*

The rat hunched up its body. Its front paws skittered on the floorboard, making a sound much worse than fingernails being dragged across a chalkboard.

Finally John's body responded to his mental command to do something! Raising the hammer defensively, he took one step back and braced himself, ready to jump forward the instant the rat came at him. He hoped to hell he could get past him!

"Go on! Get, you bastard!" John suddenly shouted. He shook both the hammer and the flashlight quickly back and forth in front of him. The rat instantly darted off to the side and disappeared under another pile of boxes, gone as suddenly as he had appeared. John's heart was thumping so loudly in his ears he could barely hear the scuttling sound of the rat's departure.

"Goddamned good riddance, too!" John said, although his voice was choked and sounded as if it were coming from somewhere in the back of his head.

Without wasting a second, John moved quickly to the other end of the attic, anchored, baited, and set the second trap, then went to the attic doorway, where he left the third baited trap. After spinning the peanut butter jar shut, he crumpled up the hardware-store bag, tossed it over by the first trap, and then hurried down the steps to the upstairs hallway. Not wanting to disturb Bri, he eased the door quietly but firmly shut and then locked it. He leaned against the solid wood for a moment, to give his racing pulse a chance to slow down.

"Everything all set up there?" Julia called to him from downstairs.

Wiping his forehead with his shirtsleeve, John took in a breath and said, "Oh, yeah . . . sure . . . everything's just jim-dandy."

But he didn't feel jim-dandy because he knew the worst was yet to come. In the morning, he was going to have to check the traps to see if he had caught anything, and he more than half suspected that he was going to lie awake half the night, just waiting, listening for *one—two—three* snaps as the traps sprung.

V

In the morning, it was worse than he could have imagined. Even before he opened the attic door, he sensed trouble. And he found it, all right, right at the top of the stairs.

That night he hadn't heard any of the traps snap, but at least one of the rats had gone for the bait, and the steel jaws had snapped shut over their prey. The problem was, the prey wasn't dead!

"You rotten son of a bitch," John said as he eased his head around the edge of the stairway and locked eyes with the creature.

The rat's reflexes must have been quick, John thought, but not quite quick enough. It looked as though, just as the trap had snapped, the rat had tried to turn and run. The teeth of the trap had clamped down on his left rear leg, which now hung from just a few shreds of torn muscle and shattered bone.

Cold, hate-filled eyes, misted with dull, animal pain, stared back at John, reaching inside his stomach with a black, icy touch. *You did this to me! The rat's eyes seemed to say. The trap didn't kill me! Look what you started. Now you're going to have to finish it!*

For the space of several heartbeats, John stood there, staring at the half-dead animal. There was an intelligence—a cold, hateful intelligence—behind those nearly dead eyes, and the accusation chilled John to the soul. He knew what he should do next; he should walk right up to the rat and step down—hard—on its head, to end its suffering, if nothing else.

But he didn't do that—he *couldn't* do it! No matter how much he knew he should, he just couldn't bring himself to go any farther into the attic. The dust-thick air clogged his throat; the dim lighting seemed to hide and distort vague, fleeting shadows that scuttled from corner to corner. And way at the back of the attic, what he *knew* was his mother's old blue wool coat didn't look at all like a coat. It looked like . . .

A body, dingy gray, bloated in death, suspended from the rafter!

The old coat, John knew, was hanging motionless on the nail; he had seen it yesterday, but now, as he looked at it . . .

The shape started to swing ever so gently from side to side . . . swing and—please, God, no!—turn around! In a second, he would see the face grinning, leering at him with eyes cold and sightless in death, but looking at him, reaching out to him with icy malice!

"What the hell?" he said, trying to force calm into his voice as he started to back down the stairs to the hallway. *Let the bastard suffer! I'll clean him out tonight when I get home from work.*

He went quickly down the stairs, looking all the while, not at the rat caught in the steel jaws of the trap, but at his mother's old coat. . . .

At the bloated shape hanging from the rafters!

He made it to the bottom of the stairs and, shutting the attic door firmly behind him, went downstairs to the kitchen for breakfast. Fortunately, Julia didn't notice the sheen of sweat on his forehead, and she didn't bother to ask him how the traps had worked. He sure as hell wasn't about to volunteer any information, either. After eating a piece of toast, that was dry and scratchy like the attic air, and practically gargling his coffee, he kissed Julia good-bye and rushed out the door.

VI

Although the day was sunny, the wind in off the water had a ferocious bite. Even with his woolen hat and gloves on, it didn't take long for John's face and hands to stiffen up as he worked, sighting through the transit and jotting down the elevations in his field book. All around him, the sounds of heavy machinery filled the air as bulldozers scooped out dirt and dump trucks put it elsewhere.

It always amazed John how fast certain phases of construction went and then how slowly others seemed to go. Laying this road seemed to be taking much longer than he thought it should. He and Barry had been crossing and recrossing the open field on the ocean side of the road all day, and they still couldn't make the staked areas agree with what was on the map. He just hoped the bosses at Atkins didn't blame any of the delay on his work.

"I think we've got to do one more setup," he shouted to Barry, who was crouched at a back site. "Then why don't we knock off for lunch?"

Barry simply nodded, but as he started to stand up, he looked out across the road. Competing with the sound of the trucks and bulldozers was a chorus of shouts, and when John turned to follow Barry's gaze, he saw several men hollering and waving to them.

"I wonder what's up," Barry said, walking quickly toward John.

"I hope it's not another bunch of protesters," John said. He wanted nothing more than to get to the closest restaurant and start pouring in the coffee. He simply shrugged and, shouldering the transit tripod, said, "Let's get to the next setup—"

Before he could continue, though, he was cut off by the men's yelling, which seemed to indicate they had found something over by the woods.

"Wanna go take a look?" Barry asked.

Sighing heavily, John shook his head. "Not really. I'd rather get this last elevation done so we can break for lunch. How important could it be?"

"I dunno," Barry said. By this time, he had already started up toward the road, so John, still carrying the tripod, followed along behind him.

As they clambered up onto the asphalt, one of the men who was coming toward them across the field shouted, "Where's Watson's truck? I need to use the radio."

"Someone get hurt?" Barry asked.

The man shook his head vigorously. "No . . . not recently, anyway."

"What?" John asked, feeling a sudden coldness in his groin. "What happened?"

"Dug up some bones," the man said. He didn't make eye contact with either of them; he was too busy scanning the area for a truck with a radio.

"No shit," Barry said. "So what's the panic?"

The man said, "Remember last summer, when them workers out to Old Orchard uncovered the body of that man who'd been missing for a coupla weeks? Well, I ain't takin' any chances with this. I'm getting the police out here right away."

With that, he started across the field toward the truck. Barry and John exchanged glances.

"Bones, huh?" John said. The tightening in his stomach was an actual physical pain now as he looked across the road to where several men had gathered near the tall oak tree not far from Haskins' derelict barn. They were huddled close together, looking down at a deep gash in the ground. Twisted, arm-thick roots of the oak lay exposed to the air in a tangled heap beside the now silent backhoe.

"Want to go take a look?" Barry asked, raising an eyebrow.

John's neck felt as if it were welded into place as he tightly shook his head. "Not really," he said in a voice that sounded unusually high. "We've still got our own work to do."

"Come on," Barry said as he started out across the field, his boots crunching the frozen earth. "A little excitement to break up the afternoon."

Reluctantly, John followed him over to the spot under the oak tree. His mind seemed to be running on automatic, and he was barely aware of walking as he came up close to the hole in the ground.

"What you got there?" Barry asked, glancing around the circle of men.

"Looks like someone was buried out here," one of them said, pushing his hard hat back on his head and rubbing his forehead with the flat of his hand.

Looking down, John saw a single knob-end of a bone, almost the same color as the dirt, sticking up out of the ground. The blade of the backhoe had scraped along the side, exposing a thick, mushy-looking black center. For several minutes, he barely listened as each of the men offered an opinion as to what this was.

"I think it might be some Indian or something," one of them suggested. "Look how deep it was buried."

"Don't be such an asshole, Mike. Soil round here's too acidic. Bones won't last more'n a coupla hundrit years. Got to be more recent. Maybe some farmer from colonial times."

"I think it looks too thick to be human," someone else said. "I'll bet it's a cow or a deer leg bone."

"Wouldn't be too thick if it was your skull, would it, Steve?"

"Shut the fuck up!"

"Why don't all a' you guys get back to work?" one of the other men said sharply. "The cops are on their way. We can stand around here jawin' all day and not be any closer to knowin'. There's plenty of work needin' to be done."

Grumbling, the men slowly dispersed, leaving Barry and John and the man who had sent them back to work standing by the open trench. As the men walked away, they continued to argue about who—or what—might be buried there. Their words, though, hit John's ears like the garbled reception on a cheap transistor radio. He fished a cigarette out of his coat pocket, lit it, and inhaled deeply, letting the wind whisk the smoke away as he blew it out. He couldn't move; all he could do was stand there, staring long and hard at the single bone sticking up out of the ground.

And all he could think was, *Maybe they've found her. . . . Maybe they've found Abby at last. . . .*

About fifteen minutes later, the police arrived, and while they set about exhuming the single bone and digging close by to see if there were any more, John and Barry left for lunch. When they came back from lunch, the state police had arrived as well, but now they wouldn't let anyone near the site except for the job foreman and the man who had first uncovered the bone.

After John and Barry got the figures they needed, they drove back to the office in Portland. Barry insisted on listening to the radio to see if anything was mentioned about the find at the construction site. But even during the drive home after work that evening, John didn't hear anything about the discovery of bones, human or otherwise, on Glooscap Island that afternoon.

When he got home, complaining to Julia of a splitting headache, he had one more unpleasant surprise to cap off a perfectly awful day. After going up to the attic to get the dead rat, he found the trap had been pulled to the limit of the anchor chain. Still clenched in the jaws of the trap was the rat's shredded hind leg, but the rat was gone. Immediately he realized that it must have chewed off its own leg to get away and, judging by the streak of crusted blood on the floor, the rat had crawled over to the eaves of the house. No doubt it would die of its wounds—and no doubt the whole family would end up smelling the dead rat as it rotted somewhere inside the walls.

THIRTEEN
Fish Bait

I

"What's the matter?"

Coming out of the darkness behind him, the voice made John sit up quickly on the couch and spin around. Air caught in his throat with an audible click.

"Oh . . . nothing," he said as soon as he recognized Julia standing in the doorway.

"Well, *something's* the matter," she said, coming around the edge of the couch and sitting down beside him. "It's almost three o'clock in the morning. Most people don't sit up at this hour unless there's something bothering them." She put her hand on his knee and gave it a squeeze, but he twitched and pulled his leg away from her.

Outside the picture window, the steady flashing of the lighthouse drew their attention. Julia thought John seemed unnaturally stiff as she wound her arm around his neck and tried to snuggle up to him.

"Is what happened out at the site today bothering you?"

Both the six o'clock and eleven o'clock news reports had covered the discovery of the bones at the Surfside Ledges condo site. Although neither report had specified whether they were actually human bones, the implication—based on the caginess of the state trooper they interviewed—was that they *were* human. And the trooper's final comment had been, "We haven't ruled out anything."

John took a deep breath and shook his head. When he shifted

uneasily on the couch, Julia noticed a soft crinkling sound . . . like crumpling paper. It sounded as if John was sitting on something. She almost said something, but then thought better of it. He was upset about his work, or maybe . . .

"Are you nervous about going out with Randy this morning?" she asked.

"No . . . not really," John answered. His voice sounded distant, hollow.

Yesterday afternoon Randy had called to force the issue to get John to come lobstering with him in the morning, and after supper—much against his will—John had called him back and finally agreed to go. He wasn't exactly sure why . . . maybe just to get it over and done with so Julia would stop hounding him about it.

"Everything at work's going okay then, huh?" Julia said. "I mean, other than those guys finding those bones."

"Sure," John said, nodding stiffly. "Why wouldn't it be?"

"So? Why are you sitting here at three A.M., staring out the front window like a zombie?"

John turned to look at her, and even though she couldn't see his face clearly, she could tell he looked livid with anger. "I just have a lot on my mind, if that's all right with you." He shifted forward, almost stood up, but then sank back down onto the couch, his chest heaving as he took a deep breath.

"John . . . honey," Julia said, taking his hand and squeezing it. "If there's something the matter—I don't care *what* it is—you can tell me."

"There's *nothing* the matter!" This time he did stand up, and as he did, Julia again heard the crinkling sound of paper. It sounded as if there was something under the cushion John had been sitting on. He was a black silhouette as he strode over to the window and, clasping his hands behind his back, stood, staring out at the black expanse of night and ocean.

Julia stayed on the couch for a moment, but then, when she shifted to stand up, she tried to make the motion appear uninterrupted as she slid her hand in under the cushion. Her fingers brushed against a sheet of paper which she pulled out, quickly rolled into a ball, and palmed before walking over to John.

"It'll be good for you to go out with Randy today," she said, carefully keeping the hand holding the piece of paper away from him. She was burning to know what was on that piece of paper, and not being able to read it immediately only convinced her that somehow it was connected with John's agitation.

John looked at her over his shoulder and laughed shallowly. "Oh, yeah—sure. Go out there on a freezing cold morning—in the predawn, for God's sake! Get myself soaked and freeze my ass off—probably get frigging sick again, too, just to watch Randy haul up his traps, slap smelly fish bait into them, and pitch the damned traps back over. What a wild and crazy time!"

"Yeah, but the fresh air will—"

"Hey! If you think it's going to be so goddamned much fun, why don't *you* go? Huh? I can stay home where it's warm and dry, and *you* can freeze your butt off!"

"Randy didn't invite me," Julia said. "And besides—"

"I know, I *know* . . . you think it'll be a good chance for me and Randy to reconnect! Huh!" He shook his head disgustedly. "Big fucking deal!"

"Well . . ."

"No, wait a minute," John said, his hostility flashing like summer lightning in his eyes. "I know what." He slapped his hands together, making a loud crack. "We'll *both* go! I'll bet—macho man that he is—Randy wouldn't mind one more passenger."

"John, I—"

"No, really!" He held up his hand to stop any more protest. "That's it! It's final! You're coming, too. If *you* don't go, *I* don't go. A little later, as soon as I'm sure he's awake, I'll give him a call. I know. Even better, we'll ask if Ellie can come, too, so we can have a regular lobstering party out there. Sound like fun?"

Julia shifted her eyes away from her husband and back out into the predawn darkness. She was earnestly wishing she had stayed in bed, left him alone downstairs, and not seen him until he came back from his lobstering trip with Randy. And she was burning to know what was on the piece of paper she had found under the couch cushion. She couldn't help but wonder if it, rather than work, had something to do with why John was acting so strange.

Julia clenched her fists, then cringed when the paper she was holding made a rustling sound. John didn't seem to notice it, though, because he was getting so excited about his idea.

"You've been telling me what a great thing this will be," he said, practically laughing. "Well, here's your chance to experience just how good life on the ocean is. What better time than just before winter?"

Julia was silent for a moment as she considered the corner he had neatly backed her into; then she grunted agreement. "Umm. Yeah, okay. I'll go as long as you can get Randy to convince Ellie to go." Her fist hiding the piece of paper tightened. "You're supposed to be down at the wharf by four-thirty, right?"

"Uh-huh."

"Okay. You've got a deal," Julia said "I'll go put on a pot of coffee, splash some water on my face, and then whip us up a breakfast. By the time we're done, you can give Randy a call and see if Ellie will join us."

"Fine," John said. "You might want to put together a few sandwiches, too. I have no idea how long we'll be out there." He turned and headed for the stairs. "I guess I'll take a quick shower to help me wake up, although *after* we've been out on the boat is when we'll both need to be hosed down."

Julia was secretly thrilled that John was heading to the upstairs bathroom, because it would give her time to read the note and replace it under the couch cushion before he noticed it was missing. What bothered her most was the thought that there was something that John would hide from her. She had always thought they had a perfectly open and honest relationship. If what she was clenching in her hand was very serious—well, she would just have to see what was on the piece of paper before she jumped to any conclusions.

She waited in the kitchen, practically shaking with apprehension until she heard the sound of running water coming from upstairs. Her fingers were trembling as she hurriedly unfolded the single sheet of notebook paper and saw what was written there. In strong, bold pencil lines, someone—it couldn't be John's handwriting; it looked more like the work of a child still practicing lettering—were the words:

I Won't Forget What...

That was all.

Julia frowned as she turned the paper over, expecting to see something else, but the back side of the lined notebook paper was blank except for the reverse impression of the pencil marks.

Is this it? This is what's bothering him? she thought, turning the sheet back over and looking at it again. *What's the big sweat?* I WON'T FORGET WHAT . . .

From upstairs, she heard the sound of running water shut off, so with one confused last glance at the notebook paper, she refolded it and dashed into the living room. She slid the note back under the couch cushion and went into the downstairs bathroom to wash her face.

As she worked to put together a hearty breakfast, she kept turning over and over in her mind what had been written on the note. She had no idea what it meant—or if this was, in fact, what had upset John in the first place. Maybe it was something else, like those bones they had found at the construction site . . . or he wasn't getting along with someone at work . . . maybe it was something she didn't have a hint of, like an affair!

No! Impossible! she thought, even as she felt a tingling chill between her shoulder blades. *But what if it* was *something like that? Maybe he and—how about that girl he used to date in high school, Abby—what if they've met and gotten back together?*

"Naw," she said, shaking her head as she prepared to scramble up a batch of eggs. Both he and Randy had said that Abby didn't even live on the island anymore. She hadn't been seen since high school days! Besides, John wouldn't . . . he *couldn't* be having an affair with Abby or anyone else. It just wasn't in his style! It wasn't in his nature! She knew him *that* well, at least!

Seconds later, she heard the heavy clumping of John's feet on the stairs. After a quick detour into the living room . . .

For what? Julia wondered.

. . . he came into the kitchen just as she was stirring the eggs in the pan with the spatula. Leaning over the pan of eggs, he inhaled deeply and smiled with satisfaction. Then he walked over to the wastebasket and dropped something . . .

Was it that sheet of notebook paper? Julia wondered. *What the hell was it? And what the hell did it mean? Was John in some kind of trouble . . . something he couldn't talk to her about?*

. . . into the trash, jabbing at it to bury it under the broken eggshells and empty orange juice can.

"I—umm," Julia said. She had been about to ask him about the message, but then she fell silent and concentrated on the eggs, which, because she had been distracted, had just started to burn.

"Yeah?" John said, about to pull out a chair and sit down.

"No," Julia said, shaking her head quickly, "I was just going to ask if you would get dishes and silverware out for us."

"Sure . . . no problem," John said. He got the table set while Julia scooped out the eggs, buttered the toast, and brought everything over to the table.

But in the back of her mind she was thinking there *was* a problem here, a very serious problem. John was hiding something from her . . . he was keeping a secret from her! The only clue she had was that stupid note.

I WON'T FORGET WHAT . . .

Who won't forget? Forget what? Had John written this? Or had someone else—who?—written it to John? Or Bri? What in the name of Christ was going on here?

Like a tiny worm tunneling its way through an apple, that tiny doubt—that John was actually hiding something from her— could get serious, she knew. *How* it could get serious, she wasn't sure, but like they said about one bad apple spoiling the whole barrel, one little secret between husband and wife could gather strength until, like an atomic chain reaction, it reached explosive proportions!

All she knew, as she and John sat down to eat, was that sure as hell, before they left to meet Randy at the wharf, maybe while John was on the phone asking if Julia and Ellie could come along with them, she was going to try to see if the note she had replaced was still there under the couch cushion or if that was what John had thrown away.

II

At the wharf, Randy and Ellie, both dressed as warmly as John and Julia, stood waiting for them at the head of a ladder leading down onto a float, where a small dinghy was tied up. Randy directed John over to the parking area by the boat yard, then climbed down to the float and busied himself with untying the small boat from the dock while John parked. Ellie waited for them over by the dock, a tight smile on her face. It was obvious she had had other—better—plans for this morning.

"Mornin' to yah," Randy said, glancing up over his shoulder as he tossed the mooring line into the boat and, kneeling, held on to the gunnel.

John almost said something to him about sparing them the "old salt" routine, but he kept his lips sealed as he stepped back for Julia and Ellie to climb down the ladder to the floating dock.

"Have you ever gone out lobstering before?" Julia asked Ellie once they were down on the float.

Biting her lower lip, Ellie shook her head. "Not since before we got married—years ago. I'm not really nuts about the ocean," she said softly. Her voice carried well in the early morning silence, echoing from the granite pier. "I took some Dramamine so I won't get seasick." She laughed softly, glancing at her husband. "I guess I'm basically a landlubber."

"I probably am, too," Julia said, wondering if she should take something for seasickness, too.

Pausing to look around, she was surprised by the contrast between the wharf area now and what it had been like the morning she and Frank had spent down here. Then, with the sunlight and brisk breeze, boats putting into the cove and pickup trucks rattling on the dirt road, it had seemed an active, though certainly not *thriving* workplace. With the sun not yet up, the sea gently lapping the underside of the float, the air heavy with the smell of rotting fish and low-tide mud flats, it all seemed so lonely . . . so depressing. Inside the well of the harbor, distant sounds seemed oddly muffled, while the noise they made—even walking across the parking lot—seemed unnaturally magnified. Riding easily at their moorings, boats that in the daytime had looked so brightly painted and seaworthy now, in the predawn gloom, looked worn and beaten, their thin layers of paint flaking off like . . .

Like flesh off a skull, Julia thought with a shiver, surprised by her gruesome imagery. She took a deep breath to steady herself as she held her arms out for balance as the dock gently bobbed in the water.

"Well, this sure is gonna be different from what I expected," Randy said, smiling as he glanced from his wife to Julia.

Julia started to say something, but when she shifted her weight forward, the dock began to rock. She braced her feet and held her arms out wider for balance. Once she was fairly certain she wasn't about to pitch over the side and into the harbor, she cautiously approached the dinghy.

"If there isn't enough room, Ellie and I don't really have to go," Julia said. She could feel John behind her, glaring at her back for even *suggesting* that they stay behind.

"Oh, no . . . no problem," Randy said. "I only brought oilskins for myself and John, but you ladies probably won't want to bait and haul, anyway. Plenty of room up front."

"Certainly not *me,*" Ellie said with a nervous giggle.

If the rotting fish smell had anything to do with the job at hand, Julia didn't even want to consider working. She wrinkled her nose at the mere thought.

"No," she said, "this is just going to be a pleasure ride for me and Ellie. You *men* can do all the hard work."

"Thanks tons," John said as he walked confidently on the dock over to them.

"Well, I'm all baited up 'n' ready," Randy said. "Watch it now when you step into the punt. It's none too stable."

Julia placed her hand on his shoulder as she stepped over the gunnel into the little boat. She banged one of the oars with her knee and, when she tried to regain her balance, set the boat to rocking wildly. This time she knew she could pitch overboard, so she made a quick grab for the rails. Steadying herself, and with Randy adding his muscle to it, the boat quickly stabilized.

"Where do you want me to sit?" she asked, scanning the grungy floor of the boat. There were empty beer bottles, lengths of frayed rope, and assorted rusty tools scattered about.

"Either the bow or the stern," Randy said. "Just watch out for that barrel there."

"Not exactly luxury, is it?" Ellie said.

Staying in a low crouch, Julia started toward the front of the boat. When she stepped past the small barrel Randy had indicated, she glanced inside—and immediately wished she hadn't. What she saw made her stomach do a quick flip; her digesting breakfast almost made a quick exit. The barrel was half full of fish heads and tails connected only by their sawtoothed spines. The barrel was the source of the strong smell, but she tried her best not to think too much about it or else she *would* be hanging over the side of the boat, emptying her stomach.

John waited until Julia and Ellie were settled in the front before he got in and seated himself in the back. He sat stiffly with his hands on his knees and inhaled deeply.

Randy, Julia thought, apparently hadn't tried to keep up appearances with this boat. It had last seen a paintbrush maybe five or six years ago, she guessed. Dirty bilge water sloshed back and forth on the floor as their weight shifted back and forth, and all she could wonder was, would the boat fill up and sink before they even made it out to the mooring?

Once his passengers were settled, Randy pushed off, leaped into the punt, unshipped the oars, and started rowing. Julia watched his back bend, his shoulders hunch as he pulled, strong and steady, on the oars. It seemed to her as though he had eyes in the back of his head because he threaded his way between the moored boats apparently without looking. She glanced back at the rapidly receding dock and wondered why in the hell she had let John buffalo her into coming. The strong smell of fishbait and the rocking motion of the boat were doing one heck of a number on her stomach. She considered asking Ellie if she happened to have some Dramamine with her, but decided to tough it out if she could.

Before long, she thought, *I'll be giving all of you guys a little show . . . a little wet burp!* She chuckled softly to herself when she thought of Bri's euphemism for throwing up. *Wet burp, indeed!*

"I figure we can just do a short haul today," Randy said. "I don't expect we'll be more'n three, maybe four hours."

Oh, great, Julia thought as the dinghy lurched from side to side. *My stomach will never take it that long.* She faced into the wind and inhaled deeply of the fresh sea air, trying desperately to get the smell of rotting fish out of her nose. Her only hope was that, once they were on the lobster boat, she could get a bit more distance between herself and the bait barrel.

Soon enough, Randy stopped rowing, shipped the oars, and, standing up quickly, grabbed the side of a boat before they hit it.

Pulling the punt in as close as he could, he nodded toward the boat.

"Climb aboard," he said. "Welcome to the *Bait Barrel*."

Appropriately named, Julia thought as she clambered up and over the side, grateful for the relative stability of the larger boat. Her movement made the underside of the punt slap against the water, but Randy apparently didn't think he was in any danger of getting swamped. Once she was on board, Ellie and John climbed over the side, and then Randy quickly tied his punt to the mooring.

"Here—grab this, will yah?" Randy said as he muscled the bait barrel over to the side and lifted it.

Wrinkling his nose, John carefully grabbed the splintery container and swung it down to the floor. "Christ," he said, wiping his hands together. "Don't I even get some rubber gloves or something?"

"Sure, I've got some you can wear," Randy said as he leaned over the side of the punt, making sure it was securely tied to the mooring. "But it'll wreak hell on your hands if you wear 'em all day."

John brought his hand to his nose and gave it a quick sniff. "Might be worth it," he said, shaking his head, but he knew this was just the beginning of the ordeal.

Randy got up into the boat, ran though a quick check of his equipment, then started up the engine. It took a few tries to get the obviously old machinery going, but before long the *Bait Barrel* was putt-putting away. Randy cast off the mooring line and steered a course through the harbor mouth and out to sea.

In the time it took them to load up, the sun tipped its orange disk up over the edge of the horizon. With a fresh, dry wind coming in off the land, it promised to be one of those achingly clear November days—the kind you can find only along the Maine coast, and which would be perfect if there weren't the darkening threat of winter approaching.

John, having donned some oilskins and gloves, was talking to Randy as he set his course out around the harbor entrance. From the harbor mouth, Randy cut to the left—port, as he informed his passengers—and headed out at an angle away from Glooscap. Behind them, a few sea gulls circled low over the water, drawn by the prospect of an easy breakfast if any of the bait chanced to fall overboard. The slanting morning sun touched the island with a lance of gold, bringing every detail of the still-sleeping island into high relief. Beyond the gentle white curve of Sandy Beach, the smooth, bare hump of Bald Hill rose up out of the dark evergreen woods. With most of the deciduous trees stripped of leaves, Julia thought it *did* look a bit like a man's bald head. Farther along the shore, lined with picture-postcard quaint houses—at least at this distance—the rocky coast stretched all the way around the curve of the island.

"Is that where the condos are going?" Julia asked Ellie, pointing to a bright yellow and brown stretch at the tip of the island. The morning sun illuminated the freshly laid roads, making them look like dark scars on a land colored with the yellows and browns of autumn.

Ellie nodded, but John, thinking she was talking to him, leaned his head out of the boat housing and, cupping his hands to his mouth, shouted, "What?"

Julia simply shook her head and waved him away.

"If you ladies get too cold up there, you can always come inside the cabin here to warm up," Randy shouted to them. "I've got two thermos bottles of coffee."

"Maybe in a bit," Julia said, fully enjoying the brisk, tangy air. She figured, once the sun was up awhile, she would warm up a bit. Catching Ellie's eyes for a second, she turned to look out over the water. The bow of the boat was slapping into the slight chop, sending white foam to either side. Up close, the water looked cold, almost menacing. Julia wondered if she would be able to last even a minute if she fell overboard; she grabbed on to the gunnel tightly for reassurance as the boat headed farther out into Casco Bay.

One thing that struck her as strange was how different real lobstering was from the tourist image of it—which, in point of fact, was all she had had until now. Postcards and books about Maine always made it look so honest and quaint, completely covering over the dirty, smelly aspects of it. She tried to imagine if this was what Randy had to look forward to every morning, heading out to sea in cold weather like this and sometimes even worse.

The steady putting of the engine lulled her into a dreamy thoughtfulness, so she was startled when the engine suddenly cut down to a low idle. She looked around and saw Randy, one hand on the wheel, the other holding a long wood handle with a vicious hook on the end. It didn't take her long to realize that he was going to snag one of the buoys she saw rising and dipping in the swells.

Randy and John were talking, and Julia felt some interest in hearing what they were saying, but she would have felt odd leaving Ellie alone up front, so she stayed where she was and watched as the boat slowed to a stop and Randy leaned out over the side. With one quick swipe, he hooked under the buoy and started to pull in the line. When the rope connected to the buoy was close enough to grab, he leaned the hook against the side of the boat and started to pull.

John, who was standing a bit to the side, signaled to Julia to join him. So, being careful not to lose her balance, she cautiously made her way to the other side of the boat. Ellie, looking as though she would have much preferred to stay home, sat right where she was, staring out over the water.

Randy had to yell to be understood as he described what he was doing. After pulling the rope up enough so the buoy and a smaller float were inside the boat, he laced the rope—or *warp*, as he called it—around a pulley, then wound it around the drum wheel. He flipped a switch which started a motor that was much louder than the boat's. The rope caught and started to come up easily. All Randy had to do was keep it coming and guide it to make sure the rope didn't foul as the lobster pot lifted up off the ocean floor.

The drum on the pot hauler wrung water from the rope, and if Randy hadn't been wearing his oilskins, he would have been soaked through within seconds. Before long, the lobster pot banged up against the protective wooden slats nailed to the side of the boat, and Randy swung it over onto a roughly built wooden stand.

"You got one!" Julia said with unsuppressed glee when she saw a dark green, almost black lobster angrily flipping its tail inside the trap. Its claws clattered like maracas on the wet slats of wood.

Randy turned off the pot hauler and opened the trap door. Grabbing the lobster by the back, he held it up in the air for a quick inspection before banding its crusher claw and dropping it into the holding tank. With barely a glance over his shoulder, he stuck his hand—*God!* Julia thought, *his bare hand!*—into the bait barrel, grabbed one of the fish heads, stuck it onto the bait hook inside the trap, then shut and locked the trap door.

"That's all there is to it," he said just before he dropped the trap over the side and played out the line as it sank to the bottom. "That's one down and fifty-six to go."

John nodded approval, and Julia, who had been thinking it didn't look all that difficult, sighed when she considered how many more traps he had to haul today.

"At the dock, you said you had a short haul today," Julia said. "What did you mean by that?"

Randy was back at the wheel, steering a course for his next buoy. The engine was racing loudly again, so he had to lean close to her as she repeated her question.

"Altogether, I've got more than three hundred 'poverty boxes' is what we call 'em," he said. "Well, in the summer I do, anyway. Now that winter's comin', I start takin' 'em out, but I still have over a hundred and fifty. A short haul is when you do a little less than half of your traps and leave the rest for the next day. By alternating back and forth, you don't bust your ass quite so much. No reason to, now that tourist season's over."

Julia nodded agreement and then went back to rejoin Ellie at the bow of the boat, grateful to be away from the nauseating bait smell. No matter how interesting all of this was, she didn't think it was worth putting up with the stomach-churning aroma which now saturated Randy and hopefully *not* John.

Randy pulled a few more traps, and then John pitched in and started to help him. At first, Julia thought his motions seemed tentative as he reached out with the gaff and tried to hook the buoy, but after a while, with Randy's help, he started getting relatively proficient at it. Several times, either when his grip on a pot would slip or he held on to the warp too long when throwing the pot back in, he and Randy would hoot and holler, and Julia was pleased to see that it looked as if he was genuinely enjoying himself. Randy got out a thermos of coffee, and Julia and Ellie came back to share it with them, but mostly they kept to the front of the boat, letting the sounds of the men working, as well as the conversation-killing steady throb of the engine and the lapping of waves, lull her into a relaxed, almost dreamy state.

As the sun rose, cutting but not entirely removing the morning chill, the ocean turned a brilliant blue. Farther out to sea, Julia could see rough-looking whitecaps—"heavy chop," Ellie told her they were called. But here in the shelter of the islands, the water was calm. Shimmering light, so bright it hurt her eyes to look directly at it, trailed alongside the boat as Randy took them farther out to sea. Randy had shouted to them, explaining that they would make a wide loop out around Chebeague, then circle in so they could get a good view of Portland harbor . . . the "tourist trip," as Randy called it.

After a bit more than two hours, Randy had quite a catch of lobsters, and John worked efficiently alongside him, no longer a hindrance. He was opening the traps, rebaiting hooks, and sinking the traps almost as quickly as Randy could.

And as they worked, Julia noticed that John and Randy were relating better as well. The night they had visited Randy and Ellie, and even this morning when they were starting out, John had treated both Randy and Ellie with a cool distance, at best. Julia thought it had been more outright hostility. But now Randy and John seemed to have rediscovered and started to share whatever they had had as best friends in high school. There were plenty of off-color jokes, which Julia and Ellie chose to ignore, and good-natured fooling around, trading insults and verbal abuse in the manner of close friends. It made Julia doubly enjoy the morning and the fact that, even at the expense of her stomach, she had come along.

It was while they were stopped, after John had gaffed a pot and had started to haul it up, that Julia chanced to glance over the side of the boat and saw something.

"What the—?" she said aloud, shifting quickly into a sitting position but not taking her eyes off the water for an instant. There had been a flash of motion just to the side of the sun's reflection —something that hadn't looked quite right.

"Are you getting seasick?" Ellie asked, concern registering on her face as she moved closer to Julia.

"No," Julia said, "I—"

She cut herself off, and then, just as she was leaning over the rail, straining to see what might have been shimmering below the surface next to the boat, John let out a loud shout.

"Come on, you mother-humper!"

"What, did it fetch up on you?" Randy asked, leaning from the house.

John had flipped off the hauler and was straining to hold on to the warp. His mouth was set in a hard line, his teeth exposed.

"I don't know what's the matter," he said sharply. "But if you don't give me a hand here, I think we're gonna lose a pot."

Leaving the wheel, Randy came over to the side of the boat and took the rope from John.

"I think I just saw something underneath the boat," Julia said, looking past Ellie to the men struggling with the lobster pot. She realized there was a nervous waver in her voice, but all she could think about was the theme music from the movie *Jaws*. She didn't know what she had seen, but there most definitely had been *something* . . . something long and dark shifting beneath the surface, just out of sight.

Randy was still holding on to the line, trying to jiggle it free. "Might be caught up in some kelp or something," he said. "Take this and hold on tight. Lemme try—"

He didn't finish the sentence as he handed the rope to John and, easing the engine up a bit, swung the boat around to approach the pot from the other side. Once he had come about, he cut the engine again and took the rope from John, but no amount of pulling would get the trap free.

Julia meanwhile, was looking back and forth from what the men were doing to the water. Even while Randy was bringing the boat around, she could have sworn she saw the blurry motion repeated. It wasn't much, what with the rippling surface of the water refracting the light, but at one point she could have sworn she had seen something swimming right alongside the boat, even as it turned. Of course, in the ocean it was entirely possible that a fish—or maybe a school of fish that looked like one big one—would follow along beside a boat. The only part Julia was having trouble accepting was that it had looked as though whatever she had seen had *legs* . . . that it had given a quick, powerful kick underneath the water's surface.

"Could there be . . . something like a big fish—maybe a shark tangled up in the line?" she asked Ellie.

"I'm not the person to ask," Ellie said with a shrug of her shoulder.

Julia suddenly got the crazy thought that there was a gigantic lobster down there, holding on to the rope, ready to seek revenge on all the local lobstermen—starting with Randy. Her mind filled with images of giant insects and crabs from half a dozen lame-brained science fiction movies from the fifties. Why not an over-sized lobster?

Julia dismissed her wild speculations, but found no reassurance in Ellie's confused expression. She knew there was *something* down there. Looking off the lee side of the boat, away from the sun, the water was darker, even more impenetrable; it rippled alongside the boat like splotches of ink. Still, though, she could see a hint of motion, as though something was keeping pace with the boat.

Could it just be the shadow of the boat reflecting in the water? Julia wondered. That seemed possible, but even as the boat turned, now and again the flicker of motion seemed to travel in the opposite direction, darting back and forth, staying close to the boat. She couldn't shake the impression that she had seen, for just an instant, the blurred image of legs—*human* legs—kicking as though—crazy though the thought might be—there was someone swimming alongside the boat a good six feet or more beneath the surface.

"We may have to just give this one up," Randy said, glancing at John over his shoulder as he continued to try to get the pot free. "That's funny, though. The bottom here's usually pretty smooth. Huh!"

He pulled on the line so hard the boat started listing seriously to the side. Julia shivered and looked longingly at the nearest land when she started to imagine all four of them falling over the side of the boat and into the icy water.

"Well, you've gotta expect it now and then," Randy said. "Least I can save the buoys."

Taking a six-inch knife from his belt sheath, he started sawing through the strands of rope. When he was about halfway through, the tension on the rope made it snap with a loud *thwang*. The rope jerked back into the water so fast Julia had the impression something down there had yanked on it. The sound it made reminded her of the sound a bullet would make hitting the water, and she remembered the day she watched Frenchie unload his rifle at the wharf rats.

Randy coiled up the rope he had salvaged and tossed it to the stern. "The storm we just had probably stirred up the kelp beds," he said, shaking his head with disgust. "I hate like hell to lose any pots."

"Occupational hazard," John said as he shook out a cigarette and lit it.

Julia was giving them less than half of her attention, though, as Randy opened up the engine and started toward his next buoy. She was still convinced there was something under the boat, and she jumped with a startled scream when she heard a heavy thump from below.

"What was that?" she asked, looking anxiously from Ellie to John and Randy.

Ellie shrugged. John and Randy, apparently, hadn't heard her.

"I didn't hear anything," Ellie said, shaking her head. "Maybe we hit another buoy."

"It sure sounded like we did," Julia said, her voice tightening like a coiled spring.

Glancing over the side again, she froze when she saw eyes— *human* eyes!—staring right back up at her. In the instant that her body flooded with panic, she tried to convince herself it had just been her own face reflecting in the water, but staring down, she saw that the eyes looking up at her were wide. They appeared to be glowing with an unnatural brightness, but even as Julia was trying to register what she was seeing, the eyes seemed to fade away, sinking back down out of sight into the murky depths.

"John—" she started to say, but then caught herself. He looked at her, but she simply shook her head, feeling foolish.

"Is something the matter?" John asked, making his way carefully over to her. "You're not feeling seasick, are you?"

"I should'a given you some Dramamine before we left," Ellie said apologetically.

Julia tightened her lips and shook her head. She was thinking, *If only it were that simple.*

No, John, I'm not seasick. I'm watching someone following us, swimming underwater beside us!

The idea hit her that it might be a mermaid, and she almost laughed aloud. *Almost.* But that really was the impression she had . . . of a person with long, flowing hair, swimming on her back just below the surface, looking up at her. *How?* Longingly? Angrily?

And why do I think her? Julia wondered, feeling panic tug at her mind. *Why do I assume it's a she?*

"Look over the side here. Do you see anything?" Julia said, pointing down over the gunnel.

Both Ellie and John obliged her, stared for a moment at the ocean sliding past the moving boat, then looked back at her. John shook his head. "Sorry," he said. "Just water 's far as I can see."

"I don't see anything, either," Ellie said. Her face twisted between concern for Julia and caution.

"I—" Julia said, then halted, searching for just the right word. "I'm not sure. I thought I saw something moving down there in the water."

"Could have been some of the kelp Randy said the storm might've stirred up," John said. "I don't know. It could have been almost anything."

By this time, Randy had gotten to his next trap. He put the engine into neutral, bringing the boat to a stop, and set to work hauling the pot. As the hydraulic drum whined, pulling up the lobster pot, Julia sat tensed, expecting at any minute to hear the hauler whine louder as it struggled to pull free another pot that was snagged on the bottom. But this one came up easily, and Julia let out a thin sigh of relief, telling herself to calm down and not get overexcited about things.

What kind of things might be down there? Julia asked herself. For an answer, all she had to do was look—or *try* to look—over the side of the boat.

Had she really *seen a person's eyes?* she wondered, *or had it just been a trick of the interplay of her reflection with the water and sunlight?*

Julia became convinced there *was* a person down there, floating beside the boat, swimming on her back. If she looked now, she thought, she would see her down there. Her eyes would be closer to the surface now . . . so close Julia would be able to peer right into them. Tension wound through her like taut bared wire as she imagined, not just *eyes,* but *hands* as well . . . swollen, white, water-wrinkled hands slapping like dead fish on the side of the boat as they tried to find a hold, tried to get enough purchase to pull up. . . .

Julia knew it was impossible! No one—no human being— could possibly be swimming in water this cold, staying under for this long as she . . .

Why do I keep thinking she? Julia wondered.

. . . followed the lobster boat out into the bay. It *had* to be something else . . . the kelp, as Randy said, or a fish, or maybe a sea otter like that one up in Rockport several years ago. What was his name? Andre? Yeah, Andre the seal. Hadn't she read something about how Andre used to follow fishing and lobster boats, making a nuisance of himself?

Over the sounds Randy and John made working, though, Julia *did* hear a heavy, wet slap against the side of the boat. Her imagination was now spinning into overdrive, and her mind was flooded with the frightening image of those *eyes* . . . coming up closer to the surface, of those *hands* . . . reaching up to the side of the boat.

Swallowing before she sucked in a deep breath of air, Julia slowly turned away from watching Randy and John. She could feel her hands clench into fists, and her shoulder muscles bunched up as though she were about to take a punch at someone. She inched her way to the side of the boat and then, bracing herself, let her gaze dart down to the water.

In one frozen instant, her mind literally blanked, becoming nothing more than a windswept, snowy field as she tried to register what she was seeing. There *was* someone there! A *person!* And there *were* eyes—cold, blank, *dead!*—staring up at her! There *were* hands, reaching up to her out of the water. Hands as cold and white and thin as—*a skeleton's* her mind shrilled—reaching up, breaking through the surface of the water and then, slowly, gently waving to her . . . beckoning for her to lean over the side of the boat . . . to look closer . . . to *come* closer. . . .

Waves of dizziness crashed over Julia as she stared in disbelief at the figure in the water. It *was* a girl . . . a young girl.

Not much older than Bri! her mind screamed.

The girl's long, dark, flowing hair twisted and tangled in the ocean currents. Her thin legs scissor-kicked in long, languid strokes that easily kept pace with the boat. She was suspended in the water, floating gently several feet below the surface, her image distorted by the rippling waves as she bobbed like a feather riding the breeze. She held her hands almost pleadingly up toward Julia, her long, narrow fingers curling as she beckoned.

"No . . . I," Julia stammered. She took one short step backward and thumped into the boat housing. Unable to force the image from her mind, she tried with a desperate effort to tear her gaze away, but those eyes . . . those cold, staring eyes shot like coldly burning sparks into her soul. Like whirlpools, they seemed to drag Julia forward to the side of the boat against her will. Seaweed and black slime dangled like bracelets from the hands as they waved to Julia, luring . . . drawing . . . pulling her to the side of the boat.

"...*come*..." a voice whispered, rasping in Julia's mind like the hiss of metal on stone.

Julia felt caught up in a spinning darkness. She was nearly helpless as she was drawn closer to the side, her gaze transfixed by those eyes... those *cold* eyes!

"...*come*...*to*..."

One more step forward brought Julia right up against the gunnel. She gripped the rail tightly, her knuckles going bloodless as she leaned out over the water, fighting—yet deep inside herself *not* wanting to fight—the irresistible pull of those *cold* eyes... those dead, white hands.

"...*come*...*to*...*me*...."

Sunlight, shattering like diamonds on the ocean, dazzled her eyes, burning like fireworks into her retina, leaving tiny spinning afterimages that danced on the water. The dark shape beneath the surface rippled and almost resolved itself into a clearly defined human shape, but the eyes and hands reached up to her.

"No!" Julia shouted just as Randy gunned the engine of the boat and started forward. Caught off balance, she started to feel herself going over the side of the boat, but then something— someone snagged her by the arm and pulled her back.

"Julia! For God's sake! Be careful!" Ellie yelled above the roar of the boat's engine.

Julia lurched to one side, breaking free of the grip Ellie had on her. Swinging her arms wildly as she fought to regain her balance, she still felt something drawing her like a piece of iron helpless in the power of a magnet.

"...*come*...*to*...*me*...*Julia*...."

John turned when he heard Ellie shout, and he came running over to her as Julia slumped back against the boat housing.

"Honey, are you all right?" he yelled. He looked anxiously at Ellie for an explanation which she didn't have.

Julia looked frantically from her husband to Ellie and then back to John. She grabbed him by the shoulder and held him as close as she could. His breath was the only warmth she felt as it washed over the side of her face. Her eyes felt as if they were jumping out of her head. She was sure her face was pale... as deathly pale as...

As those hands! she thought, feeling her panic increase with a rush that was almost audible. *Those hands... reaching up to me!*

"No... the—umm, I think I kind of lost it there," she stammered. To her own ears, her voice had a funny distorted vibration to it. "Maybe I'm getting seasick, you know?"

"You look like shit," John said, shifting to one side and hugging her tightly. "For a second there, I thought you were going to fall overboard."

"Yeah, when the boat started up, it kind of caught me off guard. I guess I lost my balance, and my stomach just sorta went."

"Well, now's certainly not the time of year to take a swim," John said, forcing a laugh. He had only caught a glance before Julia fell backward, but he clearly had the impression that she had been about to jump, not fall, into the water.

"Yeah, I . . . well, I don't know," Julia stammered. "I think I'm gonna lose it."

She looked almost desperately at her husband, wanting to tell him what she had seen. *No!* she commanded herself. *Not saw! Thought I saw!* She wasn't exactly sure why, but she couldn't bring herself to do that. It wasn't that she was afraid he would think she was crazy.

Well, what else would you call it? her mind whispered.

"Why don't you come inside and have some coffee?" John said. His voice was strong and kindly, reassuring, and it helped dissolve some of the raging panic she was feeling. "You're really looking pale. You probably ought to sit down and rest a bit."

Randy stuck his head around the corner of the boat housing and said, "We can head on in if you're not feeling well. This ain't really a workday for me, anyway."

Julia started to walk toward the boat housing, but each step felt shaky; she was infinitely grateful to have John to lean on. She shook her head at Randy's suggestion, though. "You've got work to do," she said. "I don't want to screw up your day just because I got a little queasy."

"I could let you and Ellie off at the float," Randy said. "John and I can always come back out later and finish off." He glanced at his wife, who had followed them inside the small cabin. The look of pleased expectation on her face was impossible to ignore.

John held Julia's elbow and assisted her in taking a seat inside the housing. "You know, you may be coming down with that flu Bri and I just got over," he said. "You shouldn't take any chances."

"I'm all right . . . really," she said, reaching for the thermos of coffee and pouring herself a cupful. "I just lost my balance there for a second. That's all. I'll be all right. I'm sorry I spoiled it for the rest of you."

For the next hour, as Randy and John finished up hauling the remainder of Randy's traps, she maintained her brave front, but for the rest of the time they were on the boat, she couldn't stop wondering exactly what she had seen. Maybe, as John had suggested, she was getting the flu bug. If she was running a fever, she might have imagined it all. But she thought—and she shivered whenever she looked toward the side rail of the boat—it had *seemed* so clear, so definite . . . those *eyes* staring up at her, and those *hands* reaching for her, and that *voice!*

"*. . . come . . . to . . . me . . . Julia. . . .*"

While they finished out the morning, even the slightest little slap or thump on the underside of the boat sent waves of goose bumps rippling up Julia's arms.

By the time they had moored the *Bait Barrel* and rowed the punt back to the dock, what she had seen had begun to recede. The images were still there—those *eyes* . . . those *hands* blazing in her mind like a glowing branding iron—but she had begun to see that, rationally, she couldn't have really seen someone swimming under the water by the boat. It was impossible! And whatever rational explanation there was, even if she never discovered it, she came away from the experience with one very clear thought. She was *never* going to go out on a boat, lobstering or otherwise, for the rest of her life!

FOURTEEN
Ice Maiden

I

A blue funk, that's what Julia called it, even though it wasn't Monday and it wasn't even morning. It was Wednesday afternoon, and she couldn't shake the feeling of . . . well, it wasn't exactly depression. It was more like a fatigue, both mental and physical.

Frank had come back from visiting friends down at the wharf and, after a light lunch, was in his bedroom with the TV blaring away; no doubt asleep, Julia thought. John was at work, and Bri was at school, and Julia was bored out of her mind! She had done the grocery shopping on Monday, as usual, and done all the housecleaning she could stand. With Robert Parker's latest

Spenser novel spread open on her lap, she was sitting in the living room, staring blankly out the window.

After the cold—and frightening—ride in Randy's lobster boat on Saturday, she had come home with a bone-deep chill that she had been positive would turn into a full-scale fever by night. It only made sense that it was her turn to get what John and Bri had just gotten over. But by Sunday, although she still felt a little less energy, she hadn't gotten sick—certainly not as badly as John and Bri had. She figured she was fighting off a light touch of the flu, though, and that's what accounted for her inability to get interested in anything. Even the Spenser book wasn't holding her interest!

Earlier in the day, she had considered taking a walk, but the weather had gotten increasingly colder since Saturday, and she didn't want to take any chances of lowering her resistance if she was fighting off the flu. So, instead, after running a few loads of laundry through, she made herself a cup of spearmint tea—that "unnatural" tea, as Frank called it—and settled herself in the living room to read. The only problem was, the stillness of the house, cut only by the indistinct buzz of Frank's TV, worked on her nerves and drew her attention away from her book.

She had a lot to consider, too, and thoughts and feelings she didn't like having kept intruding on her mind.

Like, what was the meaning of that note she had found: I WON'T FORGET WHAT . . .

What?

Who wrote the note and why?

And, more importantly, why had John been hiding it from her? He had purposely stuffed it under the couch cushion and then, when he thought she wasn't around, gotten it and thrown it away.

Why?

And beyond that, why did she suddenly feel like she couldn't even trust her own husband? She was desperately wrong if something as simple as that note—*but is it so simple?* she wondered —could shake her trust in John.

But then, why hadn't she told John, honestly and upfront, what was on her mind? Even if she hadn't confronted him about the note, why had she felt she couldn't mention what she had seen swimming in the water beside the boat? She knew it wasn't just that she thought he would think she was crazy. They had always had an honest and open relationship; they prided themselves on never hiding anything from each other. But—and it hurt like hell to admit this—for the past few weeks—since they'd moved to Glooscap, if she was really honest with herself—John *had* been acting as if he was hiding something from her. Maybe it was as simple as his not wanting to live here with his father, or that he didn't like his new job. Certainly, it *couldn't* be that he loved her any less, but something was galling him; something was eating him up from the inside. She knew him well enough to know that!

Wishing desperately that she had someone to talk to about all this, she let her gaze drift to the phone. If she had felt well enough she would have dialed her friend Sue back in Vermont and talked it out. Over the years, they had been through plenty together, and Sue just might see an obvious angle that she was missing!

But something inside her made her not want to break the closed silence of the house. She felt a small measure of contentment just sitting on the couch, watching small motes of dust spiral through the shafts of sunlight filtering through the curtains. The droning of Frank's TV receded to nothing more than a distant insectlike buzz, and Julia sat there, staring blankly into space, letting her thoughts roll around in her mind until . . .

. . . she became aware of a very light *tap-tap* sound.

By the time it had intruded on her awareness, she felt as though she had been hearing it a long time before she became aware of it. She shifted her feet to the floor, letting the Spenser book drop to the floor as she craned her head around, trying to find the source of the sound.

It seemed to be coming from the kitchen . . . a steady, faint tapping, as though someone was rapping lightly on the window. Just as she walked around the side of the couch and entered the kitchen, the tapping sound stopped and she saw a fleeting shadow shift away from the window.

Her first impression was that there had been a bird sitting on the sill and pecking, for whatever reason, on the glass. But before she relaxed the tension in her shoulders, she heard the sound coming from behind her, from the living room.

Julia almost called out to Frank to ask if he was doing something that might be causing the sound, but she knew he napped every day at this time; there was no sense disturbing him. She turned and walked into the living room and almost screamed aloud when she clearly saw the silhouette of someone through the front door window. Before she could blink her eyes, though, the figure seemed to ripple and then was gone. The person's silhouette didn't duck away to one side; it was simply . . . *gone!*

Am I imagining things? she asked herself. She was torn between wanting to walk boldly to the window, pull aside the curtain, and look out . . . and simply ignoring it, going upstairs instead to lie down and pretend she hadn't seen anything.

But she *had* seen something, and as her mind began to replay what she had imagined seeing in the water alongside the boat last Saturday, she felt a chilled sense of worry.

Am I losing my mind? she wondered. *Is there something wrong with me? Maybe I do have the flu, and it's making me hallucinate things!*

The thought that perhaps the pressure of moving and trying to adjust to island life had affected her more than she realized sent a cold panic through her, but they had been in Maine for almost two months now. That excuse wasn't going to hold for much longer. Julia's hands felt clammy, and a swirl of cold air, as though the door had been left open, sucked up around her, making her shiver.

I'm getting sick, she thought, eyeing the couch and her unread novel lying facedown on the floor. The muscles in her legs felt as if they had turned to jelly. Waves of cold swept up her back, making her teeth chatter. Staggering backward, she grabbed the couch arm for support. She was starting to ease herself down when the tapping noise sounded again—from behind her, at the dining room window!

Her legs almost gave out from under her as she swung around to look, and yet again she thought she saw a hint of motion as someone ducked down beside the house.

"This isn't very funny," she sputtered under her breath. She didn't have the strength to shout as she strode over to the closet by the front door. Grabbing her heavy jacket she shrugged her arms into it and, swinging open the front door, stepped out onto the front doorstep. With her first breath, the cold autumn air hit her lungs like a hammer. She gasped, and her eyes began to water as she looked around the sides of the house.

The grass was yellow and matted and showed no sign of footprints by either the living room or dining room windows. Pulling her collar close to her neck, Julia came down off the steps and walked slowly around the side of the house. Frozen soil crunched underfoot, sounding like someone grinding away on a mouthful of breakfast cereal.

Julia walked to the corner of the house and looked down along its length, but she wasn't surprised to see that there was nobody there. She was thinking there never *had* been anyone outside the house. She had imagined it all, due—probably—to the fever she knew now for *sure* she was running. It was either that, or else Bri had gotten home from school early and was playing some kind of trick on her.

"I caught you!" she yelled suddenly, and then, turning, she quickly dashed back around the front of the house to the Oak Street side, where she could see both the living room and kitchen

windows. Again, though, there was no sign of anyone . . . no
footprints in the matted grass or anything to indicate the sound
had been other than her imagination.

With a deep sigh that came out in a thick plume of cold mist,
Julia turned and started back toward the front door, but she had
taken no more than two or three steps when the front door, which
she had left open, slammed shut with a loud bang. It sounded like
a gun going off close to her ear. Julia jumped with a startled shout
and stared wide-eyed at the closed door. And as she walked
slowly back to the steps, she was convinced that, just below the
crunching sound her feet made in the dead grass, she could still
hear that low, steady *tap-tap* sound on a window, only now it was
coming from inside the house!

Julia mounted the steps and reached for the doorknob, convinced that it wouldn't budge when she turned it.

It'd be just like my luck today to lock myself out, she thought as
she turned the knob. To her surprise, it opened, and it seemed as
though, as soon as she stepped inside, the faint tapping sound
stopped.

Shaking her head, convinced she was just letting her nerves get
the better of her, she took off her coat and hung it back up in the
closet. If she had been feeling poorly before, she felt much worse
now, and her only thought was to get to the couch and lie down
before she collapsed on the floor.

Lurching forward with her arms out in front of her like Frank-
enstein's monster, she walked slowly over to the couch, thinking
she wanted nothing more than to sink down onto the cushions and
let sleep pull her down.

Damn any tapping sounds, she thought. *Damn it all! I feel like
a piece of homemade shit!*

Her knees bumped into the couch arm and she pitched forward,
letting her arms flop out to the sides. The knuckles of her left
hand dragged on the floor, but she didn't care. There were tiny
spots of light swimming in front of her eyes like amoebas—even
when she closed them. She reached up for the afghan on the back
of the couch and pulled it down on top of her, but she knew it
wasn't going to be enough to cut the chill that was now screaming
like a blizzard through her body.

As she drifted off into a thin, disturbed sleep, the *tap-tap* sound
seemed to come again, but now not from just one window at a
time. It was louder, and it rattled every window in the house until
it sounded as though the panes of glass would come ripping from
their frames, exploding inward to shatter on the floor. It sounded
as though a howling winter storm—like the chill racking her
body—was throwing its full strength against the house. Icy

fingers knocked on the windows and reached up under the clapboards, trying to tear the glass and wood away.

Julia had no sense of how long these sounds continued, growing stronger and stronger, but suddenly another sound, as though from another world, intruded on her awareness—the screeching of the school bus brakes.

Bri's home, Julia thought, rolling her head to one side and staring dumbly at the door.

From the street in front of the house, she heard with unusual sharpness the sound of the school bus door opening and a brief burst of laughter and shouted conversation from the passengers that cut off just as suddenly as it had begun; then the sound of Bri, coming up the walkway and opening the front door.

"I'm home!" she shouted.

"And not playing with the windows anymore," Julia said as she tried, without much success, to sit up on the couch.

"God, you look *awful,*" Bri said as she walked into the living room and, slinging her backpack off, looked at her mother.

"Same to you," Julia said.

"No, I mean it," Bri said as she came over to the couch and put her hand on her mother's forehead. "God, you're burning up with fever."

Julia was trying her best to look directly at Bri, but her vision kept wavering in and out, as though she were looking through a telescope and someone else was fiddling with the focus. She could still hear a loud chattering sound, but it took her a long time to realize that it was her teeth, not someone outside tapping on the windows.

"I guess I caught a chill when I went outside," Julia said weakly. "I thought you were tapping on the windows . . . trying to play some kind of trick on me."

"I just got off the school bus," Bri said with a shrug. "Do you want me to get you anything? Ginger ale or something?"

Julia shook her head. "No . . . not really. But I saw someone out there. Maybe it was your friend Audrey stopping by looking for you."

Bri opened her mouth to say something, but no words came out. Looking nervously at the floor, she acted as though she hadn't heard her mother.

"Does she have long, dark hair?" Julia asked. She thought she had caught just a fleeting glimpse of dark hair in the window, but then she realized with a jolt that what she was remembering was the girl she had seen swimming in the ocean beside Randy's lobster boat.

Bri's eyes darted nervously back and forth from her mother to the kitchen doorway. "Uh, yeah . . . her hair's kinda long."

Julia was having trouble focusing as she looked up from the couch. She almost drifted off to sleep several times and had to force herself to stay awake.

"Did you see her today at school? Why would she be coming around here before school was out?"

"I don't know," Bri said. She picked up her backpack and started toward the kitchen. "I haven't even seen Audrey since I fell—" She cut herself off before she let her mother know about her near drowning the weekend before last. "For a long time," she finished lamely.

"Oh. So maybe it wasn't her, then," Julia said.

Her mother didn't seem to have noticed her slip of the tongue, and desperate to switch the subject to anything else, Bri asked her if she wanted some aspirin. By this time, though, Julia had drifted back to sleep, so Bri tiptoed out into the kitchen and poured herself her usual after-school glass of milk. The milk was fresh and cold, the expiration date printed on the side of the carton was still more than a week away, but just the mention of Audrey made the milk taste as if it had curdled in her mouth. She ended up pouring more than half of it down the sink; then she went up to her room to work on her homework until her father got home.

II

The worst Julia expected to happen on Thanksgiving Day was that John and his father would plant themselves in front of the TV and watch football games all day. Usually John was so good about helping her out in the kitchen, it never failed to surprise her how, on holidays, he acted as if the kitchen was her job, and hers alone!

This Thanksgiving, though, proved different. If anything, John was helpful in the extreme. He stuffed the turkey for her, kept an eye on it and basted it every half hour, cut and prepared the squash and potatoes, and even had the table set before she had to ask. Julia and Bri felt as if they had been left in the dust because, more often than not, when they went into the kitchen to get started on something, John was already doing it.

About an hour or so before they planned to eat, when Julia went out to start the mashed potatoes and found John getting them ready, she finally figured out what was going on. Glancing at the living room, where Frank sat watching the Patriots smear the Dolphins, Julia leaned close to John and whispered in his ear.

"Are you being helpful because I just got over being sick, or are you doing all of this just so you can avoid—" She cocked her thumb in the direction of the living room, and right at that moment, a loud cheer went up from the stadium crowd.

John frowned and shook his head innocently. "Huh? What do you mean?"

"I mean I think you're being Mr. Helpful in the kitchen because you don't want to spend any more time than you have to sitting in there with your father."

"Cut me some slack, huh, Jule?" He was using a wire masher on the cubed potatoes, and Julia thought she detected just a slight increase of pressure as he pushed down on the spuds.

Julia shrugged and was about to say more when Bri came dashing into the kitchen and grabbed a diet soda from the refrigerator. She picked up instantly on the fact that her parents were having one of *those* discussions, so after popping the can top and taking a glass from the cupboard, she left them alone. After dinner, she had tentative plans to visit Kristin Alexander, a girl she had started being friends with at school recently. She didn't want to say or do anything that might upset those plans.

"Look, John—I mean, since we've moved back here . . . God, it's going on two months now. Have you sat down and talked with your dad? I mean, really talked—one to one?"

John sighed and, letting go of the potato masher, allowed his hand to drop to his side. He gently placed the bowl on the table and slumped in his chair. "No," he said softly. "Not really. I guess there's not that much to talk about."

Julia looked at him sympathetically and shook her head. "Oh, but there *is*. Don't you realize it? Your father's going through a lot right now, what with having to depend on us and everything. He really *needs* you to talk to him."

John did nothing more than snort loudly, but he didn't take up the bowl of potatoes and get back to work. Julia could tell her words had reached him on some level.

"I think—especially on holidays and what with Christmas coming up—he seems to be . . . I don't know. You know him better than I do."

"Not really," John said, shaking his head, his mouth tightening into a firm line.

"I just think it would be nice if you and he could connect on an adult level. God! Ever since we moved here, you've been acting like a kid whenever he's around."

"Look," John said, his face suddenly cast over with a frown. "*I* never wanted to come back here. It was *your* idea—not mine!"

"Let's not start in on—"

John cut her off with a quick, slicing motion with his hand. "As far as I'm concerned, my father and I have nothing more to deal with. I'm his kid; he raised me, and I have to live with the good things and the fuck-ups he gave me. It's too late for either of us to change what we are to each other, all right? So why don't you just drop it!"

Julia was silent for a moment as tears began to well up in her eyes. She was angry at herself for even mentioning it to him, but now she was thinking, *There you go! You've done it! You've gone and spoiled the day!* She took a step back from the table, casting a fearful glance at the living room doorway, afraid Frank might have heard some or all of their conversation. But the TV was blaring away, and when Julia moved so she could see Frank, he seemed totally involved with watching the game. The football players on the screen were nothing more than blue blurs through her tears.

"I don't think it's *ever* too late," she said, her voice a sharp rasp. She knew John would dismiss what she was about to say, attributing it to her own situation with her parents, but she had to say it anyway. "You can *never* say it's too late until the day your father dies. Then and only then can you say it's too late!"

John was looking at her, completely at a loss for words, his eyes stinging a bit. He couldn't stop following her gaze toward the living room doorway. Although he couldn't see his father's back, as Julia could, in his mind he could picture him sitting hunched up in his wheelchair, his thin hands gripping the armrests so tightly the blue veins and tendons stood out in high relief on his pale skin. He could clearly imagine his father's thin face with its wattle of loose flesh hanging down under his chin . . . his thin, nearly colorless lips pressed tightly shut . . . his dull blue eyes, now glazed and dulled by the years, staring blankly at the TV.

"I want you to promise me one thing," Julia said as she wiped her nose with the back of her hand.

John looked at her, raising his eyebrows in a silent question.

"For me . . . as a special gift, I want you to promise me you'll treat your father like you're *both* adults."

"But I—"

This time it was her turn to cut him off with a quick chopping motion of her hand.

"No buts," she said, softly but firmly. "I want you to promise me, maybe some night when Bri and I go out Christmas shopping or something, that you'll sit your butt down and talk to your dad. Try to find out who he is now before it *is* too late."

Slowly John nodded agreement, but when he reached for the

bowl of potatoes, Julia quickly darted forward and took it from him. "And the *last* thing I'm going to put up with is your lumpy mashed potatoes. I'm not going to have you ruin my Thanksgiving dinner with lumpy mashed potatoes!"

"Lumpy?"

"You're darn-tootin', mister," Julia said as she went over to the counter and dumped the contents of the bowl into her Cuisinart and hit the high-speed button. "Why don't you get yourself a beer and go watch the rest of the game? I think I can handle it from here."

III

The rest of Thanksgiving Day went not badly, as far as John was concerned, but not great, either—especially as far as Julia was concerned. Bri was ticked off because her mother had told her she wanted her to stay home with the family, rather than visit her friend Kristin. John ended up spending most of the afternoon in the living room, and Frank was there most of the time, but what little conversation there was between them seemed strained, and quite often hostility surged just below the surface like a hungry shark.

The big dinner was fantastic. In an attempt to get into the true spirit of the holiday, Julia added boiled onions and succotash to her usual turkey, mashed potatoes, gravy, peas, candied yams, and cranberry jelly. The after-dinner desserts—apple pie with vanilla ice cream, and pumpkin pie—went practically untasted because everyone had filled up beforehand.

That evening, Julia suggested that all four of them settle down to play a game, but when they finally agreed on Monopoly and dug out the game box, they found several cards were missing and so had to put the game away. Julia then suggested they go for a walk to help their digestion so they could make room for dessert.

At first Bri didn't want to go along, saying she would rather stay at home, where it was nice and warm, and maybe have a checker game or two with Frank; but Julia persisted, so she finally agreed, grumbling as she pulled on her coat, hat, and mittens.

Once everyone was bundled against the cold, they left by the kitchen door. After a brief hesitation, they decided to turn left and head along Shore Drive in the direction which would—eventually—take them out by the Surfside condos. John silently vowed to himself that he would get them to turn around before they got that far; the last thing he wanted was to catch even a glimpse of that place. Whenever he thought about the bones that had been dug up out there, his blood ran cold. Even when he was a boy, there had been stories about Haskins' barn and the woods around it, and he never had been—and never *wanted* to be—out there after dark.

The road was strung with streetlights every hundred feet or so, but here on Glooscap, the Highway Department hadn't yet replaced the old-fashioned bulbs with modern, glaring sodium arc lights. Even directly under them, the thin light cast weak shadows over their faces. Bri tried to make a joke about how "spooky" they looked, wandering down the road, but everyone's laughter seemed thin and forced.

Their footsteps echoed hollowly in the cold night as they walked past the houses of neighbors they hadn't met. *Why isn't John out and about, reacquainting himself with the life he's known?* Julia wondered. The brightly lit living room windows, most of which didn't even have the shades drawn, flickered with the glow of TVs, looking homey and cozy; the coziness of the homes only made Julia feel colder and more alone.

As John led Julia and Bri along the road, he felt an odd mixture of the past intruding on the present. Other than the hike up Bald Hill, he realized this was the first time since they had moved to the island that he had gone out for a casual stroll through his old haunts. Until now, Shore Drive had been nothing more than a means to get on and off Glooscap and to reach the site of the condo development he was working on. But now—especially at night—the road seemed both intimately familiar and strangely alien at the same time. He could see that, in many ways, it was he, not the road, that had done the changing over the years. Even though there were quite a few new houses on the outer stretch of the road, and in some ways the road looked new, in other ways he felt an odd familiarity, as though he had never left the place . . . or that the boy he had been, the boy who had walked and run and ridden bikes and then driven cars over this road had grown up and was still living somewhere on the island, and he had simply been given that boy's childhood memories.

"Maybe it's just me," Julia said as they walked slowly along the side of the road, "but doesn't it seem to have gotten colder sooner in the winter than it did in Vermont?"

"Colder, maybe, but in Vermont we would've had snow by now," John said with a grunt. His breath was a plume of thick steam that made it look as if he were smoking a cigarette. "It all depends. Sometimes the coast gets snow real early in the winter and it snows a lot all through March. Other years, it just gets really cold and there's almost no snow."

"The cold feels *rawer* here, though," Julia said. "Is it because of the moisture from the ocean?"

"I'd say so," John replied. "What I always liked about it was that we'd get in a lot of ice-skating before the snow fell. We almost never had to bother with clearing off a patch of ice to skate on, like we did in Vermont." John sighed as an assortment of memories and images arose in his mind. "I remember one winter it got so cold, the bay between the island and the mainland froze and you could walk all the way over to the mainland."

"Wouldn't that be dangerous?" Bri asked. "I thought seawater was too salty to freeze."

John noticed, whenever they were under a streetlight, that Bri's eyes would flick back and forth nervously, as though she was trying to see something just on the fringes of the darkness . . . almost as if she was looking for someone.

"Randy and I crossed the frozen bay that winter," John said, "but only on a dare, and—yes—it was dangerous. The whole time we were out there, the ice was crackling and buckling. A couple of times it even split open near me." He chuckled tightly with the memory. "Truth to tell, I was scared out of my mind. If you fell into that water, just imagine how cold it would be! God, you wouldn't last more than a few seconds!"

He was talking to Bri, but his words sent a tremor of fear racing through Julia. As soon as he said the word *water*, she unwillingly dredged up the image she had seen off to the side of Randy's lobster boat. Of course, she knew it would have been impossible for a person to be swimming in the ocean beside the boat that day—even if it *wasn't* winter. But she had seen *something* that had looked like a person, and that didn't stop her mind from manufacturing a whole range of thoughts and images of what it might have been.

"I'd say, just guessing by how cold it's already been this year, we're going to have a really cold winter without too much snow," John said, pumping his arms to heat up his muscles.

"How do you know, Mr. Weatherman?" Julia asked, laughing softly even as her mind filled with the memory of what she had seen. "I mean, it always amazes me how the weathermen talk about what kind of winter we're going to have, and they can't even tell us what it's going to be like twelve hours from now."

"Hey! I'm not making any predictions here," John said. "But

you know, what I *am* thinking is maybe we should check out Larson's Pond. I'll bet it's frozen already and the ice is perfect."

"For skating? Oh, yeah! Kristin said something about that," Bri said, showing interest in the conversation for the first time since they had left the house. "I'd *love* to go skating! Maybe I can call up Kristin and invite her."

"Where is this Larson's Pond?" Julia asked.

"From the house, we'd head up Oak Street and take a right onto Hook Road. It isn't far. We used to go skating there all the time when I was growing up—hockey games and —" He nudged Julia with his elbow. "When we were a little older, skating parties with our honeys. What do you say we check it out tomorrow?"

"And I can ask Kristin?" Bri asked, jumping up and down excitedly.

"Sure—I don't see why not," Julia said, especially pleased by Bri's enthusiasm.

They had come more than a mile now, and were on a stretch of road where there were no more houses. Thick, dark woods lined one side of the road; on the other side, they could hear the soft rolling of the ocean as waves washed up over the rocks. The air was so cold it felt as if it were burning the insides of their noses.

John knew it wasn't too many turns in the road before they would be near the construction site. He stopped under the next streetlight, took out a cigarette, and lit it, drawing the smoke deeply into his lungs. When he exhaled, he tried to keep from staring straight down the dark road as he thought about those bones . . . those damned bones that had been dug up! The woods around him seemed to get darker and draw in closer.

"I don't know about anybody else," he said, letting his teeth chatter loudly, "but I'm freezing my tail off. I think it's time to head on back."

"Same way?" Julia asked, looking back the way they had come. "Back a ways, didn't I see where Hook Road comes out onto Shore Drive? Maybe we could walk home that way."

"We could walk by the pond and maybe check to see if it's frozen," Bri said.

John took another drag on the cigarette as he shook his head. "Not a good idea," he said. "I don't think there are any street-lights along there—or not many, anyway. Besides, Hook Road winds around. We'd end up walking more than twice as far as we would just going straight back. I wouldn't mind getting back quickly."

"What's the matter?" Julia said, suddenly leaning forward and lightly slapping John on the stomach. "Are you afraid you might wear yourself out?"

John laughed and started bounding up and down on his toes like a prizefighter warming up. "I'm not afraid of a little exercise," he said. He was swinging his hands back and forth, clapping himself on the upper arms, but then, before he could say any more, he started coughing. He let the cigarette drop to the street from his mouth and crushed it with his heel as he doubled over, hands on his thighs, and coughed so hard it started to hurt his stomach. The coughing jag lasted only a few seconds. When he was through, he looked up at Julia and shook his head. "I just want to get back and have a slice or two of pie," he said, his voice sounding thick with mucus.

"And ice cream," Bri added.

"What do you say we jog back?" Julia asked teasingly. She wanted to say something about how he should try to quit smoking again, but then she thought his coughing fit was comment enough.

"Let's not get too worked up here, okay?" John said. "If we go skating tomorrow, it'll be exercise enough."

IV

Julia's left knee hit the ice first, and she had enough forward momentum to spin her around in a lazy corkscrew spiral as she slowly fell forward onto the ice. Her skates—somewhere far behind her—made loud, crunching hissing noises as the black ice rushed toward her face. The shock of her hands slamming down hard sent jolts of pain up to her shoulders. She was only vaguely aware of John's loud burst of laughter as she glided to a stop, her face mere inches from the ice.

"You all right?" she heard John shout.

She raised one mittened hand and waved at him to signal she had survived the fall, then started scrambling to her feet. Her skates, though, didn't want to stay directly under her, and with a *swick* sound like ripping cloth her feet shot out from under her again, and she went flat onto the ice.

John's laughter got louder, and in spite of the pain she felt in her hands, elbow, and knees, the embarrassment burning her ears was worse. She was just sucking in the air to yell to him when she saw the arm reaching up at her out of the frozen depths of the pond. Instead of shouting at her husband, a strangled cry came out of her mouth.

The arm—at least it *looked* like an arm—was frozen in mid-motion, reaching futilely up through the five- or six-inch solid ice. Julia could see just the hooked fingers and part of the fore-arm. The rest, from about the elbow down, disappeared into the thick, black depths of closed-in water.

"Jule?" John called.

She twisted her head around to glance at him, but her throat was constricted, and she knew that no words would come out.

"Did you hurt yourself?"

She turned her head back and looked down at the ice, down at what sure as hell looked like a hand, suspended there in the murky depths. She instantly thought that this hand, reaching up toward her, looked just like the hand she had seen over the side of Randy's boat. The memory rose in her mind with an almost audi-ble whoosh.

It's impossible! her mind screamed. *This can't be!*

Behind her, she heard the hissing of John's skates as he skated over toward her. With a loud scraping sound that sent a spray of ice chips flying, he skidded to a stop inches from her and bent down. Resting his hand gently on her shoulder, so gently she barely felt it through the thick layers of coat and sweater she was wearing, he nudged her.

"I'm sorry I laughed," he said, his voice low and kindly. "It didn't look like that bad a fall. Did you really hurt yourself?"

Julia ran her teeth over her lower lip and shook her head, afraid that, if she tried to speak, all that would come out would be an ear-piercing scream. Her eyes were transfixed by the sight below the ice—*that hand . . . like the one she had thought was going to reach up out of the ocean and grab the side of Randy's boat!*

"Come on," John said, trying to hold her under the arms and help her to her feet. "We've been at it awhile. Let's take a break."

"Look," she said, forcing the word out as she pointed to the ice with her mittened hand. "Look . . . down there."

Confused for a moment, John shook his head as he stared at the surface of the ice. He was expecting to see—what? Blood on the ice? Something there that had tripped her?

"Let me help you up," he said.

But his words barely registered in Julia's brain. She was still staring through the ice, staring down at something . . . an indis-tinct figure . . . beckoning up to her. A wave of dizziness crashed over her, and every muscle in her body felt like old, rotting rub-ber. The darkness below the ice seemed to start spinning in an inward-turning vortex that tugged her down . . . *down.*

"Come on," John said, now more forcefully trying to yank her to her feet. "You're not used to this much exercise." He snorted with laughter. "And you said *I* couldn't handle it."

"No . . . I . . ." She started to get up, but her legs felt useless, as though they belonged to someone else. All feeling and control was gone. "Down . . . there. . . ."

John eased her back down, and the solid surface—cold though it was—felt comforting. She brought her face close to the ice and looked as if she wanted to rest her head and fall asleep.

John's first, panicked thought was, *She banged her head! She's got a concussion!*

He looked around frantically for Bri, but she was far down at the other end of the pond, silently spinning circles and figure eights with her friend Kristin. He cupped his hands to his mouth, about to call to her to go get help, when Julia said something. Her face was so close to the ice, her words were distorted and he didn't quite catch what she had said.

"Tell me where it hurts," he said, his voice edged with mounting fear. "Did you hurt your head?"

"No!" Julia said, her voice stronger. "Look . . . *down there* for Christ's sake!"

She banged against the ice with her mittened hand, and this time John saw that she meant below the surface. As soon as he adjusted his focus and his eyes registered what he was looking at, his chest went suddenly cold.

"What the—?"

Julia turned her head around and looked at him with an expression of rising fear. Her blue eyes seemed to bore directly into his mind like tiny drills, laying open every secret he had. He felt as though he was stripped naked and standing in the face of a frigid blast of arctic wind as he saw his own reaction mirrored in his wife's face.

"It . . . it can't be what it *looks* like," he stammered, looking back down at what certainly looked like a human hand, frozen in the ice, reaching helplessly up to the surface.

"What the hell else *could* it be?" Julia said, her voice sounding like a creaking door.

As his initial rush of fear subsided, John sat back on his heels for a moment and, removing one glove, rubbed his hand over his forehead. His fingers felt like hot coals on his skin.

"You tell me what you see," Julia said, feeling a bit better now that she was sharing this with someone, now that someone else had seen it and she knew she wasn't going crazy.

John swallowed with difficulty and, taking a deep breath, looked up at the vault of blue sky for a few seconds before answering. "What it *looks* like is someone's arm," he said. His throat was so raw, he was surprised the words came out at all.

Julia was nodding her head. "That's what I think, too," she said.

They both looked back down at the thing under the ice. John scrambled to one side, trying to catch it from a different angle, but no matter how many angles he tried, it still looked like an arm—*a human arm!*

"That can't be," he said, shaking his head quickly from side to side. "That just can't be!"

"Well, it *could* be a person down there," Julia said. Every breath she took sent ripples of cold through her body. "I mean, it's possible. Maybe someone was swimming out here last summer and drowned." She shrugged as though that had to be the answer. "They drowned, and no one ever found the body. Just before the pond froze, the body started to float up and—"

"Uh-uh," John said, shaking his head. "This isn't a swimming pond. It was always too mucky for swimming, and look." He pointed to the line of dead cattails along the edge of Larson's Pond. "It's practically a swamp. No one in their right mind would come swimming here."

Julia shrugged, unable to stop herself from repeatedly looking down at the frozen arm. "Well, then—maybe someone was out for a hike and fell in and drowned . . . or some kids were playing in a boat or raft and one of them went over."

"They would have sent the rescue team in diving until they found the body, I would think," John said tightly. He fastened his gaze on to Julia's eyes.

"Maybe . . . maybe the person was out here alone . . . or maybe someone on the island *killed* whoever is down there," she said, pointing at the ice, "and they sank the body out here to hide it."

With a sudden grunt, John stood up so quickly he had to wave his arms wildly to catch his balance before he fell backward. His mouth opened, but he didn't say anything; he reminded Julia of a fish that had suddenly been yanked up into the air and was trying unsuccessfully to suck water into its mouth. His hands fumbled in his coat pocket as he reached for his pack of cigarettes and his lighter. He popped a cigarette into his mouth and hurriedly lit it.

"Maybe there's some killer loose on the island, and he's sinking the bodies of his victims into the pond," Julia said. "Wasn't there something a few years ago up in Holland, Maine, where some guy was doing that to kids?"

John exhaled a wisp of blue smoke and shook his head. "Come on," he said. "You've been reading too many mysteries. That probably isn't even an arm." With the cigarette dangling from his lower lip, he suddenly dropped down onto the ice and stared down at the thing. "It's gotta be a tree branch or something, and the distortion of the ice just makes it *look* like an arm. It's too dark, anyway. Don't you think a body that's been underwater for very long would be all white and puffy?"

"How the hell should I know?" Julia asked. "I just think it looks like—"

"Glooscap isn't the kind of place where—" He was interrupted by a cough that rattled in his chest. "Where that kind of stuff happens. Come on—let me help you up. If you stay on the ice like that, you're going to get sick all over again."

"Do you think we should notify the police or something?" Julia said. All she could think was, if that *was* a body down there, the authorities needed to find out.

"Let's take a break," John said. "We can check it once the sun has shifted. With different light I bet we'll see that it's just a waterlogged tree branch. I wish we could have a campfire to warm up."

Julia was silent as she stared out over the ice, but from the angle at which he was looking at her, John couldn't tell if she was watching Bri and Kristin off in the distance or looking at the spot where she had fallen. He could easily see where that was because of the skate marks on the ice.

"If you tried lighting a fire these days," Julia said, her voice soft and distant, "you'd probably get arrested."

John snickered. "Yeah—probably that same group of nutty environmentalists who were protesting the condos would take us to court for polluting the area."

He finished the cigarette and crushed it out on the side of his skate blade and—being environmentally conscious himself—put the butt inside the cellophane of his cigarette package. He flopped back, stared up at the blue sky, and told himself he should feel contented, but he knew what both he and Julia were thinking: *What is it down there under the ice?*

What he was trying his best *not* to think was how that thing that looked like an arm under the ice might be connected in some way to those bones the workers had uncovered out at the condo site. He was *positive* Julia wasn't dwelling on any connection there . . . and he wished to hell he wasn't!

They rested on the edge of the pond for a while; then they went back out onto the ice for a few more turns. Bri and Kristin seemed tireless, so about an hour later, once both John and Julia felt completely wrung out, they took off their skates and put their shoes back on. After telling Bri they were heading home, they each tied their skate laces together and slung their skates over their shoulders.

"You want to check it before we leave?" Julia asked.

John didn't have to ask what she meant. After thinking about it for a second, he nodded agreement. Slipping on the smooth ice, not used to the feeling of not having their skates on, they made their way back to where Julia had fallen. Both of them were tense with expectation as they neared the spot.

"Well . . . ?" John said, standing back as Julia bent down and peered into the frozen depths of the pond.

She was silent for a while; then, frowning with confusion, she looked up at John.

"I don't see anything," she said, her voice raspy. "Are you sure this is the spot?"

John held his hands out helplessly. "It sure looks like it to me. You're the one who fell down here," he said before leaning over and looking for himself.

They spent the next five minutes scanning the area, searching beneath the ice, but whatever they had seen, it sure seemed not to be there now.

"So, what do we do?" Julia asked once she had given up looking. She stood up and brushed her mittens clean on her pants.

"What do you mean—what do we do?"

"Do we call the cops and tell them?" she said.

John barked a short laugh, then shook his head. "Tell them what? That we saw a crack under the ice that looked like someone's arm? Don't be ridiculous! I told you, it was just a trick of the sunlight hitting a sunken tree branch or something. There's nothing down there now."

Julia looked from him back to the ice and, shaking her head, let her breath out slowly. "I *know* this is the place," she said. "But—huh!" She rubbed her forehead with the flat of her mitten. "I guess you're right."

"Come on," John said. "We can get home and heat up some cocoa."

He started to walk away, his feet skittering on the ice. When Julia hesitated for a moment, he turned back to her and shouted, "Are you coming?"

Julia nodded that she was but still didn't move from where she was positive she had seen . . . well, *something* under the ice.

"Come on!" John shouted, his voice now edged with impatience. "Will you just forget about it?"

He turned and continued walking, but in the back of his mind, a small voice was whispering . . .

Forget about it . . . if you can!

FIFTEEN
Nor'easter

I

Exactly a week after Thanksgiving, by midafternoon on Thursday, the first real snow of the season arrived, slamming into the rock-rimmed northeast edge of Glooscap Island like a howling animal. When Bri was settling in to wash the supper dishes around six o'clock, she knew, and secretly rejoiced, that there wouldn't be school in the morning. There *couldn't* be—not if it kept up like this, she thought. Outside the kitchen window, the snow was coming down so fast and thick she could barely see the streetlight on the opposite side of the road.

"'S what the old-timers call a real 'rafter-snapper,'" Frank said, sitting in his wheelchair by the kitchen table and talking with Bri while she worked. "Jus' listen to that wind."

Bri stopped scrubbing one of the pots and listened. The blizzard whistled, low and throaty, as it swung up and under the eaves of the house, and below that sound, she thought she could hear a deeper, lower vibrating sound that was almost like... someone moaning. Actually, she thought it sounded a lot like the noise her father made when he was snoring quietly.

Julia was pacing back and forth between the living room and the kitchen. Every time she entered either room, she would go to one of the windows and peer out into the blinding gray sheet of snow. John had called her from the office over an hour ago, saying he was heading right home, but because of the storm, they shouldn't hold supper for him. He'd settle for a sandwich whenever he got there.

Well, Julia thought nervously, *we finished supper, and Bri's almost finished with the dishes. He should be here by now!* She didn't want to say anything to Bri that might upset her, but just her pacing was message enough.

"I'd reckon, if you don't have school tomorrow, maybe we'll

have an opportunity to play a few games of checkers," Frank said. "'S I recall, I've got a few games to catch up to yah."

"Sure," Bri said, smiling even though the worry her mother was feeling had been transmitted to her, too. In the back of her mind, she was thinking about the term paper she had due next week in History. She hadn't even picked a topic yet, and a long weekend might give her a chance to get it started.

Julia, who had been staring out into the snow, sighed and, turning, walked back into the living room. She had only taken a few steps, though, when the lights suddenly flickered, dimming for a few seconds before brightening again.

"Brownout," Frank said matter-of-factly.

"Do you lose the power during storms very often?" Julia asked nervously. She had seen the stack of year-old firewood in the garage, and figured—if worse came to worst—they could build a fire in the fireplace to keep warm.

If worse came to worst, she thought grimly, *John won't make it home tonight! Please let him drive safely!*

"We don't have too much trouble with it," Frank said. "You might want to get some candles handy, just in case it does go out, though."

While Julia went to the cupboard and fished around for the candles she had stored there, she repeatedly told herself that it was foolish of her to worry like this. Traffic leaving Portland on any given night was slow enough. On a night like this it would be *terrible.*

Besides, she thought, *if something does happen, I'll get a phone call from the police. It's the waiting and not hearing that's the bitch!*

She found little reassurance in that thought, though, as she found the candles and put them on the countertop. She stood beside the counter for a moment, waiting to see if the lights would flicker again. Once she was fairly certain the lights weren't going out—not *yet,* anyway—she walked back into the living room and looked out onto the street.

Already it looked as if there was at least three inches of snow on the ground. With the wind swirling the snow into drifts, it was difficult to tell. Up by the streetlight, the snow was just a thick halo around the feeble light.

"Jesus *Christ,* I wish he'd call!" she whispered to herself, slapping her fist into her open palm. Her breath fogged up the window, and she was just going to head back into the kitchen when the telephone rang. Its harsh *br-ring* cut into her ears like an ice pick.

"I'll get it!" she shouted, her voice wound up tightly as she dashed into the kitchen and snatched up the receiver, fully expecting to hear, not John's voice, but a state trooper's!

"Hello!"

"Guess who?" the voice on the other end of the line said good-naturedly.

Julia had been so startled by the phone ringing, it took her several heartbeats to register that it really was John on the other end of the line.

"Sweet Jesus" was all she managed to say as she slumped back against the kitchen wall, her body flooding with relief. For just an instant, she locked eyes with Bri, who then turned back to her job at the sink. Frank seemed as unconcerned as usual.

"Where the hell *are* you?" she said into the receiver, still not quite believing she had heard John's voice. Her frightened imagination was telling her she hadn't really heard him . . . that the next words she heard would be spoken by a state trooper, who would tell her they had found John's car wrapped around a utility pole on Route 1.

"I seem to have a real fondness for spinning out on this damned bridge," John said.

"What?"

"I just lost sight of where I was in the snow blowing in off the ocean, and I missed the turn."

"You didn't dump the car in the ocean, I hope," Julia said, feeling torn between relief that John was all right and nervousness that he still wasn't home yet.

"I'm fine . . . just fine," John replied. "I went off the road just before the bridge. It was—" He paused and had to swallow before he could continue. "It was . . . strange," he said. "As I was driving onto the bridge, I could have sworn I bumped into a person who was walking along on the side of the road."

"Oh, my God! No one was hurt, were they?" Julia asked with a gasp.

"No, no. Nothing like that," John said. His voice took on a husky edge. "I was—there wasn't even anyone there. I must've just imagined it or something. I don't know. Anyway, a neighbor saw me swerve off the road. I'm up at his house now. He and I tried to push the car back onto the road, but it's pretty stuck. I called for a tow truck, but it might be a while. I just didn't want you to be worried, that's all."

"Oh, I haven't been worried," Julia said, and she caught the sidelong glance Bri gave her over her shoulder. "Not at all. Couldn't you just leave the car there and walk home?" she asked, wishing now more than anything that he was safely home. To hell with the car, as long as John was safe!

"A guy named Smokey, he runs the Mobil station nearby, said he'd be along with his tow truck before long," John replied. "Besides, if we leave it here, it'd probably get plowed under, and we wouldn't find it till spring. I don't particularly relish the thought of trudging a couple of miles through the snow, either. It's getting pretty bad."

"Well, just be careful driving home," Julia said. "I'll have a pot of coffee all ready for you when you get here."

"'Kay," John said. "See you in a bit."

"'Bye," Julia said softly, and then she hung up, grateful that John was at least as close as the island.

II

John arrived home an hour and a half after his phone call. He sat down to a supper of re-heated spaghetti, and after that he started a roaring fire in the fireplace. He, Julia, and Frank, who still seemed impatient for a game of checkers with Bri, were sitting in the living room, quietly enjoying the blaze. Bri was upstairs at her desk, silently cursing her history text. A little after nine o'clock, the lights "browned out" again. They flickered quickly a few times, and then completely winked out.

"I'm ready for that," Julia said as she got up from the couch and went into the kitchen. With the flickering fire coming from behind her in the living room, she got the candles she had gathered earlier. Along with a flashlight and two oil lamps, which Frank kept for just such emergencies, they were ready to tough out the power outage.

"Bri?" Julia called out, hurrying over to the foot of the stairs. "Wait a second. I've got a flashlight. I'll be right up."

Alone upstairs, Bri had had a moment or two of panic as she fumbled her way out of her room and into the hallway to the stairs. It spooked her when the sound of the storm raging outside seemed—as soon as the lights went out—to increase in intensity. She imagined that the wind sweeping up under the gutters was making a faint vibrating noise that sounded like . . . the low-throated rumble of organ music.

Keeping her hand on the wall so she wouldn't lose her balance, she made her way as fast as she dared toward the distant glow of firelight reflecting in the stairwell. Her breathing sounded loud and ragged in her ears, but it was better than hearing the wind as it wrapped its cold hands around the house, sounding like . . .

Church wood! she thought against her will. A shiver danced between her shoulder blades.

Julia held the flashlight on the stairs so Bri could see her way down, and—grateful to be leaving her history book behind—she joined them in the living room.

"Ah, there you are," John said, smiling up at her as she came over and sat down heavily on the couch. He was bent over an oil lamp on the coffee table, trying to trim the wick evenly before lighting it. Julia followed Bri over to the couch and shined the light where John was working.

"Jesus!" he shouted, looking up at her with anger contorting his face. "Will you get that damned thing out of my eyes?" He squinted and waved his hand wildly in front of his face.

"I was just trying to help," Julia said mildly.

"Well, it won't help if you frigging *blind* me!"

"How long do you think this will last?" Bri asked in the awkward silence that followed her father's outburst. She looked from her father to her grandfather to her mother. She knew now—for sure!—there would be no school tomorrow, but she was thinking it would be nice to get all of her homework done tonight so she could really enjoy the long weekend.

"What—the storm or the power outage?" her father asked. His voice sounded a bit snippish, but she did her best to ignore it. She didn't reply as she watched him trim the wick just below the ragged, burned edge, then strike a match and touch it to the wick. A warm, yellow flame licked across the top of the wick and, satisfied, John gently put the clear glass globe back on. Immediately, the flame spread and brightened.

"They probably won't get the power back for a coupla hours, at least," Frank said, his voice a low grumble. He had been thinking about watching some TV, so he was angry about being cut off. "Weather forecaster says the storm's gonna be with us till tomorrow afternoon."

"Boy, that thing sure throws light," Julia said. "It's almost as good as a regular light bulb." She snapped off her flashlight and sat down on the couch, careful not to nudge John. As far as she was concerned, he owed her an apology for snapping at her like that.

"Do you think it'd be bright enough for me to finish my homework?" Bri asked. She still wanted to get the work done, but as soon as the words were out of her mouth, she regretted them. She wasn't so sure she wanted to be upstairs alone while the power was out.

"I don't think it'd be very good for your eyes," her mother said, shaking her head.

"Might be bright 'nough for a game or two of checkers, though," Frank said, smiling widely.

Bri looked at him, nodded, then went over to the closet where they kept the checkerboard. She set it up on the coffee table beside the oil lamp, and Frank rolled his wheelchair around so he could reach it. Bri plunked herself down on the couch and began sorting the pieces.

Satisfied that there was enough light—at least in the living room—and that the water pipes probably wouldn't freeze because of the fire they had going, John got up and walked over to the window. Holding the curtain aside, he looked out at the storm. The streetlights were out, and the few houses he could see were plunged into darkness. He wondered if Portland had lost its power, too. He doubted it; what he remembered growing up was that only the islands seemed to lose their power, practically with every storm.

Julia, deciding that she should make the first move toward an apology, came over beside him and, leaning her face close to his, looked out the window with him. "Pretty, isn't it?" she said. She sighed deeply as she wrapped her arm around his waist and hooked a finger through one of his belt loops.

John grunted and kept his eyes fixed on the snow streaking past the window. It might have just been her imagination, but he seemed to pull away from her.

"Kinda scary, too, though. Don't you think?" she said. A slight shiver raced through her body. "I mean, it really makes you realize how much we depend on things like electricity, how much we take them for granted."

"When *I* was a boy," Frank said, not bothering to look up while he was busy placing his checker pieces on the board, "we didn't even have 'lectricity out here. Like a lot of modern conveniences, you find once you don't have 'em, you don't really need 'em."

"You know what?" Julia said, nudging John in the side. "We ought to go out for a walk."

John looked at her, and the scowl on his face deepened. Shaking his head curtly, he said, "I had enough tromping in the snow earlier this evening."

"Come on," Julia said, giving him a playful shake. "It'll be romantic to see what the island looks like with just candles and lamps glowing in the windows. It'll be like we stepped back a hundred years. All the houses will look so cozy."

"I'm cozy right where I am," John said. "I'd just as soon stay inside on a night like this. It may *look* beautiful, but once you're out there with the wind howling and snow pelting your face, it isn't so pleasant."

"Ah, you're no fun," Julia said. Figuring he was still just cranky and wound up from his drive and walk home, she waved her hand at him in disgust and, leaving him by the picture window, walked back to the fireplace and stood behind the couch to watch Frank's and Bri's opening moves.

John almost turned and said he would go for a walk with her. He was thinking this idea of hers—like the one about going lobstering with Randy—was one of those things she would have to experience before she accepted the truth that romantic notions and reality were pretty far apart. He turned back to look out the window, and as he did, he saw an indistinct fluttering motion outside in the storm. Instantly remembering the person he had thought he had bumped into on the drive home, he felt gooseflesh break out on his arms. For just an instant—no more than half a heartbeat—one area of the solid gray wall of snow seemed to darken like a stain, and take on a familiar shape. . . .

The shape I saw by the bridge, he thought as chills slowly uncoiled through his body. *That damned shape that made me drive off the road!*

The hand holding back the curtain clenched involuntarily into a fist, and he felt the curtain rod sag and almost pull out of the wall. His eyes felt as if they were perfectly round globes as he stared, fighting a rush of panic, out into the stormy night. He didn't know whether or not he wanted to see the shape again or just tell himself it had been an eddy of the wind that, for just an instant, had broken up the steady fall of snow.

Behind him, he could hear the pleasant chatter of Frank and Bri as they played their game, and every now and then Julia would add a comment, but John's mind felt numbed. Was he imagining things, he wondered, or had there really been some*one* out there earlier on the bridge, and now in front of the house? Julia's proposed walk aside, why would *anyone* be out on a night like this? And why in the name of God would they be out in front of his house?

John glanced nervously over his shoulder at his family. In the warm glow of the fire, they did look cozy and warm, almost picture-book perfect. But he was standing away from the fire, and even at this short a distance, the warmth didn't quite reach him. He could feel thin tendrils of cold brush against him.

When he turned and looked out the window, he would have screamed except that his throat closed off as tightly as if cold hands had suddenly reached out and choked him. It was no trick of the swirling winds! It was no illusion! There *was* someone out there, and he could clearly see that *someone* was coming up the walkway toward the front door.

Panic strangled John. His breathing came in sharp, almost painful gasps that fogged the window as he watched, unable to move a muscle as the figure slowly came closer to the door, trudging step after trudging step . . . closer . . . closer . . .

There was no way he could distinguish who it was out there. All he could see was a small, slightly slouched figure wearing— apparently—a long, dark coat that hid her. . . .

Why do I think her*?* he wondered.

. . . feet. The wind whipped around her, fluttering her coat and hair. *Yes!* he could see long, dark strands of hair twisting in the wind. She was almost up to the front steps now, and still—as much as he wanted to—John couldn't move. He stood and watched with horrified fascination.

Any second now, he thought as panic flooded through him. *Any second now there will be a heavy-fisted knock on the door!*

The black shape walked slowly up the steps. As soon as the person was too close to the house for John to see through the window, he stepped back. A funny little sound came out of his throat, but neither the checker players nor Julia seemed to notice. His legs felt as if they were bound by splints as he turned and started for the front door.

It can't be! his mind was shouting. *It's impossible. There can't be anyone out on a night like this!*

But he had seen *someone*!

His hand was trembling as he reached out slowly for the doorknob.

There can't be anyone there! There can't be anyone there! he kept repeating in his mind. He was watching his hand reach for the doorknob as if it belonged to someone else . . . was under someone else's control. He didn't want to open the door. There *couldn't* be anyone out on the doorstep! Not on a night like this!

The doorknob felt like ice as his fingers closed around it and began to turn it slowly. It seemed to twist forever, but then, with a click that slammed his ears like a gunshot, the latch snapped open. The door immediately burst inward, as if whoever was out there had slammed his—no, *her*—shoulder up against it. With a loud tearing shriek, snow spiraled into the foyer; cold wind clawed at his face.

"What the hell are you doing?" Julia shouted, looking over at him as he braced his feet so the door wouldn't slam him back into the hallway wall.

The storm came roaring into the house like an animal unloosed from its leash. As the cold air spun around him for just an instant, John thought he heard what sounded like . . . yes, laughter—thin, high laughter—but he saw instantly that there was no one there

—no woman dressed in a long, dark coat stood on the doorstep
. . . no one . . . just the raw, elemental power of the storm screaming into the house, invading the warmth.

"Will you please shut that door?" Julia said as she walked
quickly over to him. "God, you're letting out all the heat!"

"I—" John stammered. He almost told her that he had been
convinced there was someone out there wanting to come in, but
he clamped his mouth shut and, pushing hard against the door,
finally managed, with Julia's help, to shut the storm back outside.

"For crying out loud, John," Julia said, glaring angrily at him.
"Are you out of your mind? It's cold enough in here as it is. What
did you think you were doing?"

Dazed and confused by what had happened . . .

—*Did I really hear laughter?* he wondered.

. . . he snapped the door lock and took a quick step away from
the door.

"No, I—uh, just wanted to see how much snow had fallen," he
stammered.

"Well, don't open the goddamned door to do that!" Julia said,
rubbing her hands vigorously together to ward off the cold. "I'm
convinced this isn't a good time to go for a walk, all right?"

John nodded and forced himself to smile. "I just thought, you
know, if you needed proof—" he said, his voice tight and high.

He was looking at Julia, trying to forget about what had just
happened, but he couldn't shake the feeling that, even now, there
was someone out there, and if he looked outside, he would see a
cold, pale face close to the window, staring in at him. And in the
very depths of his soul, he thought he would recognize the face
pressed up against the freezing glass!

III

Other than Frank, who opted for his own bed, the rest of them
decided it would be fun if they slept in the living room by the
fireplace. John figured it would be an easy way to keep the fire
tended, and Bri—although she didn't admit it to anyone—didn't
relish the thought of sleeping alone in her room with just a flashlight to find her way around. So after Frank had gone off to
bed—with three out of four satisfying wins at checkers under his
belt—John and Julia folded out the couch, and Bri spread her
sleeping bag out on the floor by the hearth.

Trying to get to sleep, though, with the storm still raging outside was difficult, and long past midnight scattered conversation

was still going back and forth. Finally everyone drifted off to sleep and stayed that way until sometime in the night Julia woke up with a start and nudged John.

"Huh? . . . What?" he muttered, more asleep than awake.

Julia rolled over and looked at him. In the fading glow of the firelight, his face was lined with deep shadows; he looked as if he was frowning.

"Did you hear anything?" she whispered close to his ear to keep from disturbing Bri.

John smacked his lips and said, "No—Christ, I've been asleep."

In fact, he had been having a disturbing dream that he was lost in a rickety old building and was desperately trying to find his way out while a blizzard—suggested, no doubt, by the northeastern howling around outside the house—tore the building apart. The most vivid part of the dream had been the sensation he had of choking; that was so vivid, he woke up with a sickeningly warm taste in his mouth. He was silently grateful that Julia had brought him out of the dream, and as he drifted up to wakefulness, he realized his dream had simply distorted what had happened earlier that evening at the front door. The only difference was that he hadn't been in his father's house. It had been someplace else, but now the dream was fading, and he couldn't hold on to the fragmented images.

"I thought I heard something," Julia whispered. Her voice was wire-tight. "Something like—I don't know . . . it sounded sort of like music."

"Umm . . . church wood," John said, his voice gravelly with sleep.

"What?" Julia said, sitting up suddenly and leaning over him.

"Huh? I don't know what you're talking about," John said. He felt himself being yanked closer to consciousness, but he fought it, wanting to drift back off. He had had enough trouble falling to sleep in the first place, and even a disturbing dream was better than waking up at whatever ungodly hour this was.

"I said I thought I heard music, and you said something," Julia said.

"The wind," John replied, keeping his eyes tightly shut even though he knew his sleep had been shattered. "It's just the wind. The storm's not over yet."

"I thought you said something else," Julia said.

"Give me a break," John said. "Go back to sleep, will you? I'm beat."

Julia eased herself back down and closed her eyes. She let the low whistling of the wind and the pebbly hiss of snow beating against the house lull her, and before very long—once no other sounds came to her in the dark—she fell back to sleep.

John, meanwhile, realized that he was getting farther and farther away from sleep. Earlier in the evening, he had felt uncomfortable about sleeping on the couch again. The memories of the hanging figure he had seen reflected in the window rose up in his mind. Now and again the image began to resolve, and he could imagine seeing the cold, bloated face of the dead person. . . .

She was hanging by her neck. . . . . The frayed rope—as gray and rotting as her skin—had dug deeply into her neck, so deeply it was almost buried in the folds of blackened flesh. . . . . Her tongue—a thick, purple wad of flesh—protruded from between her teeth, almost bitten clean off. . . .

Whimpering softly to himself, John rolled over and stared at the fire. When he closed his eyes, he watched for a while as the insides of his eyelids glowed with orange light. He prayed that the flickering light would dispel the images that were swirling in his brain.

Finally, though, he knew it was too late—he wasn't going to be able to drift back to sleep, so he opened his eyes and just lay there, staring at the warmly glowing embers on the hearth. He listened to the wind shrieking in the darkness outside, but—unlike Julia—he wasn't lulled back to sleep by it. She may have heard music, but he lay there, waiting to fall asleep and dreading that the next sound he heard would be a heavy hand knocking on the front door. . . .

IV

Overnight the world was transformed. Bri was the first to wake up, and she ran to the living room window and looked out at the thick blanket of snow, blindingly white in the slanting rays of the morning sun. Out by the headlands, the sea was roiling blue-green water, smashing into the rocks and tossing white spray high into the air. There was a purity, a freshness to the world that she could feel even before she dressed and went outside. She decided that—Audrey be damned—she was going to take a walk out on Indian Point just to see how beautiful it was.

"Are you going to help your father shovel the driveway and front walk?" Julia asked as she trudged into the kitchen where Bri was already half finished eating her breakfast.

"I wanted to go for a walk first," she said, busily chewing the last bite of toast. "I can't *believe* how beautiful the snow looks! I want to go down to the Point. I'll bet it doesn't even look like the same place anymore."

Julia sniffed and nodded as she fumbled to get the coffee brewing. Without waiting to hear her mother's response, Bri cleared her place and started tugging on her heavy coat, hat, and mittens.

"You just make sure you're careful down there," Julia said once Bri was bundled up and ready to go.

"Oh, don't worry so much," Bri replied. "And tell Dad he can save some of the shovelling for me to do later, all right?" With that, she swung open the door and stepped out into the razor-sharp air.

The closer Bri got to the ocean, the louder the sound of the waves got. Sometimes, depending on the wind, she could hear the muffled roar of the surf from her bedroom, but nothing, she thought, compared to being this close to the sea and surrounding yourself with the sound, the *feel* of its surging power. . . .

The power that almost pulled me under, she thought, and that thought finalized her decision to stay well up on the headlands, away from the water. She could enjoy the brisk air and hear the waves just fine from up there.

She had been right, though, about the snow changing things on Indian Point. It covered everything with an unbroken white sheet. Only down by the water had the waves stripped the snow away and exposed black rock to the bright sunlight. In the twining branches of the scrub brush, thick clumps of snow were caught like distorted baseballs. The rocks and branches on the seaward side were crusted with thick ice—frozen salt spray. Bri started humming the tune of "Winter Wonderland" as she plowed through the snow out to the tip of land. But she hadn't gone more than twenty or thirty feet along the trail before she saw that she wasn't the first person out on the point this morning.

"Audrey . . . ? she whispered as she stared down at the footprints entering the trail from the right. Of course, there was no way to tell who it was, but Bri was pretty certain she wouldn't enjoy her walk, not if Audrey was out here. No way!

The tracks in the snow were fresh—it looked as if small feet, possibly Audrey's, had made them, Bri thought. The edges where the snow was broken were still sharply defined, so whoever had passed through here had done so no more than a few minutes ago!

Bri strained to see through the winter-stripped trees out to the point. There was no reason to shout or to try to hear because of the pounding roar of the ocean, but suddenly Bri wanted to—she *had* to find out if these tracks were Audrey's. If Audrey was out here on the headlands, then she was all set to turn around and head home. The walk could wait!

"No, damn it!" Bri said, slapping her mittens together and ad-justing her woolen hat low over her eyes. "I have just as much right to be out here as *she* does!"

She started forward, struggling through the knee-deep drifts, and she couldn't help but wonder why the tracks she was follow-ing looked as if they had been made so . . . easily—as if whoever was walking out here had lightly skipped through—almost *over* the snow. She was finding it quite a job to plow her way along the trail.

As she went along, Bri had to acknowledge to herself that she *was* following the tracks. She told herself she didn't want to meet with Audrey; she wanted to *avoid* her. She also admitted to her-self that she was more than a little curious to find out who—if not Audrey—would be out here so early after a storm. Maybe it was someone else, someone she could meet and *really* make friends with besides Kristin.

The tracks wound out along the edge of the cliff overlooking the pounding surf. Soupy white foam shot up high into the air as wave after wave smashed into the rocks. Bri paused to watch, feeling equally thrilled and scared by the power of the ocean. Far out on the deep blue water, she saw sea gulls bobbing in the waves like miniature icebergs, heedless of the danger closer in to shore. Bri found herself wondering if sea gulls or seals ever did get swept up and smashed against the rocks to die. She shivered when she thought that that's exactly what might have happened to *her* that day she had fallen into the water. Trying to put such morbid thoughts from her mind, she turned and continued follow-ing the tracks, which had begun to fill in with windblown snow.

The tracks swung back along to the west side of Indian Point, and just before they got to the ledge with a clear view of the harbor, they swung back in under the trees.

"It's Audrey, all right," Bri said under her breath, recognizing the place where, not so long ago, Audrey had stopped their walk and turned around, saying she didn't want anyone down by the fishing boats to see her.

In under the snow- and rime-laden trees, Bri followed the sin-gle set of footprints. She knew that not more than a couple of hundred feet ahead she would come back to where she had first picked up Audrey's tracks, so she was looking for the trail to veer off to the left. She grunted with surprise when the trail continued straight back to where she had initially picked it up.

"What the . . . ? That's impossible!" she said, squinting as she looked back the way she had come, then forward to where she could clearly see where she had started following the trail.

"How the heck can that be?" she wondered aloud, scratching her forehead with the rough wool of her mitten.

There had only been one set of footprints, and she was positive she had followed them around in a circle until they came back to where they started, making one big circle. But that was impossible! She figured she either must have missed where the tracks branched off or...

Is this another one of her tricks? Bri thought. She could feel her heart pounding in her chest, and she was taking little sips of air, like water, through her mouth. Knowing Audrey, the only surprise was that the trick wasn't *meaner*!

Bri suddenly straightened up and, turning her face away from the wind, shouted as loud as she could, "Audrey! I know you're out here." Her voice seemed to whisk away like a dandelion fluff caught by a breeze. "I know you are, and I know what you're trying to do!"

Behind her, the ocean surged and roared, and closer to her, the wind whistled shrilly as it tore through the ice-covered branches, but that was all—no reply came to her...none that she could hear, anyway.

The sun glinting off the snow and the knife-sharp wind brought tears to Bri's eyes, blurring her vision as she looked back and forth along the circular trail in the snow. She supposed it was possible that Audrey—or whoever—could have made a loop around the point and then smoothed over the snow to hide where she had gone. Bri remembered how, back in Vermont after a snowstorm, she and her friends as a joke used to hop on one foot around the base of a tree to make it look as if a person had straddled the tree—walked right through it like in those cartoons.

Or maybe Audrey had simply done one complete circuit and then, while Bri was following her first set of tracks, come around and gone down over the rocks, where the surf had washed away her footprints. She supposed that was a possibility, but it didn't explain why, looking back and forth, she still could only see two sets of tracks—her own and...whoever else was out here.

"Audrey!" Bri shouted again, letting the word tear from her lungs. Her voice sounded frail against the sound of the ocean.

"The heck with you, Audrey!" Bri shouted as her anger boiled over.

Whatever was going on here—even if Audrey was running around in a *million* circles—Bri wasn't about to waste her time playing follow the leader! She had better things to do than try to figure out where Audrey had come from or where she was going! With an angry *harumph*, she turned and started back along the path toward the road. She had promised her father she would help him shovel, she told herself, so to heck with it!... to heck with Audrey!... to heck with *everything*!

As she made her way off the point and back to the road, Bri paused halfway and, looking back over her shoulder, still able to see a portion of the tracks she—and Audrey—had made, she shouted one last time, *"To heck with you, Audrey!"*

SIXTEEN
Father and Son

I

The following Saturday and Sunday were beautiful... sunny and cold with temperatures reaching into the lower teens. "Darn-right seasonable for December," Frank commented when he returned from church and visiting on Sunday afternoon. By Sunday night, though, the sky was overcast, and Bri found herself hoping against hope that the storm roaring up the East Coast wouldn't veer out to sea; she wouldn't have minded another day off from school. By midnight, though, two hours after she had gone to bed but wasn't able to sleep, the snow hadn't started, so she resolved to get up in time for the school bus at seven o'clock.

On Monday morning, Bri and John both agreed that it was a perfect Monday—overcast, cold, and gray. By now the freshness of the snow had been broken by snow plows and footprints and melting. The island took on a desolate atmosphere that made Bri, at least, think this was how life was in Russia all the time.

On his way to work that morning, John slowed after crossing the bridge and, looking down to his left, was surprised to see evidence of his skid off the road. A lot more snow had fallen, and the snowplows had cascaded snow off the road, but still he could see traces of his tire tracks and the tracks left by Harry's tow truck. He shivered and sped past the site, trying as best he could to put the incident out of his mind.

In the office, he lingered for only a few minutes around the coffee urn, then went straight to his office and began work on

drawing the plan for a septic system for an apartment building on
Maple Street in Westbrook. He was finding—as long as he didn't
have to deal with Surfside condos—that the office was the only
place where he felt he could begin to relax.

With blueprints and logbooks and computations spread out over
his drawing board, he tried to immerse himself in his work; but
even though the system he was designing wasn't all that complicated, he found his mind kept drifting back over events of the last
few days, and his feelings of uneasiness grew steadily stronger.
He found himself swearing at the slightest thing—a dropped pencil, a blueprint that wouldn't stay flat.

First and foremost, there was Julia. Something was coming
between them, of *that* he had no doubt. He could see it as clearly
as if someone, literally, had driven a wedge between them. For a
while now she had treated him as though she *mistrusted* him—as
if she didn't believe half of what he said to her, even when it was
about relatively innocuous things.

Of course, in many ways, she was correct in feeling funny
about him because he *was* keeping secrets from her. Several
things had happened lately that he *couldn't* discuss with her. What
happened on Thursday night, for instance, when he had skidded
off the road . . . How could he tell her—and expect her to believe
him—that he had seen a person who one minute was walking
along the side of the road, and the next was sailing up over his
car. And then, when he had gotten out to check on her—*yes,
her!*—she was gone. How could he expect Julia to believe something like that?

Or—worse—those notes he had been finding around the
house. Who was writing them, and what in the name of Christ did
they mean? So far, he had found four, and so far they spelled out
the message: I WON'T FORGET WHAT . . .

Was this someone's idea of a practical joke? The thought had
crossed his mind more than once that it was Randy playing some
elaborate joke on him. But whoever was doing this, he just wasn't
getting the humor. What it made him think of, the memories it
stirred, simply weren't funny. So he had kept this away from Julia
because, first of all, he didn't know who was doing it or why, and
second, he didn't know what it meant—if anything. Why give
Julia anything more to worry about?

And there were other things gnawing at his heart, things a husband didn't like to think about or acknowledge . . . such as Julia's
wanting to have a baby.

On the surface of it, the idea was ludicrous. They had a teenage
daughter—not his own, but he loved her as if she were his own
—and that should have been enough. At their age, the very last

thing they needed was to be strapped down with an infant. God! Just the thought of diapers and teething and "baby-proofing" the house sent shivers up his spine, but Julia's wanting a baby went deeper than that. It also put a harsh light on their sex life.

They had been married more than five years now, and sure, it was reasonable that the romance would diminish. No one can live together day after day and maintain that unique level of being totally bowled over by love . . . not and stay grounded in reality. But ever since they had decided to move back to Maine, their sex life had gone rotten. Maybe it was simply that every damned time they started something, Julia would talk about not using birth control, and that would ruin it for him. It made him feel like a performer instead of a lover . . . or that they weren't as sexually compatible as they had thought. Maybe five years together had doused the flames of passion, and her eyes—as his increasingly were—had begun to wander elsewhere, looking at strangers and fantasizing. Hell, for all he knew, she and Randy had been getting it on.

No, he dismissed the thought as too ridiculous. But maybe Julia's messing around with Randy had something to do with those frigging notes he'd been finding around the house. Maybe they were rough drafts of Randy's frigging *love* letters to Julia!

"Don't be absurd," he cautioned himself, but a seed of doubt had already become firmly implanted in his mind.

But beyond that, there were other things—deeper and darker things—that bothered him. Some he could pinpoint easily enough . . . maybe a little too easily; others made him feel like the proverbial blind man trying to describe an elephant by touch.

Moving back to where he had grown up hadn't been—and still wasn't—his idea of a smart move. His feelings about the people who lived on Glooscap—especially his father—hadn't changed in the least. He didn't think they ever would. He thought he had left all of them and their narrow-minded ways of thinking behind. After all, it had been his father who had pushed him so much, demanding that he go to college, get a decent job, and not end up married to some island girl and finish his days spinning his wheels deeper and deeper into the ground . . . until he was deep enough to bury!

Of course, seeing Randy Chadwick and then experiencing all the high school memories that dredged up wasn't his idea of fun, either. At work he had made a few new friends—especially Barry. He enjoyed that particular relationship, partly because it was new; it wasn't just based on having grown up together, or having been high school buddies. Reconnecting with Randy and seeing how island living had aged him and Ellie both saddened and angered him. He knew that he and Julia could never feel comfortable socializing with the Chadwicks. Just knowing that they had chosen to stay on Glooscap made him feel uncomfortable. He wanted to associate with people who had never known him as "Frank Carlson's boy."

And the workmen finding those buried bones out at the construction site by Haskins' barn! That whole business sent cold, numbing waves of blackness through his mind whenever he thought about what had happened when he was a teenager out there in that barn. There was no possible way Julia—or anyone else, for that matter—could have found out about that night late in the spring of his graduating year.

No way!

It was the one secret he knew he would keep until he died! But things that had happened since he and Julia came back to Glooscap had stirred up those long-buried memories, like a ladle gently stirring up the bottom of a witch's black brew. Just seeing the barn, or simple, innocent remarks by people like Randy Chadwick struck deeply into his mind, sending out dark spiderweb rays of fear and guilt.

"Yo! My man!"

The voice suddenly intruding on his thoughts made John jump straight up out of his chair. His elbow knocked the pocket calculator from the desk. When it hit the floor, the black plastic housing shattered and skittered under the desk.

"Christ! Don't sneak up on me like that, all right?" he said, glancing up at Barry as he bent down and started scooping up the broken pieces.

"Hey, sorry, man. I didn't realize you were so jumpy," Barry said, getting down to help him. "I guess that one's a goner. If you want, I'll buy you a new one." He handed John the few scraps he had collected, and John dropped them into his paper-filled wastebasket.

"No, no. Forget it!" John said, shaking his head. "It was just an inexpensive one I picked up at K-Mart, anyway."

"Been drinking too much coffee or what?" Barry asked. He glanced at the design John had been working on, then locked eyes with him.

"I was just—" He took a deep breath and finished, "Just thinking." He started rubbing his forehead with the flat of his hand. "I've got a few problems at home, is all."

"Nothin' serious, I hope," Barry said, frowning with concern.

John shook his head and tried to sound casual. "Naw. You know how it is."

Barry, who had been married for sixteen years and had four

children, nodded his understanding. "Hell, man, I haven't seen you that jumpy since . . . well, least since that day out at Surfside."

Squinting, John looked at Barry, hoping what he was feeling didn't show on his face. Barry was chuckling softly under his breath and shaking his head.

"I don't think I've *ever* seen anyone get so freaked out. I mean, Christ, you must've been on jobs that uncovered bones before. Any other time, we'd just keep on working, figuring whatever was buried there didn't give a shit no more."

John simply nodded and, as much as he didn't feel like working today, stared blankly at his current project, hoping Barry would get the hint and disappear.

"You know, half of those guys were looking at them bones like they were going to get up and dance, for Christ's sake," Barry said, still jiggling with laughter. "Maybe it was 'cause it was so close to Halloween or something."

"What, uh—whatever became of that, anyway?" John said. He wanted to make the question sound casual, but his throat felt as though it was pencil-thin, and—at least to his ears—his voice sounded unnaturally high.

Barry scoffed and waved his hand in front of his face. "How the hell should I know? I didn't call around and ask. I figured once they called the police in, they'd do their thing. *My* thing was to get as much of the work done out there as I could before the snow covered everything."

"Who would know what they found out about those bones?" John asked. The back of his legs felt rubbery, the way they had that day after skating with Julia, so he eased himself back into his chair.

Barry shrugged. "Call the state police if you're wondering. Actually, I came in to ask you what you think the office should do for a Christmas party this year. The consensus is that it might be too late to plan something before Christmas 'cause everyone's made plans already. Most everyone thinks we should have a New Year's Eve party instead."

John shrugged. "Sounds good to me," he said, still wishing his voice would loosen up.

"If it's no problem, then, I'll put you down in favor of New Year's Eve," Barry said. "It pretty much looks like that's what it's gonna be." He turned to leave, but then paused for a moment at the door. "Sorry 'bout your calculator. Maybe *Sanity* Clause will get you a new one for Christmas."

"Don't sweat it," John said.

It took a major effort not to sigh with relief as Barry wheeled around the corner and was gone. If it hadn't been too obvious, John would have gotten up and closed the office door behind him, but instead, he turned back to the plans he was working on, telling himself he had to get working on them and not just sit there, pondering things that were probably better left alone, anyway.

As he shuffled through the pages of notes he had, jogging them into order, he noticed a single sheet sticking sideways out of the stack, and as soon as he saw it, his hands began to tremble. He recognized it immediately—a single sheet of notebook paper.

Slowly, his teeth clenching and his breath stopping so long his lungs began to ache, he took hold of the edge and slowly pulled it out from his pile of notes.

It can't be! his mind was screaming. *It isn't!*

But as he slowly exposed the sheet of paper, his chest began to burn, and he could hear a steady, rapid pattering sound in his ears, as though his ears were stuffed with cotton. He unfolded the paper, and in an instant it felt as though someone had dashed his eyes with a splash of acid. There, in the middle of the paper, in heavy-handed pencil marks, were the words:

I WON'T FORGET WHAT YOU...

With a low whimper, he shredded the paper, ripping it over and over until it was practically confetti.

Save it for the New Year's Eve party, he thought as a crazy laugh tried to get out of his mouth.

He crumpled the shreds of paper into a tiny ball and jammed the ball into the bottom of his wastebasket. A sharp piece of the broken calculator nicked the back of his hand, but he barely noticed the thin jolt of pain or the tiny beads of blood. His mind was racing along dark, narrow lines . . .

How the fuck did this get here?

And who the fuck is doing this to me?

II

The night was cold and clear when John went out to the garage for an armload of firewood. Overhead, the stars were as bright as chips of diamonds scattered across the rich black velvet of the night. The first breath John took froze the inside lining of his nose, making it sting as if he had inhaled water. Even though his nasal lining was hurting, his teeth were chattering, and his misted breath hung over his shoulder like a scarf, he preferred this moment of arctic cold to being inside the house. Julia and Bri had gone to the mall, leaving him—for the first time since after his mother had died—alone with his father.

The logs he carried clunked together in his arms, sounding exactly like a baseball bat solidly whacking the ball over the center field fence. He wished, somehow, he could stay out here all night, rather than go back inside and sit in front of the fireplace while his father read *Readers' Digest* and he just stared into the flames.

But the cold cut like a knife right through his sweater. Within seconds his hands were so numb he was afraid he was going to drop his load of wood as he dashed back to the kitchen door and hurried inside, kicking the door shut behind him.

"Oughta leave some of the glass in them door windows," Frank said, not bothering to look up from his magazine as John went over to the hearth and dropped the load of wood.

"It's *freezing* out," he said by way of apology. His teeth were still chattering as he pulled open the fire screen and, wincing from the sudden blast of heat, dropped two fresh logs onto the bed of glowing embers. Sparks corkscrewed up the flue as he took the poker and jiggled the logs into a better position, then stirred the coals.

"Should always put three logs in at a time," Frank said. "Burns better that way."

This time Frank *did* bother to look at John, who stared back at him, wanting more than anything to tell his father to mind his own business, but the reflection of the flames in the chrome of his father's wheelchair made him hold back his comment. Sighing, John straightened up, put the poker back, and sat down heavily onto the couch.

"You know—" he began to say, but then he stopped himself and rolled his head back and forth to relieve the tension he felt building in his neck. His entire body felt wound up like a tiger ready to spring at its prey.

"Huh?" Frank said. He stuck his index finger into the middle of the magazine to mark his place and leaned forward a bit in the chair. One of the wheels made a squeak that set John's teeth on edge.

John opened his mouth, wanting to say more, feeling he *had* to say more, but he didn't want to because he knew he would sound like . . .

Like a kid, he thought, feeling a flush of heat that had nothing to do with the fire in the fireplace. He recalled what Julia had said about how ever since they had moved in, he had acted like he was still a boy around his father—as if he weren't an adult. In an ironic way, he could see that it was his father now who was the child, who had become dependent on them. Still, that didn't remove the feeling John had that he would always be the kid and his father would always be the adult.

"You were going to say nothing," Frank said. He reached out to the side and placed the magazine on the end table beside him.

"No—I . . . it was nothing," John said, stammering as he shook his head. He found himself wishing to heaven he hadn't already gotten the firewood; he needed something to do.

"Would you like a beer or something?" John asked as he hoisted himself up to his feet.

Frank nodded and said, "Sure. A beer'd be fine 'bout now."

Grateful to be out of the room, John went to the kitchen, got two cans of beer and two glasses, taking his time about it before walking slowly back into the living room. He handed a can and a glass to his father, who simply grunted his thanks, popped the top, and poured, raising a several-inches-thick head of foam.

"That's not how you pour a beer," John said, wishing, even as he spoke, that he had kept his mouth shut.

"Oh?" Frank replied. "And just how d'yah pour a beer *correctly*? I mean, I always pretty much assumed if yah got it into the glass and from there into your mouth, you were doin' all right." As if a demonstration was needed, Frank tilted his head back, took a long swallow, then smacked his lips with satisfaction.

Not wanting to carry this any further, John simply slouched back on the couch and, dispensing with the glass, popped the top and drank. He wanted to stop bristling at every little thing his father said and yet he also wanted to tell his father how he had made him feel all those years he was growing up. What he had just said, about always putting *three* logs in the fire, was a perfect example of how he had always driven it into him that if he didn't do something *his* way, he wasn't doing it the *right* way!

Especially now, John felt an urgency to talk with his father. After the stroke, he knew he didn't have all that many years left. As tough a nut as he was, his system had suffered quite a shock, and John didn't think he would last more than five . . . maybe ten years. The man had lived his life and it was nearing its end, but before he died, John knew he had to clear the air about certain things. Otherwise, after his father was gone, he honestly felt as though he would spend the rest of his life resenting his father.

Clearing his throat, John shifted forward and, looking from the fire to his father's lined face, said, "You see, Dad—if you want me to be honest with you, that's always been something you've done that drives me crazy. You're always telling me how to do things, rather than letting me find my own way."

Frank made a deep rumbling sound in his chest, and John had the momentary impression he was going to spit at him. He didn't, though; instead, he rubbed his hand over his face and sighed.

"I'm just tryin' to give you the benefit of what I've learned," Frank said softly. "I ain't got much money in the bank, 'n' when I go—what'll you have? This old house and a handful of unpaid medical bills Medicare won't cover. I'm tryin' to pass on to you certain things, ways of doing and looking at things that I think are the right way—"

"*Your* way," John snapped. "What works for you isn't necessarily the right way for me or anyone else!"

Frank took a long, shuddering breath. "Well, what works *always* works, in my mind. I'll tell yah—what breaks my heart more'n anything is how you still won't take your family to church. Now you've got a wife and a child, you should be going to—"

"No! No way!" John said, making such a quick slicing motion with his hand he almost spilled his beer. "I don't want to talk about that!"

Frank's expression hardened, and in the glow of the fire, the lines on his face deepened. "'S far as I can see, that's where you've gone wrong," he said. His voice was a thundery growl. "If you could only see that—"

"No, if *you* could only see!" John shouted, suddenly sitting forward. The sudden motion made beer splash onto his lap, but he ignored it as he turned on his father. "If you could have seen what it was doing to us—to me and to Mom—you might have eased up on that—that *church* bullshit!"

"You'd better watch what you say," Frank said.

"I know what I'm saying," John shouted, his face flushed with anger. "You just didn't—*Christ*, you *couldn't* see it!" He shook his head sadly from side to side. "But you drove both of us fucking *crazy* with this church—church—*church* crap! All the time! As if going to fucking church was somehow miraculously going to change things!"

Frank's mouth opened to say something, but he was so choked up with anger, all that came out was a strangled gasp. His hands tightened on the wheelchair armrests, and when he looked at his son, he saw tattered waves of darkness sweeping in around the edges of his vision.

"I know this may sound spiteful," John continued, apparently ignorant of his father's rising anger. "But that isn't how I mean it. I think your pushing about it all the time—I don't know, maybe going to church gave you some kind of idea that *your* way was the only way, but I think that's a lot of what got Mom started drinking in the first place—"

"That had nothing to do with it," Frank said. His voice was low, steady, almost under control, but John could see his father's knuckles turning white as he increased the pressure on the armrests of the wheelchair.

"I think it had *something* to do with it," John said. "I know it did! You never even realized how I felt so pushed about it. I didn't want to have a thing to do with your fucking church—or with you!"

"You'd better watch your mouth, boy!" Frank snarled.

"I'm not a boy!" John snapped back. "Jesus! Don't you see it? Once even *you* couldn't deny that Mom was drinking too much, what did you do? Pray for her to stop?" He snorted and, for a breather, took a swallow of beer. "I mean, what kind of husband would let his wife do a thing like that—drink herself to death?"

The glimmer in Frank's eyes burned harder and colder as he stared at John. As John was speaking—yelling at him—Frank felt his face, his whole body, even the nerve-dead left side, tighten as a dull tingling ran through him. His son's words hit his ears like the rapid, deafening punch of a jackhammer.

"And tell me just what kind of husband *you* are to Abby, huh?" Frank asked. His voice was harsh and steely, his mouth a thin, bloodless line. His eyes were rolled upward, and the firelight caught a wicked gleam in the exposed whites of his eyes.

John hadn't missed his father's slip of the tongue, calling Julia Abby. In the awkward silence that followed, he looked away from him and stared into the fire. For a moment, he imagined he could see faces rippling in the glowing bed of coals.

"From what I been seeing," Frank continued, "ever since you got here . . ."

"I don't want to hear anything you've got to say," John said, suddenly standing up and walking over to the fireplace. He took the poker, opened the screen, and jabbed angrily at the blazing logs.

Frank's mouth tightened into a grim line as he watched his son. Although the thoughts were vague in his mind, he couldn't help but feel both disappointment and sadness—disappointment because he didn't like what he saw of what his son had made of his life, and sadness because he knew there was nothing he could do or say to John that would change anything.

Maybe back when John was young—God knows he had tried

to raise him right—he might have been able to change things. . . . Maybe the sadness was that he knew he couldn't go back and do things differently. Or maybe, down deep, he realized that even if he could go back, things probably would have worked out this way, anyway, because of who—and what—they were.

John turned and looked at his father over his shoulder. The firelight cast one side of John's face into high relief, and staring back at him, Frank had the dizzying sensation of seeing himself when he was younger. He saw, in many ways, his own disappointments and failures written on his son's face, but as much as he wanted to reach out and communicate with him, his next words came out like honed-steel blades.

"'S far as I can see, you ain't much of a husband to Julia, and you ain't *no* kind of father to Bri."

John scowled, thinking, *Well, at least you remembered her name!* He frowned deeply, and the firelight burned wickedly in his eyes. He was thinking how all his life he had to put up with slams like that, but there was one thing Julia was right about—he was no longer the boy growing up in this house. He was an adult, and he didn't have to put up with shit like this from *anyone* . . . not even his father!

"I don't think you're any kind of judge as to what kind of husband—or father—I am," he said. He felt so tense his voice wavered, but he held his gaze steadily on his father, letting himself dredge up and feel all the years of hurt and frustration.

If there was only some way to let you know, let you feel what I've been through, he was thinking.

"If you ask me, I think Bri's too damned good to be your kid," Frank said. "And although it saddens me to think the family name's gonna die out with us, I spose it's as God intends it to be. I spose it's the punishment I get for—"

"Did you ever think that maybe your stroke and your being left in a frigging wheelchair was part of God's punishment? Huh? Did you?" John asked.

He got up out of his crouch and, walking over to the fireplace, glared at his father. He picked up the poker in his right hand, and he squeezed the handle so hard his fingers began to ache. But if he had felt any desire to try to communicate with his father before, felt any need to try and settle things between them—*before he dies*, he thought with a chill—that was all passed. Just like before—like *always!*—his father had said things that had cut too deeply to be forgotten . . . or forgiven.

Frank's hands, gripping the armrests, began to shake. As with many things in his life, he regretted some of what he had said, but in his mind, John never had, and wasn't now showing him the proper respect due a parent. John didn't go to church! Maybe that's where it started, or maybe that was just an outward symptom of something deeper that was wrong inside his son. It didn't matter after a while, Frank thought, feeling a deep, painful bitterness. It just didn't matter.

"I think," Frank said, his voice so low John could barely hear him above the crackling of the fire, "that having you for a son is just 'bout all the punishment God needs to dish out to me."

"I could say the same!" John shouted, clenching his hands and shaking them in front of his face. The poker, still in his right hand, clanged against the mantel. "You've *never* been any kind of father to me! All I ever got from you was criticism! Do this *my* way or else . . . !"

Frank shook his head, trying as best he could to slow his racing pulse. It had always been this way between them, from the time John was a baby. He had always been willful—"bullheaded," as his mother used to say. He and his wife used to think a certain amount of that would serve him well in life, but in Frank's eyes, John had never had anything to balance that bullheadedness, had never shown the proper respect to authority, either to his parents or to God.

"It's true!" John wailed. "You never gave me room to breathe. Christ! You were always hounding me, telling me I had to go to college, get an education, get a good job so I could get off this island. If you hated it so fucking much, why the Christ did you never leave?"

"All I wanted was what any parent wants," Frank said tightly. "For you to have a better chance at life than I did."

"Oh, yeah—sure! And you want to know something else? I'll never forgive you for what you did—practically *forcing* me to break up with Abby when we were dating in high school!"

"Abby. . ." Frank said, his voice dropping to barely a whisper as he tilted his head back and stared up at the ceiling. Something —a vague thought—danced just out of his reach, like a shadow that shifts every time you turn and try to see it.

John paid no attention to what his father said as he continued his tirade. "Oh, you broke us up, all right! Always telling me she wasn't good enough for me. That if I ended up married to her, I'd ruin my life. You drove me to—" He caught himself, took a deep, shuddering breath, then went on. "Christ! I couldn't wait to graduate from high school, but not because I could leave this goddamned island! I just wanted to get out of this fucking house! Out from under your shadow! All my life, I never felt like I could measure up to *your* standards. I couldn't even come *close!*"

With that last word, John cocked back his arm and swung the

poker viciously at the mantel. The metal handle bent as it cut deeply into the wood. John's eyes were stinging; his breath was coming in shallow, fitful gasps that burned all the way down to his stomach. All he could think was . . .

How simple it would be! How easy just to go over to him, sitting there so helpless in his wheelchair, and whack him with the poker!

A whole lifetime of anguish and feeling inferior would explode in that single, vicious swing that would crush his father's skull like it was an eggshell.

Maybe that's what he wants! John thought, not daring to look at his father because he knew the jolt of hatred he would feel might really make him do it. *Maybe he's so damned tired of living in a wheelchair he* wants *me to end it all for him!*

"You watch what you're doing there, boy!" Frank shouted angrily. "You've got no right to go banging things around *my* house!"

"You've been a *bastard*!" John wailed. He swung again and hit the mantel with the poker, feeling the impact numb his arm up to his shoulder. "Nothing but a mean, rotten, lousy *bastard* to me all my *life*!" Again he swatted the mantel. This time, the tip of the poker hit the edge and removed a piece of wood the size of his hand. The iron bar was now bent around almost ninety degrees.

I could do it! he was thinking as his mind was swept up in a flood of red-hot anger. *I really could kill him! Right now!*

"If you don't calm yourself," Frank said, "I'll get on the phone 'n' call the cops. You ain't got no right to stave up *my* house!"

John suddenly stopped and looked at his hand holding the poker, at the veins and tendons standing out in sharp relief, the twitching muscles that he knew with one quick swipe could end his father's life.

He's driving me to this! he thought. *All my life, he's been driving me to this!*

"Look, son, I don't think we ever really liked each other," Frank said. "'N' I'm beginnin' to think maybe we never will." He released the brake on his wheelchair and gripped the wheel rails. "I think we're gonna both just have to learn to live—and die—with that. But I'm warnin' yah—" He pointed his gnarled forefinger at John as if it were a loaded and cocked gun. "If you think you can pull horseshit like this in my house and get away with it, you're dead wrong!"

His piece said, he spun his wheelchair around and, without a backward glance, rolled across the floor to his bedroom, shutting the door firmly behind him.

With a sudden, gut-deep grunt, John threw the poker to the

floor and, taking a long, trembling breath, walked away from the fireplace to the living room picture window. His vision was blurred and his mind was a torrent of raging thoughts, tangled emotions, blazing anger as he looked out at the night. Beyond the reflection of the firelight in the window, he couldn't see much of the starry sky he knew was out there, but as he stared outside, he thought he saw something beyond the glass, emerging from the thick, black night . . . a fleeting glimpse of—his mind went suddenly numb when he registered what it was—the outline of a person standing right outside the living room window, close to the house, looking in at him.

"Jesus Christ!" he said as he stumbled backward. Air rushed from his lungs in a painful gasp. He glanced back toward the fireplace, to the spot where his father had been sitting. Even though he knew his father was close by in his bedroom, John was filled with the dread cold of loneliness, as though someone . . .

Who?

Him? His father? Maybe Julia or Bri?

. . . *someone* was in danger!

He tried to convince himself it had been just a trick of the eye. No one would be out there looking in at him. But when he looked again, the shape was still there! There *was* someone out there! A face close to the glass was staring him straight in the eyes. And in a flood of panic, he instantly recognized the cold, dead-white face. This was the same person, the same figure he had seen before, reflected in the glass late at night . . . the same person he had seen hanging from the ceiling . . . the same person he had seen coming up the walkway the night of the blizzard . . . the same person he had seen walking along the side of the road while he was driving home during the storm.

"No!" he said, his voice no more than a whimper. "Impossible!"

The face leered at him, smiling as it locked eyes with him with a glance like an icy spear. Impossible as it was, he was looking at Abby Snow—his girlfriend from all those years ago, and she was watching him through the thin pane of glass that separated them.

Abby Snow!

John staggered away from the window, almost tripping on the rug edge. The room spun around him, throwing him entirely off balance. The skin on the back of his neck was tingling, and he thought he could hear, just at the edge of awareness, a low, hollow laughter. Back by the fireplace, his eyes came to rest on the bent poker, and he quickly bent down and picked it up. Holding it in front of him like a crazily bent sword, he stood staring at the glass.

She couldn't really be out there! he thought, and panic raged inside him like a storm-tossed sea. *How could she be? How in the name of everything holy could she be?*

Using a shuffling sidestep, he cautiously approached the picture window, not knowing if, when he got there, the person—the *illusion*—would be gone or if the window would suddenly explode inward in a shower of razor-edged shards. He felt foolish holding the bent poker out in front of him, but if there was someone out there . . .

It can't be Abby! It can't possibly be Abby! his mind screamed.

. . . he wanted them to know he didn't take kindly to Peeping Toms. With a sudden rush, he charged the window holding the poker high over his head, ready to swing. If there *was* someone out there, they were going to be sorry when he caught them!

But as soon as he got to the window, he saw that there was no one there. Beyond the dim reflection of the fireplace and furniture—and his own terror-stricken face—there was nothing but the snow-covered lawn and the black, frozen night. The streetlight, he saw, cast a veined shadow onto the glass from one of the bare maple trees in the front yard, and John suddenly burst out with laughter.

Is that all it's been all this time? he thought. *Just a shadow from a tree?* Loud, crazy-sounding laughter filled the living room. The poker dropped to the floor with a clang.

No Peeping Tom!

. . . and *certainly* no Abby Snow!

Just the streetlight throwing a shadow onto the picture window. In his frenzy of anger at his father, John realized he must have been half crazy and had imagined seeing Abby's face. He *had* to have, because one thing he was sure of was, no matter how much Randy Chadwick or anyone else around town speculated, he *knew* that Abby Snow, his high school girlfriend, was dead. He had seen her body!

PART THREE

Atropos—the Cutting Fate

And now how abhorred in my imagination it is!
My gorge rises at it. Here hung those lips that
I have kissed I know not how oft.

—*Shakespeare*

Justice foreshadowing the event shall come, in her hands
a just victory. Yes, she will come, my child, in vengeance
and soon!

—*Sophocles*

SEVENTEEN
Wish List

I

In the two weeks before Christmas, Julia felt at times as though she were living in a Norman Rockwell painting. The temperature stayed well down in the teens—and lower at night—and several light dustings of snow, never more than an inch or two at a time, kept the ground sparkling white. Even some of the more tedious holiday chores, such as writing and sending Christmas cards and untangling the strings of outdoor lights, were less tiring. And if, back in October when they had first moved in, the house had seemed old and dingy, now that she and John had finished with the necessary "paint 'n' paper," it seemed positively homey in an old-fashioned way, in spite of the tensions that still existed, especially between Frank and John.

Julia was thankful that Bri, at least, had finally started to make friends at school. She spent almost every afternoon with Kristin, either at Kristin's house or the two of them at Bri's. They seemed to enjoy each other genuinely. Several of the local kids had shoveled off a large area of Larson's Pond, and Bri went skating there just about every Saturday. What Julia was happiest about, though, was that Bri had stopped her lonely walks out on Indian Point. She had never liked the idea of that, and she certainly didn't have a very good feeling about that girl Audrey that Bri had met out there. Kristin and she seemed to be developing a true friendship.

Things with John, on the other hand, were not going as well. Julia had started inviting Ellie Chadwick up to the house once or twice a week for coffee and conversation, but she certainly didn't feel close enough to Ellie to tell her about her problems and concerns with John.

Most of them centered around how he was still not relating well to his father. If anything, their relationship had deteriorated, and Julia found herself wondering what might have caused it. As far as *she* was concerned, she got along just fine with Frank—even now, with the colder weather and him at home more because he was unable to go visiting down at the wharf. And although Bri was doing more things with Kristin and had less time to spend at home, she still found time to have a few games of checkers with her grandfather. Both of them had pierced Frank's gruff exterior.

But John . . . well, his relationship with his father was still a problem, just as it was difficult for her.

Actually, the more she thought about it, the more Julia wasn't entirely sure the problem was just between John and his father. It seemed as though ever since October, John had been steadily building a wall around himself, at least at home. From what little he told her about his work, it seemed as though things were going along just fine there. It was a different story when he got home in the evening. If he wasn't sullen and quiet, he was grumpy and sometimes outright hostile, snapping at the slightest irritation—even when Bri was involved—and swearing about the most minor things. She had tried to mention—offhandedly and usually jokingly—that she still wouldn't mind getting pregnant; but whenever she did, John would simply glower at her, as though she had asked him for a million dollars or something equally impossible.

Her wanting to get pregnant was at least one thing she felt open enough to talk about with Ellie, even though it made her feel more and more as if she were becoming part of the *Donahue* crowd.

"If I was you," Ellie said one morning as they sat at the kitchen table drinking coffee, "I'd just stop using birth control and not tell him. You get preggo, and then—!" She shrugged her shoulders. "Whether he likes it or not, he'll have to adjust to the idea."

Julia shook her head. "I don't know," she said. "I mean, I don't really like to operate that way. John and I have always been totally honest with each other."

Julia could tell by the wry expression on Ellie's face that she didn't have to say aloud what she was thinking—*Come on . . . totally honest?*

"I mean, that's pretty much how I got Randy in the first place," Ellie said, smirking into her coffee cup. "Course, back then, the idea of birth control was pretty much limited either to not doing it, or the guys using rubbers—"

Julia's chuckle interrupted her. "Yeah, and that's how it's getting to be again, what with AIDS and all. If Reagan didn't bring us all the way back to the fifties, AIDS has."

"Next we'll be seeing huge tail fins on cars, I suppose," Ellie said, and they both laughed heartily. "But I was saying that's how I got Randy to marry me in the first place. I mean, I think the last thing he wanted was a family and all right after high school, but I knew if he went off to college, I'd lose him for sure."

"You mean to tell me you got pregnant on purpose?"

Ellie shrugged innocently. "I just used my 'womanly wiles,'" she said. "I figured—you know one of the classic lies—*I'll only put it in a little way?* well, one night—actually, now that I think about it, we were on a double date with John and Abby—I decided to let him go all the way, as they say, figuring if I got pregnant, he'd have to marry me and not go to college."

Although Julia laughed along with Ellie, she also found herself wondering how anybody could do something like that to someone they supposedly loved . . . let yourself get pregnant just to hang on to them, ruin their chances to go to college and get ahead. All in all, it was a testament, she supposed, to their love that, like so many other couples she knew who had gotten married straight out of high school, they hadn't gotten divorced. In fact, they seemed to be reasonably happy together, and they had two healthy kids.

"Wait a minute," Julia said. "I don't want to get too nosy here, but my math's good enough to tell me that your oldest is only twelve; that's not old enough to be—" She cut herself off as the realization of what she was getting at hit her.

Oh, Jesus! Me and my big mouth. What if she lost the baby?

"Life's full of ironic little twists, I guess," Ellie said. She was still smiling, but Julia couldn't help but wonder if she had hit on a long-dead but still raw nerve. "I miscarried a week after we got married. I dunno—maybe it was God's way of punishing me for being so sneaky."

For just an instant, Ellie's guard dropped, and Julia could see the lingering pain in her eyes. "I'm sorry," Julia said. "I didn't mean to be so—"

"Hey! Come on. It was *years* ago," Ellie said, forcing a smile. "I was only a coupla months along. It wasn't like I lost a child, you know? Most people around town never even suspected it was a shotgun wedding, and once I could get birth control pills, I didn't get pregnant until eight years later. It was the trying that was fun, anyway."

Julia frowned and looked down at her coffee cup. *Even trying isn't that much fun for us anymore,* she thought sadly. And that's when it hit her that she couldn't deny it—things weren't just rotten between John and his father. Things were rotten between the two of them, too. She felt a sudden urge to be alone and wished Ellie would hurry up and leave so she could sit down and think.

"But that's what I'd do if I was you," Ellie said. "Men!" She made a disgusted sound in the back of her throat. "They don't know what they want, anyway. I mean, Randy is so predictable."

She nailed Julia with a hard look and, pointing her index finger at her, said, "If you want a baby, get one! John'll have nine months to adjust to the idea."

Julia glanced up at Ellie and smiled weakly. What she was wondering was, did she really want a baby in the first place, or was she latching on to this idea because she knew, deep down inside, things weren't very good between her and John and maybe she was hoping a baby would pull them back together. Was this —yes, it felt like a *need* to get pregnant—simply a refuge from a marriage that she saw was heading toward the rocks but was too afraid to admit it?

Their conversation turned to other things, thankfully, and they made tentative plans to go to a local crafts fair together over the weekend. Ellie told her about a place up in Windham where they could select and cut their own Christmas tree, and suggested that a week or so before Christmas both of their families could go out together and maybe have supper together afterward.

Julia agreed that it sounded like a good idea, but she was still dwelling on this "baby business," as John referred to it. There was nothing wrong with wanting to do something that would bring them closer together as a family, she decided, and maybe Ellie was right—John *would* have nine months to get used to the idea. She hardly paid attention as Ellie went on and on, chattering about this family and that situation. Finally, just before lunch, she left, saying she wanted to get home in time for *Donahue*. Julia was glad to see her go, but the whole time she fixed lunch for herself and Frank and throughout lunch, she was unusually quiet. Frank even commented on it.

II

On Thursday, with Christmas only nine days away, John took the afternoon off from work and went shopping down on Exchange Street. When he had been rushing out to work that morning, Julia had given him a slip of folded-over paper, saying it was her Christmas "wish list." He hadn't taken time to look at it then, and didn't until he had left the office, deposited his briefcase in the car, and was striding down Exchange Street. When he saw what she had written, he didn't know whether to get angry or laugh with relief. Printed in small, neat letters in the middle of the page were the words:

A BABY!

That was all.

The instant before he opened and read her note, he had had the panicked thought that he was going to see, in heavy-handed pencil lines, something like—*I won't forget what you*...The measure of relief he felt had been so great, he actually found himself not getting as upset with Julia as he might have otherwise.

"Some help you are," he said, resisting the temptation to crumple up the paper and toss it away. If this was her idea of a joke, it was only passable, at best! He remembered her best joke of all time—when she had sent him grocery shopping. She had wanted chicken breast meat for an Italian dish she was going to make, so on the list, she had written, "*chicken tits*." That had made him laugh so hysterically, several customers turned around and left the aisle just to avoid him.

On the other hand, if this *wasn't* simply a joke . . . well, he knew they couldn't talk about it rationally. He had tried his damnedest to make her realize how foolish it was to start in again with babies. And anyway, none of this gave him any idea what to get her for a present. Looking at the generally overpriced goods in the Exchange Street shop windows, he didn't know where to start.

The wind in off Casco Bay was cold, and the sky was darkening to a rich gunmetal gray. It looked as if it might start spitting snow—again. As John walked up and down Exchange Street, he actually found himself feeling a little bit of Christmas spirit. The decorations and the quaint shops and the gentle strains of Christmas carols from outdoor speakers all combined to make him feel as though he had taken a step back in time and was wandering the streets of Dickens's London. People walked by, bundled up against the cold, and more than a few actually smiled at him and nodded, giving him friendly holiday greetings. It was enough—*almost,* he thought—to make him forget for a while all about the problems he felt hanging over his head.

After a couple of hours, in spite of Julia's lack of help, he had quite an armload of presents—some fancy soap and perfume, a silver pendant sea gull, a new pair of Laurel Burch earrings to replace the ones which Julia had lost . . . or which the rats in the wall had "borrowed," and a package of nice writing paper and envelopes, all for Julia. For Bri, he bought a large stuffed alligator, a designer T-shirt emblazoned with the Portland skyline (the logo read: LONDON—PARIS—ROME—PORTLAND), and—against his better judgment—the new album by Bon Jovi. His father was the only problem, but he was content with the shopping he had done so far and took his pile of loot back to the car. He considered leaving everything in the trunk and trying to find something for his father, but in the past two hours he had come up dry, so figuring he was burned out, he paid his parking fee and went home.

His good mood was destroyed as soon as he got home and walked into the kitchen.

"What the hell is this?" Julia said. She had obviously been waiting for him at the door. In her hand was a sheet of notebook paper, which she flapped so rapidly in front of him, he couldn't see what was written on it. By the cold clutching around his heart, though, he had a pretty damned good idea.

"What's what?" he asked, aware of the tremor in his voice.

"This! What the hell does this note mean?"

She stopped shaking the paper under his nose long enough for him to see, scrawled in heavy pencil across the middle of the paper,

I WON'T FORGET WHAT YOU DID...

"Any ideas?" Julia said after giving him the note.

He had left the bags of presents in the car, intending to get them later so he could hide them until he got them wrapped. Feeling a cold tingle travel up his spine as he clenched the piece of paper, he shivered as he shrugged off his coat and went into the hallway to hang it up. He had instantly noted the addition of the word *did*, and the gnawing in the pit of his stomach told him, now more than ever, that there was more to come.

"I . . . I haven't got the faintest," he said as he rejoined Julia in the kitchen. He turned the sheet of paper over in his hand, as though inspecting it for more. After handing it back to Julia, he went to the refrigerator and took out a beer, snapped it open, and took a big swallow. His mind was raging, but all he could think was, he didn't really have anything more to say to her. He was just as confused—maybe more so—than she was.

"Where'd you find it?" he asked, forcing the tremor from his voice.

"It was right here on the kitchen table when I got back this afternoon. I was visiting with Ellie."

John willed his hand not to tremble as he reached out and took the sheet of paper again from his wife. As he studied it, it struck him as remarkable how every sheet looked identical except for the addition of a new word each time. He knew—he was *positive*—he had thrown away the other notes, but this sheet looked exactly the same, even down to the torn ring holes on the side. The heavily scrawled letters, each of which had been gone over several times, still made him think of a child practicing lettering, but deep inside, he knew it was more serious than that—*much* more serious!

"I haven't got the foggiest," he said with a snort. As he handed the note back to Julia, he could feel the beads of sweat that stood out on his brow.

"Well . . . how about the other ones, then?" Julia asked, nailing him with a hard look.

"What—what do you mean?" John said. His mouth felt as if it were full of sawdust, so he tipped his head back and took another healthy swallow of beer, letting it bubble down his throat.

"I mean the other note—or possibly other *notes*—just like this one that you might have found around the house," Julia said. Her grip wrinkled the paper, and John found himself wishing she would throw the damned thing away and forget about it.

"I still don't know what you mean," he said, shaking his head with confusion. He lowered his voice so, if his lie was too obvious, she might not notice it.

"Oh, I think you do, John," she said, "and it really bothers me to think that you would keep *anything* from me. The day we went out lobstering with Randy, remember? I came down around three in the morning and found you sitting on the couch, staring out the living room window. Remember?"

John gave her a slight nod of the head.

"You had a note almost identical to this," Julia said, her voice taking on a steely edge. "And when I came into the living room, you stuffed it under the couch cushion so I wouldn't see it. Right?"

Again, John nodded. He was unable to maintain eye contact with her for very long. Just to do something, he took another long sip of beer.

"That one said, I WON'T FORGET WHAT . . . Now this one has a few more words added. I WON'T FORGET WHAT YOU DID . . . So tell me, what does it mean?"

"I told you—I have no idea," John said, shrugging. "Maybe it's something of Bri's."

He wanted to go over to her and hug her . . . tell her to forget about it, that everything was all right, but there was a black chill creeping through his gut that told him otherwise. Each additional word that was being added to the message pushed his mind farther and farther along a certain path that he didn't want to—didn't *dare* to follow!

"Bri's not going to write something like that," Julia snapped. "And anyway, this one wasn't here when I left for Ellie's, and Bri went over to Kristin's straight from school. It's not hers and it's not your father's!" Julia said, her voice almost breaking. "I think it's yours. You may be telling the truth—that you don't know what it means—but do you want to know what bothers me the most?"

Unable to form a single word in his throat, John nodded his head.

"That you would hide something—*anything* from me. I thought—" Her voice choked off, and John saw tears welling up in her eyes.

John felt as though someone's icy hands were squeezing his heart until it was about to crush inward. If he could have looked deep inside himself, he thought, he wouldn't have been surprised to see anything more than dark, dry powder where his heart should be, because he *did* have an idea what those notes meant, what they were leading to. He might not know who was writing them—not *yet*, anyway—but he was positive he knew what they meant. And he knew, as deeply as he knew the dark secrets of his heart, that he could never let Julia know.

"I thought we were honest—totally honest with each other," Julia said as tears ran down her cheeks. "But you found that note that morning and you hid it from me."

"No, I—"

"You hid it under the couch cushion, and don't tell me you didn't!" Julia shouted. "You didn't know I saw you do it, but when you went upstairs to get dressed, I took it out and read it. And then later, after I had put it back, you took it out and threw it away because once we were back from our lobstering expedition, I checked and it was gone. Can you deny that you threw it away?"

Biting his lower lip, John nodded his head. "Yeah," he said, his voice registering hollowly in his ears, "I did. I didn't know what it was, so I just chucked it."

"So then why did you try to hide it from me? You didn't tell me!" Julia said, her voice almost breaking as more tears coursed down her cheeks. "You didn't tell me about it. You *hid* it from me and didn't tell me, as if it was some . . . *secret* of yours!"

"It wasn't that at all," John said. "I'm just as confused about all of this as you are. Yeah—sure I found the other note that morning—"

"Only one other?" Julia said, nailing him with a cold stare.

"*Yes!* Just that one! I swear. And I don't know what this one or the other one meant. I have no idea."

"I want to believe you," Julia said. "I *really* do."

She rubbed her eyes with the back of her hand, but all that did was make them red and puffy. Her breath came in sharp hitches that shook her shoulders. She was still holding the notebook paper, now balled up in her hand, and she stared at it as if she expected it, somehow, to give her more of an answer.

"I don't know what to think," she said, her lower lip trembling. "I mean, how can we have a . . . a marriage that works if I don't feel I can trust you?"

"But you *can* trust me," John said, his voice low and—he hoped—convincing.

"But you *kept* this from me," Julia said. "And if there are any secrets between us, what I thought was . . . *love* just isn't going to last."

John was fighting back a flood of panic because he knew, as surely as he knew there would be a sunrise tomorrow, there would *have* to be another note to finish the sentence. If he felt a chill in his soul now, he was just beginning to imagine the arctic blast that would come when the message was completed.

I WON'T FORGET WHAT YOU DID . . .

Did what? . . . Who did what?

Maybe just one more word or two—or a name—would complete the message. John found himself dreading what the next note would say, but more than that, he knew, when it came, there was no way in heaven that Julia would find out about it.

"Can we just forget about it?" he said.

He put his nearly empty beer can down on the countertop and came over to her, wrapping his arms around her waist and pulling her close. She collapsed into him, burying her face in his chest, and he could feel deep sobs wrenching her body. He ran his hand up her back and, lacing his fingers in her hair, gently rubbed the back of her head.

He was going to say more, about how she could trust him and believe him as she always had . . . that there were no secrets between them—never had been and never would be—but even as the words formed clearly in his mind, they wouldn't leave his mouth.

"I love you, you know," he said, leaning back so he could look down at her upturned face.

She looked at him, her eyes glistening with tears. She sniffed and wiped her nose with her palm.

"I love you, too," she said, her voice no more than a hoarse whisper.

John didn't like the way she looked at him, though. He could see her eyes narrowed with suspicion, as though if she squinted while she looked at him, or caught a glance out of the corner of her eye, she would see someone different from the person she expected to see, see who he *really* was. He could sense that, even if it was just the tiniest chink in the wall, he had lost a measure of her trust, and he was going to have to work hard to regain it. . . .

They kissed, but even after they broke the kiss off and he took the crumpled note from her and tossed it into the trash can, he caught her, from time to time throughout the evening, looking at him *funny*, as though she was no longer sure who he was.

EIGHTEEN
Christmas Eve

I

It had always been a tradition in Julia's family to wait until Christmas Eve to decorate the tree, and John had readily adopted that tradition because, for one thing, he thought it helped counteract what he saw as the increasing commercialization of the holiday. Another, more practical reason had always been that, until recently, he had usually been so damned busy right up until Christmas Eve, he rarely had time to get to it before then.

Julia knew school was getting out for the week sometime around noon, and she suspected that John's office—since they weren't having their holiday party until New Year's Eve—would let out early for the day as well. While Frank watched, adding his own pleasant small talk, she busily decorated the house, taping the cards they had received around the living room doorway and nailing the family stockings to the mantel. Because the day was overcast, she turned on the electric candles in the windows before sunset. Their warm orange glow made the living room look as if it were filled with cheery firelight.

The night before, John had cut their tree to size and set it into the tree stand in the living room so the branches would drop. Julia was on her knees, testing and replacing the burned-out bulbs in several strings of lights.

"One favor I've got to ask yah," Frank said.

"What's that?" Julia asked. They still had one of those old-fashioned strings of lights where, if one went out, the whole string stayed off. After trying for fifteen minutes to locate the offending bulb, she was close to throwing the whole damned string away.

"I was wonderin' if you folks'd accompany me t'church this evenin', it being Christmas Eve 'n'all."

Julia didn't look up as she let out a deep sigh. "I—uh."

"Far's I'm concerned, it's the only thing you have to do for me for Christmas this year," Frank said. He looked past her, his eyes dimming as they focused on one of the lights in the window. "It'd mean a lot."

His voice was low and earnest, and when she looked up at him, the expression on his face made her see how ridiculous it was that she was getting so worked up about something as stupid as a set of tree lights. *If the holiday isn't for doing things to make your family feel good*, she thought, *then what good is it?*

Before she could say anything, though, Frank continued, "Now I know John won't take to the idea. Never has." He turned and looked at her expectantly. "But I thought, even if he didn't come along, maybe you and Bri'd join me."

"I think that would be nice," Julia said. Maybe it was something about the holidays that made her feel sentimental, but it took a great effort on her part not to burst into tears and rush over to hug him.

"Oh, 'n' by the way," Frank said, nodding toward the floor by her foot. "You ain't ever going to get that string of lights to work if you don't plug it inta the socket."

Julia looked behind her and saw that, while she had been untangling the lights, her foot must have pulled the cord from the wall socket. As soon as she plugged it back into the wall, the whole string lit up.

"I owe you another one," she said, smiling at Frank, who was chuckling so deeply his wheelchair started squeaking. Without another word, he spun around and went to his room, closing the door gently behind him.

Long before John and Bri got home, Julia had everything done except for the tree. The boxes of decorations were all sorted out and waiting on the floor beside the tree, and she had even finished wrapping the gifts she had gotten for the family. The sky was lowering, and it looked as if there might be a bit of snow headed their way, but she thought that would be too much to hope for on Christmas Eve.

A little after noon, Bri slammed in through the door and, slinging her backpack to the floor, collapsed at the kitchen table. "I can't believe it!" she wailed, leaning back and shaking her fists at the ceiling. "Mrs. Endicott gave us a term-paper assignment due the week after vacation! At least *five* pages! She's nuts if she thinks I'm going to ruin my vacation researching *Shakespeare*! Dad was right—she *is* a battle-ax!"

"Is that the only homework you have over vacation?" Julia asked mildly.

Bri nodded, her mouth set in a grim line. "Yeah . . . the rest of the teachers are at least *partially* human."

"Count your blessings, then," Julia said. "I'm sure you can find some time to get it done."

Shaking her head with disgust, Bri stood up, picked up her backpack, and trudged up the stairs to her bedroom, grumbling to herself something about that *woman* not having a *heart*.

A few minutes after Bri had moved like a whirlwind through the kitchen, John arrived. Julia greeted him at the door with a smile and a kiss, hoping that he would quickly lose the frown that wrinkled his forehead.

"Rough day at the office, hon?" she asked, wishing to God she didn't sound like a stereotypical housewife on TV.

"Yeah, you might say that," John replied as he stamped his feet on the rug and took off his coat. Clumps of snow fell to the floor and immediately started to melt into dirty puddles. "Even rougher getting out of town with all that traffic."

What he didn't tell Julia . . . what he *couldn't* tell her was that, once he had left work and gotten to his car, he had found another note, just like all the others. It had been right smack-dab on the middle of his car seat, even though all the doors had been locked and all the windows had been rolled up snugly. In the same handwriting, were the words:

I WON'T FORGET WHAT YOU DID TO...

He had torn up the sheet of notebook paper and sprinkled it on the ground in the parking lot, grinding it into the slushy snow with his heel. And as he had driven home, he had known and dreaded that when the next message came, the last word—a name—would be added. And he knew, more than ever, what that name would be.

"Well," Julia said as she busied herself making a sandwich for him, "after you have a bit of lunch, I was thinking we could get the tree decorated this afternoon."

John cocked an eyebrow as he looked at her. "After supper won't be time enough?" he asked. "Christ! I mean, I just walked in the frigging door! Will you give me a chance to unwind?"

"Well, I was just thinking we'd get it done this afternoon so—maybe—we could go to church tonight with your father," Julia said. "He—"

Glaring at his father's closed bedroom door, John sucked in a breath, held it, and let it out with a hiss. "Jesus H.! He put you up to this, didn't he?" Julia could only stammer.

"Oh, I know he did. You don't have to make excuses." John

was scowling as he leaned back on the counter, his arms folded across his chest.

"It's Christmas," Julia said, looking at him with pleading in her eyes. "It means a lot to him."

She came over to him and, smiling, wound her arms around his waist. With a sudden clenching of her arms, she pulled him so close to her it forced his breath out. Caught by surprise, he had to laugh when she reached down to his crotch and grabbed him firmly but not too tightly.

"Now, I don't want to have to resort to any *extreme* measures of persuasion," she said, tightening her grip just a bit. "But I will if you don't see reason. Can I make myself any clearer?"

Wincing his eyes in mock pain, John groaned and said, "All right . . . all right. I'll go."

Julia released the pressure but didn't let go. Instead, after a quick glance over her shoulder to make sure Bri wasn't standing in the doorway watching, she began to rub up and down on his crotch. She was satisfied when she felt him beginning to stiffen.

"And who knows," she whispered close to his ear as she maintained the steady friction. "Maybe *after* church, once all the little children are tucked into bed, waiting for Santa Claus to come, we can have our own little . . . *fun*." She said the last word with a deep, throaty growl.

John ran his hands up and down her back, molding the curve of her hips beneath his fingers. He was still feeling wire tight, but he made himself relax a bit. Bringing his mouth close to hers, he whispered, "We'll just have to wait and see, now, won't we?"

"Well," Julia said just before their lips met, "you know what *I* want under the tree. . . ."

"I always knew you had a dirty mind," John said, almost laughing. "And here you are, talking about going to church!"

After John had a sandwich and beer for lunch, they called Bri down. Frank even came out of his room and watched as they strung the tree with lights and then hung ornaments from the branches. Julia was glad to see John starting to unwind; he joined in, joking and laughing with them. Actually, he seemed so relaxed, she started remembering how much fun he used to be. She was pleased to see that he even directly addressed his father a few times, asking his opinion of how this or that looked on the tree.

Throughout the rest of the afternoon and during supper, everyone seemed filled with holiday cheer. It was only after supper, while they were getting dressed for church, that Julia began to feel guilty. She didn't know when she had decided, but as they were driving to church, she knew she had made up her mind—she was going to take Ellie's advice and tonight, if they did make love after Bri and Frank were asleep, she was conveniently going to forget to use her birth control.

II

John had *never* liked going to church. There were a whole host of reasons why, but one of his strongest reasons—especially on Christmas Eve, the night of the candlelight service—was that he got *scared* in church. There was no other word for it. He could barely admit it even to himself, but that was it—he got *terrified* . . . especially during the candlelight service, when they darkened the church.

He had been—what?—maybe ten years old the first time his parents (this was back before his mother began drinking) took him to a Christmas Eve candlelight service. The beginning of the service had been typical—boring and long, with the minister and congregation responding back and forth and everyone joining in on the hymns; but then, after the sermon, someone at the back of the church had turned off the lights, plunging the whole church into darkness. A single candle had still burned on the altar, and the minister had still been talking, going on about the promise of hope and light that the season brought but it had taken John several seconds to realize that he hadn't suddenly lost his sight. His first terrified thought had been, *I can't see! I'm dying!*

For just an instant, ten-year-old John had felt as though he were spinning—falling backwards and spinning completely out of control, his mind a swirling blackness except for one tiny sliver of light. While the minister was going on about a light in the time of darkness, a black, nameless dread . . .

I'm not dead . . . but I'm dying!

. . . had gripped John in its icy clutch. Before he knew what he was doing—before he could even clamp his hand over his mouth —he had let out a high-pitched, warbling screech that had echoed through the church. Needless to say, the entire service had been disrupted by John's cries.

He remembered what happened next only in fragments. He knew his father had grabbed him by the arm and roughly jerked him down the aisle and down to the church basement. He knew he had been in tears, flailing his arms and legs, screaming as loud as he could—partly because of the licking he knew he was going to get, but mostly because he could still feel that cold, dark terror squeezing his heart. He knew that everyone in the church must be wondering what was wrong with him . . . if he was sick or if he was out of his mind. And he knew he had told his father, down in the church basement, that he had had an awful jab of pain in his stomach, that he felt like he was going to throw up. As it turned out, that had spared him the whipping he had expected; and ever since that day, he had never been able to enter a church without feeling at least the stirrings of that black, nameless dread. . . .

I'm not dead . . . but I'm dying!

This Christmas Eve, pushing Frank in his wheelchair, he and Julia and Bri walked into the church and sat down, a little too close to the front, John thought, eyeing the doors at the back of the church—his escape route if he needed it. He gritted his teeth, trying his best not to let his nervousness show. It took effort to stay calm, and he knew it would get worse when the church went dark for the candle lighting, but he kept telling himself it was only going to be for an hour . . . he could make it. He had only been ten years old, after all. The church's sudden plunge into darkness had caught him by surprise, had scared him. He was an adult now, he kept telling himself, he could handle it.

There were several familiar faces in the congregation, and many people came over to Frank to wish him and his family a merry Christmas. John had to struggle to put names to some of the faces, and he even got a few, but he felt awkward trying to smile and look cheerful when all he could think was, *Am I going to scream again when the lights go out? Will I feel like I'm dying?*

The minister—still Pastor Vernon, looking old and tired—came out, and the service began with a rousing "Joy to the World." John was surprised at how much of the service was still in his memory, and he mouthed the congregational responses with only a few glances at his opened hymnal. He halfheartedly joined in the carol singing, although he did have to admit it felt quite nice being there with Julia and Bri. But his mind was rushing ahead, waiting— *dreading* the moment after the sermon when the church lights would go out, and he would be standing there alone . . .

Yes! Alone, no matter how close I'm standing to Julia and Bri!
. . . in the dark, waiting for the ushers to move down the aisles so all could light their candles, wondering if that same cold dread he had experienced so long ago was still there, still waiting for him. . . .

I'm not dead! . . . But I'm dying, his mind whispered, thoughts from more than twenty-five years ago.

The sermon was drawing to a close, its words and message completely lost to John. Gripping the hymnal tightly, he felt his hands slick with sweat as he waited . . . waited for the sudden drop into blackness. He heard Reverend Vernon say, "A light in the time of darkness." That was the cue, and suddenly the church lights silently winked off.

But John was ready for it this time.

He kept his eyes focused straight ahead at the single candle still burning on the altar as blackness rushed down around him with an almost audible whoosh. He felt a cold jab in the pit of his stomach, as though he had been skewered by an icicle, but he was biting down so hard on his lower lip, he knew a tiny whimper was the only sound he would make. In his mind, he *was* ten years old again, and—*yes!*—the cold dread was there. It sprang like a tiger out of the darkness at him.

But with his eyes on the single burning candle, he watched as Reverend Vernon reached forward with a large white candle and touched the wick to the flame. With the second candle burning, adding its light to the dark church, John felt a small measure of reassurance. Memories and fears were still rushing like a whirlwind in his mind, but now the ushers had touched their candles to the one the minister was holding, and soon they were moving down the center aisle as everyone passed the flame and lit the small candle he or she had been given when entering church.

John turned to peek at Julia. Her face was bathed in the warm glow of the candles, looking peaceful and content. Even the rough crags of his father's face appeared to be smoothed out, softened. The rising tide of dark, oppressive fear inside John seemed to crest like a towering wave, and then, ever so gently, begin to recede, but then, when John looked straight ahead again, he saw something—some*one* that made his heart thump in his chest.

Standing in front of him just three pews away was a woman, a young girl, really, who he was positive hadn't been there a moment before when the church lights had been on. She was wearing a rough-looking gray sweater—certainly not fancy Christmas Eve attire—and her long, dark hair swept down her shoulders in a swirl that gleamed like a crow's wing in the flickering candlelight.

In a frozen instant of panic, John thought he recognized her. Her hair, the stoop of her shoulders, her stance—everything seemed so familiar. All around him, the congregation made noise —hushed whispers and muffled shuffling of feet as each person passed the flame to his neighbor. But below the crowd noise, John thought he heard something else—a low, rippling giggle that danced just at the edge of his hearing. He wasn't positive, but it sure looked like the girl's shoulders were shaking.

As though she's laughing, John thought, suddenly filled by the necessity of seeing the girl's face.

The ushers made their way slowly along the aisles. Once Frank had his candle lit, he nudged John to get his attention so he could light his. John then passed the flame along to Julia and Bri, all the while struggling to keep his hands from trembling.

Who the hell is she? he wondered, unable to pull his eyes away from her back as he watched her, concentrating his gaze so intensely he was sure she must feel his eyes boring into her back like lasers.

John sensed more than saw a stirring beside him and, looking to his left, saw that his father was watching him, his eyes glistening like glass in the candlelight.

Maybe he's also remembering what happened that Christmas Eve when I was ten years old, and he's expecting it to happen again, John thought as a frantic helplessness churned inside him.

When Frank followed John's gaze, and he, too, saw the girl in the gray sweater, John saw an expression of confusion sweep across his father's face. The lines around his eyes and mouth suddenly deepened until they looked like dark ink marks. His lower lip began to tremble, and his eyes rolled backward in his head, gazing blankly for a moment at the ceiling.

"Isn't that . . . ?" Frank whispered, more to the ceiling than to his son.

John could see his father's hand clench the hymnal as wave after wave of what looked like—concern? No, *worry*, then stark fear—swept over Frank.

With a sudden twist, Frank looked wide-eyed at John, snapping his head for him to lean close so he could say something to him. After glancing around to see if they were disturbing anyone, John leaned down to his father.

"*That's* what I was going to tell yah before," Frank said, his voice no more than a strangled whisper. "I was tryin' to remember. That's . . . that's . . ."

Again a blankness swept like a banner across Frank's eyes as he reached into his mind for the words he knew were there but weren't forming for him. His face reflected the struggle going on inside him.

"What?" John asked, prodding. He could feel his stomach churning as his eyes kept flicking back toward the girl in the gray sweater.

"That's who I saw before . . . at the house," Frank said.

"Who?" John hissed. The only answer Frank made was to jerk his head in the direction of the girl standing in front of them.

John looked back at her, and his own fear grew, compounded by whatever his father was trying to communicate to him. He felt a dread coldness reaching out to him from the darkness of the church where the candlelight didn't reach. He was absolutely convinced the girl hadn't been there when the service began, and although the logical explanation was that she had arrived late and had slipped unnoticed into place with her family, there was something totally unnerving about her sudden appearance—something that obviously bothered his father, as well.

John's first impression had been that—at least from behind—she looked like someone he knew very well . . . someone who couldn't *possibly* have been here tonight!

Everyone in the church had a candle lit now, and the church organ began the rousing strains of "Hark, the Herald Angels Sing." As the congregation joined in the song, John found himself dumbly mouthing the words as he looked frantically back and forth between the girl's back and his father's confused expression. The girl appeared not to move. She just stood there, her head bowed, apparently not singing.

The memory of the panic John had dreaded earlier seemed like nothing compared to what he felt now, staring at the girl. John tried to tear his gaze away from her, but he couldn't. For just an instant, as he glanced at the candle in his hands, the flame appeared to burn a deep blue.

Beneath the swelling chorus of voices singing the carol, John thought he could still detect a faint ripple of laughter—cold and icy, like the darkness he had dreaded earlier, only worse because it wasn't just cold—it was *cruel*!

With all the candles lit, the church was almost as bright as it had been with the ceiling lights on, but this light had a peculiar flickering glow that made it seem somehow unnatural. John felt a prodding in his ribs and, turning, saw Julia looking at him.

"You okay?" she whispered, her brow creasing with concern.

Tight-lipped, John nodded his head. "Yeah—" He stopped himself from mentioning his father's sudden confused panic, and looking at Frank now, he seemed just fine, singing along with the carol.

"Then sing," Julia said, holding her hymnal so he could see the page number. "Come on."

John quickly riffled through his hymnal until he found the correct page, but all the while he was positive he could hear that faint trace of laughter nibbling at the edges of his awareness. Once he found the carol, he scanned the lines and found where they were, but then when he lifted his head—aware that Julia was still watching him—started to sing, his throat closed off with a strangled gag.

The girl wasn't there anymore!

John looked at his father to see if he had noticed or reacted, but Frank was singing along, oblivious to his son's confusion. John quickly looked down the aisle to see if the girl . . .

It couldn't possibly be who I thought it was!

. . . was leaving, but she was nowhere in sight. There wasn't even a gap in the crowded pew where she had been. John saw the wide back of a man in a dark blue sports coat where, seconds before, the girl with black hair and the gray sweater had been standing.

Am I imagining things? he thought as a chilly rush went up his back. The tips of his fingers began to tingle with pins and needles, and he was aware that he was taking very shallow breaths.

How could she just vanish like that? he wondered.

Leaning close to his father's ear, he whispered, "Did you remember who you wanted to tell me about?"

Frank pulled away from him and looked up with anger in his eyes. "What—? Who?" he whispered harshly. "Don't go botherin' me during the service!"

John straightened up, now thoroughly confused by his father's earlier reaction.

"Are you sure you're feeling all right?" Julia asked, nudging John in the side and leaning close to him. "You don't look so good."

"I'm fine—fine!" John said, forcing his voice to stay low. He shook his head vigorously from side to side. "Honest. . . ."

Julia turned back to her own hymnal and continued singing loudly.

John tried to push aside the thoughts that kept rushing in on him. He tried to tell himself that the girl in the gray sweater had been there all along; he just hadn't noticed her. And finally, once the candles had been lit, she had left, either to go downstairs to the bathroom or to go home. Maybe in a while, he told himself, she'll be back; but even if she didn't return, she *had* been there all along. That was her father in the dark blue sports coat.

But what the hell was my father doing? he thought, looking at him from the corner of his eye. *Why did he act so weird . . . and then pretend he hadn't said anything?*

"That's what I was going to tell yah before."

"I was trying to remember."

"That's who I saw before . . . at the house."

The thin laughter John had heard had been . . . *must* have been —like the momentary blue glow of his candle—just his imagination playing tricks on him. The fact that, from behind, the girl had reminded him of Abby Snow was nothing more than a coincidence. His earlier fears, remembering what had happened to him during that Christmas Eve service when he was ten years old, had just sparked his imagination and made him *think* she looked like Abby, because, bottom line, he *knew* Abby Snow, having been dead for almost twenty years, couldn't be here—or *anywhere!*— this Christmas Eve!

III

The too-good-to-hope-for snow Julia had wanted had started falling sometime during the church service, and as the people walked out into the night, thick flakes were sifting down, tumbling like coins in the streetlights. Lit from the inside, the stained-glass windows of the church stained the piled-high snowbanks with soft blues and reds. The night was filled with shouted holiday greetings, and even John, who still felt the tingling residue of panic, tried his best to feel elated.

"Should've put snowies on my chair," Frank said, chuckling as John struggled to push his wheelchair down the snow-slick walkway. Julia and Bri followed close behind.

"I think this is neat," Bri said. She bent down, scooped up a handful of snow, and tossed it playfully at John's back.

He turned around and said to her, "I'll get you for that. Or maybe Santa will just leave coal in your stocking." As he looked back at her over his shoulder, a shadow under one of the yew bushes beside the church seemed, for just a second, to shift, but he pretended not to notice.

"Well," Bri said, skipping up close to him, "*I* happen to know that Santa got you nothing but neckties this year."

"Oh, no . . . not *again*!" John wailed dramatically.

They crossed the street to their car, and while Julia swung open the back door, John helped his father get in. He collapsed the wheelchair and went to put it into the back of the staion wagon, but just as he was raising the hatch, a sharp peel of laughter filled the night. For a frozen instant, his mind went blank. Looking up at the church, not knowing what he expected to see, maybe the girl he had been watching, he felt a rush of relief when he saw two boys racing across the church parking lot and throwing fistfuls of snow at each other. A few paces behind, a man and a woman were walking; the man shouted out, "Aaron! . . . Jesse! You boys stop that right now!"

Smiling weakly and shaking his head, John got into the car and drove back to the house, grateful that church was finally over!

"Anyone feel like taking a peek under the tree?" Bri said as they all burst into the kitchen, stamping their feet to remove the snow. Almost instantly, Julia was over by the stove, asking if anyone wanted coffee or hot chocolate.

"Let's all have some cocoa, and then we can each open a present," Bri said, jumping up and down excitedly.

"Sounds good to me," John said. On his way into the house, he had scooped up a small handful of snow. After he swung the door shut behind him, he turned and tossed it at Bri. "Here's yours."

Bri tried to duck to the side, but the snowball caught her on the side of the face. It splattered and fell to the floor with a plop.

Julia looked at them and scowled. "If you two *children* are going to play, would you mind doing it outside? I don't want my kitchen floor all wet."

"I'll wipe it up," John said, reaching for a paper towel.

While Julia heated the milk for cocoa and Bri went upstairs to put on her nightgown and robe, John and Frank both went into the living room. John plugged in the tree lights and then sat down on the couch, trying not to think about the girl he had seen in church or wonder what his father had been trying to tell him—and then why he had totally forgotten about it.

"Ahh, what the hell," he muttered softly to himself, thinking at least now church was over and the sooner he got that girl out of his memory, the more he would enjoy the rest of the holiday.

Bri came tromping downstairs, her arms loaded with the presents she had wrapped for her parents and grandfather. She went over to the tree and added them to the gifts Julia and John had spread out just before they left for church. They had waited until Bri and Frank were in the car because Julia said she wanted to maintain a bit of the illusion of Santa Claus. Frank had gone to his bedroom for a moment and returned with three envelopes, one with each of their names on it. He handed them to Bri, who put them under the tree.

"Didn't have much chance to get out shoppin'," he said by way of excuse.

John almost said he could have picked up something for him but he decided not to.

"Here we go," Julia said, entering the living room holding a tray with four cups of steaming cocoa. She placed the tray down on the coffee table and plunked herself down beside John.

"So—who goes first?" Bri said. She was kneeling in front of the tree with her hands on her knees, looking anxiously from one person to another. "Granddad, why don't you take a peek inside of this?" She got up and handed him a small rectangular box, giving him a quick kiss on the cheek as she did.

"Ahh, you didn't have to get anything for me," Frank said, looking a bit embarrassed as he fumbled with the ribbons and paper until he exposed a box. When he opened the lid, his face broke out into a wide smile. "Son of a gun," he said, holding up a pair of fleece-lined slippers. "I was needin' a new pair." He put them back into the box and place the box on the table beside his wheelchair.

John and Julia were sitting back, smiling as they sipped their cocoa and watched Bri. It struck Julia as charming that, even though Bri was already thirteen and growing up right under their noses, Christmas still had the magic to turn her into a little girl again. Maybe, she thought, that was the true magic of Christmas —that even though you were much too old to play with toys, you could act like a kid again at least once a year.

"Bri," Julia said, "why don't you check out that green box?"

"You mean the one that says *'From Santa'*?"

Julia nodded.

Bri chuckled as she reached for the box. Before she opened it, thought, she held it up and gave it a gentle shake. "It sounds like something from Cherry Webb," she said, smirking. "I hope it's a green something."

"Just open it. You'll see," Julia said, smiling. "Hold it! Before you do . . ."

She got up and went into the kitchen, returning a second later with her camera in hand. After popping up the flash bar, she took aim and nodded. "Okay—go to it."

As Bri ripped open the paper and burst into a grin when she saw that it *was* the green blouse she had wanted, the room filled with a burst of bright light. Bri blinked her eyes in a daze and, holding the top up against herself, said, "Geeze, I'm not sure it's worth getting *blinded* for. Thanks, Mom and Dad."

"I didn't get that for you. Santa did," Julia said, moving so she could get a different angle for another shot.

Laughing out loud, Bri leaned toward the fireplace and, looking up the flue, shouted, "Thanks a lot, fat man!" Before she pulled back, the room again filled with the flash of Julia's camera.

"You know, while you're at it," Frank said gruffly, "you might's well hand out those envelopes I gave yah. No sense waitin' till tomorrow."

Bri gave her mother and father a quick glance to see if she had their approval as well, then gave one each to her mother and father, keeping the one with her name scrawled on the front. The handwriting was done in pencil lines and, she noticed, was so faint it almost looked like a tattered spiderweb.

"Go ahead. Open 'em," Frank commanded when all three of them just sat looking at the envelopes.

Bri was the first. She slid her finger in under the flap and tore it along the top. Inside was a money card—the kind with the little oval in the center so you could see the face on the bill peering out at you. Bri felt a dash of excitement when she opened the card and saw that it wasn't a president; it was Benjamin Franklin smiling up at her. Written on the outside was: *"To Bri—with love and Merry Christmas—Granddad."*

"Oh, Granddad," she said. "You didn't have to do *this*!" She jumped up and wrapped her arms around his neck so hard she almost pulled him from the wheelchair.

Meanwhile, Julia and John had opened their envelopes and found that they had one-hundred-dollar bills inside theirs. Both of them expressed their surprise, but in spite of himself, John couldn't help thinking, *You never used to be this generous. Why now?*

"Thanks a lot, Frank," Julia said, coming over to his wheelchair and giving him a kiss on the cheek. "I agree with Bri—you didn't have to."

"Ahh," Frank said, waving her away with his hand, "it's the least I could do. I ain't ever gonna get out to spend it."

"You got out enough to get to the bank and get crisp new bills and gift cards," John said, eyeing his father slyly.

To prevent having to respond, Frank picked up his cup of cocoa and took a slurping sip.

"Well, that just leaves the two of you guys," Bri said, turning to rummage around under the tree. After pawing over the stacks of gifts, she turned around with one in each hand and held them out to her mother and father. "Here you go. Now take your time opening it. Don't just throw the paper all over the place in your excitement."

Both Julia and John snickered as Julia came back to the couch and sat down beside John. "You go first," she said, nodding her head to indicate the present he was holding.

"Oh, no. Ladies first," John replied.

Shrugging, Julia looked at the name tag. *"To Julia—Love John,"* it read. She slipped her fingers in under the paper and peeled it back. Smiling, she pulled out the box of White Shoulders perfume. "My favorite," she said as she opened the box and, unscrewing the cover, brought the small bottle up to her nose and sniffed. Her eyes flickered with satisfaction as the fragrance filled her nose.

"Quick! Where's that camera!" Bri shouted. She saw it on the coffee table and grabbed it, aimed, and shot while Julia, with a wide, silly grin, held the perfume bottle up close to her cheek.

"One person left to go," Bri said. She looked back under the tree and started shifting back and forth, pawing through the stack of presents like a woodchuck burrowing in the ground. Brightly wrapped packages shifted back and forth as she lifted them up, inspected them briefly, then put them back down.

"Are your *sure* you've been a good boy this year?" Bri asked, turning to look at her father. "I don't seem to see a *thing* under here with your name on it."

"Come on, Bri," Julia said, smiling tightly.

Shrugging, Bri took a present and, holding it out to her father, said, "Oh, here we are."

"You're too kind," John said, smiling as he took the present. It was small and very light. Actually, it felt as though it was empty. Inspecting the name tag, he read aloud, "To John . . . from a *secret* admirer."

Julia looked at him with upraised eyebrows, as if to say, *It's not from me*. She was also thinking that, since she gave Bri all of her extra wrapping paper, she would have recognized if it was from her.

John took a sip of cocoa and, sitting back on the couch, began slowly unwrapping the gift. The tabs of Scotch tape pulled away easily, exposing a plain white box. When he flipped open the cover, all he saw inside was a wad of crumpled-up tissue paper. After a few seconds pawing through the tissue paper, he looked up, first at Julia, then at Bri.

"Is this some kind of joke?" he asked. His hand was still fishing around inside the box, but by now he knew it was empty. He pulled all the tissue paper out and looked through it, but nothing fell out.

"What do you mean?" Julia said.

"It's empty . . . unless someone thinks a box of tissue paper is a gift. Bri, did you do this?"

Bri shook her head, and from her furrowed brow, John was convinced her denial was honest.

Shrugging, John put the box beside him on the couch. "I don't know. Maybe it was from someone at the office or something and the store forgot to put the gift in before they wrapped it."

"Hmm . . . it *is* kind of strange," Julia said. "Bri—why don't you grab something else for your father. Maybe later we'll figure out what happened."

While Bri busied herself inspecting the remaining presents under the tree, John dropped the empty box onto the floor and started balling up the tissue paper. When he picked up the wrapping paper from his lap, he noticed some marks on the inside of the paper. At first he only saw two words:

WHAT YOU

His heartbeat sounded suddenly loud in his ears as he carefully unfolded the paper the rest of the way and, shielding it from

Julia's view, looked at the message scrawled in pencil on the inside.

Same heavy-handed printing as before . . . same message . . . with one more word added!

I WON'T FORGET WHAT YOU DID TO ME !

But it wasn't the name he had been expecting!

ME?

John's throat made an involuntary click as he gasped for breath. He had been expecting more messages, more words, and he had been ready to deal with them. He had been so positive the last word would be a *name*. But this! *This*, with the last word—ME—underlined so heavily the pencil had almost torn right through the paper. . . .

The last word should have been ABBY!

The whooshing sound of his heartbeat in his ears got so loud it was like the roar of the ocean. He could feel the drops of cold sweat breaking out on his forehead. His hands were trembling and they looked milky white as he rolled the wrapping paper up into a tight ball and squeezed it, making sure none of the writing showed.

"Hey, Dad! Did you fall asleep or something?" Bri said. She was jabbing at him with a brightly wrapped box. "Here, this one's from me. I swear there's something in this one."

Her voice came to him from far away, and turning to look at her, he had the curious sensation of being distanced from his body. He saw his hand reach out mechanically, as though it belonged to someone else. He spoke, even though the words he said were barely formed in his mind.

"Oh—thanks, but you didn't have to get me anything," he heard himself say automatically as his hand closed on the package. The sudden weight of it as Bri let go caught him by surprise, and he almost dropped it.

All he could think about was what he had seen written on the inside of the present. His mind was roaring with questions. . . .

Who was writing these messages?

How did they get them—the note in his car this afternoon . . . and now the one in this package in the house under the Christmas tree?

And why? Why was . . . whoever it was doing this to him? The memory of what had happened to Abby was torment enough. . . . Why was someone tormenting him?

He had become increasingly convinced that it was Randy who

was doing this to him, but if so, why end the message with the word ME?

"A new set of wrenches, I'd say by the feel," he said, forcing a laugh to cover up the shaking in his voice. He glanced at Julia, and although she didn't say anything, he was positive she was looking at him strangely, as though she suspected what was going on.

Is she in on this with Randy? he wondered. And then it hit him so hard he felt it in his mind like the concussion of a cannon shot. *It has to be Randy! Randy Chadwick is the one! He's known all along what happened, and now that I've moved back he's using it against me. Maybe Julia's even helping him! How else could these notes be appearing in places they shouldn't be? Maybe Randy's trying to steal my wife away from me!*

"Well, come on . . . open it up," Julia said. "It's getting late and I want to get to bed so Santa Claus will come." Her voice was spritely, but when he looked at her again, he became convinced he saw something dark moving behind her eyes like a hungry shark.

His hands felt rubbery, almost out of control as he tore open the paper. All the while, he was thinking, *What if the same message is written on the inside of this, too?*

I WON'T FORGET WHAT YOU DID TO ME!

But as he peeled the paper away, he glanced at the blank inside, grateful there was no handwritten message there. All he saw was a small white box, heavy for its size, with the word *Norelco* stamped in gold on the bottom left corner.

"An electric razor," he said flatly. He took a deep breath fighting to control the trembling he was positive everyone heard. "That's a really neat idea. Thanks." He slid open the cover and looked inside, but didn't bother to take the razor out of its case.

Bri leaned forward, presenting the side of her face. "You are allowed to kiss me . . . but just on the cheek," she said, waving a cautioning finger at him.

John gave her a quick little peck on the cheek and then put the box down on the coffee table next to his empty cocoa cup.

"Well, I'm beat. I'm hittin' the sack," Frank said, pulling back on the wheelchair wheels to turn around. "I'd say, all in all it's been a fair to middlin' evenin'." Glancing at Julia, he nodded and added a soft, "Thanks for comin' to church with me, Abby."

Julia opened her mouth, about to correct his mistake, but then decided to let it go. "My pleasure," she said; then she turned to Bri and said sharply, "You! Get your teeth brushed and your butt in bed now, or *else!*"

"Don't you want me to help you clean this mess up?" Bri said as she stood up and surveyed the crusted cocoa mugs and torn gift wrappings strewn around.

"You need your sleep," Julia said, glancing at her watch. "It's already past eleven. Your father and I can take care of this."

John noticed that, again, she looked at him strangely.

"G'night, everyone," Frank said tiredly as he rolled down the hallway to his bedroom. His door slammed shut behind him.

"Go on," Julia said, waving her hand at Bri. "Get upstairs."

"I hope I can get to sleep," she said as she started slowly up the stairs, dragging her feet on each step. "I'm so excited about Santa coming."

"Get out of here!" Julia said. She took some crumpled-up wrapping paper and tossed it playfully at her.

John still hadn't moved from the couch. He was sitting there, staring blankly at the lights on the Christmas tree as though hypnotized. The ornaments caught and fragmented the colored lights into thousands of dazzling sparkles. Beside him on the couch, he could sense the balled-up gift wrap with the penciled message on the inside, it seemed to burn against his leg like a hot coal. He was only vaguely aware of Julia as she bustled about, clearing away the empty cups.

"Here—you want me to take that?" she said, standing at the end of the couch with her hand out.

"Huh?"

"That paper you've got," she said. "I'll throw it away for you."

He picked up the paper ball, fully expecting it to sear his hand as soon as his fingers touched it. But nothing like that happened —it was just a crumpled-up piece of paper that he held out to his wife; but for a few tense seconds, he looked at her, trying to fathom that curious, dark look in her eyes, trying to read if she *did* know what he had seen written on the inside.

"Okay. I guess that's just about it," she said simply as she scooped up the other discarded wrappings and, crumpling it all together, went into the kitchen and stuffed everything into the trash can.

She went around the house, turning off all the lights except those on the Christmas tree, and then she plunked herself down on the couch. Snuggling up under her husband's arm, she laced her fingers through his and held him tightly.

"Did you have a nice time tonight?" she asked, giving his hand a jiggle.

John shrugged, not taking his eyes away from the tree for an instant. "Okay, I guess," he said, his voice hollow and distant.

"I think you've been really uptight all evening. Come on. Tell me—what's the matter?" She tightened her grip on his hand and reached up to his shoulder, pulling him around so he would have to look at her. They looked intently at each other, while the brilliant tree lights reflected in their eyes.

"Nothing's the matter," he said, taking a deep breath and letting it out slowly. "I'm just beat—that's all."

"Well . . ." She pulled him closer and brought her face up close to his. "You know, I was wondering if you were going to give me what I wanted for Christmas."

"What? Oh, you mean what you had on your list?" he said as he noticed the hazy look in her eyes.

"Yeah," she said, *"that."* They brought their faces even closer, their lips less than an inch apart. She pressed her mouth against his and gave him a long, lingering kiss. His body felt rigid in her grasp, but the longer they kissed, the more he seemed to loosen up. Eventually she felt his tongue flickering between her teeth, and she took that as a signal to proceed. Rubbing her hand on his chest in long, lingering circles, she let herself melt into his arms.

IV

Half an hour later, naked and bathed in sweat, the two of them were slouched side by side on the couch, their arms wrapped around each other's shoulders as they stared out the picture window at the cold night. The snow, apparently, had stopped, and through the breaks in the clouds, they could see a sprinkling of stars.

"That did it—I just *know* it did," Julia said as she ran her fingertips up and down John's inner thigh. In the last moment before he penetrated her, she admitted that she wasn't going to use the diaphragm, but he had simply muttered, "What the hell . . .?"

John chuckled weakly. The sex, he had to admit, had been good. All evening, ever since Julia had first told him she wanted to go to church with Frank, he had been feeling the tension building inside of him. And then, remembering what had happened during the candlelight service when he was ten years old, and trying to figure out what his father had meant to tell him, and then seeing that note on the inside of the wrapping paper . . . *everything* had gotten on his nerves. He had needed a release.

But now, after a healthy dose of sex—and he had to admit it *did* feel nice not having to use the diaphragm—he was unwinding . . . beginning to, anyway. The other memories were just that—memories. They might be unpleasant, but he was convinced he could deal with them, ignore them as much as possible and dismiss them when they arose. The note, though . . .

I WON'T FORGET WHAT YOU DID TO ME!

. . . was different. It, unlike a memory, was something real, *too* real. Someone was doing this to him, leaving notes around to remind him about what had happened to Abby. As far as he had known, no one other than himself had known a thing about it. The notes he and Julia had been finding indicated otherwise. Once he was convinced it was Randy—and actually, the more he thought about it, he had started to suspect Randy way back when he and Julia had gone to the Chadwicks' for supper—it all started to make sense . . . maybe *twisted* sense, but sense nevertheless.

What he determined to do was simply to make sure he didn't give Randy or whoever was doing this the satisfaction of seeing that it was getting to him. After all, it wasn't as if he had done something actually wrong.

It wasn't as if he had *killed* her or anything!

He had to admit, though, that it was a nice, chilling touch, using the word ME, when he had been expecting to see her name. The note should have read: I WON'T FORGET WHAT YOU DID TO ABBY!

In the warm glow of the Christmas lights, John held his wife close to him, feeling her smooth, sweat-slick skin rubbing against him. He tried to let himself feel totally content. If she was right, if this pop had gotten her pregnant, well, then . . . so what? It was what she wanted, and God knew they had tried often enough before, so she must have her mind made up pretty firmly on this. And anyway, if tonight was like so many other times back when they had first gotten married and both had wanted to have another baby, it hadn't worked, and she still wasn't pregnant.

"How can you be so sure," he said, looking at her, her skin glowing from the multicolored tree lights. "I mean, you can't feel it or anything."

"Oh . . . women have ways of knowing things," she whispered before kissing him on the chest and shoulders. Her lips were warm and wet on his skin. "When it happens, you can just *feel* it."

"Yeah . . . sure," he said, laughing softly. "Men can feel it, too. It's called *orgasm*."

"Ahh—cut it out," Julia said. She slapped him playfully on the bare stomach, making a loud smack sound. "You men are all the same—so insensitive."

For just an instant, John found himself wondering what she meant by that: *You men are all the same*. He tried not to let the thought form in his mind that, maybe what was going on here was that Julia had been seeing Randy Chadwick. Was something like that possible? Could his wife, who was home all day while he was at work in Portland, be having an affair with his best friend from high school? Had daytime soap opera come to Glooscap Island, Maine? Stranger things than that have happened, he supposed. He felt a sudden dash of chills, as though a cold breeze were wafting over his naked body when he thought next . . .

Maybe that's why Randy's leaving those notes around! He's trying to drive me crazy so he can steal my wife!

"Well, if we're going to get up sometime before noon tomorrow, we ought to be getting to bed," Julia said. She stood up and stretched her arms over her head, and John couldn't help but admire her shapely body in the bright glow of the tree lights.

Shifting forward, he was bending over to collect his clothes from where they had tossed them onto the floor when a sudden, loud groan interrupted the silent night. Startled, John and Julia looked at each other, their eyes widened with fear and surprise. Neither of them was positive they had heard what they thought they had heard.

"What the—?" John said, and then, in an instant they both grabbed their clothes and started to dress. While they were scrambling to get into their clothes, a second, louder noise—a ragged shout—rang through the house, and this time both of them knew where it was coming from.

"My father . . ." John said. He jumped up and down as he pulled his pants on and ran bare-chested down the hallway. Quickly buttoning her blouse, Julia was only a few steps behind him.

The door to Frank's bedroom was shut, and when John tried to turn the doorknob, it wouldn't budge.

"Shit! He's got it locked," he said. "He never locks the door, does he?" He was looking frantically at Julia when, for a third time, a sound—a loud scream this time—came from the bedroom. John clenched his fist and hammered on the door as hard as he could. "Dad! Dad! What's the matter? Are you all right?"

He gripped the doorknob and shook it violently. The door rattled on its hinges, but it wouldn't give.

"Oh, Jesus! Oh, Jesus!" Julia said when, below the sound of John's pounding on the door, she became aware of a strangled, gurgling sound coming from behind the door.

"*Dad!* For Christ's sake! Open up!" John wailed. He stopped trying the doorknob and instead pounded with both hands on the door. Then, hauling back a few steps, he coiled himself and suddenly threw himself at the door. He hit with a resounding thump, but still the door didn't budge.

"Why would he lock his bedroom door?" John shouted frantically as he looked at Julia. She was staring at him with eyes that looked like shiny coins, holding her hands up in front of herself, a gesture of helplessness.

"Come on, Dad! *Open up!*" John shouted, but he and Julia could both tell from the sounds coming from his room that something was seriously wrong—something bad was happening to Frank.

Another stroke . . . or a heart attack, John thought, and already his mind was darkening with thoughts of everything that would be left unresolved between them if his father died now.

"Is there a spare key or something? Maybe in the kitchen somewhere?" Julia said. Her voice sounded pinched and high.

John grimly shook his head and then threw himself at the door again. He hit it hard and bounced back with a grunt.

"Jesus Christ! Jesus Christ!" he shouted. For a third time, he slammed his body so hard against the door he was positive the whole door frame would give way. But he felt the door give just a fraction of an inch and no more. Meanwhile, from inside Frank's room, they could hear a loud rustling sound, as though Frank was violently struggling with something. They could hear his raspy breathing, and his throat was making a deep vibrating sound, as though he wanted to scream even louder but couldn't find the breath to do so.

"Get me something!" John shouted, turning to Julia as he continued to rain heavy-handed blows on the door. "Anything! A hammer! An ax."

Frantic, Julia turned to run out to the garage; and as she did, she ran straight into Bri, who had come downstairs to find out what all the commotion was about. Surprised, Julia let out a piercing shriek.

Turning and seeing Bri cowering in surprise and fear, John shouted to her, "Quick! Call the rescue unit!"

While Julia went out to the garage to find the ax, Bri hurried into the kitchen and dialed the emergency phone number taped to the telephone. Convinced the door was giving way, John levered himself against it by bracing his legs against the opposite wall and pushing with everything he had. He could feel his muscles straining, his veins bulging.

The door seemed to be sagging inward, just barely. It was almost as if the wood were swollen with water and was wedged inside the frame. The door creaked loudly every time John smashed into it, but not loud enough to mask the strangled, choking sounds coming from inside the room. Sweat—this time not the sweet sweat of sex, he thought—dripped down his forehead and stung his eyes as he pushed for all he was worth. The sounds of the struggle within the room seemed to grow louder and louder in his ears until that was all he could hear. A flurry of motion beside him caught his attention.

"Here," Julia said, her voice no more than a bark as she thrust the ax into his hand.

John gripped the ax handle, braced his legs, and flailed at the door like a madman. The blade bit deeply into the wood with each swing, removing splinters of wood and making the door reverberate. Julia stood back and watched, horrified at what was happening and thinking crazily, *What a hell of a Christmas Eve!*

At last the door gave way with a loud inward explosion of shattering wood. John threw it wide open. The ax fell to the floor as he staggered into his father's darkened bedroom, his eyes straining to see what had happened. So far, all he could see was a shapeless mass wrapped up in a tangle of sheets.

"Dad!" John shouted as he fumbled for the wall switch. He could still hear deep, ragged breathing coming from the bed; it sounded like someone crinkling paper. He found the wall switch and clicked it on, ready for just about anything; but what he saw made him step back until he was stopped by the wall.

"What?" Julia said from behind him, leaning in through the shattered door.

After a second, John regained his self-control and went over to the bed, knowing as he did that this was it—his father was dying. Wasn't that raspy breathing sound what they called the death rattle?

"Did you call the rescue?" he yelled, barely glancing at the doorway over his shoulder.

"Bri did," Julia said as she cautiously approached the bed and looked at Frank. The sheets and covers looked as though he had been wrestling with someone; they were untucked and strewn all around. Frank lay crosswise on the bed on his back, his arms and legs spread wide. The buttons of his pajama tops had ripped off, exposing his white, bony chest that rose up and down with his rapid panting breath. His eyes, milky and white, stared blankly up at the ceiling.

John was on his knees beside the bed, his hands hovering helplessly over his father, as if he wanted to touch him, to help him, but he didn't dare to.

"Dad? Can you hear me?" he whispered, coming close to his father's ear.

The old man's harsh breathing reminded him of the sound of metal scraping against metal. He didn't blink; he didn't move except for his labored breathing. His face had an almost translucent cast to it, like waxed fruit.

"We called the ambulance, Dad," John said soothingly. He reached out gingerly and, just to do something—*anything*—

began to button up his father's pajama tops. When his fingers brushed against his father's chest, he was shocked at how cold and clammy it felt.

Julia came over to the bed and stood beside John. They exchanged knowing glances, silently acknowledging that they both thought this was it—the ambulance wasn't going to arrive in time.

Tears of thick, almost milky fluid formed in each of Frank's eyes, ran down the sides of his face, and soaked into the sheet. A trace of pink foam dribbled from the corner of his mouth. His pale lips moved, but neither John nor Julia could tell if he was trying to speak or if it was just a muscle spasm.

John turned to Julia and nodded at the sheets, indicating that the least they could do was cover him, make him as comfortable as possible until the ambulance got there. Julia went to the other side of the bed and, trying her best not to move Frank, untangled the sheets from his legs and pulled them up with John.

"She—" Frank said, his voice nothing more than a whisper of wind.

"You just relax," John said as he tucked the sheet up under his father's chin. "The ambulance is on its way."

A faint flicker of light seemed to brighten Frank's eyes for just an instant as he broke his steady stare at the ceiling and looked over to John. At first John thought it was simply a spark of recognition, of realization that he was dying and, although he never had and couldn't now say to his son what he wanted to, it was all right . . . everything was all right . . . he was beyond pain. But as John looked deeply into his father's eyes, he saw something else —a spark of . . . *fear* . . . *pure terror*!

"It's okay, Dad," John whispered, knowing now—just as he had dreaded—that the things they should have said to each other would never be said now.

Frank's mouth made a loud smacking sound as he tried to form words. The pink foam kept bubbling out onto the sheet. "She was . . ." he rasped. "She . . . was *here*!"

"Who was?" John practically shouted. "What are you talking about?"

Frank tried to answer, but his back suddenly arched as his chest heaved with a roaring intake of breath. For a moment he seemed to rise above the bed, but then he sank down, melting onto the mattress with one last shuddering groan. Just at that moment, from far off, John and Julia heard the wail of the approaching ambulance.

NINETEEN
DOA

I

By the time the ambulance and police arrived, Bri was sitting on the couch, crying with her face in her hands. Julia, herself teary-eyed but trying to be strong for Bri, was sitting next to her, patting her on the back and saying whatever comforting words came to mind. She knew from what she had experienced when *her* parents had died that it almost didn't matter what was said, so long as there was someone there to hug and comfort you.

John, still stunned from having his father die in his arms, was standing in the kitchen, looking out at the driveway as the cruiser and ambulance came speeding around the corner of Oak Street and pulled into the driveway. Their flashing blue lights strobed across the freshly fallen snow, reminding him of the sudden flash of Julia's camera earlier that evening.

Christmas Eve . . . he thought, sadly shaking his head when he saw four men, no more than dark silhouettes as they hurried up the walkway to the kitchen door. John went to meet them there, to tell them there was no longer a need to hurry; his father was dead. When he opened the door, his jaw dropped in surprise when he saw that one of the men was Randy Chadwick. The other three he didn't recognize, but one of them introduced himself as Officer Pelkey.

"Your dad?" Randy said, looking at him with a twisted, worried expression.

Eyeing Randy darkly, John nodded. "Yeah," he said, even as his mind filled with angry thoughts about Randy and what he had been doing to him. "He's in his bedroom." John's throat was raw from yelling earlier, and his arms and shoulders ached from his wild ax swinging. "I think it was his heart."

Randy nodded, then followed silently as John led them down the hallway to his father's bedroom. Julia came and stood in the living room doorway, nodding a silent greeting to Randy as he passed. John, doing his best to fight back his dark suspicions at a time like this, tried not to wonder if there was any other, deeper meaning in the glance Julia and Randy had exchanged.

"What in th' hell happened to the door?" Pelkey said, staring in amazement at the splintered remains hanging from one hinge.

"It was locked," John said, shaking his head as though dazed. "I—uh, had to bust it open."

"Did he make a habit of locking his door at night?" Pelkey asked, running his fingers over a particularly deep gash in the wood.

John shrugged. "I can't say as I ever checked before."

"Do you want me to get the stretcher?" Randy said, his voice low as he looked at the dead man—the father of his high school best friend—lying on his bed. Randy's mind suddenly filled with scrambled memories of Frank while he and John had been growing up. Turning to John, he said, "If you want to wait in the living room, we can take care of this."

"Might's well wait until Chuck gets here," Pelkey said as he looked at the body. "You plan to use Lang for the funeral?"

"I suppose so," John said with a shrug. "I hadn't given it much thought." He was feeling hollow inside, as though nothing he could say or do would make a difference, anyway. But he decided to stay as Randy and the policemen went over to the bed and did a brief examination to confirm Frank's death.

Pelkey picked up the containers of medicine on the bedstand and inspected the labels. "Had a stroke, huh?" he said. "We'll have to take these to the lab and have 'em checked. You don't mind, do you?"

"Not at all," John said weakly.

Pelkey stood, shaking the containers, making them rattle. The sound reminded John of the rattling noise of his father's breathing just before the end.

John watched blankly as Randy opened up a medical bag, took out a stethoscope, and reached up under Frank's pajama shirt. He listened for a moment, then took the stethoscope off and shook his head.

"Could you stand back, please, while we get some shots here?" Pelkey said. One of the other policemen raised a camera and started snapping pictures from different angels. Each glaring blast of white light made John think, *Jesus! Christmas photos!*

"So," John said, turning to Randy while the policemen did their work, "I didn't realize you were a medical man." He was leaning back against the bedroom wall, mostly because the backs of his legs felt like rubber and he was afraid he would fall down if he didn't.

Randy shook his head. "I'm not, really. I've had a minimal amount of training. I just work as a volunteer—mostly in the winter, once I put the lobster pots up for the season."

John nodded his understanding, but all the while, as he watched the policemen examine and photograph his father, he couldn't stop thinking, *He's got to be the one who's doing it. Leaving those notes around.... And worse, I'll bet money he's been messing around with Julia.* The more he thought about it, the more convinced he became that, when Randy had passed Julia in the hallway, they had looked at each other *strangely*, as though a secret had jumped the gap between them like a spark.

"I'd hazard to guess it was his heart," Randy said, looking squarely at John. "I'm sorry."

"Appears you're right, Randy," Pelkey said. "I've got to call the medical examiner. Can I use this phone?" He indicated the telephone on the bedstand, and John nodded that it was all right. Pelkey dialed a number and stared up at the ceiling while he waited for an answer.

"Al ... sorry to ring you so late, but we have a—" He cut himself off and, looking at John, said, "If you want to wait out in the hallway..."

John shook his head and muttered, "No ... I'll wait here, if you don't mind."

Pelkey shrugged and spoke into the phone again. "We have a possible DOA at oh one-fifteen. A Mr. Frank Carlson, at Thirty-three Shore Drive on Glooscap."

Possible? John thought. *Christ, he's as dead as a stone!*

Pelkey paused while the man at the other end of the line spoke, then grunted agreement. "Uh-huh. Appears to be heart. Had a history of heart trouble."

"He had a stroke last spring," Randy whispered, and Pelkey nodded and repeated the information. He read the labels of Frank's prescription drugs, then, after a pause, nodded again and said, "All right. Thanks.... And have a good holiday. Catch yah later." After hanging up the phone, he turned to John and said, "We have permission to move the body. Would you like me to call Lang's and have him come over?"

John could feel a deep shuddering in his body as the reality of what was happening sank deeper into his mind. His father was dead—stone cold dead at one-thirty on Christmas morning! Tomorrow, instead of opening the rest of their presents and enjoying their traditional turkey dinner, he was probably going to be at Charles Lang's Funeral Home, making burial arrangements.

"Yeah," he said, his voice sounding strangled. "We've used Lang's before ... when my mother died."

"Let me give Chuck a call, then," Pelkey said. He took a small notebook from his shirt pocket, looked up the number, and began dialing.

The other cop, meanwhile, had finished taking pictures, and now that they had permission to move the body, he and Randy were busy straightening Frank out so they would be able to move him onto the stretcher when the funeral director came. Frank's limbs were stiffening, but certainly rigor mortis hadn't set in yet. Without the spark of life, his father seemed diminished somehow —small and almost frail. The icy pit in John's stomach got worse as he watched the men shift his father's body around as if it were a piece of useless meat.

But that's all it is now, anyway, he thought as blades of ice cut through him. *That's what I used to think he was, and now that is really all he is!*

The stinging in his eyes got worse, and his vision began to blur. He hardly noticed the buzzing of Pelkey's voice as he spoke on the phone with Charles Lang at the funeral home.

After Pelkey had finished on the phone, and while they waited for Lang to arrive, John went out into the living room to be with Julia and Bri. When he saw Bri's tear-streaked face, his heart almost broke. He came over to them, and the three of them stood in the living room, hugging each other, seeking the reassurance of warm, living bodies in the presence of death. As far as John knew, this was the first time Bri had actually seen a dead person. For himself . . . well, besides his mother's funeral, there *was* that other time. . . .

As soon as he thought, again, about Abby . . .

I WON'T FORGET WHAT YOU DID TO ME!

. . . another memory rose in his mind.

The gray shape he had seen reflected twice in the living room window . . . that person hanging from the living room ceiling . . . gray, frayed rope buried deep in the fold of the swollen neck . . . the body, slowly turning . . .

John knew who it was now and the realization hit him so hard, he wanted to cry out loud.

In his memory, the body spun slowly around until he could see the face. . . . It was swollen a bloated gray. . . . The tongue hung out between clenched teeth, bitten almost clear through. . . . It was Abby Snow . . . with a twisted rope strangling her neck!

"Why'd . . . why'd this have to happen?" Bri asked. Her voice was strained as she glanced back and forth between her mother and father.

Julia silently shrugged, knowing there wasn't any rational, reasonable answer. John could do nothing more than shake his head.

They remained where they were, hugging and sobbing, until they heard another car—the funeral director, no doubt—pull into the driveway. Pelkey went to the kitchen door and let the man in. John left Bri and Julia and walked with Lang back to his father's bedroom. Lang was followed by his assistant, who was pushing a collapsible stretcher. While Lang's assistant and the policemen shifted Frank's body onto the stretcher, Lang spoke kindly and sympathetically with John in the corner of the room.

Back in the living room, Julia stayed with Bri, still hugging her daughter as she was racked by deep sobs. "Honey," Julia said, her own voice husky with emotion when Bri started toward the hallway. "You might not want to watch. Why don't you go upstairs. I'll be right up."

Her face pale, her eyes and nose running, Bri sniffed loudly and shook her head. "Can't I go see him . . . say good-bye to him?" she asked.

Julia shook her head. "No," she said firmly. "I want you to remember him the way he was when he was alive. That's the best way."

Bri put her hand to her mouth and started gnawing on the knuckles as they both stood there, listening to the sounds coming down the hallway. There was a loud clanking of metal and the soft rasp of fresh sheets shifting. A moment later, Bri's eyes widened when, looking over her mother's shoulder, she saw the sheet-covered shape wheel past. The sound of the stretcher wheels instantly reminded her of the sound her grandfather's wheelchair used to make and she burst into tears again, collapsing into her mother's arms.

"You take care of her," John said tightly when he came back into the living room. He rubbed his hand on Julia's shoulder. "I'm going with him to the funeral home."

Randy, who was standing in the doorway, said, "John—if you'd like, I can come with you."

The offer seemed genuine, but John simply shook his head. "I can go alone," he said. "Thanks, though." A small corner of his mind was beginning to wonder how he ever could have suspected Randy of leaving those notes. He must have been crazy to be so paranoid about such an old friend.

"I could stay here," Randy said, "with Julia and Bri until you got back."

Instantly John's fragments of doubt disintegrated, and before Julia could respond, he snapped, "That won't be necessary."

Julia looked at him, dumbfounded, but before she could say anything, John left her standing there as he followed his father's body out to Lang's station wagon. The cold grabbed the back of his throat and made his eyes sting even more as he watched the men slide the stretcher into the back of the hearse.

"Let me run in and grab my coat. I want to come along," he said after Lang had closed the hearse doors.

"Fine," Lang said. "You can either ride with me or follow in your car."

Nodding, John went back into the house and came back out a moment later, wearing his heavy coat and gloves. Telling himself he didn't want to make anyone else go out of their way to bring him home later, he got into his own car and started it up, waiting as Lang slowly backed out of the driveway into Oak Street. That's what he told himself—that he didn't want to inconvenience any-one—but deep inside he knew the real reason. He was filled with dread at the idea of riding in Lang's station wagon with his fa-ther's body.

Besides, he told himself, *it won't do my father any good now, anyway!*

II

John got home from the funeral home about two hours later. Julia was waiting for him in the living room, sitting cross-legged on the couch, staring blankly at the winking Christmas tree lights. She had a cup of tea in her hand, but it had long since gone cold. Julia told him Bri was upstairs in bed, but she doubted that she was asleep yet. They sat on the couch for a while, talking but mostly just sitting, looking at the bright tree and the dark night outside and thinking . . . remembering . . . trying to make some kind of sense of what had happened, but neither of them succeeded.

No one slept well in the house where death had so recently brushed his cold hand, and as the light of dawn brightened the bedroom window, both Julia and John stopped pretending to be asleep and went downstairs. Even the aroma of fresh-brewed cof-fee and the butterscotch bars of sunlight spilling onto the kitchen floor couldn't dispel the gloom of the house.

"You know," John said, sitting at the kitchen table and glancing down the hallway, "every time I look down there, I expect to hear him thumping around in his room, getting into his wheelchair to come for breakfast." He could see several splintered boards litter-ing the hallway floor. The memory of breaking through that door seemed somehow distant, almost as though it had happened to someone else.

Julia, who had had to deal with the loss of her parents when she was twelve years old, nodded silently. Sometime during the long night, her stomach had started churning and, although she had at first thought it was from the tension and grief of last night's events, she still felt as though she was going to be sick to her stomach. In the back of her mind, she was wondering if she had another touch of the stomach flu they had all suffered not so long ago.

"When I think of all the times I—" John started to say, but then his voice choked off, and he lowered his gaze so his wife wouldn't see the tears forming in his eyes. He was remembering all the times while he was growing up, and especially after his mother had died . . .

After his father had let her drink herself to death!

. . . he had wished—he had closed his eyes and fervently *prayed*—that his father would die!

And now—after all these years—he had his wish, and with it came guilt as sharp and stinging as salt poured onto a festering wound. When he looked at Julia and saw the grief in her eyes, his heart felt as though it was twisted into something black and cold because all he could think was, *Are you screwing Randy?*

The sound of footsteps coming down the stairs made both of them jump. Turning, they saw Bri, her face drawn and pale, walk into the kitchen and plop herself down into her usual chair. She propped her chin in her hands and sat there, staring blankly at the tabletop.

"Didn't sleep too well, huh?" Julia said, coming over behind her and gently massaging her shoulders.

Bri shook her head and sighed, a deep, shuddering breath. She tried to look around at her mother, but the stinging in her eyes was too strong. When she shifted her gaze, though, and found she was looking down the hallway toward her grandfather's bedroom door, she burst into tears and let her head drop forward onto the table, her shoulders shaking as she cried.

Julia looked at John helplessly, both of them silently acknowledging that this was what they would all need in order to get over it—tears . . . tears and time.

After eating a light breakfast of toast and coffee, Julia cleaned up the kitchen while John went to his father's bedroom to clean up the mess from the night before. The door couldn't be repaired. Its shattered remains, along with pieces of the door frame, were strewn on the floor. It took him two trips to carry the debris out to the garage. The second time, on his way back to the room, he peeked into the living room and saw Julia and Bri sitting side by side on the couch, staring at the array of presents on the floor under the tree.

Cleaning up the broken door, he found, was the easiest part. Looking at the tangled mess of his father's bed, the pile of church clothes he had worn last night and had kept on for Christmas Eve, while they sat around the tree, distributing gifts, the pair of slippers he had gotten from Bri . . . everything about the room had an aching melancholy. John was surprised he didn't feel as though his father was just gone from the room, that he was still alive and would return. His entire room vibrated with loneliness and a cold sense of his being gone forever.

Moving mechanically, and trying—but not succeeding very well—not to think too deeply, John stripped the soiled sheets and blankets from the bed, rolled them into a ball, and stuffed them into a plastic trash bag. He assumed Mr. Lang at the funeral home would want to dress his father for burial in his church clothes, so he neatly folded them and placed them on the bureau. Other things, such as his dirty underwear and socks, he tossed into the bag with the sheets and blankets.

He didn't take the time to sort through his father's valuables or to tidy up the room. His only regret, after he had taken the trash bag out to the garage, was that the bedroom door couldn't be locked. The memories and regrets that had died with his father, he thought, should stay in that dingy, dark room.

But once the work was done and the room was as straightened up as he cared to make it, one thing continued to weigh on John's mind. It had been sitting there in the back of his mind ever since last night, but no matter how much he thought about it, he just couldn't come up with an answer.

What, he wondered over and over, *did his father mean when he said, "She was here"? Who was here? He couldn't have meant Julia or Bri. Maybe, just before he died, he had a vision of his dead wife waiting to greet him on the other side. Or maybe . . .*

John shook his head, trying to dismiss that thought, but it, like the guilt produced by those notes Randy—*it had to have been Randy!*—had been leaving for him, wouldn't go away. It echoed in the dark recesses of his mind, over and over. . . .

She was here! . . . She was here! . . .

III

Visiting hours at Lang's funeral home were the next day, Sunday afternoon. That morning, Julia had felt a bit queasy when she woke up, and as the day progressed, the churning in her stomach got bad enough so she considered not even going to the funeral home; but she realized she *had* to be there along with John and Bri. Dressed in their Sunday best, while hushed organ music filled the dimly lit room, they spoke with the surprisingly large number of people who showed up. Several people from the island had sent flower arrangements, and there was even one from CMP, acknowledging Frank's years of service to the company.

The cloying smell of flowers made the air in the room heavy and close as people came by and offered their regrets.

"What a terrible thing to have happen right at Christmastime. . . ."

"He was a good man . . . a *damned* good man . . ."

"Such a shame . . . but he struggled so hard after that stroke. He's better off now. . . ."

"He's with Dianna now; you have to believe that. . . ."

The only time Julia came close to breaking down in public was when Frenchie came down the aisle, swinging himself on his battered crutches. He was wearing a shabby brown tweed suit which he had obviously not worn in many years. The left pants leg was pinned up over the stump of his leg, and his necktie was cocked to one side. He stopped beside the casket. As he looked down at Frank, his lower lip trembled and his amber eyes misted over. Twin streams of tears fell from his eyes and wound down through the white stubble of his beard. To Julia, he seemed unnaturally diminished, as though looking at his dead friend reminded him that his time was due soon, too.

"I'm gonna miss him," Frenchie said, his voice almost cracking as he shook his head from side to side, looking directly at Julia. "He was one helluva cardplayer."

That was it—Frenchie's eulogy for Frank—and Julia knew that no one was going to do better. Frenchie turned and went rapidly back down the aisle and out of the funeral home, not bothering to stop and talk with anyone else.

"We—umm, we shot rats down at the wharf one day with your father," Julia said by way of explanation to John, who looked at her curiously once Frenchie had left.

The two-hour stretch of visiting seemed more like four or five to Julia. Throughout the afternoon, her stomach felt as if some giant had reached down inside, grabbed her guts, and was squeezing with all his strength. Several times she had gone to the rest room and, locking the door behind her, leaned with her head over the toilet bowl, praying she would throw up so she would be done with this yucky feeling. It wasn't just a reaction to grief, she knew; it was something physical . . . that damned flu coming back!

She thought John seemed to be handling things well enough—too well, actually. Just about everyone who had come knew him by name—some even called him "Johnny." She wished he would loosen up and not deal with all of these friends of his father's as though he either didn't know them or didn't *want* to remember them. He stiffly shook their hands and listened to their words of condolence as though nothing was registering with him.

Bri, on the other hand, spent the whole time sniffling and wiping her eyes with her handkerchief. Her eyelids were red and swollen, and her face had a waxy paleness. Her thin shoulders never stopped heaving and shuddering as she cried. When people from the island, some she had never even met before now, would say a few words to her, she would embrace them and sob.

Just before the afternoon visiting hours were over, Julia noticed that Randy and Ellie Chadwick had arrived. As soon as John saw them, she physically felt him stiffen, and looking down, she saw that John's hand had clenched into a fist. He shifted nervously from one foot to the other as Randy and his wife made their way over to them.

"I'm so sorry," Ellie said, leaning forward and hugging John. She brushed his cheek with a trace of a kiss, then turned to Julia and gave her a hug.

"I wish it hadn't been me on duty that night," Randy said simply, obviously at a loss for words. He and John were shaking hands and looking intently at each other.

"It's just the way things go," John said, his voice little more than a whisper.

He let go of Randy's hand but kept staring at him, searching his face waiting for him to reveal . . . *what?* he wondered. *Is Randy really feeling the sadness that's on his face . . . or is his face nothing more than a mask, hiding the fact that he's been screwing my wife!*

Maybe it had all started that day they had gone out lobstering with Randy—or maybe it had started sooner. Maybe they had started their affair right after that day they were moving into the house and Randy had stopped by.

John still wasn't positive—he didn't have *proof* that Randy and Julia were "getting it on," as they said, but he *was* positive that Randy was the one who had been leaving those notes around the house, in his office, and in his car. . . .

I WON'T FORGET WHAT YOU DID TO ME!

That was a nice touch, adding ME. Very nice touch. Cold . . . almost ruthless!

Somebody knew *something* about what had happened, John thought, and who could it be if it wasn't Randy? Back in high school, no one had known him better than Randy had. They had shared secrets together that, even now, John hadn't revealed to Julia. It was entirely possible that Randy had somehow figured out what had happened at Haskins' barn that night! And if he had, and if he was writing these notes, trying to drive him crazy, he must have *some* reason to be doing it!

What better reason than to try to steal my wife?

"Usually, you know," Randy was saying, drawing John's attention back, "when you get an ambulance call on an island as small as Glooscap, you gotta figure it's someone you know, but it ain't often that it's someone—well . . ." He let his voice trail away as his glance slid over in Julia's direction.

"It must be tough," John said, not knowing what else to say, mostly because he was barely listening. He was watching Randy, just waiting for a tiny chink to appear in his facade, waiting for a silent flash of communication between him and Julia . . . the proof he needed.

If he's trying to make me crack, I'll show him, John thought. *He's not going to get to me!*

By this time, Ellie was talking softly with Bri, who was crying into her shoulder. Randy had moved over in front of Julia. They simply looked at each other, neither one saying anything while John studied them, and then Randy kissed her on the cheek. In John's mind, that looked all the more suspicious. After a moment, Randy and Ellie left them, moving over to the far side of the room, where they saw some neighbors.

"You could at least be civil to them!" Julia said, leaning close to John so Bri wouldn't hear her. "Why are you acting so . . . cold to everyone?"

"What do you mean?" John said, shrugging innocently.

"You know *exactly* what I mean," Julia said. "You don't have to treat him like you think he's responsible for—" Her voice caught in her throat, and she finished lamely, "for what happened."

"I don't," John said, shaking his head. Before he could do anything else, though, some other people came up to them and spoke softly about how much they had admired Frank and how much they were going to miss him at church. And that's how it went, both in the afternoon and again from seven to nine that evening.

Frank's funeral was planned for ten o'clock the next morning, so by the time they got back to the house at nine-thirty that night, all three of them were exhausted and—especially Bri—wrung out from the strain of the visiting hours. Julia's irritation at John was blunted, but only because the twisting in her stomach felt even worse, if that was possible. While she was in the bathroom, brushing her teeth before bed, she thought she was finally going to be able to throw up and start cleaning out her system, but even though the sour churning in her gut got worse, it never came to a head. She went to bed and eventually fell asleep, but all night in her thin sleep, she could feel her stomach tossing up and down. Only once did she have a dream. She was in a boat—it seemed like Randy's, but it was bigger, almost a luxury yacht. In the dream, when she looked overboard, she saw someone—a young girl—swimming on her back and looking up at her. Julia awoke with a start and sat up in bed, her breathing raw and hot in the deep night.

IV

The ringing of the telephone startled them both awake the next morning. John reached over Julia and snagged the receiver in the middle of the second ring.

"Hello," he said, his voice thick with sleep. He could barely focus his eyes on the alarm clock, and was surprised to see they both had slept past seven o'clock.

"John, this is Randy."

"Umm . . . what do you want, Randy?" John said, his voice suddenly tightening. He made eye contact with Julia to let her know it was nothing serious.

"I didn't wake you up, did I? I'm sorry—"

"No, no," John said, shifting to a sitting position on the edge of the bed. "We were just getting up anyway."

"I was just thinking, talking to Ellie, you know, that if you wanted me to, I could drive you folks to the funeral today. I could pick you up whenever you were ready to go."

Frowning, John looked at Julia and considered for a moment. On the one hand, it might nice not to have to worry about driving, but on the other, he sure as hell didn't want Randy around . . . especially if it would make him wonder all through the service what—if anything—was going on between him and Julia.

"Well—?" Randy said.

"I—uh, thanks for offering, but I guess not," John said. "I appreciate your offering, but I think it'd be best if we just went by ourselves as a family. You understand."

"Oh, yeah . . . sure," Randy replied. "We're planning on going. I was just—you know, offering."

"I appreciate it," John said. "I'll see you there."

Julia was sitting up in bed, propping herself on her elbows. He passed the receiver to her, and she replaced it and then sagged back down on the bed. Black waves of nausea swept through her like a strong tide. She thought she would throw up for sure if she moved too fast.

"He offered to drive us to the funeral today if we wanted," John said.

Standing up, he pulled on a pair of pants and a shirt, then went to the window and stood looking out at the day. As it had yesterday, bright sunlight glanced off the snow with a blinding glare. On the horizon, the open ocean was a tossing dark blue mass with whitecapped waves. It was so cold, thin strands of steam—what the locals called "sea smoke—twisted up into the sky.

While John was staring out the window, Julia prayed that today she would feel a little better than yesterday. Finally, knowing she had Frank's funeral to face, she let out a low groan, tossed the covers aside, and swung her feet to the floor.

"We probably ought to start getting ready," she said. It sounded as though someone had his hands wrapped tightly around her throat.

"Are you all right?" John said, looking at her over his shoulder.

She was about to say, *Of course I am,* but even as the words formed in her mind, her stomach clenched up hard. When she opened her mouth, all that came out was a deep belch. A thick, bilious taste flooded into her throat and stung the inside of her nose. The best she could do was nod her head.

"Are you sure?" John said, coming over beside her. "You look like crap."

"Thanks a bunch," Julia said, smacking her lips in an attempt to get rid of the sourness in her mouth.

John placed his hand on her forehead and grunted. "You don't seem to have a fever."

He didn't say any more, though, because Julia suddenly bolted from the bed, raced down the hall to the bathroom, and ended up kneeling with her face over the toilet. For a few seconds she waited, feeling her nausea condense until it was a hard, burning ball under her ribs. Then, with a sudden wrenching, just as John followed her into the bathroom she open her mouth and let it rip. Hot vomit shot from her mouth and splashed into the toilet. The smell of it only made her stomach worse, and she heaved until she thought her sides would collapse.

As soon as she started throwing up, John grabbed a washcloth and wet it with warm water. As she leaned over the toilet bowl, he pulled her hair straight back and rubbed the cloth over her brow. Wave after wave racked her body until there was nothing left to spew out, and she knelt there dry-heaving. Each contraction made her eyes feel as though they were about to pop out of her head. She tried not to imagine them plopping like fat grapes into the puky water in the toilet bowl.

"Jesus H., that was a mean one," John said, once the worst had passed, and Julia, still sitting on the floor, turned around and looked up at him. Her face was drained of color, and thin strands of wet hair clung to her forehead.

"Off to a good start," she said. Her throat felt as raw as hamburger. "Could you get me a glass of water?"

John ran the water until it was cold, then filled the bathroom cup and handed it to her. She wanted to gulp it down greedily but restrained herself and merely took a single sip. The last thing she needed was to trigger another round of heaves.

"Do you have the flu again?" John asked, his face creased with concern. All he could think was, *Here it is, the day of my father's funeral, and my wife gets as sick as a dog!*

Julia found it difficult to focus on him, but she shook her head. "No. You know what I think it is?"

But she didn't tell him what she *really* thought. She knew it was too soon . . . *much* too soon for her to be experiencing morning sickness. That came during the second or third month. If she was feeling anything like that, she knew it had to be psychosomatic. She kept reminding herself that every pregnancy was different, but there was no way she could have morning sickness yet . . . not unless she had gotten pregnant sooner than Christmas Eve.

"I—umm, think that pork I had for supper in between visiting hours didn't sit so well with me," she said to John.

"That's an understatement," John said, forcing a chuckle. He was about to say more when a muffled knocking from downstairs caught their attention. They looked at each other questioningly.

"Sounds like there's someone at the back door," Julia said. "Would you run down and see who it is?"

John nodded, turned, and was gone, his footsteps clomping rapidly down the stairs. Still feeling weak-kneed, Julia gripped the sink edge and pulled herself up off the floor. The shock of what she saw when she looked into the mirror made her think for just a split second that there was another face reflected there. This couldn't be *her* face, pale, drawn, and hollow eyed, reflected in the mirror. She turned on the faucet until the water ran ice-cold, then splashed several handfuls onto her face, blowing and blubbering with each. When she straightened back up, she almost screamed when she *did* see another face reflected in the mirror, staring at her over her shoulder. Only after the first jolt of panic did she realize that it was Bri standing in the bathroom doorway.

"Are you all right?" Bri asked faintly.

Julia grabbed a hand towel and patted her face dry. "Yeah," she said, feeling short of breath. "Good Lord, you scared the crap out of me. Don't go sneaking up behind me like that, okay?"

Bri nodded as though she had a stiff neck. "Yeah—sure. I was just worried about you. I heard you wet-burping in here."

"Well, don't worry," Julia said, still feeling her heart racing in her chest. "I'll be just fine." She tried to smile but found she couldn't. She was afraid that if she really let herself feel what she thought was truly happening, she'd start laughing like an idiot and not be able to stop.

If I can make myself feel this sick just thinking *about being pregnant, I* hope *to hell this doesn't go on for the full nine months!*

V

When John got downstairs, he saw Randy Chadwick standing outside the kitchen door. He was wearing a heavy coat and had a woolen hat pulled down to his eyebrows. Cold air blasted in at John when he opened the door for Randy to come inside. John reached past him and swung the door shut. He looked at John with a twisted little half smile, but he came no farther inside than the rug by the door.

"Ellie, uh, wanted me to bring this over for you, so right after I hung up I decided to shoot on over," he said. He was holding out a covered casserole dish. "It's her homemade lasagna."

The casserole was warm in John's hands when he took it from Randy and placed it on the countertop.

"Thanks," John said simply, and he found himself wondering if he'd find another note on the bottom of the dish. What would *this* one say?

"If you want to reconsider, the offer's still on," Randy said. "I wouldn't mind driving you folks to the funeral home."

Biting his lower lip, John shook his head firmly. "Uh—no. We'll be fine," he said, feeling a sudden flood of anger at his former friend. Even with his father's funeral just a few hours away, and Randy apparently earnestly offering his help, all John could think was, *He's got to be the one who's writing those notes.*

I WON'T FORGET WHAT YOU DID TO ME!

"Tell Ellie thanks for the lasagna," John said. "I'm sure it'll be good."

He was anxious for Randy to get going, mostly because he felt as though there was nothing else for them to talk about . . . not unless he decided to ask him, *Why the hell are you writing those notes to me? Oh, yeah—by the way, you aren't fucking my wife, are you?* He honestly surprised himself by not saying anything as he reached past Randy and opened the door for him. The sudden blast of cold air made him shiver, and Randy stepped back outside.

"I'll be seeing you at the funeral, then," Randy said. He started down the walkway to his car, which he had left parked down by the road.

"Sure . . . thanks," John said, smiling grimly. He was watching Randy carefully, trying to see one slight misstep, one tiny motion that would reveal what he was really thinking.

Was he watching me like a hawk, waiting to see if I was starting to crack? he wondered as he heard Randy's car start up and watched it pull away slowly. The car's exhaust was heavy in the cold air, like the steam rising from the ocean.

"Who was that?" Julia asked.

Her voice coming from behind him so suddenly caught John by surprise. He made a startled little yelp and wheeled around to face her.

"Jesus! You scared the shit out of me!" He eased the door shut behind him, then walked over to where he had left the casserole dish. "That was Randy," he said, letting his hand rest on the still-warm dish cover. "Ellie sent over a dish of lasagna."

"Oh, wasn't that sweet of her," Julia said. She picked up the dish and lifted the cover, taking a deep sniff of the contents. "Umm—even feeling as lousy as I do, this smells great."

"Oh, I'll just bet it is," John said, his voice taking on an irritating singsong tone. "It's so *sweet* of him to bring it over, too."

Julia put the casserole back on the counter, all the while frowning. When she looked back up at John, her frown deepened. He glared back at her.

"What the hell is wrong with you?" she said. She was still feeling a bit limp from throwing up, and the last thing she needed was an argument with John.

"Oh, nothing's the matter . . . nothing's the matter at all! I'm just feeling jim-dandy! My father's going to be buried this morning, and dear, sweet Randy is running over to do these darling little favors for us! *Would you like me to drive you to the funeral today? Here's a little something the little lady cooked up for you!* Goddamn! I don't need his horseshit!"

"He's just trying to be neighborly," Julia said as she pulled a chair away from the table and sat down. The backs of her legs were throbbing.

"Neighborly . . . oh, sure," John said, his voice practically snarling.

And is it neighborly to be popping the wife of your former best friend behind his back? he thought. *Is it neighborly to be leaving*

*little notes around, intending to drive that same former friend out
of his mind with guilt?*

He stood leaning against the counter, squinting as he looked at
Julia and wondered, *And are you in on this with him? Maybe
you're working together. That's how those notes could end up in
my car and office. You're helping him!*

"I'm sure that, if it had been his father instead of yours, you
and I would want to help as much as we could," Julia said.
"Come on, John—he was your best friend, for crying out loud!"
She made an effort to keep her voice low and steady. She didn't
want a fight right now, but she knew she couldn't let him feel and
say such things unchallenged.

"Was! That's the important word here," John flared back at her,
jabbing a pointed finger at the center of her chest. "Randy and I
don't have anything in common anymore."

Or do we? his mind whispered, filling in the brief pause.

"He doesn't know who I am anymore, and I don't know who
he is. And for all I care, that's the way it can stay!"

Julia shook her head, wishing to God this wasn't happening—
especially now, on the day of Frank's funeral. She had no doubt
that Bri, who was still up in her room, could hear every word
through the floor. She figured this was just one way John had of
expressing his grief. Randy had been on the ambulance crew that
night, and John was twisting it in his mind, somehow putting the
blame for his father's death onto Randy simply because he had
been there.

"I mean, who the hell does he think he is?" John shouted. "He
comes in here acting like we're still best buddies or something."

Even buddies don't share wives, his mind said. *That's called
"buddy-fucking"!*

"We don't fucking *need* his goddamned help! We can handle
this by ourselves! So *fuck* him!"

If you're not already fucking him, his mind whispered.

"Keep your voice down," Julia said as mildly as she could. "I
don't want you getting Bri any more upset than she already is."

John opened his mouth to say something, but all that came out
was a loud snort. He shook his head and then, setting his eyes on the
casserole, walked over to it and picked it up. With both hands raised
over his head, he spun around and flung the dish as hard as he could
against the kitchen wall. Instantaneously, there was a loud crash and
a sickening splat as glass and lasagna exploded into the air. The
whole mess slid to the floor, leaving a bloody-looking asterisk on
the wall just beside the phone. For one sickening instant, when she
looked at the bright red mess on the floor, Julia had the impression

that it was flesh and blood, not tomatoes and noodles. Her stomach tightened violently, threatening to start heaving again.

"*John! Stop it!*"

It was frightening to watch as he closed his eyes tightly and, clenching his fists, shook them above his head. His lower lip was trembling as his breath came in short, stuttering gasps. For a frozen moment, she sat there, waiting to see if the rage had passed or if he was going to do more. But then, with a sudden sagging of his shoulders, he brought his hands down and, slamming them hard against his legs, let out a long, low wail.

For now, Julia forgot all about her own raging nausea as she went over to John and threw her arms around him. Feeling as limp as a straw scarecrow, he sagged into her arms and sobbed, his body shaking uncontrollably. She braced the back of his head with a gentle but firm grip and, because words failed her, simply breathed deeply and evenly beside his ear.

TWENTY
Suspicions

I

John decided to have Frank's funeral at Lang's Funeral Home rather than at the Lutheran church, but he did, of course, ask Pastor Vernon to conduct the service. He and Julia and Bri were sitting in the front row as people quietly entered and took their seats. There was a small, white lectern set up at the front near the open casket, where Frank lay, his hands folded across his chest, the harsh lines of his face smoothed and softened by the mortician's art. Frank was dressed in the same suit he had worn to church on Christmas Eve, and with the curtains drawn, the lights dimmed, and organ music playing softly in the background, John could easily imagine that they were at the church.

Bri was sitting at her mother's right-hand side, and from time to time she found it necessary to clench her mother's hand tightly —especially when she looked at her grandfather's body. In her mind, she kept telling herself that this was it—this was real; he was dead and soon to be buried. But every time she looked at her grandfather, she could have sworn she saw his frail chest rise and fall with shallow breaths. The illusion—*that's all it is,* she told herself, *just an illusion!*—was overpowering . . . and frightening. She tried not to think it but couldn't stop herself from imagining her grandfather suddenly sitting up in the casket and shouting, *"Hey, everyone! Surprise!"*

John, on Julia's left, sat with his head bowed, his hands clasped together, and his eyes closed more often than opened. Whenever he looked at his father's body, the waves of guilt and regret that swept up inside him were almost too much. They made him want to get up and scream just to release the black, coiling tension. He also still regretted the scene he had pulled this morning in the kitchen, throwing Ellie's dish of lasagna against the wall, and even though Julia had told him dozens of times that she understood why he was upset and that she forgave him, he knew, in the center of his darkening heart, that she *didn't* know why he was upset . . . could *never* know why.

I WON'T FORGET WHAT YOU DID TO ME!

At precisely ten o'clock, Pastor Vernon, who was seated across the aisle from John, stood and went to the podium, his forefinger stuck inside his hymnal, marking the page for the burial service. After clearing his throat and smiling benevolently at John and Julia, he signaled for the organ music to stop and began the service with a brief eulogy. Unlike that given the day before by Frenchie—*"He was a helluva cardplayer!"*—Pastor Vernon's focused entirely on Frank's faith, his attendance at church, and his belief in a better world beyond.

Bri and Julia, both teary-eyed, listened to what Pastor Vernon was saying, and at first John did, too, but after a while he noticed that he was beginning to feel uncomfortable. It wasn't the simple fact of his father's funeral, or that all the people sitting behind him were, no doubt, looking at him as much as they were at Frank, or even the knowledge that Randy was sitting somewhere behind them. It was more a feeling of . . .

—*of being watched! That was it!* he realized with a sudden jolt.

The back of his neck and scalp felt as though cold, clammy fingers were brushing lightly up to the top of his head. The words Pastor Vernon was saying faded until they were no more than a distant, buzzing drone. The air in the room, already thick with the scent of flowers and perfume, seemed to thicken and tighten in his throat until he wasn't even sure he could breathe.

John glanced nervously at Julia and shifted in his seat, trying to break the creeping sensation of somebody watching him, but nothing he could do, short of standing up and looking around, would get rid of the feeling. It was there like a dark presence, hovering in the corner of the dim room, flitting just out of sight in the corner of his eye.

I WON'T FORGET WHAT YOU DID TO ME!

Suddenly everyone in the room began to recite the prayer that was printed in the funeral service handout, and the sudden sound of everyone speaking together caught John by surprise. He tensed, his eyes flitting to the piece of paper in his hand. He had been holding it so long and so tightly, it was limp in his hands.

"Our Father who art in heaven . . ."

Mechanically, John moved his mouth along with the words, but even as he listened to the dull rattle of his own voice, he heard something else that sent a cold dash along his nerves. From behind him, very faintly, he heard the same sound he had heard on Christmas Eve during the candlelight service—a faint ripple that sounded like . . . *laughter!*

John could feel beads of sweat break out on his brow as everyone continued with the prayer.

". . . on earth as it is in heaven. . . ."

It felt as if there were a hot coal lodged in the back of his throat, blocking any air he tried to draw into his lungs. A scream was building inside of him, seeking any opportunity to break out. With rising fear, he looked again at Julia, but she seemed completely oblivious to his rising state of panic.

". . . as we forgive those who trespass against us. . . ."

And below the sounds of everyone speaking in unison, like a frigid current of air, the other sound seemed to grow in strength until there was no doubt in John's mind. Someone was *laughing*!

Finally, when he couldn't stand it any longer, John, keeping his head lowered, turned around slowly and scanned the crowd of people. Everyone, it seemed, was intent on what he or she was saying—some read from the paper; others had their eyes closed and their heads bowed. But then, way back by one of the two entrances, John saw something that made him gasp. A young woman with long black hair and wearing a heavy gray sweater was standing in the last row. She had her head bowed so he couldn't see her face, but he instantly recognized her as the same person he had seen, only briefly, at the candlelight service. Her shoulders were shaking, and it appeared for an instant that she was sobbing, but then it hit John with a force that was almost physical: *her shoulders were shaking because she was laughing!*

". . . for Thine is the kingdom, and the power . . ."

No! his mind wailed. *It can't be!*

John turned his head back around so quickly, he felt for a moment as though he was going to lose his balance. That same cold, cruel laughter he thought he had heard on Christmas Eve now filled his ears . . . or was it just his mind? Every joint and muscle in his body felt as if it had been frozen as the soft, almost feathery sound hit his ears like hammer blows. Barely aware of his movement, he lurched to the side, bumping into Julia.

". . . forever and ever. Amen."

"John?" Julia whispered, leaning close to him. "You okay?"

She was suddenly afraid that he was about to pass out. His face had paled, and his eyes had an unnerving blank look. He didn't seem at all steady on his feet.

For just a moment, he locked eyes on her. In the silence that followed after the prayer he could hear it even better—that low laughter!

"Yeah, I'm . . . I'm okay," he said, forcing himself to smile even though it felt more like a grimace. His mind filled with an image of his face as nothing more than a grinning skull. He became convinced the young woman had raised her face and was looking at his back, drilling him with her cold, piercing, *dead* eyes! He also was convinced that, as soon as he turned and tried to see her, she would again lower her face, hiding behind the cascade of dark hair.

The service was nearing an end, and as the organ music began once again, people began filing forward to pay their last respects to Frank. John, Julia, and Bri all stood and simply stayed where they were as people moved slowly past the open casket. Other than Frenchie and the Chadwicks, Julia didn't know anyone other than a few people she had noticed around the island. John introduced her to several people, including Barry Cummings, who had taken off from work. Bri did her best not to break down and cry, but before long her face was glistening with tears and she was furiously wiping her eyes with her handkerchief.

John shook hands with each person as he or she went by, and most everyone called him by name. He accepted their expression of sadness with a curt nod of the head—particularly, Julia noticed, when Randy and Ellie went by. Julia whispered her thanks for the lasagna and, wincing with the lie, told Ellie they would probably have it tonight. She was already concocting another lie to explain how the casserole dish had gotten broken when it was time to return it.

The whole time they were standing there greeting people, the back of John's neck felt as if it were on fire. He wanted to turn to see if that young girl was still there, waiting in line to shake hands with the family, or if she had left right after the service. John couldn't shake the sensation that her cold eyes were still boring into him, but at least—*thank God!*—he didn't still hear her laughing! He was wondering why no one else seemed to have noticed it during the service, but he wasn't about to mention it to Julia.

Finally the last few stragglers went past the casket, shook hands and hugged the family, and went out into the cold, clear morning. John and Julia, with Bri between them, went out to their car and brought it around to wait behind the hearse while Lang and his assistants carried the coffin out the back door of the funeral home.

"I can't believe he's really in there," Bri said, sniffling as she watched the men slide the casket into the back of the black limo. Sunlight glinted off the polished wood and metal. The men's breath shot out like smoke in the cold air. "I mean . . . whenever I think about how we used to play checkers and stuff, I—" Her voice cut off with a wrenching intake of air.

"There, there," Julia said, patting the back of Bri's hand. "You just have to remember that for the last year or so, he wasn't really happy. Once he wasn't able to get around and visit with his friends as easily as he used to— He didn't like living like that."

"I wish I'd known him before," Bri said. She shook her head, unable to accept that *anyone* could be better off dead. As gruff as her grandfather could be at times, all she could remember were the good times they had had, and although she had certainly been aware of the tension between Frank and John, she had never felt any bad feelings toward the former.

Only a few other cars lined up behind theirs as they waited to begin the procession out to Whispering Pines Cemetery. Once the casket and flowers were loaded, they drove slowly out of the funeral home parking lot. At the cemetery, Pastor Vernon read a few more passages from his service book, took a handful of frozen earth, and sprinkled it on the coffin. The dirt rattled on the coffin lid like hail. Bri felt emotionally drained, so she went to the car and waited while several men slowly lowered the coffin into the ground. While the cemetery work crew waited to one side for everyone to leave so they could fill in the grave, John and Julia thanked Pastor Vernon and walked slowly back to the car.

"Well, that's that," John said, taking a deep breath and blinking his eyes rapidly as he looked up at the sky. He lit a cigarette and inhaled deeply.

Julia grunted and nodded her head, then opened the car door and slid into the front seat. John came around to the driver's side and started up the car. After only a few puffs, he crushed the cigarette out in the ashtray.

"Seeing as how we don't have that lasagna dinner anymore,"

Julia said, her voice laced with submerged anger, "we might as well eat somewhere in town." John grunted his agreement as he pulled slowly away from the grave site. Beneath her own thoughts about death and funerals and grief, she was satisfied with herself for mentioning John's outburst this morning. *There, I said it and it's over,* she thought.

As John turned from the cemetery drive out onto Route 1, she looked back over her shoulder at the grave site. Unconsciously, her hand was stroking Bri's hair.

It sure is over, she thought. *Just like it's all over for Frank.*

II

On the drive home from Frank's funeral, the mood in the car was somber. As the car pulled into the driveway, John was surprised by how small the house looked to him now. Just as, even after he became an adult and was physically larger than his father he still *felt* smaller than him, the house his father had lived in most of his life had always seemed so big.

Until now.

Just *knowing* his father wasn't living there any more made it look and feel cramped. Everything about it was diminished somehow.

"I'll tell you what I think," John said as he cut the engine and nailed Julia with a cold stare. "I think we should sell out now; get out while we can and move back to Vermont. I'll bet I could even get my old job back at—"

"Did you leave the door unlocked?" Julia asked. Her voice had a sharp edge of apprehension.

"I was the last one out," John said. "I'm *positive* I locked it."

"I think we've got some trouble," Julia said.

John frowned as he looked past her to the kitchen door. It was hanging open, swinging silently back and forth in the breeze.

"You wait here while I check it out," John said. He got out of the car, slid the car keys into his coat pocket and, easing the door quietly shut, started up the walkway to the house.

"Hey! Anyone here?" he called, his eyes darting from side to side, taking in as much as he could without entering. Even from here, he knew there was trouble—*big* trouble. The kitchen table and chairs were overturned; plates, pots, and pans were scattered all across the floor; the refrigerator door was open, and fruits and vegetables had been tossed out onto the floor. A gallon of milk had tipped over and gurgled onto the floor, leaving a wide, white puddle.

"For Christ's sake," Julia said, staring in disbelief at the mess. "What the hell happened?"

John didn't reply as he went to the garage, grabbed the ax—the one he had used to break down his father's bedroom door—and cautiously entered the house. Gripping the ax tightly in both hands, he stepped gingerly over the wreckage, heading toward the living room. Bri and Julia followed three steps behind him.

"Who could have done something like this?" Bri said, her voice hushed because she was afraid whoever had done it might still be hiding in the house.

John hushed her, then gasped when he saw what had happened in the living room. The Christmas tree was knocked over, and all about it were smashed ornaments and lights. The couch and all the chairs and tables were overturned. Magazines and books had been torn open, and pages had been ripped out and strewn everywhere. Even the rugs and carpet were twisted and pulled out of place, laying about in bunches. All the pictures had been knocked off the walls and lay on the floor in piles of shattered glass and wood frames.

"I can't believe what I'm seeing," Julia said as she bent down and picked up one of her favorite tree ornaments—an angel who had seemingly had surgery to remove her wings. The sight of it only made her stomach worse. In the back of her mind, she remembered the time she had come home and found the furniture shifted out of position, but it hadn't been anything like *this!* This was outright vandalism!

"Someone knew we weren't going to be home today and took the opportunity to trash us," John said. He hit the ax head in the palm of his hand, making a wet slap sound. "I'll bet you the upstairs is just as bad."

"Who'd want to do something like this?" Bri asked, her voice whining up the scale. She had always heard about housebreaking and street crimes, but—until now—had never experienced it. She felt curiously as if she were in a dream and as soon as she woke up, everything would be back to normal.

Frank's bedroom, the downstairs bathroom, the dining room, and all the rooms upstairs were the same. It looked as though a tornado had ripped through the house, pulling out and overturning everything in its path. Julia and John felt a slight measure of relief when, upon checking their valuables, they found that nothing had been taken, but it was going to take them the rest of the day and most of the night to get everything that wasn't broken back into place.

"Do you think we should call the cops?" Julia asked once they were upstairs and it was obvious whoever had done this had come and gone. Positive that she was safe now, Bri went to her room and started cleaning up the mess there.

John, struggling to turn his bureau upright, grunted. "I don't know. I suppose so, but then again, why get them involved?" He braced his feet and pushed the bureau back into place against the wall. Then he knelt down and began resorting the clothes and putting them back into the drawers.

"Why get them involved? Because someone planned this!" Julia said. Her voice pitched upward into a wail that almost broke. "Someone was waiting to be sure we weren't going to be home before they did this!" Holding her chin in her hands, she sat down heavily on the bare mattress, staring blankly at the twisted knot of sheets and blankets on the floor by the closet door.

"But other than a few things broken, nothing's really been taken," John said, a measure of calm in his voice. "I think we should just take it as one more reason to consider what I suggested—sell the house and move the hell back to Vermont!"

"Come on, John!"

"Hey!" He indicated the mess with a side sweep of his arms. "I wouldn't exactly call this a welcome home."

"I just can't believe that someone—anyone would do this . . . *knowing* we were at your father's funeral and coming in here and wrecking everything. Why?"

John had his hand to his mouth, biting on the knuckle of his forefinger so he wouldn't say what he was thinking, but finally he decided there was no way he could keep it back. "I think I've got a pretty good idea who did this," he said, his voice a low growl.

Julia looked at him, her eyes twin ovals of fear. "Could it have anything to do with that condo your company's building?" she said. "Maybe this was done by someone who's really pissed off about that."

John shook his head, looking at her with a cold, intense expression. "Nope, not that," he said. "I think it might have been Randy."

For a flickering instant, Julia looked at him wide-eyed, then smiled weakly and almost laughed aloud. "You're kidding, right?"

"No, I'm not," John said firmly. "I think good old buddy Randy Chadwick might have had a whole *lot* to do with this."

"Come on, John. You're being ridiculous now," Julia said. "You saw him at your father's funeral this morning. How could he have—"

"Did you see when he and Ellie got there?" John said sharply. "I didn't. For all we know, he might have come at the last minute, slipped into the back just so he *could* have an alibi."

"You and Randy were best friends, for God's sake! Why would he want to do something like this?" Julia asked. She sat on the bed, staring at her husband, wondering how he could even suggest something like that.

John's first thought was, *Hell, I can think of plenty of reasons!* But that wasn't what he said. He stood up slowly and walked the length of the room, his hands clasped behind his head.

"I've told you this a hundred times already, but apparently it hasn't sunk in yet. Randy and I were friends—in high school. Other than maybe once or twice when I came home from college, I haven't seen him or talked with him or written to him until we moved back here. You see—maybe it was just me and my imagination, but I always felt like Randy held it against me that I went off to college and he ended up married to Ellie and staying here on Glooscap."

"He seems happy enough living here," Julia said. She felt a twinge of guilt, remembering that day Ellie had revealed to her how she had trapped Randy by letting herself get pregnant. She also wondered a bit guiltily if that wasn't pretty much what she had done to John . . . if, in fact, she was pregnant now.

"I mean, he was always the smarter one when it came right down to it," John continued. "He was National Honor Society, captain and star pitcher for the baseball team—all of that stuff. I was always second best. But *I* was the one who got out. Maybe just because my father always pushed so hard, but *I* was the one who went to Orono, got my engineering degree, and didn't have to stay here, and make my living hauling lobster traps until my hands were as tough as asphalt and my back was broken."

"I don't think Randy hates his life, if that's what you mean," Julia said, thinking about the day she and John had gone out lobstering with him. "Certainly I don't think he holds *you* responsible for anything that's happened to him . . . not enough to do something like this, anyway!"

John shrugged. "I don't know," he said, cautiously eyeing Julia, trying to see if she would let on in any way that there was something more between her and Randy that she wasn't saying . . . something like some serious fucking!

"Come on, John," she said. "Whoever did this was—well, I certainly don't think you can blame Randy! He wouldn't be crazy enough . . . or *stupid* enough to do something like this."

"I guess you just don't know Randy, then," John said softly.

"And *you* don't, either," she snapped. "Not anymore, you don't."

"And you're saying you do?" John said, narrowing his gaze at her. Casting her glance downward, Julia shrugged. "I've spent quite a bit of time talking with Ellie, and we got together with them those couple of times. I think I'd be able to recognize it if he were whacko."

"Yeah, well, don't be so sure of yourself," John snapped. "People aren't always what they appear to be, you know. Everybody's got their deep, dark secrets!" His mind finished the idea for him. . . .

Ain't that the goddamned truth!

"Well, sitting around trying to pin the blame on Randy or whoever isn't going to get this mess cleaned up," Julia said. Even though her stomach was a raging storm of acid, she stood up and began sorting through the pile of clothes on the floor.

John joined in with her, and they worked together silently for a while before he cleared his throat and said, "One thing, though— does this make you want to move any sooner than spring?"

Julia thought for a moment, then shook her head. "Not really, but I want you to promise me you'll stop by the hardware store when we're done with this and buy some good, solid dead-bolt locks for the front and back doors. I know your father always said it wasn't necessary, but"—she glanced around at the mess in their bedroom—"I'd say it's necessary now."

"I suppose I could do that," John said, although in the back of his mind he was thinking whoever bought the house from them would want to put on their own locks, anyway.

III

By the Wednesday morning after the funeral, the family seemed to be getting back into the groove of normal living. Although Barry told John he could have the entire week off—and more, if necessary—he decided that getting back to work, even if it meant working on the Surfside condo project, was best for him. Bri had already gotten up and left to spend the day at Kristin Alexander's house by the time Julia—who was still feeling nauseous and was convinced that she either had an intestinal flu or one hell of a case of psychosomatic morning sickness—came downstairs and joined John in the kitchen. He was rinsing his plate off at the sink, staring blankly out the window.

"You know, I just can't get used to him not being here," Julia said. "Every time I turn around, I keep expecting to see him there like he always was."

She had a single piece of buttered toast and a cup of coffee in front of her, but she barely touched them. Every few seconds, it seemed, she heard something—either a faint rustling or sometimes a dull, metallic clank—from down the hallway by Frank's empty room, and she looked around, fully expecting to see Frank wheeling his way toward the kitchen.

John was silent as he put on his heavy coat and gloves and went out to warm up the car before leaving for work. When he came back inside the house, he stood for a moment, leaning against the counter and looking silently at Julia. He picked up the cup of coffee he had left there and took a last, thoughtful swallow.

"That's exactly what my dad said the morning after my mother's funeral," he said, his voice hushed as he stared vacantly at the ceiling and thought that was probably what everyone who lost a family member said for weeks after the funeral.

Julia opened her mouth to say something about how she had felt when *her* parents had died, but all that came out was a little grunt. The first few bites of toast had just hit her stomach, and they felt like hot metal bubbling in her gut.

"Well, if I don't get a move on, I'm going to be stuck in the inbound traffic all morning," he said. He rinsed his cup under the faucet and put it on the sideboard, grabbed his briefcase from next to the door, came over and gave Julia a kiss, and then went out the door. The glass panes rattled as he swung the door shut behind him, and she sat there at the table, listening as the car pulled out of the driveway.

"All alone now, my girl," she said softly to herself as her eyes skimmed across the kitchen floor. *Bri's gone over to her friend's house. . . . John's gone to work . . . and Frank's gone for good! Just you and your thoughts, kiddo!*

The dishes John and Bri had already used that morning were rinsed and stacked; everything was put away. As Julia inventoried what *didn't* need to be done in the kitchen, she was suddenly swept up by a feeling of complete uselessness. Already, with John probably no more than a mile from the house, she was beginning to realize how much of her day had depended on having Frank around for company . . . not that she had done all that much in the way of taking care of him—Judy Bartlett, the nurse, had done most of that—but she realized now how she had taken for granted Frank's being there so she had someone to talk to, to do things for. Without him and the rest of her family, the house felt to Julia like a vast and hollow shell.

When she wasn't gazing down the hallway to Frank's room, Julia found herself sitting with her elbows on the table, her face cradled in her hands as she stared emptily at her coffee cup. She picked up the cup and took a sip, but it had long gone cold. She wrinkled her nose and, just as she got up to dump it out in the sink, a jolt of pain hit her so hard in the stomach it was like a blue flame shooting up behind her eyes. Groaning, she leaned over the sink, positive her two or three bites of toast were on their way back up.

Sweat broke out on her forehead as she stood waiting. She considered jamming her finger down her throat, just to speed things along—*barf and get it over with!*—but she couldn't bring herself to do it. The pain transformed itself into spiraling waves of nausea.

"Jesus H.!" she hissed, leaning over until her eyes were level with the faucet. "If this is how it's going to be for nine months, maybe I don't want a baby after all! It's *got* to be the stomach flu again!"

She fumbled for the cold-water tap, turned it on, and filling her cupped hands, splashed her face several times with water. Sputtering, she straightened up and was reaching for a paper towel to dry her face when the phone rang. She jumped and turned around quickly, and her hand knocked the pile of dishes over into the sink. Something broke, but she didn't see what it was as she lurched across the floor to the phone.

"Yeah—" she said.

"Julia?" It was Ellie Chadwick's voice. "Is this a bad time to be calling?"

Pausing briefly, Julia licked her lips and said, "Oh no—not at all." She couldn't believe how good it was to hear a human voice.

"I can call back later if you'd like," Ellie said.

"No . . . no," Julia replied. "I was just washing my hair at the sink, and the phone surprised me. Oh, but guess what—" Holding the receiver to her ear with her shoulder, she went back to the sink and looked down at the two broken plates. "I'm sorry, but I knocked over your casserole dish. It's completely shattered." The lie tasted like the sourness bubbling in her stomach, but she was silently grateful for the opportunity to explain why Ellie wasn't going to be getting her lasagna dish back.

"Oh, don't worry about that old thing," Ellie said. "Just as long as you got to eat the lasagna first."

"Umm," Julia said, wincing even more with the second lie. "We had it last night. You'll have to tell me what you used for spices. It had a really unique flavor."

"It was nothing special," Ellie said.

"Well, thanks for thinking of us."

"How are you and everyone doing?" Ellie asked. "I haven't been by to see you 'cause . . . well—"

She let her words trail away, but Julia filled in the rest of the sentence for her: *Because Randy told me what a jerk John acted like the morning he brought the lasagna over!*

"Oh, you know—it's difficult learning to accept it all," Julie said. "I think Bri's taking it the hardest, though."

In her memory, she was replaying the morning of the funeral, when John had flung the full dish of lasagna against the kitchen wall. She had insisted that he clean it up, but even afterward, once he had apologized and said he felt like a fool and she had told him to forget about it, she knew the incident was going to fester in her mind as one of those little things she would hold against him for a long time to come.

"Aww, that's too bad," Ellie said. Then, after a pause, she said, "Are you *sure* you're doing all right? You sound kind of funny."

"I'm fine . . . *really*," Julia said. "It's just . . . well, today's the first day John's gone back to work, and it's pretty quiet around here."

"Do you want me to come over?" Ellie said. "If you want me to come over, I will."

For a second or two, Julia considered saying, *Yes! Of course!* but then she realized, if she got sick to her stomach while Ellie was here, she might have to tell her that she thought—no, she was *positive*—she was pregnant. Because he had been so wound up lately, she hadn't even hinted at it to John, other than what she had said the night *it* had happened. . . .

That did it. . . . . I just know it! . . . Women have a way of knowing!

Christmas Eve, she thought, barely aware she was still on the phone with Ellie, when they had made love on the couch a mere hour or so before Frank died! She momentarily entertained the notion that, if there was such a thing as a soul, what if Frank's soul, so recently freed from his body, had somehow transferred to her womb and was now growing with the embryo inside her. Carrying the thought a bit further, she wondered if the universe might not be chock full of disembodied souls drifting around . . . waiting to be born.

Whatever, she thought, one thing she was sure of—when she was absolutely certain she was pregnant, once she was over this intestinal flu and it was time to let people know, John was *definitely* going to be the first to know!

"I—don't mind being alone," Julia said, cringing with the thought that there it was—her third lie of the morning! A sour bubble came up into her throat and made her burp. She covered the receiver with her hand so Ellie wouldn't hear.

"Well, I just wanted to see how everyone was," Ellie said. "But you don't hesitate to call if you want some company, all right?"

"I will," she said. "Maybe I'll drop over this afternoon." She cut herself off quickly as she burped again, and felt a flood of panic when she thought, *Oh, Christ! Here it comes!*

"Whatever you want," Ellie said, but Julia barely heard her. Saying a sharp "good-bye," Julia practically threw the receiver onto the hook as she spun around and raced back to the kitchen sink. With three convulsive gags, her minimal breakfast and a thick, yellow mucus shot from her mouth and covered the broken dishes in the sink.

IV

"Has anyone been in my office?" John asked, walking up to the knot of people ritually gathered around the coffeepot in the conference room. Barry was there, and he along with everyone else shrugged and looked at the others questioningly.

"Oh, is it about your electric pencil sharpener" Barry asked with a guilty grin. "Mine broke a couple of days ago, and I had to borrow yours. I thought I put it back, though."

John stood a few feet away from the group, his hands clenched at his sides. He was trembling, and everyone watching him thought it was either because of his father's funeral or because he was angry.

'No . . . no," he snapped, shaking his head vigorously. "My pencil sharpener's there. I mean has someone who doesn't work here—someone off the street—been up here poking around?"

"I don't know what you're talking about, man," Barry said. He felt deep concern when he saw what he took to be a deep sadness etched on John's face. Coming over to him, he placed his hand gently on John's shoulder and guided him over to a corner away from the group. "You know," he said, "I wish you'd taken my advice and stayed home a week or two. It takes time to get over—"

"It isn't *that!*" John said. His voice carried so loudly, several people looked over at them. "I just want to know if anyone's seen someone in my office. Someone who didn't belong there."

Barry shrugged and shook his head. "I dunno. I mean, there have been plenty of clients and other people up here. Are you expecting someone or something?"

"No, I—" John wiped his hand over his face, then fished his pack of cigarettes from his shirt pocket. He had to fight to control his shaking hands as he lit up, and even after the first drag, he felt as if he wanted to scream with frustration.

"I'm telling you, my man," Barry said, lowering his voice, "it ain't good for you to even be here. Everyone knows what you've been through, and—"

"No—no! It's not that," John said, shaking his head. He had his cigarette dangling from his mouth, and the thin blue smoke curled up over his shoulder like a scarf. He hesitated for a second, then reached into his pants pocket. "Do you recognize this?"

With trembling hands, he smoothed out a piece of notebook paper which had been crumpled up into a tight ball, and held it up for Barry to see.

Barry's eyes took just a moment to register what was written in heavy pencil lines; then he looked John squarely in the eyes and shook his head. *"Meet . . . That's all? So what the hell does that mean?"* Barry asked. *"Meet!"*

"That's what *I* want to know," John said. He took a quick, nervous puff on the cigarette, then flicked the lengthening ash into the nearby trash can. "Somebody was in my office and left this on my desk. I want to know who the hell did it."

Frowning with confusion, Barry said, "What's the big deal? I mean, someone started to jot down a note and didn't finish it. So what?"

"This isn't the first one," John said. "I've found a couple of others around." His voice took on a jittery edge, and he suddenly wished he had never mentioned it to Barry or *anyone!*

I WON'T FORGET WHAT YOU DID TO ME!

"Just like this?" Barry asked. "Saying *'meet'* ?"

"No . . . there were other messages," John replied. "And, frankly, I don't like the idea that just anyone can wander in here off the street and come into my office. I think I can expect a little more privacy that that!"

"Look, John," Barry said, resting his hand on John's shoulder again. "I haven't noticed anything unusual going on, all right? I mean, if someone's coming up here to bug you, I don't know about it. It looks to me like just a piece of scrap paper someone meant to throw away."

John winced as he inhaled on the cigarette, thinking, *Yeah, sure! You don't know the half of it!*

"You've been under a lot of stress lately," Barry said kindly. "I think you should take my advice. Go home—be with your family for a few more days. There's the company New Year's Eve party coming up this Friday night. Show up for that, and maybe you and your wife—who I still haven't met, other than briefly at the funeral Monday—can unwind a little. Until then—"

"I'm fine, all right?" John said, his anger practically boiling over. For added emphasis, he sliced the air between them with a sharp chopping motion of his hand. "I have work to do, and I'm going to fucking-A do it. I just want you to know that I don't appreciate feeling like my office is a place where just anyone can walk in off the street."

"Fine," Barry said, stepping back a pace. "I understand. But if you won't stay home like I tell you, I sure as hell don't want you coming over and unloading your bullshit on me. Understood?" he was bristling, and he frowned deeply as he stared at John.

Clamping the cigarette firmly between his lips, John nodded curtly and turned to go back to his office.

I sure as hell do *understand,* he thought angrily. Barry's reaction only further strengthened his resolve to convince Julia they had to move back to Vermont as soon as possible.

TWENTY-ONE
"See what *he* did..."

I

The whole week following Frank's funeral, everyone in the family seemed tense and out of sorts, as though, in order to deal with Frank's death, they each turned inward. Julia knew from terrifying experience as a child that it was better to share their thoughts and feelings, but she also kept reminding herself that different people had different ways of handling the reality of losing someone in the family.

Bri, it seemed, was bouncing back the quickest... maybe simply because of her youth, which couldn't dwell too long or too morbidly on death... maybe for other reasons. But whatever her reasons, she was spending a large part of the week off from school over at Kristin's house. Suspecting she did it partly to be out of the house where Frank had died, Julia didn't mind, even though it left her alone much of the time. The important thing, in her mind, was that Bri wasn't dwelling on the negative aspects, and more and more, whenever she mentioned Frank, it was usually within the context of how much fun they had had together, not how much she missed him.

John began the habit of leaving early for work and coming

home later than usual; and each successive evening, he seemed increasingly tense, losing his patience and yelling about the simplest things. His irrational outbursts were completely out of line, Julia thought, but at least so far—thank God!—he hadn't actually gotten violent. There were no repetitions of the lasagna-throwing incident. As each day went by, Julia became increasingly sure of her pregnancy—she could feel subtle changes in her body as new hormones kicked in to support the life she was bearing. The early morning nausea—she knew it couldn't be morning sickness—had lessened, and she was convinced it had been another touch of the flu.

It wounded her deeply, though, that she couldn't tell John that, like it or not, he was going to be a father—a *real* father—for the first time; but being honest with herself, she questioned how he would react. For all she knew, it might be just the thing to set him off. Just as time would gradually dull the pain and guilt and regret he must be feeling following his father's death—*must be feeling,* she thought, because he certainly wasn't talking to *her* about it—there would be time later to let him know what had happened on Christmas Eve . . . time for him to get used to the idea of her having a baby.

Alone in the house most of every day, Julia had plenty of time to think, not just about Frank's death, but about the other tragedies she had suffered in her life.

There were memories, sad reflections . . . her parents' deaths, her divorce from Sam Mullen, Bri's real father. The pain and misery he had put her through before finally admitting that, for the past three years, he had been having an affair with a girl half his age. And there was the time when Bri, only nine years old, had been hit by a car and—*thank God!*—received no more than a broken leg. The weeks and months of casts and crutches had been a strain that had affected Julia more than she had admitted. And there were other painful memories, but none of them touched as deeply as the rift she felt now deepening between her and John.

Yes, by Jesus! She had to admit it! As Ellie had done with Randy back in high school, she might have used getting pregnant as a last, desperate means of hanging on to him. As much as she wanted to deny it, maybe she did see that, ever since they had moved back to Glooscap, John had been acting more and more . . . foreign to her. Even before his father died—*hell!* On the day they moved back to Maine, he had seemed darker—more withdrawn . . . as though he was hiding something from her, and his secret was eating him up like a wildcat trying to claw its way out of a burlap bag.

These and other thoughts kept her awake long into the night, hours after John had sunk down into the deep, steady breathing of sleep. She would lie in bed, her hands clasped behind her head, and stare uselessly at the dark ceiling for so long that at times she couldn't be sure if she had her eyes opened or closed. She would blink her eyes and not have the slightest physical sensation that she had done anything. The thick darkness of the room . . . of the insides of her eyelids . . . stayed unvaryingly the same. There was no sleep, and certainly no rest in darkness like that.

On Thursday evening, well after dark, John had arrived home from work as wound tight as usual. After supper and long, drawn-out hours of awkward silence as they sat in the living room with the TV blaring uselessly away, they all went to bed but—as usual—sleep didn't come to Julia. She lay in bed, feeling the heavy warmth of her husband beside her, and she started thinking how nice it would be—as it used to be—if she could just nudge him and he, rolling over groggily, would wind an arm around her and hold her close to him. And then—as they used to—she would respond, making low sounds in the back of her throat, and he would come more awake until, after some luxuriating foreplay, they would be making soft, slow love in the darkness.

Not tonight, Julia thought, only distantly aware of the warm streams of tears that ran down her face. *Not tonight . . . maybe not ever again.*

The thought gave her a dull chill, like being cut with a blunt knife. Heaving a deep sigh, she swung her legs out from under the covers and sat up on the edge of the bed. The bedsprings creaked beneath her weight. Through the window, she could see the dusky black night sky sprinkled with stars. The light almost hurt her eyes with its brightness as she stood up and walked slowly toward the bedroom door.

If I'm not going to sleep, she told herself, *I might as well go downstairs and do something to make myself tired.* She was thinking maybe a cup of warm milk would soothe her as she glided silently down the stairs and turned toward the kitchen.

But at the foot of the stairs, she paused—frozen in midstep as though she were a frightened rabbit in the headlights of an on-coming car. She could feel her eyes widen as she slowly turned her head and looked down the length of the hallway toward Frank's room. As dark as the house was, she could barely make out the darker rectangle where the shattered remains of the bed-room door had been removed. The blackness in the doorway was so intense, Julia had the unnerving impression that it was flicker-ing with barely perceptible flashes of dull blue light.

She stood stock-still, her hand resting on the stairway railing as a thin ripple of chills zipped up her arms, across her shoulders to the back of her neck.

Could the stair railing really be this cold? she wondered, as her whole body shivered. Looking down at her hand, it appeared to be vaguely translucent . . . pearly white in the diffused light of the night.

Her breath came in short, nervous gulps as she stood there, staring, straining her eyes to see what could possibly be in the doorway.

Maybe just the moonlight, she thought, but a quick glance behind her at the living room picture window showed her that the night was thick and dark; there were no moon-cast shadows in the front yard.

But when she looked back at Frank's opened door, she saw— undeniably—that there was *something* . . . some kind of light, filtering weakly out into the hallway. It seemed to be pulsating in time with her racing heartbeat.

"Julia . . ."

Her name came to her from the darkness, no more than a fleeting ripple, a whooshing in her ears that could have been—*had to be!* her mind said—nothing more than blood racing through her ears. The coldness on the back of her neck was spreading, sliding down her back between her shoulder blades like cool water. The knot in her stomach tightened as she placed one foot in front of the other and started, ever so slowly, down the hallway.

Don't go down there! her mind was screaming. *You don't want to go down there! You don't want to see what's in there!*

But the pale blue light was there! The open rectangle of Frank's door had the illusion of being a solid gel of blue light. As she took one—two—three steps closer to it, the light got brighter! And when she had taken another few steps closer, the voice— *Christ! No! It sounded like Frank's voice*—whispered her name again, just the way he had always pronounced it, as though it had two syllables instead of three.

"Jule-yah . . ."

She could feel every muscle, every nerve in her body vibrate with the sound, as though a low current of electricity were tingling up from the floor through her feet. As she neared the door, the corner of her mind whispered, *Don't go in there! You don't want to go in there. You don't want to see what's in there!* But then another thought intruded, and Julia became convinced that Frank was still alive. He was lying in bed, and he needed her help!

"Jule-*yah!* . . ."

The voice was louder, more commanding, and Julia knew no matter how impossible this all was, no matter how much she knew Frank couldn't be there . . . that she shouldn't enter the room, her feet kept shuffling forward, almost as though someone else was directing them.

At the open doorway, she reached her hand out and touched the splintered door frame. She knew why it was broken and the door was gone!

John smashed the door down with an axe, the quiet corner of her mind whispered. *He broke it down on Christmas Eve . . . when his father was . . .*

"No," she whispered, surprising herself by the nearness of her own voice.

Frank's not dead. He's in there! . . . And he needs help!

The whooshing sound in her ears was now as loud as thunder as she stared at the blue light streaming through the bedroom doorway, lighting up a kiltered rectangle of the floor and the opposite wall. Julia turned the corner and, looking into Frank's room, gasped with surprise. *He was there! He was lying in his bed!* He had the covers pulled up to his chin, and he was turned so she couldn't see his face clearly, but she *knew* it was Frank!

"*Jule-yah! . . .*"

The voice was coming from the bed, and on impulse, Julia moved toward him, her hands out in front of her. All around her, the room glowed with eerie, shifting blue light that, oddly, cast no shadow. All she could think was, *Frank's there. He needs help!*

When she was beside the bed, she reached out gently, prepared to roll Frank over and see what he needed. It was in the instant just before her hands touched the figure that she noticed something . . . odd. Frank was wearing a thick sweater. It looked gray in the strange light . . . a heavy, bulky knit sweater.

And then, just as she touched it, the figure under the bed covers began to roll over. In an instant flood of horror, Julia saw that it wasn't Frank! The skeleton face on the bed looked up at Julia with black, eyeless sockets that, deep within, seemed to radiate a cold, red light. Loose strands of long, dark hair hung down to its shoulders, and flaps of gray skin were peeling away, exposing the white bone beneath. Tiny worms—maggots—were squirming in the decayed flesh, and when the figure sat up in the bed, the motion sent them raining down on the sheets and pillow like hard, dry rice.

So frightened she couldn't grab enough breath to scream, Julia felt herself falling backward as though someone were pulling her roughly by the collar from behind. The blue light in the room hurt her eyes as she watched the figure on the bed slowly heave itself into a sitting position. Thick, dark clots that could have been dirt or lumps of decayed flesh rained onto the sheets. The bedsprings creaked beneath its weight, but below that sound was another sound—a harsh, grating sound. It took Julia a moment to recognize it—dry bones rubbing against each other!

"*Jule-yah . . .*" the figure said, its lipless mouth moving mechanically up and down as those empty eye sockets looked up at her. They were spinning pools of black where even the ghostly blue light couldn't reach.

"*He* did this to me, Jule-yah. . . ." the skeleton mouth whispered, its voice thick and muffled, as though the tongue had swollen and now blocked its throat.

"See what *he* did to me? . . ."

"No," Julia said, her voice only a hint of sound. She still felt herself falling away in a slow, backward spin.

"*See what he did to me, Jule-yah? . . .*"

The thing on the bed reached out to her. Thin, bony fingers with long, cracked fingernails clicked like insect shells as they clenched and unclenched. The bulky sweater, Julia could see, was green with mold and coming apart in places. Her nostrils were filled with a damp, earthy smell that almost choked her.

Then, in an instant of hot pain that flashed red across her vision, Julia backed into the bedroom wall. Frank's room—and the thing sitting up in his bed—suddenly kiltered sickeningly to one side, and Julia's lungs finally took in enough air so she could let out a piercing wail. The scream cut off abruptly when she hit the floor, and it was some minutes later, after John had heard her and raced downstairs to find her, that she came to.

When she did regain consciousness, she found herself propped up on the couch with both John and Bri leaning over her, their faces twisted with concern. The back of her head felt tender, and when she tried to move, her shoulders and neck burned with pain.

"What the hell?"

John's face was sidelit by the single light he had switched on. Julia could read the concern in his eyes, and she was filled with a warm love for him—*like I used to feel,* she thought sadly as she shifted forward and wrapped her arms—*damn the pain!*—around him. She could feel heart-wrenching sobs trying to build up inside of her, but she clamped her jaw tightly, not letting them out. When she closed her eyes, though, blinking back the tears, she clearly saw in her mind the horror that had been on Frank's bed. The need to cry and scream became almost overwhelming.

"There . . . there," John cooed, close to her ear. She couldn't believe how reassuring the warmth of his breath was down the side of her neck. "You had a bit of a fall," he said, "but everything's all right now."

They stayed that way, embracing almost desperately for several minutes. Eventually the burning need to scream subsided as the strength of her husband's arms held her, and with a shuddering breath, she pulled away and looked at him.

"I was—I can't really remember," she said, her voice sounding unnaturally thin in her ears. "I couldn't sleep, and I came downstairs for a drink. I must've . . . it had to have been a dream." Her voice trailed away as she took a peek into her memory of what she had seen. . . .

No! she commanded herself. *Not seen! What I dreamed! It had to have been a dream!*

"You must have tripped on the bottom stair there, or maybe you bumped into the couch in the dark," John said, indicating the stairway with a curt nod of the head. "You didn't twist your ankle or anything, did you?"

"The bottom of the stairs?" Julia asked, looking at him with surprise. "I thought I was in—" Again she cut herself off, thinking—at least for now—it was better not to mention what she had imagined.

"Hey, babe—all I know is, I was sound asleep until you let out a horrible scream." John chuckled and shook his head nervously. "I think I must've jumped right up into the air."

"Yeah, I—I hope I didn't scare you guys," Julia said, looking from John to Bri.

"Oh, no . . . nothing like that," Bri said. Her tight smile let Julia know that she felt the exact opposite.

"Well," she said, shrugging helplessly, "I have no idea what happened. I mean, the last thing I remember was I wanted to heat up some milk to help me sleep. The next thing I know, I'm on the couch with you two goons leaning over me."

You're getting pretty damned good at lying, girl, she thought bitterly to herself.

The horror she had seen in Frank's bedroom was still as clearly etched in her mind as if it were a movie she had seen a dozen times. Every sight, every sound, even the heavy earth smell of that decomposing sweater—*and those eyes!*—were a clear memory.

As clear as if it really happened, she thought, looking deeply into her husband's eyes and trying not to see spinning wells of black, eyeless sockets glowing with a dull, fiery red.

"It's almost four o'clock," John said after glancing over his shoulder at the clock on the mantel. "I think what we all need to do is get back to bed."

Bri stood up slowly, leaned back, and yawned widely. Julia, watching her, commanded herself not to think it looked as if her mouth was frozen in a long, silent scream.

"Yeah, I think I'm tired enough now," Julia said as she heaved herself up off the couch. Every muscle complained, and the back of her head still throbbed, but she forced herself not to let it show.

"You're sure you didn't get hurt or bang your head?" John asked, still watching her with concern. "I mean, if you banged your head really hard, maybe you should go to the hospital for an X ray."

"I'm fine . . . really," Julia said, and she followed her assurance with a yawn that was only half forced. "I'm just glad no one has school or work to go to tomorrow, 'cause I feel like sleeping till noon."

II

It surprised Julia, but once she fell asleep, she stayed asleep until well after sunrise the next morning, and when she finally got out of bed a little after ten o'clock, she actually felt rested. The dream—she was still trying to convince herself that's all it was—she had had of that *thing* in Frank's bed had lost only a bit of its clarity. It still hovered in her mind, sharply lit by blue-edged light. Whenever she caught herself dwelling on it, she would shake her head and, to anchor herself, look outside the nearest window at the bright, snowy day.

It was New Year's Eve day, and the family spent most of it lazing around the house. It was too cold outside to do much of anything, and Bri—who was upset because Kristin was off visiting relatives with her family—had gone for a walk by the ocean but soon turned back because of the biting wind off the water.

"Are you sure you don't mind staying home alone?" Julia asked Bri during supper. They were eating early because of John's office party in Portland that evening.

"What—do you mean am I *afraid* to stay here by myself?" Bri said. The only thing that bothered her about it was remembering how they had found their house trashed after Frank's funeral, but her father—as promised—had put new dead-bolt locks on both doors, and she figured she would keep turning lights on and off all evening, so any prospective burglars would see that someone was home.

"I just mean—" Julia said, but she paused when, again, the memory of the *thing* in Frank's bed, raising itself up and staring at her, blossomed in her mind.

"Yeah?"

"Huh?" Julia shook her head, trying to force the memory away. "Oh, yeah—I mean, if you'd like, we could have someone come stay with you. I'll bet Ellie Chadwick wouldn't mind."

"Yeah, great," John whispered, but neither of them heard him.

"I'll be fine," Bri said. "Actually, I probably ought to get started on that paper for English class."

"You haven't started that yet?" Julia said. She shook her head with mild disgust.

"I've been busy," Bri said, and that—thankfully, she thought —was the end of it.

"Well, then, if you don't mind cleaning up the supper dishes, maybe your father and I will get ready to go," Julia said.

John looked up from his plate. "I've been looking forward to this all week," he said. The sour-looking downward turn of his mouth spoke otherwise, but Julia, who also wasn't keen on going to the party, smiled at him.

"If you want to sit around and moan, fine," she said, pushing herself away from the table and standing up. "It just means I'll get the shower first."

"Fine," John said.

Once upstairs, Julia—even knowing that both Bri and John were downstairs—felt subtle waves of uneasiness. All day, no matter how hard she tried to put the events of last night out of her mind, they kept intruding almost constantly. The most ridiculous thing would remind her of some aspect of the dream, and she would find her attention wandering far afield, thinking about that odd blue light, that skeleton face with peeling, rotting skin, that horrible, choking stench of rotten flesh, those black, bottomless eyes glowing with a dull red glow. . . .

She hurriedly undressed and went into the bathroom, but as soon as she turned on the shower and stepped in under the warm spray, she felt even tenser. Maybe it was the hissing sound of the water, she thought; it could mask any other sounds so she wouldn't hear . . .

What? she thought, chastising herself. *Am I expecting someone to come sneaking up on me from behind?*

She wet her hair and started shampooing it, but as long as possible, she kept her eyes opened, focused on the translucent shower curtain, expecting at any second to see a dim, distorted shadow shift by on the other side. Her imagination went into overdrive, and she further imagined seeing the figure raise a long-bladed knife over its head and then start to bring it down to slice through the shower curtain with a watery hiss.

She hurriedly rinsed her hair and decided to skip her customary second lathering. She told herself she had to hurry to get ready for the party, anyway.

The warm water felt soothing on her skin as she rubbed the bar of soap over her body. Taking a washcloth from the railing, she was just beginning to work up a soapy lather when she felt an odd sensation deep in her stomach. It wasn't much—as a matter of fact, she almost took it as nothing more than the warm rush of water over her belly and legs, or maybe a last knot of fear unwinding. But then she looked down, and her heart did a cold little flip. The insides of her thighs were streaked red with blood.

"Oh, Jesus! Oh, shit!" she said, staring in disbelief as the thin trickles of blood ribboned over her white skin. The suds down by her feet turned pink before being sucked down the drain. From deep inside the pipes, there came a hollow gurgling sound. . . .

Almost like laughter, Julia thought in her panic. *Or satisfaction!*

Arching her back, she gently probed her pubic hair with her fingers, afraid—and positive—that the source of the blood wasn't a razor cut from shaving her legs; it was from *inside* her.

I can't be having a period! she thought, feeling her eyes begin to burn. *I'm going to lose the baby! I'm losing it now!*

Frantically she looked from her bloodstained legs to the shower curtain. Her imagination was whirring into high gear, and she fully expected to see the thin plastic get torn aside as a grinning skull face leered in at her, laughing with deep, bubbling glee.

Like the shower drain, laughing as it drank my blood!

"Jule-yah . . ."

The voice whispered like tearing paper in her mind.

"*See what* he *did to me? . . .*"

"No," she said, *her voice a feeble wail.* "I'm *not* going to lose it!"

Gently probing her lower belly with her fingertips, she pressed in on her pubic bone, trying to feel if it was true, that the embryo —*what? Only five days old?*—was tearing away its anchor on her uterus wall. She drew her finger up under her vagina and stared numbly at the thick clots of blood, so deep red they were almost purple.

It's normal to show a little spotting, she told herself as she rinsed the blood away under the full stream of the shower. It was just a little bloody show from the period she was supposed to be having but wouldn't, now that she was pregnant. A last little kick from her recently fertilized body.

"I *can't* lose it," she said aloud, barely hearing herself above the rushing sound of the shower. *I just can't!*

She remembered the idea she had had awhile ago, that the universe was full of wandering, drifting souls just waiting to be born. Perhaps they were the souls of people who had already died—like Frank—and if the concept of reincarnation was true, they were waiting to be reborn. She closed her eyes, praying silently that the little soul that had drifted into her womb would hang tough, hold on to the promise of life nine months from now.

When she opened her eyes again, she told herself it looked worse than it was. Already the water slipping down the drain was almost completely clear. No deep-throated laughter rang up from the drain. Her legs had only a few traces of thin blood—*very thin*, she told herself. *A little bit can look like a lot because it can scare you.*

"This is normal," she said, still unable to keep her hands from probing below her belly. "This *has* to be normal!" She laughed nervously to herself when she wondered how *normal* it was to feel morning sickness the morning after getting pregnant. Wasn't that supposed to come only after you missed your first period? But, no—that had been the flu. Morning sickness and the rest of it was all ahead of her.

"If it's one last period you want, here you are," she said.

"What?" a voice spoke out suddenly.

Julia let out a startled shriek. "What the hell are you doing out there?" she shouted. Gripping the shower curtain tightly in one hand, she tore it aside, almost ripping it off the curtain rings. It was only with a slight measure of relief that she saw John standing in his undershorts by the bathroom sink, his face slathered with shaving cream.

"I'm shaving," he said, holding up his hands innocently. "What's it look like I'm doing?"

Right away, Julia's eyes fastened on the tiny razor nick on his chin. A trickle of blood not much thicker than a hair snaked down the curve of his jaw.

See! she told herself. *Just a little bit of blood looks like a lot!*

"Well," she said, fighting to control the trembling in her voice, "you scared me. I didn't hear you come in."

Shaking his head, John looked back at his reflection in the mirror and ran the razor blade down his cheek.

"I'll be done in a second, and you can have it," Julia said as she ducked back under the stream of water. Taking the wet washcloth, she rubbed between her legs and smiled gently to herself when she saw only a trace of pink.

False alarm . . . I hope, she thought, even though her stomach was still tingling . . . *with tension,* she told herself, *not the walls of her uterus sloughing off!*

III

The party was loud . . . *too* loud, Julia thought as they walked into the plush home of William Atkins. Mrs. Atkins, a frail but still attractive woman in her midfifties, greeted them at the door and took their coats. Although it was still early—only a little before nine o'clock—it looked like just about everyone had arrived already and things were getting into high gear. From the plushly furnished living room came the raucous sounds of so many conversations going on at once Julia could hardly make out a word. Some unrecognizable music was playing low on the stereo.

"There's plenty to eat and drink on the dining room table," Mrs. Atkins said after John introduced himself and Julia. "Please —relax and have a good time."

John nodded and, holding Julia by the crook of her elbow, guided her through the crowd toward the huge spread of food. Along the way, he paused and introduced her to several people— all, she assumed, from work—but the only person whose name she remembered was Barry Cummings. He was smiling widely, his eyes red-rimmed, looking as though he, at least, had started celebrating the New Year quite a bit earlier that afternoon.

"Now we know where last year's profits went," Barry said, smiling as he nodded toward the table. He was unsteady on his feet and almost spilled the drink he was holding.

John nodded and moved away from him as fast as he could without being rude.

"I'm not going to last long here," Julia said as they moved slowly along the length of the table, loading up their plates with sliced roast beef, Swedish meatballs, lasagna, fresh-baked Italian bread, and an assortment of condiments. As good as the food looked, the pit of Julia's stomach was in turmoil, and she knew she wasn't going to be able to eat much. After what had happened in the shower, she had put on a pad, and now she was anxious to excuse herself and go to the bathroom to check it.

Please, God, when I do, let there be no more blood! she silently prayed.

"I'll be right back," she said, putting down her plate and edging away from John. "I have to find the little girl's room."

"Can I get you a glass of rosé while you're gone?" John asked as Julia walked away from him. He was standing beside the table where the drinks were being served.

Julia paused and shook her head. "I think I'll stick with ginger ale tonight," she said. The muscles in the backs of her knees felt as though they were unstrung, and all she wanted to do was get to the bathroom.

John looked at her with wide-eyed surprise. "Ginger ale? Really? You usually don't—"

"I'll be the designated driver tonight," Julia said. "This is your crew; you can unwind with them."

"Do you want that ginger ale straight up or on the rocks?" John said. He gave her a low, snorting laugh, then turned and ordered their drinks from the tuxedoed bartender. *Julia may be on the wagon tonight,* he thought, *but not me.* He asked for a double whiskey and took a big gulp before turning to give Julia her ginger ale.

Julia noticed how he poured down the first gulp, but she acted —for now—as if she hadn't. All day John had been acting as if he wanted desperately to find an excuse not to come, and now it seemed to her he had decided, if he *was* going to be here, he might as well get hammered at company expense. Leaving her drink next to her plate of food, she made her way through the throng to the bathroom. After locking the door, she hiked up her dress, pulled down her panties, and saw—with a flood of relief —that the pad was only slightly pink.

"Thank God!" she muttered. She pulled her panties up, smoothed out her dress, and flushed the toilet for good measure before leaving to rejoin John. As they mingled with the co-workers, their spouses and dates, several people offered, along with the New Year's wishes, their condolences to John concerning his father's death. He accepted them gratefully, but Julia could tell—both by the way he stiffly nodded his head and by how fast he put away his first three drinks—that he was nervous about something. Like her, he left the food on his plate mostly untasted, but his reason was that he seemed so busy drinking.

Conversation, as usual at parties like this, was mostly superficial and tended to revolve around work, no matter how much people protested that they wanted to leave the office behind. Small knots of people were discussing this or that particular project, the relative merits of this or that building material, and whether or not they had seen the peak of Portland's development boom. Only in the living room, on the couch by the picture window with a wide vista of the Portland skyline across the bay, were there people—obviously the younger co-workers trying to impress their dates—talking about other things, generally either politics or astrology.

About an hour into the party, after John had finished off his fourth drink and was acting decidedly unsteady, Julia nudged him and whispered in his ear, "Can we head home now?" She tried to keep any trace of desperation out of her voice, but the longer she was on her feet, the worse she felt. The unsettled feeling in her stomach was still there in spite of the ginger ale.

John looked at her, bleary-eyed, for a moment, then shrugged. "What's the matter?" he said, his voice slightly slurred. "Aren't you having a good time?"

Julia stopped herself from saying, *No . . . I love talking about how the concrete footings for practically every condominium along the shore will be underwater by the turn of the century.* Instead, she gave a helpless little shrug, as if to say, *Get me out of here!*

"I don't think we can split before midnight," John said. Someone knocked into him from behind, and he turned around, glaring, until he saw who it was and then smiled a greeting.

"Well, then, maybe we could finagle a seat in the living room," Julia said. "My feet are *killing* me." She really didn't care anymore *how* the evening went now that she was sure the blood flow had stopped.

Just some normal spotting, she told herself, and smiled with satisfaction.

"Lemme get us each a refill," John said, taking her glass from her even though she hadn't offered it. "You see if you can find someplace to sit."

Unable to find a seat on the couch, Julia hunkered down on the floor by the picture window. Whenever the conversation stopped holding her interest, she would turn and look out at the brightly lit city across the bay. A myriad of building lights and blinking holiday lights reflected in the cold, black water. Everything outside seemed crisp and clear compared to the smoky blue haze in the Atkins's apartment. Twisting the lock, Julia opened the window a crack and took a deep breath of frigid air, trying to ignore the dull ache deep in her belly.

"Ahh, there he is," one of the men on the couch said. "You can ask him yourself."

Looking up, Julia saw John making his way over to her, carefully sidestepping the intervening people until he got to where she was sitting. He handed her both glasses before sliding down onto the floor next to her. His drink was already half gone, she noticed.

"Ask me what?" John said, looking up at the two young couples on the couch. He recognized the man who had spoken as someone from around the office, but he couldn't place his name. He knew he worked downstairs in the blueprint department.

"Well," the other man on the couch said, looking shyly down at his feet for a second, "I heard the state police have been asking some questions out at the Surfside project site."

"Really?" John said. "What for?"

His first thought was that the man he had heard about who had been punched by a truck driver while protesting at the construction site was suing the condo corporation.

"You know," the young man said. "Because of those bones they found—"

"Hah!" The sudden burst of laughter made them all look around at Barry Cummings, who had turned his attention toward their conversation. "Dem bones, dem bones gonna *rise!*" he said, adopting a deep-South black accent and raising his hands menacingly. His face wrinkled with mirth as he looked from one person to the next, finally ending with John.

"The last I heard," John said, "they'd determined those were cow bones." Apparently only Julia noticed the tightness in his voice, but she hadn't missed how, as soon as the man had mentioned the bones, John's face had paled and he had put his drink down on the floor and clasped his hands together between his legs. He shivered and, turning around, slid the window closed.

"Hah! You shoulda seen it," Barry said, wobbling drunkenly on his feet. "I was out there when they found 'em, 'n' *nobody* knew what the hell was goin' on. Those friggin' staties looked just as confused as everyone else . . . everybody thinkin' they was *human* bones. Huh! As if that's the first time someone with a backhoe's uncovered bones, fer Christ's sake!" Turning to John, Barry smiled widely. "Christ! John, you was there, 'n' you was as freaked out as th' rest of 'em."

Noticeably pale, John held up his hands helplessly. "I was just —just surprised. That's all," he said, glancing nervously at Julia and wondering how much of this he had told her.

"Surprised?" Barry said, looming over him. "You just 'bout *shit* yourself. Hell, in all the years I've been doin' surveying, whenever we turned up bones, we just kept right on diggin'."

"You'd just leave them there?" one of the women on the couch asked.

Barry nodded and turned the motion into an effort to stay standing. "Sure as hell would. When you're workin' on a project, the last thing you need to do is waste time dickin' around with crap like that. 'Sides, nine times out of ten, it turns out they're nothing more'n animal bones."

"But what about that one time in ten when they *are* human?" the woman asked. "What if you find remains of, say, an Indian campsite or a colonial graveyard? Wouldn't you contact some archaeologists or somebody to check it out?"

"And slow down the project?" Barry said. "Hell, no!' "

"That seems an awful waste," the woman said, glancing at her date. "But then, what if the bones belonged to some person who's been missing? I mean, you must have to contact the police for something like that."

Barry shrugged. He looked pensively at the small amount of booze in the bottom of his glass, then drained it off before answering. " 'N' how are we supposed to tell? I don't know what other people do, but my experience has been that you just keep right on workin'. We're there to get a job done, not screw around with anything we find . . . 'less, I suppose, it was a briefcase with a million dollars in it. Then I might take some interest." He snorted with laughter. "Hell, I'm runnin' dry."

As he turned to go get a refill, John tried to signal him to ask if he'd refill him at the same time, but Barry didn't hear him and was soon swallowed by the noisy crowd. Glancing at Julia, John held up his glass and asked, "You ready for another?"

Biting her lower lip, Julia shook her head. "Don't you think you've had enough?"

For a second, John sagged back down onto the floor and considered. Then, with a huff, he shook his head. "No," he said as he struggled to stand up. "Just one more."

"Make it a weak one, okay?"

"Sure," he said as he started to push his way toward the bar. He felt a little unsteady, but he also felt in a somewhat better mood . . . as long as he didn't let himself think too much about the discussion they had just finished. He was angry at Barry for making him feel like such a fool, but on the other hand, he was grateful that Barry's drunken mumbling had diffused the topic. The *last* thing John wanted to think or talk about was those bones uncovered out near Haskins' barn and what he—or *anyone*—thought about them!

Contrary to Julia's request, he ordered another double. As he was turning to go back to Julia, though, he spun around a little too fast and bumped into the woman standing behind him. His hand knocked back, spilling his drink onto his chest.

"How clumsy of me. I'm so sorry," the woman said. As with just about everyone else here, he didn't recognize her.

"My fault entirely," John stammered as he brushed his hands down his jacket front. He could feel the cold whiskey soaking through his shirt. "Maybe I'll get lucky and absorb it through my skin."

The elderly woman laughed as she reached for a handful of napkins from the bar top and handed them to him. He immediately started blotting his chest and hands dry, sheepishly glancing at her now and then.

"I really should watch where I'm going," he said once the pile of napkins was nothing more than a soggy mess in his hands.

"Let me get you another drink," the woman said. "What did you have?"

"Whiskey—a double," John said, looking around for someplace to toss the wet napkins. He didn't see a wastebasket nearby and was just about to hand them to the bartender when he noticed a thin black streak on the back of his hand. Confused for a moment, he turned both hands over and looked to see what might have made the mark. Suddenly he froze. His heart gave a cold thump in his chest, and his throat closed off.

"What the—" he muttered, turning over the whiskey-soaked napkins. Carefully, so they wouldn't dissolve in his hands, he unfolded the napkins and saw that there was something written on the bottom napkin . . . two words printed in bold, dark pencil marks.

MEET ME...

John had the physical sensation of hands closing tightly around his throat as he stared unbelievingly at the two words. He instantly recognized the printing; it was the same as that on all those other notes he'd found.

"Jesus Christ!" he muttered, hearing his voice only distantly.

"Excuse me?" the woman he had bumped into was turning around—carefully—and holding his fresh drink out to him. Her heavily made up face was wrinkled with her smile, but in his panic, John suddenly saw her cheerful expression as a grimace— a taunting, evil grimace!

"No—I, uh . . . nothing. Thank you," John said, shaking his head. His hand was trembling as he reached for the drink, positive he would spill this one, too.

"I hope you can get your jacket clean," the woman said.

"Oh, don't worry about it," John said mechanically. "It's just an old thing, anyway."

He still couldn't shake the impression that, as nice as this woman was trying to be, she had somehow known about the message written on the napkin. . . .

MEET ME . . . !

Did she slip it into my hand? John wondered, giving her a sidelong glance. Maybe she was gleefully enjoying his rising panic; beneath the sparkling friendliness in her eyes, was there a wicked gleam of pleasure at his expense? Any second now, he fully expected her to throw her head back and laugh long and loud at him.

Positive only a whimper or a scream would come out if he tried to say anything more, John nodded his thanks and walked back to Julia. All the way, he felt as though the woman was watching his back, thoroughly enjoying the churning black panic the note had stirred up inside him.

"I saw that," Julia said, smirking as John sat down beside her.

"Can't really say that was one of your better moves, can we? I hope you didn't get any on her dress; it looks expensive."

"Give me a break, all right?" John said as he took a sip of his drink. It burned the back of his throat, but for the first time tonight, it seemed to make him more uneasy. He felt tensed and ready, as though he was expecting a fight with someone. In his right hand, on the side away from Julia, he was still clenching the ball of whiskey-soaked napkins; and to his fevered imagination, he was positive he could feel those two words—MEET ME—searing the palm of his hand as if they were written in fire instead of pencil.

"I'll finish this and we can get going," he said, raising his glass in her direction.

Julia nodded her agreement. "Happy New Year!"

IV

In spite of what she had told her parents—that she didn't mind being alone while they went to the party—Bri *was* nervous all evening. As soon as her folks pulled out of the driveway, and then again several times during the evening, she went to both doors and double-checked the locks to make sure they were secure. But even then, she didn't like being in the house—*alone* for the first time, she realized, since Frank had died.

Drawing all the shades in the living room, she sat on the couch and watched TV for most of the evening, but nothing really caught her interest. She tried calling Kristin on the phone, even though she knew she was visiting her grandmother, and for the most part just sat on the couch, fighting back the tension she could feel coiling inside of her.

She knew her discomfort had to be primarily because of her grandfather's death. Even though she kept reminding herself Frank hadn't been her *real* grandfather, in the short time she had known him, she had developed a deep attachment to him. She missed his dry sense of humor, which only she—and her mother, sometimes—seemed to catch, as well as their evening checkers games. And Granddad seemed, in turn, to have opened up to her—certainly as much, if not more, than he had with her mother, she thought.

And there were no two ways about it—it was *creepy* being in a house where someone had died so recently. In her overactive imagination, every rumble of the furnace, every clank of water pipes, and every creak of the floor became magnified, became something else. She found herself thinking it wouldn't be very difficult to become convinced a house was haunted when your mind distorted one sound into another simply because you expected to hear the ordinary sounds of the other person—the one who was dead! She could easily see how someone who had lost a husband or wife or child would continue to hear the sounds of that person's activities. And, sure, looking into a dimly lit room or down a dark corridor, it would be normal to think you saw the person still there.

As much as she tried not to think along these lines, Bri's mind kept wandering back to how every little thing reminded her of Frank. After all, this had been *his* house for so long, it would only be natural if it had somehow stored up traces of his presence. Several times during the night, Bri would find herself sitting bolt-upright on the couch and looking around, trying to nail down the source of the creaking or clanking she heard. She would stare down the hallway, her heart thumping in her throat, expecting to see Frank rolling his wheelchair down toward the living room!

As the evening progressed, Bri's imagination kept getting tweeked by the lonely quiet of the house. From thinking about her grandfather, she then started remembering Audrey and some of the other things that had happened to her since she had moved into the house. Before long, she was so scared she hurried over to the easy chair in the corner, where her back would be against a comforting solid wall, the afghan pulled tightly up under her chin.

She tried not to think about the time she and her parents had climbed Bald Hill and she had seen Audrey off in the woods, beckoning for her to follow her in under the shadows of the trees . . . and what she had tripped over!

She tried not to think about the time after the snowstorm, when she had gone for a walk out to Indian Point and seen Audrey's footsteps in the snow . . . footsteps that went in a circle with apparently no beginning or end!

She tried her best not to think about how, even during the first few nights in the house, she had heard that low-throated organ music—*church wood*, her grandfather had called it—vibrating softly in the wooden frame of the house. Or the time she had gone to the window and, looking out, had seen Audrey standing down in the street, looking up at her, her face a ghostly pale from the moonlight.

She tried her best not to think about *any* of these things, but it did no good. They arose in her mind unbidden and—especially after Frank had died so horribly in this house—she was convincing herself that somehow all of these things were related. Somehow Audrey and the church wood and the *thing* she had tripped

on in the woods and her grandfather dying were all connected—
she could *sense* that they were; she just couldn't quite see how!

Across the TV screen, faces and New Year's Eve party scenes
in Times Square flashed by silently. The loneliness inside Bri
began to build until, before she knew it, she was silently crying to
herself. She cried because she missed her grandfather. She cried
because she missed her former life in Vermont and all of her
friends there. She cried because she knew, until her parents came
home, she didn't *dare* move from where she was!

And that's how she stayed until half an hour before midnight,
her knees tucked up against her chest, her chin wrapped in the
afghan. When she finally heard their car pull up into the driveway, she dashed over to the couch and flopped facedown with the
afghan over her shoulders. When her parents came in, her father
obviously having had too much to drink, she joked about how she
must have fallen asleep right after supper. She told her mother
several times how she hadn't been lonely at all. . . .

Maybe I said it a few too many times to be convincing, she
thought, and having spent some of the Christmas vacation working on a paper on *Hamlet,* she almost laughed aloud when she
thought, *"Methinks the lady doth protest too much."*

All she could think about now was how happy she was, now
that her parents were home. After wishing each of them a happy
New Year, she went upstairs to bed, telling herself to get those
foolish thoughts she had been having out of her head!

TWENTY-TWO
Storm Watch

I

"You mean I can go?" Bri said, incredulous. She had the phone
pressed to her ear, braced by her shoulder, and was looking at her
mother, who was sitting at the kitchen table. Into the phone, she
said, "She said I can come! . . . I dunno. I'll see if my father—"

Julia signaled her to silence with a wagging finger.

"Wait a sec," Bri said, frowning as she looked at her mother with raised eyebrows.

Julia leaned toward her across the table, her eyes shifting toward the living room doorway. From the living room, she could see the flickering light of the TV and hear its low, indistinct buzz.

"I'll drive you over," Julia whispered. "I don't want you bothering your father."

"Kristin? My mom says she'll give me a ride over," Bri said, her voice rising with excitement. "Okay—great! Give me ten minutes to get packed, and we'll be right over . . . Okay? Yup, 'bye."

Bri let out an excited whoop as she hung up the phone. Spinning on her heel, she started to run out of the kitchen but then checked herself and, turning back to her mother, smiled widely and said, "Thanks a *million*, Mom!"

Julia waved both hands at her amd muttered, "No problem." With that, Bri was heading upstairs, taking them two at a time.

As she listened to her daughter's footsteps on the stairway, Julia cringed and looked back toward the living room. The last thing she wanted right now was for Bri—or *anyone*—to bother John.

Ever since he got up this morning, the day after the New Year's Eve party, John had been quiet and sullen. After a light breakfast, he had complained of a headache and, mumbling something about having some of the "hair of the dog that bit me," had sat down in front of the TV with a glass of whiskey in his hand. That had been at ten o'clock in the morning, and he had been like that right into the afternoon. That worried Julia more than anything else right now. She was secretly relieved that Kristin Alexander had invited Bri for an overnight stay at her house. Some deep maternal instinct warned her that it might be best if Bri wasn't around the house . . . at least until John got out from whatever cloud was over him.

But Bri's not the problem, Julia thought, staring at the living room doorway. *John's the problem! . . . A serious problem!*

The night before, while they had been getting ready to go to the party, he had seemed edgy.

No, she thought, *admit it to yourself, at least. He has been acting downright wired!*

She had had high hopes that he would unwind at the party, finally loosen up a bit. Sure, she understood that he was still feeling gloomy about his father's death. Hell, she and Bri were certainly not over it, either. But John seemed to be internalizing it too much—dwelling on it and not talking it out. Sure, there were a lot of unresolved conflicts between John and his father which now would never be worked out . . . sure, John could regret things he had said and done—or *didn't* say and do—but she was positive he shouldn't bottle it up. There was something smoldering inside of him like a white-hot coal, just waiting to burst out in a blinding flare of heat and flame, and in her opinion he was taking things too far if he thought he could spend the entire weekend drinking and sitting in front of the TV.

From upstairs, she could hear Bri as she dashed around her room, collecting her things for her overnight. For some reason, the distant, thumping sound made Julia remember the time back in the fall, right after they had first moved in with Frank, when she had heard rats scampering around inside the walls.

God! she thought. *That feels like years ago!* and she shivered at the memory.

Of course that thought instantly stirred up other memories . . . of the day she and Frank had met Frenchie down by the harbor . . . of how happy she felt watching Frank and Bri play checkers . . . of the pure joy on Frank's face when they had attended church with him on Christmas Eve. Before long, Julia's eyes were brimming with tears.

And now look at us, she thought, not caring as the tears carved slick tracks down her cheeks.

Frank is dead and buried . . . Bri, although she has made one friend, is still basically homesick for Vermont and lonely . . . and John is depressed, quietly fuming with repressed anger and drinking too damned much, and even talking about selling his father's house!

"And what are you going to do about it?" she whispered, cradling her head in her hands. Her breath, smelling faintly sour, rebounded onto her face from her cupped palms. "Just what the Christ are you going to do about it, Julia?"

Emotions twisted and coiled inside of her like hot, wet strands of flesh. She thought of the famous scene from the movie *Alien* where the creature burst out of a crewman's chest, and for the first time in her life thought she understood what it must really have felt like to have something alien growing inside her.

And I do *have something growing inside me,* she thought, gently rubbing a hand over her lower stomach. *For the second time in my life, I've got a new life growing inside me, and what in the name of sweet Jesus am I going to do? I'm so damned scared, I don't even dare to tell my husband I'm carrying his baby!*

But no matter how much she thought about it, she had no idea what she was going to do. There was no way she could answer her own question, *What are you going to do about it, Julia?* Maybe John was right after all, and they *should* sell the family home. Back in Vermont, they had jobs and friends and schools and *everything.* They could pick up their lives again as if this stay

on Glooscap Island had been nothing more than a brief interlude
. . . a short, sad interlude; but now that Frank was dead, she realized she hadn't seen or planned anything beyond that. Foolishly,
she had just assumed that Frank would need their help, and they
would be there to give it.

So *now* what?

But no matter what they did, she had the gnawing fear that their
lives wouldn't be the same ever again. Even if they packed up this
weekend and moved back to Shelburne Falls, they had lost things,
misused and misplaced things—like affections and emotions.
And even more basic than that, there was going to be a new baby
in their lives. Any patterns they had had before would certainly be
altered by that simple fact!

And, so far, John didn't even know he was going to be a father
for the first time in his life! As much as she despised her own
reaction, Julia cringed whenever she thought about telling John
that she was pregnant. The way he had been acting lately—*God!
If he was drunk already at noontime!*—she honestly didn't know
how he would react . . . *with anger and hostility, no doubt! Certainly not with joy!* And it cut her to the quick when she realized a
negative reaction was *all* she was expecting from John.

With her eyes closed, she could imagine that she was alone, far
out to sea, being tossed back and forth by towering waves. The
memory of her seasickness the day she and John had gone out in
the *Bait Barrel* with Randy came back, and that was exactly how
she felt now!

"It's the pregnancy," she whispered softly. "*That's* what's
screwing me up! I've got to get a doctor's appointment."

But even as the words came out of her mouth, washing over her
hands, she knew that wasn't it at all!

Julia suddenly jumped up when she heard Bri come clomping
down the stairs. Breathless with excitement, Bri entered the
kitchen with her suitcase dragging from one arm and her rolled-up
sleeping bag under the other.

"I'm all ready," she said brightly, but then she noticed the pale
look on her mother's face and pulled up short. "Mom? Are you all
right?" she asked, coming over to her, her face wrinkled with
concern.

Julia forced herself to smile and nodded her head. "Yup. I'm
okay," she said, her voice sounding low and gravelly. "I was just
thinking about Frank, and . . . well, it's that time of the month for
me, too, and I guess I'm a little bit emotional. You understand."

The lie tasted like acid in the back of her throat, and she
thought bitterly, *Boy, oh boy, are you getting good at this lying!
This is getting to be downright habitual!*

Bri's mouth was set in a firm, straight line as she nodded her understanding. "Yeah," she said, "I know what you mean. I'm still not used to Grandad not being here."

"Come on," Julia said. "Let's not keep Kristin waiting any longer than we have to." She picked up the car keys and headed to the front hall closet for her coat. For just a second, she paused in the living room and almost said something to John about where she was going; but even from the side, the scowl that darkened his face forced the words back down her throat, and without another word she went out to the car with Bri.

II

On the drive over to Kristin's, Julia was burning to tell Bri that there was more to her emotional state than her missing Frank and having her period. She was dying to tell someone that she was pregnant, but she held herself back only because of her personal vow that John would be the first to know . . . when—and if—the time was ever right.

When she got back to the house after dropping Bri off, John met her at the door.

"Where in the hell have you been?" he shouted, his face flushed with anger. When Julia told him, he snorted, refilled his glass from the bottle on the counter, and then without another word, walked unsteadily back to his place on the couch, muttering something unintelligible under his breath.

And that's how they spent Saturday night and most of Sunday —John putting the whiskey away until he ran out of that, then starting on beer; and Julia sitting by herself, usually in the kitchen or silently in a corner of the living room, wishing she could cut through to John but knowing she couldn't . . . not until this black mood passed.

When Bri called on Sunday afternoon, asking if she could spend another night at Kristin's and if she could go to school from there, Julia readily agreed. "You just make sure you come home right after school, okay?" she said. All she could think was, she didn't want Bri to see John the way he was, and maybe he would stop drinking tonight so he could go to work in the morning. If he didn't pull himself together soon . . . well, she tried not to think along those lines until she had to.

As on Saturday night, that Sunday night Julia went up to bed around her usual time. She tried several times to coax John out of his sullen rage; but every time she spoke to him, he would flare back at her and tell her to leave him alone. Both nights he fell asleep—or passed out—on the couch and woke up—or came to—sometime early in the morning and crawled upstairs to bed. Both nights Julia, who had finally drifted off to sleep, woke up as he climbed under the covers fully clothed, but she feigned sleep and lay there in the dark, staring at the gradually lightening ceiling.

Over the weekend, Julia cried silently to herself more than she had since . . . since her parents had died, she figured. The one thing she and John had always prided themselves on in their marriage was their communication—both sexually and emotionally. They had always been able to talk things through, express themselves with each other and communicate.

But not anymore, Julia thought as tears burned her eyes. *Not anymore!*

"It's over, you know," a thin voice whispered to her in the dark. *"If he keeps this up much longer—any longer, you'd better buck up and face it—it's all over!"*

III

"I feel like such an *asshole*," John said.

He was sitting at the breakfast table, listlessly stirring his scrambled eggs with his fork and trying to look at Julia, who sat across the table from him but unable to maintain eye contact for very long. Through the kitchen window, the early morning light was thin and gray, and Julia could see specks of snow spitting out of the sky.

"You should," Julia said, feeling her brow tighten as she looked at him. "You *were* an asshole, and if you want the whole god-damned truth, you had me scared witless all weekend."

"I—I don't know—" he started to say, but when he shook his head, he winced from the sudden jolt of pain that shot like a sparkling light up the back of his head.

"You deserve every bit of pain from that hangover," Julia said, and even though her voice was mild, almost joking, John could tell she meant it.

Trying not to move too suddenly, John signaled his agreement. "I know . . . I *know*! It's just that—I don't know, once I started drinking at that damned party, I couldn't stop. Look, I jumped down into the well. Maybe I guess I figured if I just wallowed in it for a while, I'd work it out. I don't know. . . ."

"And?" Julia asked. "Do you feel any better?"

John's smirk looked pained. "Not much, to tell the truth," he said, "But I think I might be coming around."

Should I . . . could I tell him now? Julia wondered, feeling a sudden buoyant rush in her lower abdomen. Maybe while he was feeling so repentent was the best time to hit him with the pregnancy news.

"Well . . . do you want to talk about it?" she asked, pushing aside—for now—the thought of telling him. "What was getting you?"

John shrugged and again squinted with pain. His hand holding the fork dropped to the table, and his gaze drifted past Julia to the living room doorway. It struck him as funny how overpowering the idea was that, any minute now, his father would come rolling out in his wheelchair.

"I don't know," he said, his voice hushed. "I mean, everything just piled up all at once . . . my father dying, stuff at work—just . . . *everything.*" He almost said something about his suspicion that she and Randy were having an affair but let it drop.

"Do you feel good enough to go to work?" Julia asked. She got up from her chair and, leaning over the sink, looked outside. Since she had last gotten up to check, the gray clouds had thickened and lowered. "I had the radio on earlier, and they're saying we might have a pretty big storm this afternoon and tonight."

"No. I've got to get in to work," John said, although he knew Barry wouldn't mind if he took off a few days—hell, he had practically insisted he take them.

"Well, pay attention to the forecasts, and if it starts getting bad, I want you to come home early," Julia said. "I certainly don't want a repeat of what happened the last time we had a storm."

Neither do I! John thought with a sudden flush of panic. He managed to keep his voice even when he said, "Don't worry. I'll be careful." He got up from the table and came over to her. Wrapping his arms around her waist, he pulled her tightly against him and gave her a lingering kiss. When they pulled apart, he looked at her, smiling thinly, and asked, "Forgive me?"

Julia couldn't help but think that, although he was looking right at her and smiling, it was as if there was a thin curtain over his eyes, veiling his true feelings . . . as if his face was as thin and unsubstantial as a plastic Halloween mask. And as warm and strong as his hug was, something about it made her feel cold inside . . . cold and *trapped.*

"Well?" he said. "Am I?"

Not really feeling it, but thinking to herself that she wasn't going to let her guard down that easily—not yet, anyway—Julia slowly nodded her head and said, "Yeah . . . you're forgiven. But if you *ever*—" She grabbed him by both arms and squeezed him as hard as she could. "If you *ever* do something like that again . . . !"

"I know—I know," he said. "God, don't shake me like that! My head is *killing* me." Looking around, his eyes suddenly widened as he noticed the clock over the refrigerator. "Hey! I've gotta get going." He started toward the closet for his coat, then stopped short. "By the way—where's Bri? She didn't leave for school already, did she?"

"No," Julia said. "Not exactly. In case you don't remember, she spent the weekend at Kristin's and went to school from there."

"Oh, yeah . . . right," John said, even though his face betrayed that he had no memory of it. He headed for the closet again, saying, "I've really got to get going."

"You just remember what I said," Julia warned him, shaking her finger as he shrugged into his heavy coat and went to the door. "If this storm picks up, you get your skinny little ass home *pronto!*"

"Don't worry. I will!"

IV

After a minimum of socializing at the coffee urn, where most of the conversation revolved around what everyone had done over the holiday, John did manage—with some effort—to throw himself into his work. Barry interrupted him briefly to apologize for acting like a fool and embarrassing him at the company party, but John dismissed him with a wave of his hand, joking that it was exactly what he had expected of him. John figured he was starting to feel better simply because concentrating on a sewer design was at least *some* kind of refuge from the steady hammering pain in the back of his head.

By the time lunch was rolling around, John was pleased to discover that his headache had receded to nothing more than a dull roar, and he was actually beginning to have hopes that—just as he had told Julia this morning—the worst really might be over! He was just clearing his desk, preparing to leave for lunch, when his intercom buzzed.

"Yeah?" he said, holding down the TALK button.

"There's a Mr. Chadwick here to see you," Ellen Buchanan, the secretary, said. "I don't see his name on the appointment book." Generally Ellen's voice sounded only slightly tinny over the intercom, but when she said the name Chadwick, her tone seemed suddenly to take on the sharp whine of a dentist's drill.

John stared long and hard at his finger depressing the button. The fingernail had gone white. He knew he could easily tell Ellen to tell *Mr. Chadwick* that he was busy, or that he had gone home early because of the threatened storm, but then he thought, *Hey, what the hell? If we're really ever going to clear the air, we might as well start right now!*

"Uh, tell him to wait there," John said. "I'm just on my way out."

A few minutes later, John walked out into the office and, smiling, greeted Randy with a hearty handshake. "So, what brings you into town on a day like this?"

Randy scratched his head, looking decidedly uncomfortable in the plush office. "I had to pick up some engine parts for my boat at Harris's and thought I'd swing by 'n' see if you were free for lunch. Should I have called first?"

John shook his head, willing himself not to wince from the echoing pain that snapped like a string of firecrackers behind his eyes. "Oh—no, no." He glanced at his wristwatch, then added, "Why don't we zip over to Carbur's? That's not too far a walk."

"Sounds fine with me," Randy said. "You'll want your coat. The snow's starting to pick up now."

They left the building and walked side by side up Fore Street and then over to Middle Street. Thick flakes of snow were falling, blowing at a hard angle straight into their faces. Already the sidewalks were slick with an inch or two of fresh snow, marred only by a few recent footprints. The wind whistled down the street, and from somewhere there came a low, vibrating hum.

John and Randy barely spoke as they crossed the street and entered the restaurant. The whole time John was thinking, *This is it! This is it! I'm gonna feel him out on this shit and nail the bastard!* but he smiled and chatted pleasantly to the waitress as he and Randy sat at a table and ordered their drinks. As much as he wanted—*needed*—something strong, John satisfied himself with a ginger ale. The last thing he wanted to do was cloud his mind *now.*

"So," Randy said, leaning back in his chair and sipping from the beer he had ordered, "how have you folks been doing? Is everyone—you know—doing okay?"

"Sure," John said. "As well as can be expected."

Randy nodded. "Yeah—I know it can be tough sometimes."

John noticed that his eyes always shifted to the side, never maintaining contact with him for more than a second or two at a time. The dark weather outside the window made the soft orange glow inside the restaurant feel warm, comforting; but John could feel an icy tension in his stomach as he watched his high school friend. John was just waiting for an opening to pounce.

"Actually," John said, "we've been thinking we might be moving."

"Off the island?" Randy asked. His face registered genuine surprise.

And was that also a trace of disappointment? John wondered.

"Off the island and out of the damned state," John said. "Christ! What reason is there to stay now? We only came here to help out with my dad, and now that he's dead—why stick around?"

Randy stroked the side of his face, his beard stubble making a harsh sandpaper sound. "Well, I thought you folks liked it here," he said. "'Specially Julia."

Hit him with it now? John thought, his stomach tightening. *Ask him point-blank if he's been fucking my wife?* But just as he was forming the words in his mouth, the waitress arrived with their sandwiches. Both John and Randy sat silently as she placed the dishes in front of them, asked if they wanted a refill, and then left.

No, not yet. It'll probably be better to hit him with those notes about Abby first!

John waved his hand casually above his head, then took a sip of his ginger ale. "Ahh, there's nothing but a bunch of rotten memories in that house for all of us. I said it right after high school and I'll say it again—I can't *wait* to get the fuck off that island!"

Randy leaned one elbow on the table and cupped his chin in his hand. Now—for the first time—he looked long and hard at John, as though he was trying to fathom him. After a moment, he took a bite of sandwich and chewed thoughtfully before speaking. "You know, I guess I just don't understand you," he said, shaking his head.

"What do you mean by that?"

"Just what I said," Randy replied. "Back then, in high school, I really knew you—at least I *thought* I did. Hell, maybe I didn't even back then, and I'm so fucking dense I'm just now beginning to realize it."

John chuckled softly. "Oh, you knew me, all right," he said, leaning forward and folding his hands on the table in front of him. "You knew me . . . but you know what I've been wondering?"

In the silence that followed, the two high school friends locked eyes. John felt a thin sheen of sweat break out on his brow. His first impulse was to let it all drop. He told himself he should just pick up his sandwich, try to enjoy it, even though his stomach felt about the size of a walnut, and just bullshit the time away with Randy. They were leaving the island—if not soon, certainly by spring. Let it all just drop! The pressure he felt in his chest, the cold sweat on his brow—they were just the result of his week-end-long drinking bout.

Lowering his voice, John leaned across the table and said, "Ever since I got back to Glooscap, I've been wondering my ass off about what you really know."

"What d'you mean by that?" Randy asked, shrugging help-lessly. He took another bite of sandwich and chased it down with a swallow of beer.

"Come on, Randy! You can cut the innocent I-don't-know-a-thing shit with me, all right?" John said. "I mean, it may work with some people, but you can't bullshit me, okay?"

Frowning, Randy nodded and said, "Yeah . . . sure. Okay."

"You can't bullshit me and tell me that you never knew what happened to Abby," John said. Leaning even farther over the table toward Randy, he scowled deeply.

"Is *that* what this is all about?" Randy said, his voice sliding up the scale.

"You know damned right well it is!" John said. "I'm willing to bet you know *exactly* what happened, and I'd place a pretty hefty bet you're the one who's been leaving those notes around my house."

"I haven't got the faintest idea what the fuck you're talking about," Randy said, his anger beginning to rise. "Look I was in town and I thought it'd be a friendly gesture to drop by and see if you wanted to have lunch. And yeah—I'll admit it; I *do* feel a little bit 'funny' about you. But I mean, it's not my idea of a great Christmas Eve, answering an ambulance call at my best friend's —my *former* best friend's house because his father is dead!"

"Sounds good," John said, his voice taking on a cool edge as he leaned back in his chair and hooked his thumbs through his belt loops. "Real convincing."

"Hey! You can think whatever you want. It's not *my* problem," Randy said, thumping himself on the chest. He raised his voice but glanced around to see if they were bothering anyone.

"Well, if you want to know what I think," John said. "I think you've known all along that Abby killed herself—"

"What the hell are you talking about?" Genuine shock—at least it *looked* genuine—registered on Randy's face.

"I think you knew back when it happened that I'd gotten her pregnant. Oh, yeah—sure . . . sure. Look *real* surprised!" He jabbed an accusing finger at Randy. "You knew I knocked her up, and I'll bet she told you exactly what I said—that there was no *way* I was going to fuck up my life by marrying her. I'll bet she confided in you because you were my best friend, and she thought maybe you'd say or do something to make me change my mind!"

"Jesus Christ, John, you got to believe me. I—"

John cut him off by pounding his fist onto the table, making the silverware jump. Several people at nearby tables glanced over at them, and Randy shifted uncomfortably in his seat.

Lowering his voice to a hiss, John said, "Come on! I'll bet she told you fucking *everything!* I'll even bet she told you she planned to kill herself if I didn't marry her!"

"Come on, John—for Christ's sake, calm down," Randy said. He reached across the table to put a restraining hand on him, but John tore himself away and glared at him.

"Just cut the bullshit with me, all right?" he said, his voice snarling. If earlier his headache had retreated, it was back now in full force. A tight pressure was building inside his chest, making spinning little dots of light track wildly across his field of vision. In the back of his head, he felt more than heard a faint crinkling . . . like paper being torn and crumpled.

"She may have even told you how she was going to do it, huh?" John snarled. "Did she? Well—*did she?*"

Randy sagged back in his chair, trying—and not succeeding—to absorb everything he was hearing.

Well, the mystery's solved, Randy was thinking as he shook his head bitterly. *Abby Snow is dead . . . has been for almost twenty years now!*

"Abby never told me *anything*," Randy said, forcing his voice to stay steady and low. "You've gotta believe me!"

John snorted with laughter, and a thin line of snot ran from his nose. He wiped it away with the back of his hand. "You must think I'm a real fucking idiot," he said, "but I don't believe you. Not for one fucking second! You knew *then* just like I know *now* that you've been leaving those notes around."

"What notes?" Randy asked. "I have no idea what you're talking about!"

"I won't forget what you did to me!" John said in an irritating singsong voice. "I've gotta hand it to you—writing *me* instead of *Abby* really gave me a jolt for a minute there."

Randy tried to say something, but John cut him off.

"And you probably *do* know damn right well what I did with her," John said, smiling wickedly. "But I couldn't let something like her being *pregnant* ruin my life, now, could I? After all, I had a scholarship to Orono. I was going to get the fuck off Glooscap! So after I found her dead, hanging from the rafters in Haskins' barn, do you think I could let anyone else find her like that? Huh?"

John was looking straight at Randy, but Randy had the unnerving feeling that John wasn't seeing him—he was looking right through him!

"The stupid bitch had even written a note and pinned it to the pocket of her sweater," John said, his eyes staring wide open with the horror of the memory. "*You did this to me!* That's what the note said. Did you know about that? Did she tell you about it? *I* did it to her! *Me!* The stupid, fucking *bitch!*"

"I had no idea," Randy said, his voice hushed with shock and awe.

"So, do you know where I buried her?" John said, as if he hadn't heard Randy. "I'll bet my fucking life you know!"

Randy sat back, took a deep breath, and let it out slowly. His mind was overloading, and he found himself speechless. He could tell that John wasn't making any of this up—this was what had happened—and the thought that Abby had been dead all these years was like a point-blank gunshot to the gut.

Unable to check himself now that the pressure of hiding that horrible discovery for all those years was flooding out of him, John gripped the edges of the table so hard his knuckles turned white. There was a roaring in his ears that sounded like crashing surf. His breath came in sharp gasps that stitched his sides painfully.

"That's right!" he said, his voice nothing more than a raw growl. "I found her hanging in Haskins' barn, and I cut her down from the rafters and buried her out by the oak tree behind the barn! This fall, when they found those bones out there in the field—fucking-A!" He shook his head and wiped his forehead with his napkin, pausing to look at the heavy wet streak it left. "That was too fucking close for comfort. I thought for sure they were her bones! It turned out they weren't, but I figure sometime this spring, once the ground thaws, I'm gonna have to dig her up so they *won't* find her. But you can't tell me you didn't know she was buried out there! You had to have known!"

"Honest to Christ, John, I never—" Randy said, casting his eyes back and forth to see if anyone could overhear them. "You've got to believe me, man. I had no *idea.*"

John slumped back in his chair, and for several stunned seconds he just stared at Randy, his mouth hanging open. The pressure inside him was so strong he felt as if his head was going to explode. His throat felt flayed, and his hand shook as he reached for his drink. His sandwich lay untouched on the plate.

"You've got to be fucking *kidding* me," he said. His voice had a low, disturbing tremble, and it felt as though strong, dark fingers were closing off his windpipe.

Randy was leaning with both elbows on the table, his head in his hands. As much as he told himself to breathe evenly and deeply, he couldn't slow his rapid panting. Looking up slowly at

John, knowing now that he absolutely didn't know this man, he shook his head.

"Never! Never in my life did I suspect *any* of that," he said, fighting for control. "I know you may not believe it, but I did—I *do* consider you my friend, whatever the hell that means anymore. If you had told me back then what you just told me—Christ! I don't know what I would have done. I mean—Jesus! She *killed* herself!"

Unable to catch his breath to speak, John nodded solemnly.

"And blamed you for it," Randy said, still awe-struck by everything John had said. "Because you got her pregnant."

"I—I couldn't let anyone find her . . . not like that," John said, his voice almost breaking. His eyes were stinging as long repressed emotions tried to escape. "How *could* I?"

"But Jesus Christ, man! She was fucking *dead*! She *killed* herself because of you!"

"Not because of me!" John shouted, clenching his hands into white-knuckled fists. He raised his fists up but didn't know whether to smash them onto the table or into his eyes. "Not *because* of me! She was . . ."

"It doesn't matter what she was," Randy whispered, leaning close to John. "She's dead. She's been dead for twenty years. I dunno. Even after all this time, I think you ought to do something about it."

He's going to use it against me, John thought with a brilliant flash of panic. *He may not have known it before, but now he does . . . and he'll use it!* Looking long and hard at his former friend, John tried to see beneath the surface expression of surprise and concern, and read what Randy was thinking.

"I haven't done anything wrong," John said. "I mean, I didn't kill her—I just buried her."

"Without *telling* anyone!" Randy hissed. "Think of how her family must've felt all those years, wondering if she was alive or dead. Think of what her mother and father and sister must have gone through!"

Biting his lower lip, John nodded. "Yeah, I heard from my father that her mother died . . . what? Maybe ten years ago. And that her father died a year or so after that. Her sister . . . I don't know." He shook his head, but whether in confusion or dismissal, Randy wasn't sure.

"Well, I've been living here on Glooscap all that time, and I can tell you—her parents went absolutely nuts trying to find out what happened to her. I think it's what eventually killed them—both of them," Randy said sharply. "And her sister, Sally . . . she got married to some guy from Westbrook and lived—I think on

Spring Street in Westbrook until she moved out to the Midwest somewhere. Every year she'd run a memorial notice for Abby in the newspaper, just as if she knew she had died. But I heard a few months ago that Sally—"

"Wait a fucking minute," John snapped, sagging back in his chair, stunned. As soon as Randy mentioned Sally's name, John barely heard anything else Randy said.

It's been her sister all along! he thought, feeling a cold rush up his back. *Here I've been suspecting Randy all along and I never even thought about Sally! It was probably her I saw on the bridge during that last storm . . . and she's probably the one who's been hanging around outside the house all this time! And she has to be the one who's been leaving those notes around!*

"Jesus Christ, Randy," he said. "I've been a goddamned fool! What am I gonna do?"

Randy's mouth opened, but nothing came out.

A fool? No—crazy is more like it, he thought but didn't quite dare say it.

"Here I've been thinking all along that you knew what had happened, and because you've—" He stopped himself from saying anything about his suspicions of him and Julia, and just looked down at his clenched fists. "Jesus Christ, man . . ."

"Hey, what's done is done," Randy said with a mildness he didn't feel. "But I think you've got to report what happened. Even though it's been twenty years, I think you *have* to."

"No way, Randy," John said, shaking his head firmly.

"They'll find her eventually," Randy said. "If not when they dig out there for the condo, then later. Someone will be out for a walk with their dog, or some kids will be out playing, and they'll find her bones. If you don't come clean with what you did, when they *do* find her, they might think you *did* kill her."

"Is there something wrong with your sandwich?" The waitress's voice, speaking so suddenly behind him, made John jump and look around quickly.

"Huh? Oh, no . . . not at all," he said. "We were just—" Smiling weakly at Randy, he finished, "having a pretty intense discussion."

"Would you like me to wrap it for you to have later?" the waitress asked. "With this storm getting stronger, the manager's been talking about closing early today."

"Yeah—sure. That'd be fine." John handed her the plate, but he didn't take his gaze away from Randy's face as he took a bite of his own sandwich.

Once the waitress left their table, Randy looked at John with intensity and said, "You've got to do it, man. You've *got* to report what happened!"

John shook his head in vigorous denial. "No way! I can't let any of that come out. Julia doesn't know a thing about it, and I'm not about to tell her now."

A small voice in the back of his mind was whispering, *All you have to do is make sure you get Sally off your back. Make sure she doesn't do anything to blow it. How much could she know, anyway?*

Plenty, another, fainter but somehow colder voice whispered. *She could know everything if Abby told her before she hanged herself!*

In a weird way, it all made sense that it was Abby's sister who was doing this to him—leaving those notes around, sneaking around outside the house at night, trying to make him—what? Give himself up, or destroy himself with the guilt of what had happened? He wasn't sure what she was up to, but then again, he didn't intend to find out, either. What most surprised him, shocked him, actually, was that he hadn't thought of Sally, hadn't even *remembered* her until now!

Sally had been three, maybe four years ahead of Abby and John in school—enough so John had barely paid attention to her. But now that he thought about her, he remembered that she *had* looked quite a bit like Abby. If he had seen her outside at night, maybe during a snowstorm or with her back to him in a candlelit church, he could easily have mistaken her for her sister. Okay, so he had been wrong about Randy, and it was too bad he had blown it here, spilling his guts to him, but . . . well, *someone* had been tormenting him, stirring up things he thought were long buried and forgotten, and he had to find out who so he could put a stop to it!

Randy let out a whistling sigh as he scratched his forehead. "I just don't see how you can do it. I mean—how can you live with it, knowing someone who *loved* you, killed herself because of what you did—or what you *wouldn't* do?"

John took a deep gulp of his ginger ale and for the first time actually tasted it. He smacked his lips, wishing it was something stronger—a beer or, better still, some whiskey.

"I've had to learn how to live with it," he said with a shrug. Then, leaning forward and nailing Randy with a cold stare, added, "And I sure hope to hell you can too."

There was a long, tense silence as Randy considered the obligation his former friend was putting on him. He acknowledged that he didn't know John anymore, and truthfully, since John had moved back to Glooscap, he didn't like what little he had seen. His wife and daughter—*stepdaughter*, he reminded himself;

John's only true child died when its mother hung herself twenty years ago!—seemed nice. So nice, in fact, Randy had guiltily wondered how Julia had ever fallen for John. But John wasn't anywhere *near* the person Randy had known back then, and he certainly wasn't who he thought he would become.

Slowly, and resenting himself for doing so, Randy nodded his agreement. "Okay," he said, his voice so low John barely heard it above the other sounds in the restaurant. "I'm telling yah, though —if it was anyone else—absolutely *anyone*—I wouldn't agree to this. But because you were my best friend—" He chuckled tightly and, looking ceilingward, shook his head. "God, that seems so long ago it's like another lifetime. But I won't mention it to a soul—not even to Ellie."

Smiling thinly, John held out his hand for Randy to shake. Their clasp was cold and hard.

Like his smile, Randy thought bitterly.

"It's a done deal, then," John said, still holding tightly on to Randy's hand and smiling a smile Randy thought looked crazy. "And you'll carry that secret with you to your grave!"

V

But this isn't the end of it, John thought as he and Randy left Carbur's and walked out into the dark afternoon. While they had been inside, the storm had picked up considerable strength, and now the snow was falling in one wind-whipped, blinding sheet. The streetlights were on, illuminating the sidewalks, which now were slippery with several inches of accumulated snow. The few cars that passed them were moving at a crawl, and at the corner of Exchange Street, a Volvo had skidded into a telephone pole, denting its front fender.

As they walked back up toward John's office building, both men were huddled into their coats and silent. Each was thinking about what he had learned and how distant they were, even though they shared such a horrible secret. At the front door to the office building, they stopped and awkwardly looked at each other.

"So," John said, holding his hand out again for a handshake, "we understand each other?"

Randy nodded and quickly broke off the handshake, sticking his hand back into his pocket.

"Yeah," he said, his voice almost drowned out by the throaty howl of the wind. "I'm parked down on Commercial Street. Probably ought to get home before the roads are completely ridiculous."

"They probably are already," John replied, smiling tightly as he considered his own drive home. He figured people had already started leaving the office but decided he'd go upstairs for a minute to clean up a few things.

"I'll—uh, see you later," Randy said tightly as he started to back away from the doorway. Even with only a short distance between them, his features were lost in the falling snow. John felt a menacing chill when he remembered that *other* figure he had seen looming at him out of the snow.

"Yeah," John said, reaching for the door handle. Before he went inside, though, he suddenly turned and called out to Randy, "Oh, hey! By the way, what's Sally's married name?"

From out of the swirling snow, Randy's voice drifted back to him from the swirling snow with an odd, disembodied distance.

"Curry . . . her name was Sally Curry. But I told you, she—"

Randy's words were sliced off cleanly as the door slammed shut and John raced upstairs to his office, fully expecting to see another pencil-written note on notebook paper. The hammering in his ears only softened a little when he saw a *While-U-Were-Out* note informing him that Julia had called three times while he was having lunch with Randy.

His hands were shaking unaccountably as he dialed his home number and waited five rings before Julia answered.

"Oh, good—it's you," Julia said, sounding as if she was out of breath. "Are you still at the office?"

"Yeah," John replied. "I'm just leaving."

"If you can't tell by looking out the window, we're in for a doozy of a storm," Julia said. "I was hoping you'd already left."

"Ahh—yeah. Everybody's bailing out now," John replied. "I was just getting some things off my desk."

As he spoke, though, he wasn't cleaning up his desk. He was flipping through the pages of the Portland phone directory, looking for someone named Curry who lived in Westbrook. Hadn't Randy said she lived on Spring Street before she moved to somewhere in the Midwest. He was hoping, if he found a number, that by calling it he would get a taped message telling him the new number. If indeed Sally *was* somewhere in the Midwest. John had a pretty damned good idea she was right back home in Maine!

"All right," he whispered when he found the listing.

"What?" Julia said.

"Oh—nothing," John replied. "I just got everything put away." He took a drafting pencil and, turning over the *While-U-Were-Out* note, scribbled down the phone number. Looking at his own handwriting, he couldn't help but wonder what Sally Curry's looked like. Perhaps like that on all those notes he had been finding?

He folded the note in half and stuck it into his pants pocket.

"Okay, Jule, I'm heading out now," he said. "But don't get all agitated. The roads are pretty slick, and I'm going to drive *extra* careful. It may be an hour or more."

"Just be careful," Julia said. "See you then."

"Yup. 'Bye."

John hung up the phone and, figuring that tomorrow was going to be another snowed-in day at home, decided that he sure as hell wasn't going to bring home any work. Another day off would be just fine with him. Maybe he would even paw through the junk in the garage and see if he could find his old Flexible Flyer, if his father hadn't trashed it, and take Julia and Bri sliding in the morning.

"Night, Barry," he called as he walked out into the main office. His boss was hunched over his desk, busily drawing on a plan. Without even looking up, he waved to John and muttered, "G'night."

On his way down the stairs to the street and to the parking lot, John continually patted his leg with his gloved hand. It was just a thin piece of paper in his pocket, and through the layers of pants material and his glove, he knew it was impossible to feel it, but just knowing it was there, and that tonight—when Julia couldn't hear him—he would get Sally Curry's forwarding phone number and give her a call, made him feel light-headed. Of course, he didn't expect her to be home, wherever the hell she lived out in the Midwest, because he knew that she was already back in Maine.

VI

The drive home had been terrible; this blizzard was at least as bad as the one before it. Being so close to the ocean made the snow wetter, and all the roads felt as if they had been greased. When John finally arrived home after almost two hours, he was relieved to see both Julia and Bri. He hugged them and, clapping his hands together, eagerly asked them what was for supper.

"I guess just hamburgers and a veggie," Julia said. She scowled when she saw John pull a paper bag from his pocket and extract a fifth of whiskey.

"Care for a before-supper drink?" he asked, smiling widely.

On the one hand, Julia was relieved to see him safe at home and in such a good mood. She was thinking, as she unconsciously rubbed her stomach, that maybe tonight she would give John the news that she was pregnant. But, on the other hand, she didn't like seeing that, as bad as the weather was, it hadn't prevented him from stopping at the liquor store before coming home.

Perish the thought of being snowbound without a fifth, she thought bitterly as she shook her head.

"No, and I—"

"Don't get all worked up. I'm just going to have a little one to steady my nerves after a drive like that," John said. He followed his explanation with a laugh that seemed forced and unnatural.

Julia watched closely as he broke the seal on the bottle and poured just a splash into the glass, adding enough water to turn the whiskey a thin amber.

"So," John said, looking at Bri after taking a sip and smacking his lips with satisfaction, "I haven't seen you for a while. How was your visit with Kirsten?"

"Kristin," Bri corrected him. "And it was fun. There probably won't be any school tomorrow, and I was wondering if maybe I could have her over tomorrow."

"As long as you get your homework done tonight, I don't see any problem," Julia said. She went to the refrigerator, took out the hamburger patties she had made, and set them on the broiler pan.

While the storm gathered even more strength outside, slamming the sides of the house and rattling the windows, the family sat down and shared a warm and relaxing meal. Julia was surprised—and pleased—that John seemed so much better; even his appetite seemed to be back. As she ate her supper, she found herself thinking that maybe the talk they had had this morning had really done him some good. Maybe—although she hated even to think it—last weekend's binge *had* been what he needed to work his anger and grief out of his system. Whatever it was, she decided she wasn't going to examine it too closely. It seemed as if John—the John she knew and loved—was back, smiling and laughing the way he used to before their move back to Maine.

"It's kinda neat, isn't it?" Bri said. "So cozy inside while it's snowing like crazy outside."

"Maybe we can convince your father to get a fire going," Julia said as she stood up and started to clear the table. She was still thinking tonight would be when she'd tell him she was pregnant, and she wanted to make sure he stayed in a relaxed, jovial mood . . . just as long as he didn't keep drinking.

"Sure, sure," John said. He signaled her to stop as he mopped up his plate with his last bit of hamburger roll. "Stop right there! I'll do the cleaning up. Why don't the two of you just go sit in the living room and watch the snow fall. This won't take me a minute."

Julia and Bri exchanged glances of exaggerated surprise, but neither of them complained as they stood up from the table and let John scrape and stack the dirty dishes while they went and settled down on the couch. From the living room, they could hear John whistling to himself as he set about the work.

The whole time he stood at the sink, washing and rinsing each plate and glass and then carefully lining them up in the dish drainer, John was convinced he could feel the piece of note paper with Sally Curry's phone number, heavy and thick, in his pants pocket. He barely paid attention to the work he was doing. The clank of dishes and jangle of silverware barely invaded his awareness as he stared out the kitchen window at the thickly falling snow, long white streaks showing against the soot-dark night. He was considering whether he would say anything to Sally or just hang up on the off chance he got her on the phone. He certainly wasn't going to come right out and ask her if she knew what he had done to her sister. He wasn't going to make the same mistake he had made with Randy, so he wanted to think everything through very carefully.

Before he realized it, he was done with the dishes. He pulled the drain plug and watched as the now nearly sudsless water was sucked down the pipe. He had phrased everything in his mind; how—if Sally answered the phone—he would explain why he was calling: *Just moved back to town and had been thinking about Abby and wanted to contact someone who had been close to her.* Maybe he would hint at why he was calling: *He had been thinking about Abby, as he often did, and wondered if Sally had ever heard from her.* Oh, he would be crafty and shrewd this time and not let on that he suspected anything . . . unless Sally blew it and spilled her guts.

But, of course, he didn't think he would get an answer, because Sally Curry wasn't somewhere in the Midwest. Her phone would ring, unanswered, and—John tensed with the thought and squinted out at the storm—for all he knew, Sally Curry was right outside the house now, hiding in the blizzard, watching the house of the man she was convinced had killed her sister!

Using the spray attachment, John washed the soap residue down the drain and reached for a paper towel to dry his hands. As he spun the roll and tore off a single sheet, his stomach flip-flopped when he saw something—a small, white square—drop from inside the paper towel roll and fall onto the counter. It was a single sheet of notebook paper, folded in half.

John's breath cut off sharply as he stood staring in amazement

at the piece of paper. He had no doubt that inside he would find a
message written in heavy-handed pencil strokes. . . .

How the Christ did she get this here? he wondered as he stared
at the paper on the counter. He didn't dare pick it up. He could
hear his heart thumping loudly in his ears, and again that tightening constriction closed around his throat.

Don't pick it up! he thought, his wet hands making squishy
sounds as they clenched and unclenched. *Don't touch it! Don't
even* think *about it!*

But he knew he would pick it up . . . he knew he would read
it—he *had* to!

Slowly he reached for the paper, the tips of his fingers tingling
as they drew closer. . . . When he touched the note, he was surprised by a sudden wash of coolness that on contact shot up his
arm like a spike of ice. With one fearful glance over his shoulder
to make sure Julia or Bri wasn't standing there watching him, he
grabbed the paper and, shielding it with his body, practically tore
it as he unfolded it and read

MEET ME... TONIGHT

John let out a low gasp, and the choking sensation around his
throat got even tighter. His hand reflexively clenched tightly shut,
wrinkling the paper, but he couldn't tear his eyes away from the
message.

MEET ME . . . TONIGHT!

"You goddamned lousy *bitch!*" he whispered harshly under his
breath. "You rotten *bitch! Where? Where* the fuck do you want
me to meet you?"

The sudden shrill ringing of the telephone made him jump and
spin around. Without thinking, he shouted out, "I'll get it!" and
walked quickly across the kitchen floor to the phone. He shoved
the wrinkled note into his pocket.

"It's probably Kristin," Bri hollered from the living room.

"I've got it," John snapped. "Hello." His voice sounded unnaturally high to him.

At the other end of the line, there was nothing—absolutely
dead silence! No voice—no hiss—*nothing!* Only a black, cold
silence so deep it was almost dizzying.

"Hello!" John repeated tensely, feeling his hand slick with
sweat on the phone. "Who is this?" The silence on the other end
of the line seemed almost to mock him.

Finally, after several seconds, there was a faint click, and just on the edge of hearing, John detected a low huffing, as though someone was taking in a deep breath with great difficulty.

"Meet me ... tonight," the soft voice whispered. It sounded like the crackle of fire. In his mind, John saw the three words of the note sparkle with deep orange flame.

"Who the hell—?" John stammered, but then his throat closed off, and in his mind he got an instant, vivid image of a building —a weather-stained, falling-down building. He hadn't meant to think of it, but then, inexplicably, it was simply *there.*

"Meet me ... *tonight,*" the voice repeated with labored intensity. "You know where. . . ."

Haskins' barn!

The thought tore into John's mind as if it had claws. He found himself staring at the blank kitchen wall not more than a foot from his face, but all he could see was the blank, gray, moonlit side of Haskins' barn surrounded by a deep, cold night sky that practically vibrated with intensity.

"You know where!" the voice repeated, and then the line went dead. After a moment of chilling silence, the rasping dial tone hit John's ear like a drill. With a low grunt, he slammed the phone back into the cradle so hard it made a little *br-ing* sound.

"Who was that?" Julia called from the living room.

Frantic, John looked around and felt only a slight measure of relief when he saw that neither she nor Bri had come into the kitchen. His ears were still echoing with the hollow sound of that voice.

"Meet me ... tonight. . . . You know where!"

His face was dripping with sweat. He tried to wipe it away with the back of his hand.

"Ahh—wrong number, I guess. They asked for ... a Sally Curry," John said, almost laughing aloud. He would have, but his chest felt as if it were bound by tough steel bands that were squeezing ... *squeezing.* . . .

He glanced at the clock, then looked out at the snow streaking past the kitchen window. Clenching his fists, he took a deep breath, enough to make his lungs ache. Then he went to the hall closet and grabbed his coat and gloves. Julia looked at him over the back of the couch, a surprised expression on her face.

"I've got to go out," he said sharply.

"Are you going to get wood for a fire?" she asked brightly. She had seen the dark tension on his face, and she knew—even as she asked—what his answer would be.

"No!" John snapped as he jammed his arms into the coat sleeves and yanked on his gloves. Before either Julia or Bri could respond, he went out the kitchen door, letting the door slam shut behind him, and got into the car. He shoved the key into the ignition and ground the starter until the engine caught. Slamming the car into reverse, he slewed down the driveway onto Oak Street, then stepped down hard on the gas and fishtailed down to the intersection of Shore Drive. He took the turn without even slowing.

"Once and for all," he muttered to himself as he hunched over the steering wheel, trying to pierce the darkness and the blowing snow with his eyes. His headlights jabbed no more than a few feet ahead, and it was only with effort—and guesswork—that he kept himself on the road.

"Okay—I'll meet you out at Haskins' barn, you bitch, and we can fucking settle this *once and for all!*"

TWENTY-THREE
The Blizzard

I

John couldn't see Haskins' barn, but he knew it was there—straight across the field in front of him. The night and the storm howled around him like a raging beast. The wind was so cold it burned his lungs as he breathed rapidly in and out. As he trudged through the snow, now almost knee-deep, the beam from his flashlight feebly illuminated the spiraling snow around him. From every direction at once, the night was filled with the deafening roar of the wind.

More than once, he had the horrifying sensation that he had lost his direction and would walk right past Haskins' barn and off into the woods without even knowing it. He knew he had to find the barn soon, if only to get out of the biting wind. No one could last long outside on a night like this!

And just what the hell am I doing this for? he thought angrily as he lurched ahead, the snow tugging at his legs like a powerful undertow. Thin but powerful fingers yanked at his coat collar and slapped him from behind. Snow stung his face, numbing it.

Then he saw the dark, massive bulk of the barn, blacker than the night, in front of him. In the swirling snow, it seemed somehow taller than he knew it really was. It loomed up out of the darkness like a tower threatening to crash down on him. He felt a clutching chill when, looking up, the building seemed for a moment to teeter in the gusting wind, its ancient wood creaking from the stress of the storm. He knew where the door was and went straight to it, shouldering it open with an almost blind panic.

As soon as he stepped inside and swung the door shut, the sound of the storm receded, dropping down to a steady roar. Anxious with mounting fear, and wondering why the hell anyone —Sally Curry or Randy or whomever!—would want to meet him here on a night like this, he swept his flashlight beam around the inside. Through the many cracks and gaps in the walls and ceiling, he could see the storm raging outside, but here inside there was a stillness, a quiet peace . . . as if he had entered another world that provided him a distanced view of the outside world.

Grunting softly to himself, John walked slowly across the hard-packed dirt floor, his flashlight dancing over the angled ridges of snow that had drifted inside. The ribbed walls rose high up above him with tatters of dark cobwebs drifting in the eddies of wind. He couldn't help but wonder what kind of creatures had found refuge up there in the dark rafters.

John knew he was foolish to be out here in the first place—and not just because of the storm. As he surveyed the barn, his mind couldn't help but go back to the night twenty years ago when he and Abby had arranged to meet here. . . .

For the last time, as it turned out, he thought, and the memory made his stomach flood with sour acid.

So far he hadn't dared to look up toward the hayloft. Up there, he knew, was the rafter Abby had used to hang herself. He found himself wondering if there was still a trace of the frayed rope wrapped around the thick beam. He remembered he had come out here that warm spring night to meet her—they had planned to talk things through, work things out if they could—but they never got to talk. He had found her swinging from a length of rope . . . swinging like those sickly gray clots of cobwebs, with a hand-printed note pinned to the pocket of her gray sweater.

YOU DID THIS TO ME!

All around him, the barn creaked and groaned as the storm buffeted its sides. Indistinct whisperings came to his ears, almost sounding like words—vague, angry accusations. He never had a chance to determine the direction of one before another would catch his ear. Before long, he was frantically turning this way and that, trying to locate the sources of the sounds.

"This is fucking ridiculous," he said under his breath, letting his flashlight beam swing around—but not quite daring to point it up to the hayloft.

"No," he said, his voice raw. "No one's going to be—"

"*John . . .*"

That single sound—*had it really been his name?*—drifted out of the dark, sending a hot bolt of fear up his spine. Suddenly aware that he had been holding his breath, he let it out slowly as he pointed the flashlight up. . . . He finally dared to look up into the hayloft.

Although Haskins was dead, and his barn was going to be torn down soon to make way for the condo project, John was surprised to see that the loft was still piled high with bales of hay. The dirt floor was littered with dull yellow chaff that had fallen through the cracks in the loft floor. On one side of the barn wall, two-by-fours had been nailed across the inside studs, forming a crude ladder.

The ladder Abby climbed up that night . . . with a coil of old rope over her shoulder, John thought. He felt a hard, dry lump form in his throat.

"*John . . .*"

He tensed, positive now that someone *had* called his name. It seemed to have come from up in the loft.

"Sally?" he called out, his voice barely vibrating in his throat. "Is that you up there?"

There was no reply, and for several seconds—seconds that seemed to stretch into long minutes—John stood there staring up at the bales of rotting hay. He still hadn't dared to shine his light on the rafter, the one Abby had slung the rope over.

Was there someone up there? he wondered, flooded with fear. *How could there be? Not tonight! Not on a night like this!*

"I don't think this is funny, you know," John shouted, forcing strength into his voice. "I don't think it's one damn bit funny!"

"*John . . .*"

Again the voice came, faintly and, seemingly, from several directions at once. John was trying to convince himself that it was just a trick of the wind whistling through the cracks in the barn. He was just imagining that someone was calling his name. There *couldn't* be anyone up there in the hayloft.

"*Come up. . . .*" the voice whispered.

As crazy as it seemed, John suddenly became convinced there *was* someone up there. And it *had* to be Sally Curry. In a perverted sort of way, it made sense that she would do something like this. Abby had told her sister everything, and now, after waiting for twenty years, Sally had heard that John was back in Maine, and she had come from wherever she lived out in the

Midwest and set all of this up—the notes, creeping around the house, the telephone call—*everything* just to get her revenge! It was crazy, but it was possible.

"I—I'm not coming up there, Sally," John shouted. He smiled a little to himself, thinking that maybe there wasn't anyone up there, that the tiny voice he heard was a product of his overworked imagination.

Talk about crazy, he thought, chuckling to himself. *I'm nuts just to be out here tonight, not to mention talking to myself!*

"Come up . . . here."

"Sally? Whoever you are up there, if you're not going to let me see you, I'm not staying," John said.

He was staring at the underside of the loft floor, and his heart froze in midbeat when he head the floorboards creak overhead. Fine grit sifted down, a miniature version of the blizzard outside as it was caught and swirled by an errant breeze. Heavy, dragging footsteps moved slowly from the back of the loft toward the front, the open end. John's hand involuntarily clenched the tube of the flashlight. Inside his glove, his hand was slippery with sweat.

Slowly, feeling every heavy thump his heart made, John directed the flashlight beam upward. At first there was nothing—just piles of pale yellow straw and the dark wall of the barn, but then he saw a subtle shifting of the darkness above him, as though a portion of the swirling black night had somehow entered the barn, and then, dissolving out of the darkness, he saw a face. When it registered who—or *what*—he was looking at, he wanted to scream, but his throat was closed shut.

Long, black hair framed a thin face so pale it hovered in the darkness of the loft like a cloud-masked moon. Dark circled eyes stared down at him, and the mouth—harsh, bloodless lips set in a firm line—slowly widened into a smile that showed yellowed teeth. Beneath the cascade of black hair, a heavy gray sweater hung loosely over the shoulders. Thick globs of moss and dirt stained the sweater, and it hung heavily, as though it was damp and moldy with age.

"Jesus Christ . . . *no!*" John whispered, taking an involuntary step backward.

The face looming above him widened even more into a cruel smile, and the lips parted to speak.

"You still recognize me . . . after all this time," she said. Her voice had a razor edge to it that cut cleanly into John's awareness.

"No . . . it can't be! . . . *Abby!*" John said.

There was a sudden rushing noise inside his head that masked every sound other than her voice. He recognized the face—the same one he had seen outside his house, looking at him through the window!—*the same one he had seen, pale and staring at him from inside the noose twenty years ago!*

YOU DID THIS TO ME!

The thought rolled in his mind like tumbling thunder.

"This can't be!" he wailed, taking several more steps backward. As much as he wanted to, he didn't dare take his flashlight beam away from Abby's face as she smiled coldly down at him. It was no hallucination! It was *real!*

"Oh, yes . . . it *can* be! It *is!*" Abby said. With that, she threw her head back and let out a long, cackling laugh that swept around and through John as if he had suddenly become immaterial.

John's breath was coming in sharp, painful jabs. The sounds of the raging storm outside dropped off almost to nothing—just a distant memory as his mind reeled around, trying to grasp the actuality of who—or *what*—he was looking at. The pale face, he saw, like the gray sweater, was smeared with dirt and mold.

"*See* what you did to me?" Abby said. She raked her fingers down across her cheek, carving deep furrows in her rotting flesh. Gray swatches of skin peeled away in strips from the side of her face, exposing the dull gray bone beneath. The flesh, John saw, was seething, crawling with . . .

No! It can't be! Not worms . . . not maggots!

It isn't possible! his mind wailed, seeming to take on its own internal lunatic giggle. *It's absolutely impossible!*

"You made me kill myself because you didn't want my baby . . . *our* baby, John!" Abby said in a low, evil rasp. "And then you buried me. But did you think you could get rid of me . . . as easily as that?" Her voice was as sheer as black pond ice—and much colder. "You actually thought you could hide what you had done . . . that you could just *bury* it? What a fool!" Again her laughter filled the barn, spinning around John like a black whirlpool.

"You can't be Abby!" John said. His voice wound tightly up the scale. "Abby's dead! I saw her dead! I *buried* her!" He was thinking—to save what few shreds of sanity he had remaining—that this had to be Abby's sister, this was all an elaborate show to get him to admit what he had done, to drive him insane with guilt!

"You buried *me*," Abby said, chuckling hollowly. "And you thought if I was dead and buried, you'd be through with me . . . that you could go right on living. But you were wrong!"

A sudden fury flashed deep within her eyes, and she raised her hands into the air—thin, talonlike fingers with cracked and yellowed nails. Her black hair was caught in an updraft and twisted around her head like raging storm clouds, like a tangled knot of snakes.

"You were *wrong*, John!" Abby said, her voice low and measured, chilling in its hollowness. "Spite and anger don't die! They can't be buried! They *grow* in the dark. They *feed* in the dark until they become strong!" She clenched one hand into a fist in front of her face and shook it viciously. Thin tendons worked beneath the layer of rotting flesh.

"And in all that time, I waited, growing stronger in the cold and the dark where *you* left me." She jabbed a pointed finger at him in accusation. "But I was patient. I waited because I knew you'd come back eventually. I knew I'd *have* you again!"

"I never did anything to you," John wailed. Tears were flooding from his eyes, blurring his vision. Abby's face shattered into dozens of sparkling reflections. Everything around him—the barn, the hayloft, the face leering above him out of the darkness—all whirled around, smearing and blending.

"You had your chance!" Abby wailed.

John had the momentary impression that now there was no flesh on her face—she was nothing more than a grinning skull face.

"And now—*after all that time*, that *eternity* in the dark spent waiting—I'll get my revenge! On you . . . on your daughter . . . on your wife . . . and *best of all*, on the baby she is carrying right now!"

John shook his head, only vaguely understanding what Abby had said.

"You didn't even know that, did you?" Abby said, laughing deeply, the sound seeming to come from the bottom of a deep well. "You didn't even know your wife was pregnant!"

"No, I—" John stammered, but words failed him.

"Before, I would have been content just to get my revenge on *you*, for what you did to me, but as soon as it happened, as soon as I sensed that baby growing in her womb—*like the baby growing in my womb that* you *killed!*—I knew you would *all* have to die! I've already killed your father. Remember his face? Do you remember how he struggled the night he died?"

Stunned at the memory, John could do no more than nod.

"*I* killed him!" Abby said, smiling wickedly. "He saw me that night at church, and he almost remembered . . . he almost told you I was back, so he had to be the first to die! You remember that night, don't you? How he suffered? How he screamed as I tore his soul apart? Yes—*I* was in the room with him. It took me awhile to gain the strength I needed. Even though people could see me, I couldn't *do* anything . . . not at first, anyway. But the more I saw you and your family, the more I let the cold darkness, the *hatred* grow inside me—*like my baby that you killed!*—the stronger I got . . . the more I could do."

"The notes..." John said with a gasp. "*You* wrote those notes?"

Slowly Abby nodded, a cold, red glow burning in her eyes. "*I WON'T FORGET WHAT YOU DID TO ME!*" Her laughter rose shrilly. "Of course I did. I had to learn how to use things again," she said. "I had to grow stronger so I could make things *happen*. At first, the best I could do was scrawl those notes and—" She laughed, a cold, thin laugh. "It brought me such pleasure to feel your panic, your gnawing fear grow as you read each new word. And as I grew stronger, I found I could move things around...like the furniture in your house. Your wife was so confused by that."

"After the funeral," John said, more to himself than to Abby.

"And so—first your father...and eventually your whole family. I have to destroy the baby your wife is carrying, just as *you* destroyed the baby I had inside me. But first, it's *your* turn to die!"

With a sudden forward lurch, she jumped off the edge of the loft. For one frozen, sickening moment, John expected to see her fetch up and snap backward at the end of a rope. He was prepared to hear the broken-board snap of her neck. But with her arms upraised and her mouth open wide with laughter, Abby's dark form seemed to drift, rather than fall, as it swooped down toward him like a black hawk. She landed lightly on the barn floor only a few feet from him.

The circle of his flashlight underlit Abby's face as she leaned toward him. Her skin—skin he remembered as soft and smooth and healthy—was mottled and blotched with rot, crawling with white worms. Through the shreds of torn skin on her cheek, John could see her dirt-crusted teeth. When she opened her mouth to speak, a sickly wash of foul breath made his stomach revolt.

"Blood will answer blood!" Abby shouted. "You *all* will die!"

She raised her hands above her head again, and with a bone-chilling whoosh, she vanished. The space in the barn where she had been standing just a second ago sucked in with a dull concussion, and John stood, amazed, as he glanced back and forth. His only thought was that he must have imagined it all. Out in the storm, his overwrought nerves had tricked him, making him hallucinate everything because of his twenty years of guilt.

But then, first faintly, but steadly growing stronger, he heard something that drew his attention upward. The oval of light from his flashlight swept back and forth across the stacked bales of hay, over the rotting rafters. At first he saw nothing, but below the howling of the storm outside, he heard a high-pitched squeaking sound that soon took on the sound of a chorus, like...

Like rats, he thought. Again, the cold fear tightened around his heart. *Rats in the wall!*

The stacked bales of hay in the loft seemed to move, to throb as the squeaking sound rose in intensity, and before long, there was no doubt in John's mind—the hay bales were *vibrating*! He took another two steps backward but stopped when he hit the barn wall. A jolt of pain shot up his shoulder, but that was nothing compared to what he felt when he saw the hay bales suddenly explode into a dark, quivering mass that spilled out over the loft floor.

"Mother of Christ!" John shouted as he watched the hay bales surge to life. Suddenly the shattering realization hit him—it wasn't the hay bales! It was something coming *out* of the bales. In an instant, he saw what it was—a tangled mass of rats scrambling over the hay toward the edge of the loft. Dozens—maybe *hundreds*—of beady eyes gleamed wickedly in the glow of his flashlight.

John turned and started to run, but his foot snagged on something and he fell to the floor. The flashlight flew from his hand and rolled away, its beam spinning wildly. Above and behind him, the chattering sounds of the rats—*hundreds* of them!—rose until it filled his ears like a storm wind. In the darkness behind him, he could hear them as they shot out from the loft and fell to the barn floor, their bodies making dull *plump* sounds when they hit, like heavy rain.

The first jolt of pain was like a hot, bright sliver of metal jabbing into his leg. Within the space of a single heartbeat, he felt an ever-increasing weight pile up, first on his legs, then up to his hips as the tide of squealing rats crashed over him, threatening to overwhelm him. Tiny claws raked at his exposed face and ripped open his pants and coat; chisel-sharp teeth nibbled him all over. Tilting his head back, John let out a lung-ripping scream that was cut off instantly when a fat-bodied rat jammed itself into his mouth. He bit down hard, severing the body, gagging as a hot gush of blood filled his throat. He spit out the rat's body and raised his arms over his face to protect his eyes from the whirlwind of claws and teeth.

John's arms and legs worked furiously to get him out from under the crushing mass of rats, but his boots kept slipping on the dirt floor, and he flopped onto his back, unable to shake himself loose. The angled light from his flashlight, which had come to rest in the corner of the barn, only vaguely illuminated the scene of horror as more and more rats tumbled to the floor from the loft and swarmed over him.

Before long, his coat and pants were nothing more than shreds, and the rats chewed and nibbled at any portion of him they could get. His body felt as if it were being splashed with acid as the

claws raked his skin open. The flow of his hot blood drove the
rats to even greater frenzy.

The combined weight of them was crushing as John kicked and
flailed to extricate himself. As he rolled and flopped around on
the floor, every now and then he caught a glimpse of the barn
door and the solid sheet of falling snow beyond it. He knew that,
even if he made it outside, the chances of getting to his car and
making it home in the storm were slim, but *he had to warn Julia
and Bri!*

The horrible thought suddenly hit him that that was where
Abby had gone. She had left the rats to finish him off while she
went to the house to do what she had said . . . *kill Julia . . . and
Bri . . . and the baby she said Julia was carrying!*

With a sudden jolt of adrenaline, John screamed and pushed
back against the overwhelming crush of squirming, furry bodies.
Miraculously, he felt the weight lift, and with his arms free, he
scrambled to shake his legs loose. With a sudden forward lurch,
he got up and, crouching low and running off balance, his arms
pinwheeling wildly, he made a desperate dash for the barn door.
His shoulder slammed into the rough wood, and it gave grudg-
ingly against the snow that had piled up against it on the outside.

The wind and snow tore into his face as he charged outside, but
just knowing that seething mass of rats was close behind drove
him forward through the high drifts toward where he had left his
car. He ran, swinging his torn and bleeding legs high over the
wind-whipped surface of the snow.

If I can only find the frigging car! he thought frantically. *If a
passing plow hasn't buried it!*

The frigid air tore like flames into his lungs as he ran, encased
in the swirling storm. All he knew was that Haskins' barn and the
rats were behind him, and Abby was most likely ahead of him. As
he ran, he fully expected to see her decomposed face, grinning a
wide, maniacal smile, darting at him out of the dark . . . laughing
. . . screaming before her clawed fingers grabbed his throat and
squeezed the life out of him.

Time stretched into a single, numbing eternity as he ran
through the deep snow, his legs churning. Ahead, without even
the feeble security of his flashlight, he could see nothing . . . no
streetlights, no shadowed bulk of his car. He wouldn't have been
surprised to find he had run around in a complete circle and had
ended up back at the barn.

Maybe that would be best! he thought bitterly. *Let the rats
finish me! Or run right off a cliff into the freezing ocean and
drown!*

But he couldn't let that happen! He couldn't let Abby—impossible as this all seemed—get her revenge. "I didn't do anything wrong! *I didn't do anything wrong!*" he mumbled to himself.

And then he saw something straight ahead of him—the snow-covered lump that was his car! With one frightened glance back over his shoulder, he saw something else—a mind-numbing sight that, *like Abby*, was impossible . . . impossible but *there*! Closing the gap between them, leaping and burrowing through the heavy snow, came the onrushing dark tide of rats, squeaking and chittering, lusting to taste more of his warm lifeblood.

In a sudden surge of speed, John reached the edge of the field and scrambled up over the humped plow ridge. Every square inch of his exposed skin was numbed, and the dim thought chilled him that, even if he did make it home, it wouldn't matter. *Abby would have gotten them already. Julia and Bri would be dead. And Abby would be waiting for him!*

He hit the side of the car hard, almost knocking the wind out of himself. Peeling off a glove, he jammed his hand into his coat pocket, suddenly frantic that he had lost the keys back in the barn. He tried not to imagine turning around and cringing back against the unyielding car, trying to scream but unable to as the seething black mass of rats swarmed over him, their teeth and claws tearing the last shreds of life from him. He saw in his mind an image of Abby's face from twenty years ago, horribly pale, her neck strangled, her bloated tongue hanging out from between her clenched teeth, dried blood dribbling down to the point of her chin.

YOU DID THIS TO ME!

In his mind, John saw Abby's face slowly dissolve into his own face, saw himself screaming a silent death-scream as his lifeless body dropped to the ground and was covered by the drifting snow. But then the cold shock of what he felt in his pocket ripped him back to what was happening.

The car keys! I've got them!

His hands trembled wildly as he unlocked the car door, swung it open, and flopped down onto the seat. The sudden glare of the dome light stung his eyes, and he almost screamed when he caught a glimpse of his face in the rearview mirror. For just an instant, it looked as pale and rotted as Abby's! He slammed the car door shut, but something stopped it from closing tightly. From down by his feet, there was a loud squawk. When he opened the door a crack, enough to turn the dome light back on, he saw that the door had crushed the skull of a rat that had almost scrambled up into the car.

"Almost, you bastard!" John hissed as he kicked the dead rat out onto the snow. He just had time to swing the door out and pull it shut before the rest of the rats hit. In a sudden and furious barrage, they slammed into and leaped up onto the car, their claws scraping the car's side and roof like a sudden blast of hail.

"Not tonight, you don't!" John shouted with maniacal glee. He stuck the key into the ignition, praying silently that the car would start. The engine cranked loudly, almost dying, then it caught. John pushed the accelerator down hard and let the engine roar.

The car was buffeted by strong gusts of wind, and from every side now came the heavy thumping sound of rats bouncing off the car. Pumping the gas pedal several times, John let the engine warm up; he didn't want to kill it now! Then, snapping on the headlights, he popped the shift into gear. The windshield was covered with heavy black bodies, but these were soon whisked aside when he turned on the windshield wipers. With tires spinning wildly in the deep snow, John turned the car around and drove as fast as he dared back to the house. The one thing on his mind was, even if he *did* end up dying from all these rat bites, he had to warn Julia and Bri. He had to get them out of the house and off the island *now*!

II

Julia was almost crazy with worry after John had gone. She tried—unsuccessfully—to hide it from Bri, and the two of them, not knowing what else to do, sat at the kitchen table, their eyes fastened on the telephone. An hour—which felt like fifteen hours—later, the harsh ringing of the phone made them both shriek with surprise. Trembling with fear, dreading what this call would be, Julia grabbed the phone.

"Yes," she said breathlessly.

"Julia? Hi, this is Randy," the voice on the phone said. "Did I call at a bad time?"

"No—I . . ." But that was all she could say.

"Well, uh, look—I don't know if John mentioned it to you," Randy said, "but he and I had lunch in town today. I was—uh, I'd like to talk to him if he isn't busy."

Julia glanced over at Bri, her eyes signaling how helpless she felt.

"Julia?" Randy said. "Can I talk to John?"

"He . . . umm, he's not here right now," Julia said when she was unable to come up with a convincing lie.

"He went out? On a night like this?" Randy said. "Where the hell did he go?"

"I don't know," Julia replied, feeling a flood of tears spilling from her eyes. "I don't know. He got a phone call. He said it was a wrong number, but right after that he left."

"Did he say who the call was from?" Randy asked.

Biting her lower lip, Julia shook her head. "No—he said it was a wrong number, someone asking for . . . I think he said someone named Sally."

"Sally *Curry*?" Randy snapped.

"Yeah. That was the name," Julia replied, swiping at her eyes with the back of her hand. "Why? What do you know about this?"

There was a long pause at Randy's end of the line; then his voice, sounding low and tentative, said, "I don't know how much—if anything—you know about what's going on, but today at lunch when I mentioned Sally Curry to John, it seemed like he didn't hear what I said about her."

"What? Who is this Sally Curry?" Julia shouted, feeling a sudden flash of panic. "What the hell is going on?"

"Sally Curry was the sister of John's old girlfriend, Abby," Randy said softly. "But when we were talking about her, I tried to tell John that I had heard a few months ago that Sally had died. Bone cancer, I think it was."

"So why would someone call here asking for her?" Julia asked. The churning in her stomach was getting worse, and she knew she was going to throw up soon if she didn't find out what the hell was going on.

"I have no idea what's going on," Randy said, still keeping his voice mild and controlled. "Look, Julia, are you all right? If you want, I can come over there until John comes home."

Julia's eyes locked onto Bri's. As much as she wanted to push aside the swelling tide of panic, she couldn't. She knew in the core of her soul that something was desperately wrong with John . . . and maybe with them!

"I don't think that's necessary," Julia said after a long pause. "It isn't safe to be outside in a storm like this, and, anyway"—she forced a buoyancy into her voice which she just didn't feel—"I'm sure John will be home soon."

"You're sure, now," Randy said. "I don't want you sitting there worrying yourself sick."

"I'm sure," Julia replied.

"Have him call me as soon as he gets home, then, okay?"

"I will . . . I promise," Julia said. " 'Bye."

Julia carefully replaced the phone on the hook and took a deep, dry breath of air. She didn't want to turn around, fearful of letting Bri see her like this, so shattered, so uncertain.

"Who was that?" Bri asked, her voice trembling with suppressed fear. "Is Dad all right? He didn't have an accident, did he?"

Julia was about to answer her, but she and Bri both screamed when John came bursting through the kitchen door. At first, neither of them knew who this horrible, bloodied person was. Even after he called out their names, his bleeding face and hands and his shredded coat were barely recognizable. But it was his eyes—the wild, crazy look in his eyes—that sent spikes of terror through both of them.

"She's *back*! . . . *Abby's* back!" John wailed, his throat so raw he didn't sound at all like himself. "She isn't *dead*! *Not anymore*!"

Grabbing Julia by both arms, he shook her wildly.

He's out of his mind! Julia thought, torn between pity for him and fear for her own and Bri's safety. *He's been drinking and he's lost his mind!*

"I've *seen* her! She was out at the barn—Haskins' barn!" John shouted, panting heavily. His face was close to hers, and his breath washed over her. She was vaguely surprised that she didn't smell alcohol on him.

"What are you talking about?" Julia asked, trying to sound calm, but just looking at him unnerved her. Behind her, she sensed Bri watching them in stark terror. After glancing quickly over her shoulder at her daughter—and seeing her own shock and horror mirrored in her face—Julia turned back to John. Her mind was frantically searching for what she could do . . . it was pitch-black outside in the middle of a blizzard, and they were alone in the house with a madman!

"We've got to get out of here!" John shouted. "We've got to get off the island! Yeah, that's it. That's it! She won't be able to leave the island! She couldn't! Otherwise, she would have done something before now! So she must be trapped here. Come on! Get your coats on! We've got to get out of here!"

"We aren't going anywhere except to a hospital," Julia said. "Bri, call the—"

"You don't understand!" John shouted. "I've seen her, and she said she was coming here!"

"Who? Who's coming here?"

"Abby . . . *Abby Snow*!"

"Your girlfriend from high school?" Julia said, shaking her head, trying to push aside her panic and confusion. "I thought you or Randy said she didn't live here anymore. I was just talking to Randy on the phone, and he said something about Abby's sister—"

"Not her sister!" John shouted, flecks of foam flying from his mouth. "*Her! Abby* herself!"

"But I thought you said Abby was—"

"She was *dead!*" John yelled, his bloodshot eyes bulging from his head. "She was dead! She killed herself, *hung* herself, and I buried her—but now *she's come back!*"

"Jesus Christ, John, get a hold of yourself," Julia said. "Do you hear what you're saying?" There was only a trace of calmness in her voice, but she didn't feel it. All she was thinking was, John was crazy—dangerously crazy—and he could just as easily turn whatever the hell he was thinking on them! Hurt them! Maybe even *kill* them!

"*I saw her . . . in Haskins' barn! You've got to believe me!*"

Saying that, he ran to the front hall closet, grabbed both Julia's and Bri's winter coats, and rushed back into the kitchen. "Here! Put these on! We've got to get the hell off this island!"

All this time, Bri had been standing by the kitchen table, her hands covering her mouth so she wouldn't scream. She couldn't believe what she was seeing, and she was too frightened to do anything.

"Take this!" John shouted at her, shoving her coat into her hands. "Will you do what you're told, for Christ's sake? She's coming here!"

Thinking the only way they would be safe was to do what he said, Julia cast a quick glance at Bri and nodded, signaling her to put her coat on.

"Get your hats and gloves, too," John commanded as he darted over to the kitchen window and looked out at the storm. All he could see was snow streaking past the streetlight, but he couldn't shake the feeling that Abby was out there somewhere, coming closer . . . *closer*!

"John," Julia said mildly, "you're cut up really bad. You've been hurt. Why don't you sit down and let me take a look at those wounds? How did they happen?" As she spoke, she pulled on her coat and tucked her hair up under her woolen hat.

"We haven't got time," John shouted at her. "She's gonna be here any—"

"Audrey?" Bri said suddenly, turning around as a dark figure filled the living room doorway. "What the heck are you doing here?"

The question was barely out of her mouth when the figure came into the glaring light of the kitchen, and Bri clearly saw Audrey's face. It was a sickly gray that almost matched the color of her heavy wool sweater. Her dark hair was tangled and knotted, hanging loosely around her shoulders. But it was the side of her face that sent blinding terror singing along Bri's nerves. Long strips of skin hung in loose flaps from her cheek, exposing the pale bone beneath. Only Bri's hands covering her mouth muffled the piercing scream she let out.

"Oh, Christ!" John shouted. Standing by the kitchen sink, his face turned a sickly white.

Julia turned and looked at the horror facing them and felt a wash of numbing chills. Instantly she recognized the face, the hair. This was the person she had seen swimming alongside Randy's boat the day they had gone lobstering.

I didn't imagine it after all!

"You didn't really think you could get away from me, did you?" Abby said. Her voice had a curious muffled tone to it, and as she spoke, clumps of dirt and mold rained onto the linoleum floor. Abby looked from John to Bri to Julia, her rounded yellow eyes widening as her dead lips twisted up into a horrible grin.

"Did you think that?" she said, her voice rising gleefully. Slowly she reached out her hands—her arms were pale and thin, her fingernails yellowed and cracked and crusted with dirt. "But you see, don't you? All of you have to die! *All four of you have to die!*"

Instinctively, Julia's hands went down to her stomach in a protective gesture.

"No!" Julia said, thinking no matter who or what this horrible vision was in their house, she would do *anything* to protect her unborn baby.

"Oh, *yes* . . . you will *all* die," Abby said, followed by a mocking laugh. "It *has* to be that way!"

They all stood frozen in place, looking unbelievingly as Abby started walking slowly toward John. Her fingernails made tiny clicking sounds, like insects, as she held her hands out level to his throat. Suddenly Bri became aware of a low, trembling sound, barely audible below the howling of the wind around the house. It sounded like—like *organ music*, she thought . . . *distant, hollow organ music!*

"The church wood," she whispered, so softly no one could hear her. But Abby . . . *Audrey!* . . . turned and looked at her over her shoulder for just a second and laughed.

John was backing away as Abby turned back to him and kept coming toward him. As she got closer, he could feel a drafty chill emanating from her. The cold reached into his muscles and froze his nerves.

"Starting with you," Abby said, glaring balefully at John. Her shuffling steps brought her closer. Neither Bri nor Julia could move. They stood watching in complete terror as the strains of organ music rose in intensity.

"Here!" John suddenly shouted. "Get the hell out of here!"

He spun around and gently lobbed the car keys to Julia, who surprised herself by darting her hand out and catching them without thinking.

Abby tilted her head back, exposing the rotten gray flesh of her neck, and let loose a wild, warbling laugh. "As if that will do you any good! *Killer! Murderer!*"

With a sudden burst of speed, John ran around the kitchen table and headed toward the living room. Abby's face contorted into a wild expression of anger and hatred as she wheeled around and went after him. In the flurry of activity, Julia grabbed Bri by the arm and shook her violently.

"Go on! Get into the car!" she yelled, giving her a rough push toward the door that almost made her fall down.

Numbed by everything she had seen, Bri lurched across the kitchen floor, swung the door open wide, and disappeared into the swirling snow. A frigid blast of air swept into the kitchen, but the whistling sound of the wind and the pealing organ music didn't mask the other sounds coming from the living room. Julia ran to the living room doorway and looked on in stunned horror.

John was slowly backing away from Abby as she steadily, unrelentingly approached him. Her arms were waving in wild circles over her head, and all the objects in the living room, all the furniture and rugs and pictures from the walls, were spinning and tumbling around as if they were caught in a tornado. The organ music pulsated weirdly, making Julia feel dizzy. Suddenly there was an ear-shattering crash as something—Julia couldn't see what—went careening through the picture window. Snow came howling into the room and was instantly swept up in the raging circle of flying furniture.

"Get the hell out of here!" John wailed when he saw Julia in the doorway. She could barely hear his voice above the insane roaring in the living room. He held his arms up protectively and ducked as a flying footstool swung past his head.

Abby spared just an instant to glance over her shoulder at Julia. Her face split into a mad grin, and she pointed at her and shouted, *"You'll be next!"*

With that, Abby pushed both of her hands forward, as if against great resistance. The motion made Julia think she was trying to close—or open—an unyielding door. The organ music suddenly shot up the scale until it was nothing more than an irritating, high-pitched buzz. Instantly John was yanked back, his arms and legs flopping in the air as though some unseen person had grabbed him by the coat collar and tugged him. He flipped over, and with his legs flinging upward toward the ceiling, he fell through the gaping hole in the picture window. For just an in-

stant, Julia thought he had been sucked outside, but then she saw
that he hadn't quite made it. His legs snagged on the tooth edges
of broken glass. With a horrified scream, Julia watched as his full
weight came down on an inverted tooth of glass that stuck like a
spear right through his stomach.

"John! No!" Julia screamed, only distantly aware that it was her
own voice. Through the spiral of airborne furniture, she could see
John's already lifeless body impaled on the daggers of glass. There
was a loud crunching sound as slivers of glass broke beneath his
weight. Blood, looking as black as India ink, gushed from underneath him and ran down to stain the living room carpet.

As Abby slowly lowered her hands, the furniture crashed to the
floor in a wild jumble. Turning, she looked at Julia. There was a
wild, insane gleam in her eyes, but there was also a trace of—
what? Exhaustion, it looked like.

All Julia could think was, *This isn't real! This can't be happening!* but as Abby's arms sagged down, her head drooped, too.

She's had it, Julia thought. *She's losing her power!*

"You'll be . . . *next,*" Abby rasped, her voice sounding distant
and hollow as she raised her hand and pointed a bony finger at
Julia. "You and that *bastard* you're carrying!" Darkness seemed
to envelope her, sweeping over her like a dark wing. Then, in an
instant, she was gone.

For several stunned seconds, Julia stood there, looking in complete shock at the devastation of the living room. She couldn't
tear her eyes away from the limp body of her husband hanging
halfway out through the hole in the window. Already his body
was being powdered with drifting snow. One of his legs, dangling
into the living room, was twitching as the nerves in his body died.
His boot made a *tap-tap* sound on the floor like a distant drum.
By the dim light coming from the kitchen, she could see large red
splotches soaking into the snow, diffusing to pink.

John is dead, she thought. *Whatever else has happened, that is
real!*

"No . . . no," she said in a deep-throated wail as her mind tried
to register what she had seen. She started backing slowly away,
knowing there was nothing she could do. John was dead, and if
Abby—whatever in the name of Christ she was—had the power
to return, Julia knew she would make good her threat.

"You'll be next! You and that bastard you're carrying!"

She suddenly became aware that she had been clutching the
keys John had thrown to her. One sharp edge had cut into the heel
of her hand, and a thin stream of blood was dripping onto the
floor. Still feeling stunned, she slowly raised her hand and looked

at the keys, only distantly aware of what they were and what they might mean.

Suddenly, though, it hit her! Uttering a low whimper, she ran from the living room, through the kitchen, and out to the car. Her hands fumbled to open the door on the driver's side; then she dropped inside onto the car seat.

"What—what happened?" Bri asked. Her eyes were sparkling circles of fear, and her voice hit Julia's ears with a distant, metallic rattle.

"Your father's—" She gulped a breath of air and swallowed it, wincing at the pain in her throat. "Dead."

All around the car, wind and snow swirled. Even in the short time since John had gotten home . . .

When was that? Julia wondered vacantly. *A lifetime ago?*

. . . snow had covered the windshield, freezing where the windshield was still warm. Julia had the curious sense of being disembodied as she slipped the keys into the ignition and started up the car. The windshield wipers scraped loudly over the glass as they pushed aside the accumulated snow and ice. Julia snapped on the headlights but could see little more than a wall of falling snow in front of her.

"You'll be next."

The voice echoed in her mind like words shouted into a vast canyon.

"You and that bastard you're carrying."

Shaking her head, Julia looked at Bri, aware that her daughter was crying and trembling. Low, tortured moans vibrated in her throat. As she looked at Bri, though, something clicked in Julia's mind—the *only* thing, in this explosion of insanity, that made any sense.

"Come on," Julia said as she gunned the engine. "We've got to get off this island!"

"Who—who *was* that?" Bri wailed, looking at her mother as tears poured down her face. "I mean . . . I *thought* she was my friend Audrey! *What the hell was she?*" She crumpled forward, covering her face with her hands as she wailed her misery and confusion.

"I haven't got the faintest goddamned idea," Julia said as she slipped the car into reverse and started backing slowly out of the driveway. The wheels spun in the deep snow, and the tail end of the car glided back and forth as Julia tugged to keep the car moving. She got to what she thought was the road—with snow this deep, there really was no telling—and shifted into Drive. Slowly, carefully, she eased down on the accelerator, thinking the very last thing she wanted to have happen now was an accident.

"How could she do that?" Bri asked, her voice muffled by her hands over her face. "How could she just appear there like that . . . and make those things happen?" She couldn't bring herself to say the words, *And how could she kill Dad?*

Julia was chewing on her lower lip as she tried to focus her concentration on her driving. Nothing she had seen in the house made any kind of sense, but *this* was real—the snow and them in the car. Whatever she had seen in the house didn't matter now—they had to get to safety. Maybe, as John had said, they would be safe if they could just get off the island. Normally, that wouldn't have been much of a problem, but with two miles of road covered with snow that reached up over the car's wheel wells, the bridge to the mainland might just as well have been a hundred miles away.

The headlights were solid yellow cones of light as they pushed against the onrushing snow. The snow driving straight at them created the illusion that they were moving fast even as the speedometer registered no more than ten miles per hour. Even at fast speed, the wipers could keep the windshield clear for only a second or two. Julia drove, hunched over the steering wheel, playing it easily back and forth as she used the streetlights—not much more than hazy globes—to keep herself on the road.

If only a town snowplow or sanding truck would go by, she thought, but if one did, and if she managed to stop it and talk to the driver, what the hell would she say?

My husband's dead, and we have to get off the island. . . .

There's a ghost or some kind of supernatural creature trying to kill me and my daughter. . . . My husband's back at the house, dead!

Julia snickered nervously under her breath, trying to rationalize the night's events, but nothing . . . absolutely *nothing* made sense!

For a panicked instant, Julia thought she had missed it when she passed Pottle's store. It was only a half mile or so down the street from their house. She was thinking she must have gone by it by now, but there was no way of knowing. All around the car, all she could see were streaks of wind-whipped snow against a solid black night. Below the steady rumble of the car's engine, all she could hear was the howling wind blowing in off the ocean and bulldozing into the side with each gust.

Suddenly something shifted in the snow ahead of her. Julia's foot automatically went to the brake, but she caught herself before she pressed down on it hard and sent the car into a spinout. With a few quick taps, she pumped the brakes to slow down. She screamed when a face surrounded by wind-torn black hair came shooting out of the night straight at her.

"Shit!" Julia shouted, her hands clutching the steering wheel until the palms of her hands ached. Abby flew out of the storm, straight at the car. Her mouth was open wide, and her eyes seemed to glow with a wicked red glow.

Julia flinched back in her seat, waiting for the heavy thud of the body hitting the car, but before she could react, the silently screaming face, underlit by the headlights, zipped up over the car roof and was gone.

Bri was cowering on the car seat, her knees drawn up protectively in front of herself. Without a word, Julia pressed down on the gas pedal just a bit harder.

"You'll be next! You and that bastard you're carrying!"

The words rang in her memory as clearly as if the figure flying over the car had squealed them in passing. All around the car, the wind whistled like voices joined in chorus.

Gritting her teeth, Julia tried to quiet her nerves and hold the road. Her last and only desperate hope was that John had been right . . . that this *thing*, whatever it was, wouldn't be able to cross the water and follow them off the island. What had he said—that maybe Abby was *trapped* on the island; otherwise, she would have gotten to him before.

But why? Julia wondered. *Why would she have wanted to get him? What had he done? Was what he said back at the house, about Abby killing herself, true? How could it be? How could any of this be happening?*

The road unwound slowly as the car, enveloped by blinding snow swerved and slewed its way around the edge of the island. The only slight reprieve they got was when they apparently had gotten around to the landward side of the island; visibility improved slightly now that the wind was coming at them from behind. It was impossible for Julia to know exactly where they were, and her fear now became, *What if, like our missing Pottle's store, I miss the turn for the bridge? What if I drive right past it?*

Aware that Bri was still cringing on the seat beside her, crying, Julia reached out to comfort her. Instantly Bri flinched at the touch of her mother's hand and, thinking it was something else, screamed.

"You've got to pull yourself together," Julia said sharply. "Wipe your eyes and keep looking ahead. I need help if we're going to get out of this alive. Tell me if you can see the bridge."

Snorting, Bri leaned forward in her seat and peered into the dark night ahead. Every streetlight they passed had a watery halo around it. She continually wiped her eyes with the back of her glove, watching the faint lights spin and dissolve into spears of faded color.

Pointing off to the left, she suddenly shouted, "There it— No, I guess not."

"Jesus, Bri! Don't shout like that," Julia said as she jerked the steering wheel to the left, then quickly corrected herself. Her hands were throbbing with pain from gripping the steering wheel so tightly. She could hear a low, steady crunch-crunch sound, and was only vaguely aware that it was she herself, grinding her teeth in apprehension. Ice thickened on the windshield, and when the wipers tried to whisk it away, they smeared it into wide, arced streaks.

"We'd better get to that bridge pretty damned fast," Julia whispered under her breath. "'Cause if we don't . . ."

Then, up ahead, she and Bri saw it at the same time—the snow-filled turn onto the bridge, just barely illuminated by the streetlight. They were almost past it when they saw it, and Julia had to hit the brakes harder than she wanted to, to avoid missing it entirely. She tried to play the steering wheel back and forth to compensate, but the wheels didn't have any grip on the road. Before she could stop it, they were spinning out of control, heading for the edge of the road.

"Hold on," Julia said, fighting to keep her voice calm.

The tail end of the car started coming around in a slow, stomach-spinning glide. Julia could hear slush splatter up on the underside of the car, and in the glow of the dashboard lights, she registered the stark fright on Bri's face.

"We'll be all right . . . we'll be all—"

But that was all she could say. Suddenly Abby was there! Arms out in front of her like a diver, she swept out of the darkness surrounding the bridge and slammed into the windshield. In an ear-shattering explosion of glass, she burst through into the front seat. Julia tried to scream as Abby's frigid hands closed around her throat and started to choke her.

As the car shot off the road and down toward the frozen bay, the only thing Julia was aware of was the blackness, infinitely darker than the surrounding night, closing over her like a tidal wave, and a long, trailing scream that could have been Bri's. . . .

—or her own.

TWENTY-FOUR
Across the Bay

I

"...don't die!...Please don't die!..."

The words came to her as though someone...

Who?...How can I see who it is in this pitch-dark?

...was speaking to her from the end of a long tunnel. She sensed a rough rocking motion, and thought crazily for a moment that she was in a boat at sea. She expected, at any moment, to feel icy waves splash over her face.

Maybe Randy Chadwick's lobster boat, she thought. *But how can I tell where I am if I can't see?*

"Come on, Mom!...Wake up! Say something!...Please, don't die!..."

"I—"

The single word seemed to originate at the bottom of her feet and rip up to her mouth like a whirring chainsaw blade, tearing and burning her flesh as it went. She was distantly aware that trying to speak caused immense pain, but with that thought came the thought, *If I can feel pain...*

I'm alive...I'm not dead....

"Come *on*, Mom!"

In a narrow corner of her mind, she finally recognized that it was Bri's voice speaking to her, calling her back from the night-stained edge of...*what*? She saw herself as nothing more than a tiny feather about to be sucked up into a whirling, black vortex.

Although the movement sent spikes of pain through every cell of her body, Julia managed to shake her head from side to side. She felt something soft, cold, and yielding under her head when she moved.

What? she wondered. *Is that snow...or the crushed pulp of my own skull?*

She opened her eyes, but at first couldn't see anything. She figured she might just as well have left her eyes shut. Maybe she had. She was surrounded by darkness, and as she watched, the darkness vaguely shifted with a bluish, grainy look—like an old-fashioned photograph. After a few seconds, she realized that she was looking up at snow blowing past a streetlight overhead. With that realization came a sudden awareness of being cold . . . *freezing* cold.

"Mom? . . . *Mom!*" Bri shouted.

Julia tried to force her eyes to focus, and when she finally did, she made out a dark shape that had to be Bri leaning over her. She could see her daughter's eyes glowing unnaturally bright—twin spots of glistening blue.

Bri's eyes gushed with tears when she saw her mother look up at her. For a moment, she forgot all about the raw wind tearing at her back or the horror she had felt as she sat in the passenger seat when their car spun out and rolled down the hill toward the bay, and as that *thing* that had looked like Audrey—but *couldn't* have been!—came careening through the windshield and wrapped around her mother. She felt a numb, stomach-dropping sensation whenever she remembered her mother's words: *"Your father's dead!"* And now if her mother was dead, too . . .

As she slowly came around, Julia was frantically thinking, *It didn't happen! . . . None of it! . . . It was all just a dream. . . .*

But as her mind cleared and she became painfully aware that she was lying on her back in several feet of snow, she knew *something* had happened . . . something *bad!* Had she skidded the car off the road and, in the instant of blacking out, imagined everything that had happened back at the house? Or had it—*could* it have really happened? John wasn't dead, and that *thing* Bri called Audrey . . . it couldn't *possibly* have been real!

"What's the . . . ? What happened?" Julia said, shifting up onto her elbows. The snowy night sky came more clearly into focus, and she shivered wildly.

"We went off the road," Bri said tightly. "You don't remember?"

With a sudden, sickening rush, Julia's mind replayed the last few seconds before the crash. She saw the face of that girl, that horrible skeleton face, loom out of the darkness at her over the hood of the car. She heard clearly in her memory the sound of the windshield exploding inward with dazzling, diamondlike brilliance. She saw those hands, felt them—*strong, thin, skeleton hands*—reach in and wrap around her neck. Involuntarily, she reached up to her throat where the flesh felt as though it had been seared by red-hot iron. Even through her gloves, the skin felt hot and raw.

"Is . . . is *she* still here?" Julia asked. Forgetting the pain in her legs and back, she staggered to her feet, brushing the snow off herself. Frantically grabbing Bri by the arm, Julia pulled her after her and shouted, "Come on! We have to get out of here! We have to get off the island!"

The streetlight, she now saw, was at the beginning of the bridge—their escape route! The family station wagon had plowed over the embankment and down into the smooth, deep snow by the frozen bay. The car had rolled to one side and was tipped forward with its tailend sticking almost straight up into the air. The taillights glowed a baleful red, staining the snow like blood.

"How did you—?" Julia started to say, but Bri interrupted her.

"The car was going real slow when we went off the road. The deep snow must've slowed it down. I jumped out and, once it stopped, went down and dragged you out. Good thing it stopped, too, 'cause you were only a couple of feet from going into the water."

"What about . . . *her*?" Julia said, still rubbing the hot ring around her throat. She found it difficult to swallow, and breathing the freezing air didn't help.

Bri shrugged. "She wasn't there when I got to the car," she said, shrugging. "I don't know where she went."

"Jesus Christ!" Julia muttered. "She's got to be around here somewhere! Come on. Let's get the hell across that bridge!"

Struggling through snow that was well over her knees, she started climbing up the embankment with Bri right beside her. The grade was steep, and they kept slipping back down almost as much as they climbed, but eventually Julia got a grip on one of the railings and pulled Bri up after her. As soon as they were out of the shelter of the bridge embankment, the full force of the storm slammed into them, almost blowing them back once again.

"Hold on to my hand so we don't get separated," Julia said. She had to shout to be heard above the roar of the wind. Snow, like tiny shotgun pellets, whipped into her face, stinging like a blast of sand. She snuggled her face deep into the collar of her coat, and Bri's reply was lost in the sound of snow splattering against her coat.

It was obvious the town plows hadn't been by for some time; the road across the bridge wasn't any clearer than the road they'd been on. But the bridge would take them across water—they'd be safe, Julia prayed, once they were off the island and Abby or Audrey or whatever was after them would be powerless. She hoped so, anyway . . . she was betting their lives on it!

As they struggled down the road, Julia became aware of a pain deep inside her belly. At first she gave it, like the other pains she felt, little credence; but suddenly the thought struck her that *this* pain was different! This one felt like . . .

The baby!

Oh, God—please, no! Don't let me lose my baby, too!

Slowing her pace a fraction, she led the way across the bridge, tugging Bri's hand. Above them, the storm wailed as it vibrated the bridge's suspension cables. The line of lights along the bridge receded in the snow until they were little more than blue puffs of lights. The wind off the ocean was as sharp as a razor, slicing into their backs, pushing them roughly along.

At first, Julia didn't care if they stayed on the snow-blanketed pedestrian sidewalk or not. She figured if a car or truck, maybe a town snowplow, came along, they could flag it down. But then she realized that a driver might not even see them until it was too late, so they held close to the side of the bridge, using the outside rail as a guide through the blinding snow.

Although it was difficult to see it overhead, they passed by one of the two support towers. The blinking red lights at the top were lost to sight in the storm, but this told Julia they were a little more than halfway across the bridge. It felt as if they had already been walking for miles. Snow dragged at their legs like a churning tide; and the wind, pushing at their backs like a schoolyard bully, tried to knock them down. Through the curtain of falling snow, Julia couldn't see the black hump of the mainland yet, but just knowing it—and *safety*—were up ahead gave her strength and courage. Suddenly she jerked to an abrupt stop, and Bri, who had been mindlessly chugging along beside her, knocked into her shoulder.

"What's the matter?" Bri said. Her words were whipped away by the wind as soon as they were out of her mouth.

Unable to speak, Julia pointed down the length of the bridge. At first, Bri couldn't see *anything* through the snow, but then, beneath one of the lights, she saw a slumped black shape. It looked like a person, hunched over and back to them, peering out over the bay, but that was impossible . . . ridiculous! No one would be out sightseeing on a night like this!

Julia started moving forward again, taking short, cautious steps closer to the dark shape. She was wishing it was nothing more than, say, an unpainted spot on one of the trusses or a windblown piece of trash that had gotten hung up in the railing. It couldn't *possibly* be . . .

"Shit!" Julia said, gasping when she saw the figure—*yes! It was a person!*—slowly turn and look in their direction.

Was this some local crazy who just liked to come out onto the bridge during a storm and watch the snow blow across the frozen bay? she wondered. *Or was this precisely the person—the thing —she and Bri were fleeing?*

Julia didn't stop, though. With Bri right beside her, clenching her hand, she kept moving forward. They both screamed in unison when the figure suddenly raised its arm over its head and shrieked at them, its voice piercing the night like a bullet.

"You can't get away! Not *that* easily!"

Both Julia and Bri could see the figure clearly now as it began to move toward them. It *was* Abby! The wind caught her heavy snow-caked sweater and made it snap viciously at her hips. The long strands of her black hair seemed to rise, framing her pale face with an explosion of twisting black snakes.

"You can't get away!" Abby wailed, her voice rising and falling like a siren in the wind. Burning red sparks flashed from the cores of her eyes as she came closer . . . closer.

Almost paralyzed with fear, Julia started to back up as the horrible skull-faced figure closed the gap between them. Her heart sounded like a jackhammer in her ears, drowning out everything except the shrill wail of the creature. Suddenly, though, an idea struck Julia. It was desperate, but right now she was past the point of rationally analyzing things.

Turning to face Bri, she shouted, "Jump off the bridge!"

"What—are you crazy?"

"Do it! Now! Jump!" She pushed her daughter roughly toward the railing. "Can't you see? She doesn't have as much power here close to the water! Jump!"

"The fall will kill us!" Bri yelled. "What if we fall right through the ice?"

"It's frozen solid," Julia gasped. "And the snow . . . it's deep enough. It'll cushion the impact. Jump! *Now!*"

Against her better judgment, Bri clambered up onto the railing after casting another frightened glance at the thing approaching them. Needle-sharp gusts of wind tried to hold her back, but she gripped the railing, crouched, and then—trying to blank her mind to what she was actually doing—sprang out into the night and dropped into the darkness.

Julia watched as the blackness below the bridge swallowed up her daughter. Her slowly diminishing scream trailed back out of the storm like an unraveling ribbon . . . then it was gone. As she turned back to face the creature, Julia couldn't shake the terrifying thought that she would never see Bri again . . . alive, anyway.

Closer and closer Abby came, her arms upraised, her face glowing with a bone-chilling light, her mouth opened wide in a long, wavering scream. Against her will, Julia backed up, giving ground. The overhead light cast a cold wash over Abby's face, which loomed closer to Julia, revealing with hallucinatory sharpness the cold, staring eyes—the flaps of shredded, rotting skin—the coils of black hair—the glistening bone.

"She'll be next!" the horrifying visage said. *"After I'm through with you!"* Her lips barely moved, and she looked more like a talking skull than a human being. "First, though, *you . . .* and the *bastard* you're carrying!"

Abby darted forward like a cobra, but Julia quickly spun to one side and grabbed on to the bridge railing. With a nimbleness and a strength that surprised her, she vaulted over the railing and then felt herself tumbling and turning as she fell down . . . down into the darkness beneath the bridge. The landing came suddenly, and was surprisingly hard, and as the cushion of snow swallowed her up, she let out one violent grunt. Then she was scrambling to her feet, trying to get her bearings. Using the black slash of the bridge overhead as a guide, she started plowing through the heavily drifted snow over the frozen bay toward the mainland.

"Bri! Bri!" Julia shouted as she ran, staggering and tripping in the deep snow. She could only see a few feet in front of her, and nowhere was there a trace of Bri. The wind tore underneath the bridge, making a low-throated moan that horrifyingly reminded her of the last sound she heard John make as he sagged onto the spike of broken glass.

"Bri!" she wailed. *"If you can hear me, head for the mainland! Head for the mainland! I'll meet you there!"*

II

For the second or two that she was falling, Bri had the sensation that the storm winds has scooped her up into the dark, roiling storm clouds, and she was flying. She expected to look down and see the bridge below her as she sailed away, tossing and turning in the wind like a dandelion puff. The cold shock of impact hit her like a hammer, and for a while—she had no idea how long—she simply crumpled forward, her face in the snow, and lay there with the wind knocked out of her. Brilliant zigzags of light traced across her inner eye, and every time she took a breath, her lungs felt as though they had frozen solid and wouldn't absorb any oxygen. She had landed awkwardly on one side, but after struggling to her feet, a quick check proved that no bones were broken.

Snuggling her face deep into her collar, she looked up at the bridge. Even the nearest light was now almost entirely masked by the falling snow. She waited, expecting to see—or at least hear

—her mother when she jumped, but all she heard or saw was the storm as it swept in off the ocean as blinding as a sandstorm in the Sahara. Thick pellets of snow rattled like marbles on the hard crust of snow.

"Mom!" she shouted, cupping her hands to her face and looking up. "*Mom!* Where *are* you?"

The storm pressed her voice right back in on her, giving her the feeling that she was locked in a closet. The raging night was like a cold, stinging cloak. Bri almost chuckled at the thought of having claustrophobia out here in the middle of the frozen bay, and she vaguely realized that laughing in a situation like this probably meant she was starting to lose her grip on reality. But then again —after what she had seen and been through—what other choice *was* there other than to slip a few gears!

"*Mom!*" she wailed, listening to her feeble voice below the heavy thrumming of the storm. At last, convinced that her mother must have already jumped, unheard and unseen, and was heading toward the mainland, she started out across the snow-covered ice. The only other alternative was too terrible to think about. *Audrey had already gotten her mother. . . . Her mother was dead! . . . And she was next!*

As she plowed through the snow, hip-deep in places, Bri's whole body tensed, expecting at any second to plunge suddenly through the ice and into the frigid water. As much as she tried not to, she thought of her father and what had happened back at Granddad's house.

Is he really dead? she wondered. *How can he be dead, just like that? Just like Granddad? . . . And now maybe Mom!*

She remembered what her father had said about the time he and his friend Randy had crossed the frozen bay.

"*You fall in, and you'll be dead in a minute!*"

With that came the memory of when she had followed Audrey along the rocks at Indian Point and had fallen into the ocean. For the first time, she realized something with a stomach-churning jolt.

"She *wanted* me to drown!" she whispered softly. "She *wanted* me to fall in and drown! She was out to kill us, even back then!"

As if in answer, a gust of wind echoed on the underside of the bridge and seemed to say . . . "*You'll die . . . now! . . .*"

The thought began to grow in Bri's mind that it had to be the truth! All along, Audrey had been trying to hurt her, to play on her loneliness and *use* it to get to her father . . . to get at her whole family! And with that thought came the bitter realization that it might have worked after all. She knew for certain that if she and her mother didn't get out of this blizzard soon, they *would* die of exposure, and then Audrey would have her revenge on all of them!

"*Mom!* . . ." she wailed, pushing blindly forward through the snow. Her face was numb from exposure. She could feel hot sweat dripping down her back inside her coat. Her face felt flushed and overheated, and although she had heard the word *hypothermia* before without knowing exactly what it meant, she suspected that's what might kill her if she didn't find her mother and some shelter *soon*!

Suddenly, below the high-pitched hiss of the snow as it sliced across the bay and the deep-throated moaning sounds coming from beneath the bridge, Bri heard something else—a low, vibrating rumble.

Can there be thunder during a snowstorm? she wondered, looking frantically up at the sky. Tatters of clouds and shifting snow created an oddly disorienting view.

Bri paused and tensed, waiting for the rumbling sound to be repeated. Everywhere around her, the snow spiraled. Everywhere she looked, she could almost imagine seeing someone—*her mother . . . or Audrey?*—lurching across the frozen bay toward her. For several drawnout seconds, the sound wasn't repeated, but when it came again, it almost knocked Bri to the ground. From beneath her feet, she felt the ice vibrate as a long, steady rumbling sound built and built in intensity. Before long, it was as deafening as a roaring cannon shot.

The ice is breaking up! was her first panicked thought. She crouched low, holding her arms out wide for balance. It could have just been her nerves or maybe her leg muscles going into spasm, but she was *positive* she could feel the whole sheet of ice subtly heaving.

The tides! That's what's doing it! The tides are shifting the ice! It's breaking up!

In her overstressed imagination, she pictured the frozen bay suddenly heaving upward—hugh blocks and spears of ice rearing skyward like mountains—and she saw herself scrambling, trying to find solid ground and then being suddenly yanked down into the numbing black water!

You'll be dead in a minute! The words of her father rang in her memory like a hammer striking iron.

From some hidden reservoir of strength, she found what she needed to start running. Kicking her legs up high to keep them clear of the snow, she took awkward, leaping giant steps toward the mainland.

The bridge is still above me, she told herself. *I'll be safe as long as I stay under it!*

The wind tore into her lungs as she ran. The headway she was making didn't seem worth the effort, though, and she would have quit if the wind had been in her face instead of at her back. But on she went, struggling to push back her fear, thinking . . .

If I don't make it out of here soon, I'm gonna scream and scream and scream until my lungs burst!

She was running almost blindly now, her breath coming in and out in hurtful stitches that lanced her side like hot knife blades. When the ice suddenly opened up right underneath her feet, she didn't have enough air left in her lungs to scream . . . and with the storm raging around her, her mother, less than a hundred feet behind her, wouldn't have heard her scream, anyway.

III

Julia was less than a hundred feet behind Bri, but because she also was several paces farther out into the bay, she never saw the trail Bri left behind as she went. Besides, the wind quickly smoothed over the tracks, so the two of them might just as well have been walking a hundred miles apart.

Julia's overriding thought—along with Bri's safety—was concern for the baby she was carrying. It was absurd, absolutely *insane* to take the words of the ghost as fact. . . .

Yes! As crazy as it seemed, that's what it had to be . . . a ghost!

But Abby had said that she knew Julia was pregnant. Knowing she was pregnant, Julia thought, actually might have been what made Abby turn on her so suddenly and violently.

"You'll be next! . . . You and that bastard you're carrying!"

"Is it a boy? Am I going to have a son?" Julia whispered to herself.

She found almost no pleasure in the thought. The reality of where she was—even if there hadn't been a supernatural creature after her—made her realize she would die of exposure before very long. Already her face was completely numb. She knew, if she didn't make it to the mainland, if she didn't find warmth and shelter soon, she would die. And even if she *did* get out of this alive, would it matter? Not with John dead! Not if Bri didn't survive!

The storm was like a raging wolf pack, howling, tearing, and pulling at Julia as she made her way alongside the bridge. Her body was aching, every muscle cramping, every nerve tingling as she struggled through the night. She was expecting at any second to see a darker-than-night human shape swoop down at her off the bridge. Her mind was nothing more than a vibrating white buzz as she forged ahead, barely conscious of the cold fingers tugging at every inch of her clothes.

The walk seemed to stretch out, and Julia began to wonder if there really *was* an end to the frozen bay.

Maybe, she thought, feeling a sudden dash of panic, *I'm already dead! Maybe this will go on forever!*

But before the panic raging inside her as wildly as the storm could crest, she looked down at her legs mechanically churning their way through the snow, her arms strongly pumping to keep her moving, and she knew she wasn't dead . . . *not goddamned yet!*

She stumbled several times, pitching face first into the snow, but each cold dash of snow on her face revived her and made her grit her teeth to keep from screaming out loud as she struggled to stand and keep walking. The overhanging black slash of the bridge couldn't go on forever—she *knew* it couldn't! There was an end to it, and that end would bring her to the mainland . . . and safety!

And she *would* find Bri, she told herself. She *would* save herself and her daughter and her baby!

"You'll be next. . . . You and that bastard you're carrying!"

"No way in hell, bitch!" she muttered, even though she couldn't hear her own voice above the howling wind.

That bridge can be twenty miles long . . . two hundred miles long, but as long as I follow it, I'll be safe. . . . We'll all be safe. . . .

"We'll all be safe! . . . We'll all be safe! . . ."

The words became a numbing repetition in her mind, but she was barely aware she was saying them as she walked and walked. In the blindness of her effort, she even crossed Bri's fresh tracks, less than a minute old, and she never noticed the churned-up snow. When she finally walked past the second of the two bridge tower bases, she knew she was close now, and hope, like a faint spark, began to kindle again inside her.

"Bri!" she shouted, her voice weak with exhaustion. She was looking around frantically, lost in the blackout of the snow, when suddenly a loud, roaring explosion knocked her onto her back. She lost all sense of direction as the night around her was filled with a violent surging. Tremendous cracking sounds echoed like firecrackers in her ears, and Julia was vaguely surprised that the blackness of the night wasn't filled with flashes of light as well.

But she had little time to think. Completely disoriented, she felt herself thrown first to one side, then the other. The whole earth seemed to rock back and forth, pitching her with it. Suddenly an intense cold grabbed her legs; it felt as sharp as a shark bite. Only a small part of her mind registered that, right up to the knees, her legs were incredibly cold . . . and *wet*. She suddenly realized she was slipping downward, her gloved hands clawing furiously at the tilting ice, trying to find some handhold.

I'm falling in, her mind screeched. *Oh, dear God!*

Her legs felt like useless blocks as she tried to climb up the ever-steepening incline. She knew she couldn't hold on forever—that the ice was breaking up and she was going to be in over her head in seconds. Coiling her legs up under herself, she waited only a split second before suddenly pushing off. For a horrifyingly long moment she was sailing through the air—long enough to have the panicked thought that maybe all of this had been a hallucination and she was still falling from her jump off the bridge—but then she hit the snow hard . . . and it was level, solid!

Behind her, she could vaguely see where a chunk of ice had thrust itself up into the air. Snow curled like frozen mist around the sudden intrusion, and Julia could hear choppy water splashing beneath the thick ice. A black terror gripped her heart when she considered—only for a moment—how close she had been to dying instantly.

"That's what you want, isn't it?" she shouted, shaking her hands over her head. "But you're not going to get it! Goddamn you! You're *not*!"

She pitched forward into the night, confident now that the mainland could only be a few dozen feet away. When she squinted, she was positive she could make out the dark slope of the road embankment. . . .

The road . . . a house . . . safety!

The hazy yellow glow of a streetlight suddenly loomed up out of the darkness, and Julia recognized instantly that this one was different—it wasn't the blue kind they used on the bridge. It was a *real* streetlight. She *had* made it!

With a final burst of energy, Julia crossed the last stretch of the frozen bay. Tears blurred her vision, and she was distantly aware that she was cackling with laughter as she scrambled up the hillside and onto solid ground.

It was all behind her, she thought . . . everything! Her husband was dead, and . . .

Bri!

"Bri! *Bri!* Answer me!" she shouted, forcing her words into the throat of the storm. Turning to look back toward the island across the bay, the full force of the snow blasted into her face, almost choking her.

Bri can't be lost! she thought, almost wild with fear. *She can't be!*

But what if Bri hadn't been as lucky as she had been? What if Bri had fallen into the water when the ice suddenly split open?

With a violent grunt, Julia doubled over as hot pain shot through her abdomen. Her instant thought was, *This feels just like a birth contraction!* But there was also a warm, gushing sensation, as though . . .

Oh, shit! I'm bleeding!

She fell to her knees, thinking, even though she had made it across the bay, she hadn't made it far enough—she still wasn't out of the storm, and with John dead, and if Bri had died back there on the ice . . .

My God! What if Abby got her!

. . . she might just as well die here, hemorrhaging to death in the snow.

"Mom! . . ."

The voice came to her out of the storm, so faint she *knew* she must have imagined it. It couldn't possibly be . . .

Looking up, she saw the distant glow of the streetlight, and standing beneath the light, she saw a snow-masked figure.

"Bri! Oh, my *God!* Bri!" she gasped as she struggled to her feet. The deep snow tried to hold her back, but she pushed ahead as the figure by the streetlight started staggering toward her.

She made it! she thought as joyful tears ran from her eyes and froze solid on her face. *My baby made it!*

They ran toward each other, each of them slowed by the snow and their own exhaustion. It seemed to take forever to close the distance between them, but finally, when they did, and they were no more than ten feet apart, Julia shrank back in blinding white terror and screamed. Staring at her, her face framed by wind-whipped black hair, was the leering face of Abby!

"No! *No! . . . You can't!*" Julia wailed as she staggered back in total disbelief. Was is possible? Could she have been wrong, and Abby's influence extended off the island as well?

I'm hallucinating! I'm imagining all of this! she told herself, but as she stared at Abby's grinning skull face, the reality of it sank into the core of her soul, and Julia knew her death was near.

"What do you want from me?" Julia wailed, falling onto her knees in the snow and beating her fist uselessly against her legs. "What do you want?"

Abby's dead mouth twitched into a lopsided grin as her red-rimmed eyes bored into Julia, cutting like lasers.

"What do I *want*?" she said, her voice low and mocking. "What do I *want*? Why . . . nothing more than your life!"

She pointed a bony forefinger at Julia, then twisted her hand over to make a clenched fist. When she squeezed, her knuckle-bones stood out in high relief.

"I want you—and your bastard to *die!*"

Raw tears flooded down Julia's face. Her head felt as though a giant had gripped it with his strong hands and was *squeezing* until the bones began to crackle as they crushed inward.

"I never did anything to you," Julia wailed. Her throat was stripped raw and sounded like an old woman's . . . pitiful, broken.

"No—*you* never did," Abby said, bringing her face so close to Julia's she could feel the cold breath wash over her skin. "*You* didn't, but your husband did. His *father* had to pay. And *John* had to pay for what he did to me. And now you, your daughter, and your *bastard* have to pay!"

"Why?" Julia said, holding her hands out helplessly. The mention of Bri—that she had to die—told Julia that Bri was still alive somewhere in the storm. That gave her a flicker of hope. "Why us, too? John never told me anything about you. I never even heard your name until Randy Chadwick mentioned you."

"Your husband *killed* me!" Abby said, her voice nothing more than a hollow cackle. "As surely as if he had tied the rope around my neck himself, he *killed* me and the baby—*his* baby—inside me! And then, once I was dead, he tried to hide it! He buried me so no one would know! And I was dead!" Abby's voice took on a low, mournful tone. "Me and my baby were *dead!*"

"But I never knew," Julia said. Staring up at Abby with the streetlight behind her made the shadows hiding her face deepen. All Julia could see was the red glow of her eyes, but she forgot all about the raging storm as she looked up into the face of death itself and felt its cold, mind-numbing power.

Abby snickered, her laughter sounding like dry, crinkling leaves. "You never knew! As if that matters!"

"But I didn't! I never even suspected!" Julia said. "*No one* knew except John, so why do you have to punish us? Let us live! I have a baby inside me, and I want it to live!" A sudden cramp almost made her double over, but Julia maintained eye contact with this horrible thing.

"*I* had a baby that wanted to live, too!" Abby shouted, her voice rising like the wind. "*My* baby died! *Yours* has to!"

Desperate, Julia folded her hands in front of her, pleading. "I can't help what happened," she said, feeling emotion drawn up from the pit of her stomach. "No one could. I couldn't have known then, but if I had ever suspected what John had done, I would have told someone—the authorities. I would have—"

Abby laughed again, low, deep, and hollow. The storm around her, alternately hiding and uncovering her, gave Julia the disturbing sensation that she was talking to nothing more than a figment of her imagination. But then Abby leaned forward and extended her hands, and when her frozen fingers gently caressed Julia's face, she knew this was more than an illusion.

"Get up," Abby said, low and commanding.

Julia was afraid her legs wouldn't support her, but she struggled to a standing position. The wind off the frozen bay hit her in the back like an iron fist.

"You said my daughter had to die," Julia said, forcing out the words through cracked and numbed lips. "She's still alive now . . . out there."

Abby nodded her head slowly. "She's still alive," she said, shaking her head from side to side. "But not for long."

She still held Julia's face in her hands, and now she brought her face right up close to her, meeting her eye to eye. As Julia looked deeply into the cold red fire inside Abby's eye sockets, she felt as though she were standing stark naked in the raging storm. Every fiber of her body, every shred of her soul felt like exposed, raw nerves as Abby stared long and deep into her eyes.

"Why does anyone else have to die?" Julia pleaded weakly.

"You *all* have to die because your husband *killed* me," Abby said. "And tried to hide it!" She tilted her head back, as though gaining strength from the storm around them. "But I have another thought," Abby said after a moment. Looking past Julia, out over the bay, her eyes seemed to draw in the darkness and the power of the storm. "I would be willing to let you live—all three of you— under a . . . a certain condition."

"What?" Julia said, her voice almost a wail. "Tell me! Anything!"

"Like you, *I* have a baby inside me still waiting to be born," Abby said. "When I died, it died; but its life force is still with me. Now that my murderer and his father are dead, I'll let you and your daughter and your baby live . . . if you will allow the life force—the *soul*—of my unborn baby to enter your womb!"

"What?" Julia lurched back away from Abby so violently she had to pinwheel her arms to maintain her balance against the buffeting wind.

"It can be our deal," Abby said. Even in the surrounding darkness, Julia could see her wickedly gleaming smile. "You allow the soul of my baby, who never got the chance to be born, to enter *your* baby . . . so he will have a chance to live. You do this, and you can live."

"No! . . . No, I can't," Julia stammered. She was looking straight ahead at Abby, but all around her, she felt Abby's power like a dark whirlpool.

"You have a simple choice," Abby said. She tossed her head back and laughed, high and cruel. "You allow my baby's soul into your body—or you will all . . . *die!*" She said the last word with a snakelike hiss.

"You don't know what you're asking," Julia said, frantic with fear. "I can't allow my baby to—"

"Oh, but you *can* . . . you *must!*" Abby said, leering. "We can let a small part of John live—apart from the time *before* he did this to me—" Saying that, she reached up to her face and began peeling off thick strips of rotten flesh. She threw each handful to the ground, where it disappeared under the snow. Julia was sure she saw the snow hiss and steam wherever the dead flesh fell.

"I can't! . . . I *won't!*" Julia shouted, but the darkness was all around her, tearing and tugging at her like a thousand tiny hands. She saw Abby suddenly sweep her arms around, as if to embrace her. Screaming, Julia shielded herself with her hands, but instead of the expected impact, she felt nothing more than a blinding cold pass through her body. Thick, cloying darkness surrounded her like a musty blanket, carrying her back on her feet until she tripped and collapsed backward into the snow. For just an instant, her eyes caught sight of the streetlight overhead; then the light exploded into a million shards that sprinkled down and pierced her body like silver nails.

IV

Minutes . . . hours . . . *a lifetime* later, Julia awoke.

At first her mind registered only a loud, rumbling roar and, thinking she was still out on the ice as it was starting to break up, she screamed and scrambled frantically to hold on to something. What she grabbed, she saw when she opened her eyes, was the boot of a man dressed in a heavy coat with a woolen hat pulled down over his eyes. Behind him, two huge glowing lights were framed by several insanely spinning orange lights. Julia's first, crazy thought was that she looking up at a UFO. It took her several seconds to realize that she was lying on the ground in the path of a Falmouth town snow plow.

"Mrs. Carlson . . . ?" the man said, leaning close to her. With the truck lights flashing behind him, his face was lost in shadows. Julia wanted to scream out—and she would have if her throat hadn't felt stripped raw.

"Mrs. Carlson, are you all right?" the man asked. There was a tone of earnest concern in his voice that cut through the insane panic she felt, and she tried to signal by a jerking nod of her head that—*yes*, she was alive—maybe not all right, but *alive!*

"It's me, Larry Fire. Folks 'round here call me Smokey. I, uhh—found your daughter down the road a'piece, n'she—"

"Bri?" Julia said, forcing the words through the shredded flesh of her throat. "Is she—"

"She was unconscious when I found her, but she come to," Larry said, frowning as he patted Julia's shoulder. "She's wicked cold 'n' scared outta her mind some, but she's in the truck cab, drinkin' a slug of coffee."

"She's . . . all right then?" Julia said, gasping. "She's alive?"

Still, on the fringes of her awareness, she could hear the roaring of the storm, but now she felt warmer and figured the driver had put a coat or blanket over her.

"She'll be fine," Larry said. "Don't you go worryin' 'bout anyone 'cept yourself."

"I—" That was all Julia could say. The events of the night crashed in on her like a tidal wave, threatening to pull her back out onto the frozen bay and down into the cold, dark water.

"You just rest easy there, ma'am," Larry said. "I already radioed for the ambulance, 'n' it's on its way."

Julia sagged back onto the ground. She could feel the darkness pressing in on her, rubbing up against her like some gigantic cat, but now she wasn't afraid.

"I'll tell yah," Larry said, shaking his head. "'S a goddamned good thing I saw your daughter. I—Christ!" He wiped his forehead with the back of his gloved hand. "I came purty damned close to coverin' her up with the plow. Christ, I could hardly see three feet in front o' me. I almost didn't see you lyin' there in the road, either." He whistled and shook his head, looking up the length of the road to the bridge.

Bri's safe, Julia thought, taking hold of that one idea and hanging on to it as if it were a lifeline. She didn't want to struggle anymore; she didn't have the strength left. Let the darkness come down now, she thought . . . so what? It doesn't matter! Whatever else had happened—or *would* happen—*Bri was safe!*

EPILOGUE:
Waiting to be Born

I

Spring finally came after a long, hard winter; and after that, a summer with temperatures reaching record highs throughout most of July and on into August. But even after all that time had passed, with autumn returning once again and the trees on Glooscap changing to yellow and brown, the sea shifting from brilliant blue to gunmetal gray, neither Julia nor Bri had satisfactorily explained—much less accepted—what had happened to them during that January blizzard. Much of what they had been through, Bri—apparently—had blocked out; and for that, Julia was silently thankful.

The birth of Nathan Edward Carlson on the twenty-seventh of August gave both of them something new to live for, a promise of the future to help assuage the deep ache of loss they still felt for both John and Frank. Healing was slow and painful, but for Julia, at least, there was emotional scar tissue—deep and thick—that would always remain.

As painful as it was, Julia decided not to sell Frank's house right away and move back to Vermont. In many ways, the decision was taken out of her hands because Dr. Flaherty, her obstetrician, advised her very strongly against doing anything that could further jeopardize the baby's and her health. Although her recovery from the night of the blizzard didn't require hospitalization, it was slow.

But time, like physical distance, will eventually heal the body and dull at least the sharpest, most painful memories. Even before winter was gone, most of the events of that previous January had began to take on the hallucinatory vagueness of a vivid nightmare. But, although Julia never discussed it directly with Bri, she knew that it had all been more than a bad dream—it had been real. John's horrible death had been real . . . the havoc inside their house had been real . . . the rolled-over station wagon buried nose-deep in the snow beside the bridge had been real . . . and the trauma they both had suffered out on the frozen bay that night had been—and still was—real. All that—and more—had been verified by the police and medics when they arrived on the scene. But there were other aspects that only Julia knew about that still made her wonder. . . .

The state authorities investigated, and after feeble protestations, Julia accepted their official version of the night's events—at least in public. What the police pieced together was this: John, as several people from the Atkins Company testified, had been moody and irritable at work, and almost everyone who had been at the New Year's Eve party commented that he had been drinking heavily that night—heavily enough, so Barry Cummings testified, that his performance at work had been affected. Coming home late on the night of the storm, so the police concluded, John had started—or continued—drinking and, in a drunken rage, had trashed the house. After threatening Julia and Bri—enough so they felt they had to flee the house for their own safety—he had stumbled and fallen through the picture window in the living room, dying almost instantly, bleeding to death from the massive cut to his lower abdomen from the broken glass. The rest—Julia and Bri's desperate attempt to get off the island during the blizzard, their subsequent crash and near-fatal attempt to cross the frozen bay, Larry Fire's finding them—was all pretty self-evident.

As long, Julia told herself, *as I don't tell them what else I saw and heard out there in the storm! As long as I never mention—to anyone—Abby . . . or Audrey . . . and what she offered me!*

Within weeks, the authorities closed the case, ruling the incident an "accidental death." They told Julia there would be no criminal proceedings against her, and that it was all right if she wanted to sell the house and move back to Vermont. And that had been her intention, to move back to where she and Bri had friends, where they could try to pick up the pieces, until Dr. Flaherty recommended that she stay put at least until after the baby was born.

Bri, with the resilience of the young, bounced back from the physical trauma of her ordeal in fine form. On the night of the blizzard, she had suffered serious frostbite and had to be hospitalized for several weeks. For a while it had been touch and go, but she recovered fully and, by the end of February vacation, was back to her usual bright and cheerful self. The only outward physical change was a rather large bleached splotch on her left cheek where tissue and blood vessels had been permanently damaged. If she *had* suffered any long-lasting psychological effects, Julia sure as hell couldn't tell by her outward appearance or behavior.

It took an immense amount of courage for Julia to stay in Frank's house—especially alone during the time Bri was still in the hospital. And then, after that, once Bri was out Julia never let her sleep over at Kristin's house; but Bri never complained . . . not much, anyway.

Although she never mentioned it to Bri, all through the winter and spring and into the summer, Julia was plagued by nightmares and fitful sleep. At least once every night, she would wake up bathed in sweat, nearly screaming from some warped distortion of what she and Bri had been through. Sometimes late at night, she would come partially awake with the feeling that someone was lying in bed with her. Convinced it was John, she would reach for him in the dark and then, jolting to full wakefulness, would realize that John was dead . . . the bed was empty. Several times when she touched the other side of the bed, she was positive the mattress had a warm, rumpled depression in it . . . as if someone had been lying there. The worst dreams, though, were the ones in which she had to confront the combined fury of John *and* Abby, both usually in horrible states of decomposition.

The effect this lack of sleep had on her pregnancy—especially after the physical stress of that January night—concerned Dr. Flaherty, but he kept her on a regimen of vitamins and constantly reassured her that if she kept taking good care of herself, she and the baby would be just fine. And she earnestly believed him, in spite of the dark thoughts that tailed her like hungry dogs all the time.

The closer she got to her due date, though, the more Julia wondered how much of her last conversation with Abby had been real and how much she had imagined. She wanted—maybe more than she had ever wanted *anything* before—to believe that none of it had ever happened—that, exhausted from her trek across the frozen bay, she had been so far gone that she had hallucinated her final confrontation with Abby. Perhaps, she told herself, her fear for her own and Bri's survival had overloaded her mind, which had already been pushed beyond its limit. She hoped to *hell* that Abby's power—whatever it had been—had, like that of the Headless Horseman in the story by Washington Irving, stopped at the bridge. Perhaps . . .

But perhaps not! her mind whispered to her, usually late at night when she wanted to get to sleep but spent the time staring blankly at the ceiling instead. *Perhaps not. . . .*

One night in late August, thankfully after the heat wave had broken, she started having contractions that increased in both intensity and frequency, and she knew the time had come. Bri came with her when Randy and Ellie drove her to the Osteopathic Hospital in Portland where, after nearly eighteen hours of labor—hours edged with a bit more than the usual fear involved with childbirth—she delivered an eight pound, five ounce boy. He seemed hale and hearty, if the strength of his lungs and the avidness of his nursing were any gauge. She had wanted to name him after Frank or John, but heeding some deepseated fear, she opted for a name that had absolutely no family connection—Nathan Edward.

The gloom that had pervaded the old Carlson house since the night of the blizzard—the night John died—was dispelled slightly the day Julia brought little Nathan home from the hospital. Bri dubbed him "Nate," and Julia didn't mind if the nickname stuck; she liked it, too. And Bri—God bless her!—was an incredible help during the first few weeks after Nate came home. She had started school, the eighth grade, in Falmouth, even though they planned to move soon; but even with homework and being so busy with her friend Kristin, she never complained about helping out while her mother was getting her strength back. Randy and Ellie Chadwick visited almost daily, bringing dishes of food and helping with the cleaning. The Chadwicks and Kristin were probably the only three people on Glooscap island, Julia figured, who were upset the day Merilee Bryant, from Century 21, put a *for-sale* sign out on the front lawn of Frank's house.

After a few weeks, Nate began to sleep . . . well, through *most* of the night, and Julia and Bri got busy packing for their move back to Vermont. The house sold for a very nice price within two weeks, but the closing was more than a month away, so they didn't feel any pressure to hurry and get out of the house. The painful memories associated with living on Glooscap had lost most of their sting, so Julia decided to take her time packing and, as painful as it was, weed out a lot of their accumulated trash. The hardest part was the day she gathered up John's clothes and took them to Goodwill. But once that bitter job was done, the rest of the work of getting ready to move went much more easily. On the last weekend of September, they had a yard sale and put up for sale everything they didn't want to cart back to Vermont. Bri cried when someone bought her granddad's wheelchair.

II

It was gorgeous—clear but chilly—on the October Saturday before they were to move. That morning towering white clouds

rolled like cotton puffs across a blue sky that was so bright it hurt
to look at it for long. Just about every room in the house was
packed up and ready to go. The van was scheduled to arrive on
Monday morning. Julia and Bri were getting tired of living out of
boxes, and both of them were anxious now to get moved and
resettled. Julia set up a small Port-A-Crib in the living room so
Nate could take his nap while she finished packing the remaining
dishes and pots and pans in the kitchen.

"You know," Julia said as she carefully rolled each cup and
glass into a sheet of newspaper and placed it into a box. "It's hard
to believe it was a year ago to the day that we moved in here."

Bri had just finished giving Nate a bottle of distilled water. She
was sitting at the kitchen table, her eyes continually drifting to the
bright slash of sky she could see out of the kitchen window while
her mother worked away. She took a deep breath and let it out
with a slow shuddering sigh.

"We've been through a lot since then, haven't we?" Bri said,
her eyes getting dreamily distant.

Julia perked up her ears when Nate, in his crib in the living
room, started fussing. "He's not settling down," she said. "Did
you change his diaper?"

"Course I did," Bri replied, but Julia wasn't completely convinced because Bri looked so lost in her daydream. She turned
back to packing the glasses, hoping that it was just a momentary
fussiness on Nate's part, and that he would drift off to sleep so
she could finish this job.

But Nate didn't drift off; what had started as a low-level
squawking soon turned into a full-scale cry. His high-pitched
wailing set Julia's sleep-deprived nerves on edge, and before long
she found herself shoving the glasses into the box with enough
force to break something if she wasn't careful. She was fuming
when she turned and saw Bri still sitting at the table with her chin
resting in her hands.

"Well?" she snapped, crumpling up a piece of newspaper and
throwing it onto the counter.

"Huh?" Bri said, shaking her head and looking up at her
mother.

"Maybe you could do something for him so I can get this
done," Julia said. "Or take over here so I can handle him." She
knew she sounded a bit snappy, but her nerves—for some reason
—felt worn particularly thin today. That surprised her because for
the last three nights she *hadn't* had any bad dreams . . . that she
remembered, anyway. Two-A.M. feedings were keeping her busy
enough at night without nightmares.

"Uh . . . yeah, sure," Bri said, standing up from the table slowly

and looking toward the living room with a confused expression on
her face . . . almost as if she didn't know who—or what—was
making that noise in there.

"Why don't you pop him into the stroller and take him for a
walk," Julia said, forcing herself to tone her voice down. "Give
me another half hour with this, and then maybe we'll drive into
Portland for lunch. I've got most of the cooking stuff packed now,
anyway."

"Yeah . . . sure," Bri said as she started walking slowly toward
the living room. "Lemme just . . . uh, get a sweater or something
first. It looks kinda cold outside."

"Make sure you bundle Nate up good and warm, too," Julia
said. "And would you mind getting a move on? That crying's
driving me *nuts*!"

Nate was still wailing away in the living room as Bri trudged
slowly upstairs. Julia turned back to her work, but she couldn't
keep her attention from drifting back to the living room as she
waited to hear Bri's returning footsteps. After what seemed much
too long a time, while Nate's crying rose more shrilly, she finally
heard the heavy tread of footsteps coming down the stairs.

"You should probably put that white hooded sweatshirt on
him," Julia called out. "If the wind is really cold, I don't want
him getting a chill."

Bri didn't respond, but, figuring she knew what she was doing,
Julia kept on packing. After another five minutes or so, Nate was
still crying, and it seemed to Julia that Bri was taking much too long.

"Are you two all right in there?" Julia called out.

"Sure . . ." Bri answered, but there was a vacant, hollow tone in
her voice that bothered Julia. In fact, when she thought about it, it
sounded as though Bri was still upstairs . . . not in the living room
at all.

"Bri . . ." Julia said as she walked over to the living room doorway and into the living room. Bright daylight filtered in through
the windows, and soft, gauzy shadows shifted across the carpet.

"If you— What the hell?"

Julia couldn't help but shout when she saw Bri leaning over the
portable crib. Her hands, looking unnaturally pale and thin, were
gripping the crib's side rail, and she was jiggling the crib gently
while she made soft, cooing noises. What surprised Julia and sent
a wave of chills through her was the thing she saw Bri wearing—
a long gray sweater. It hung down heavily at her side, as though it
was saturated with water. There were white patches all over the
sides and back that looked like . . . mold. The sweater brushed
against the side of the crib with a soft thump-thump sound as Bri
shook the crib, trying to calm Nate.

"Where the hell did you get *that* old thing?" Julia asked as she took a few cautious steps into the living room.

The fuzzy-edged shadows on the floor seemed to shift subtly, making her feel off balance, disoriented. Had a cloud covered the sun, changing the light, she wondered, or was it her vision? An alarm went off somewhere deep in the back of her mind as recognition dawned. She gasped aloud, unable to believe what she was seeing.

"*Bri—!*"

"You know," Bri said, her voice sounding muffled, distant. "When he's crying like this, I can see that he has your mouth and chin."

"Jesus Christ, Bri! What are you doing?" Julia shouted as panic raged inside her like a flaming blast. "What in the name of God are you *doing*?"

Moving stiffly, Bri shifted her shoulders as she began to straighten up. The heavy folds of the gray sweater rippled like sludgy, scum-topped water. Her mouth dropping open in horror, Julia tried to take a deep breath, but she couldn't manage anything more than a gulp of air.

"But I think . . ." Bri said, slowly turning around to face her mother.

When she looked at Julia, a cold, numbing darkness swirled around her, pulling and tugging at Julia like an irresistible wave, like groping, clawing skeletal hands.

Bri's face was gone, and in its place was the rotted, peeling visage of Abby Snow. Her long black hair, tangled and stringy, dangling clumps of dirt and crawling things, hung loosely down around the sides of her pale face. Exposed bone showed between shredded strips of dead flesh, and her eyes were glowing with a wild, intense red glare that burned into Julia's mind like blazing coals.

Julia backed up until she hit the living room wall. Then, as her knees gave way, she crumpled slowly to the floor.

"I think, though, that he has *my* eyes," the *thing* . . .

That's not Bri! Julia's terror-numbed mind shrieked. *That can't be Bri!*

. . . said. Its jaw made hollow clacking sounds as the blackened lips peeled back exposing the top row of yellow, dirt-crusted teeth.

"Don't you think so?" the creature said. "Definitely . . . *my* eyes!"

Julia's throat was making odd little clicking sounds as she watched the creature throw its head back, exposing the mottled gray flesh of its neck, and begin to laugh. She felt herself falling, spinning backward into madly churning darkness as the laughter spiraled higher . . . and higher. . . .